Praise fo

"You should read *Behind He*
— Stephen King, #1 *New York Times* bestselling author

"Pinborough shrewdly transforms a romantic suspense novel into an eerie thriller calculated to creep you out. . . . Pinborough keeps us guessing about just who's manipulating whom—until the ending reveals that we've been wholly complicit in this terrifying mind game." — *The New York Times Book Review*

"*Behind Her Eyes* is a cunning puzzle box of a novel, a masterfully engineered thriller that brings to mind Hitchcock at his most uncanny and Rendell at her most relentless. Lean and mean, dark and disturbing, this is the kind of novel that takes over your life. Sarah Pinborough slays." — Joe Hill, #1 *New York Times* bestselling author of *The Fireman* and *Nos4A2*

"The season's twistiest thriller . . . Like all powerful over-the-counter drugs, *Behind Her Eyes* deserves its own warning label. . . . Mind-blowing, genre-bending, breakthrough psychological thriller . . . Avoid any contact with the growing buzz concerning the novel's ingenious, to-die-for twist." — *BookPage*

"*Behind Her Eyes* is a dark, electrifying page-turner with a corker of an ending. Sarah Pinborough is about to become your new obsession." — Harlan Coben, #1 *New York Times* bestselling author of *Fool Me Once*

"This is a mindf*ck—psychological thriller, with a sprinkling of magic realism—that will keep you asking WTF and turning the page. You might want a reading partner for this one, so you can share your guesses and discuss the ending." — Book Riot

"A vertiginous tale of obsession, manipulation, and betrayal . . . The writing is evocative. . . . The characters are so sharply rendered they

could draw blood; every thought, word, action, and reaction rings 100 percent true, and their emotions are so palpable that it's painful. Pinborough's prose is peppered with stunning turns of phrase and insightful observations. Her pacing is deliberate, but deliciously so, and . . . no one can claim her plotting lacks originality or ambition."
—*Mystery Scene*

"Twisty thriller *Behind Her Eyes* energizes genre. . . . If you like an intricately plotted thriller that will keep you turning pages . . . this book is quite entertaining."
—*The Florida Times-Union*

"One of them is hiding a secret, revealed near the end of the book, which will leave you (and another of the characters) gasping. . . . Your patience and indulgence will be rewarded in spades when you get to the ending(s), which will have you simultaneously swallowing your tongue and screaming. Seriously. You'll be stuck in that nanosecond between seeing a car's bumper slide up to you and the moment of impact for a long time to come after reading it."
—Bookreporter

"A masterpiece of suspense . . . A rare joy . . . Creates a sense of disorientation and dread that is highly satisfying. But it is with the plot, so tight and yet also intricate, that Pinborough shines. No detail or character is extraneous. Every word comes back into play and matters as the story moves to the disturbing conclusion that everyone is talking about. . . . Readers will likely never see it coming. . . . Give this intense book to patrons freely, but especially target those who are fatigued with the current spate of female-driven psychological suspense. It will be enough to shake things up for them."
—*Booklist* (starred review)

"A modern love triangle with so many mindscrews you start questioning if maybe this particular triangle has more than three points. It's funny, it's cold, it's modern. A master class in juggling moods and the two sides to every story. And, wow, that ending. Pinborough's latest had me questioning *everything*. And the answers that

"A dark, electrifying page-turner with a corker of an ending. Sarah Pinborough is about to become your new obsession."
—HARLAN COBEN, #1 *NEW YORK TIMES* BESTSELLING AUTHOR

"Deserves its own warning label . . . Mind-blowing, genre-bending, breakthrough psychological thriller . . . Ingenious, to-die-for twist."
—*BOOKPAGE*

"A masterpiece of suspense . . . A rare joy."
—*BOOKLIST* (STARRED REVIEW)

"A master class in juggling moods and the two sides to every story. And, wow, that ending. I loved *Behind Her Eyes*."
—JOSH MALERMAN, BESTSELLING AUTHOR

"Has everything a thriller needs . . . It takes a lot to catch me out, but this one did. It'll get you, too."
—JOANNE HARRIS, BESTSELLING AUTHOR

"If *Behind Her Eyes* isn't the thriller of the year, there is no justice. Hugely entertaining, utterly compelling, and the ending will leave you reeling."
—SARAH LOTZ, BESTSELLING AUTHOR

eventually came frightened me more than the unknown preceding them. I loved *Behind Her Eyes*. It's a modern love triangle thriller, and it would make one helluva movie." —Josh Malerman, bestselling author of *Bird Box*

"*Behind Her Eyes* is as twisty as a steep mountain road and just as nerve-racking. The shocks just keep coming around those blind curves." —Charlaine Harris, #1 *New York Times* bestselling author of the Sookie Stackhouse series

"Walking the tightrope between psychological and supernatural thriller with effortless ease and delicacy, *Behind Her Eyes* has everything a thriller needs: fully realized characters, peerless writing, a tank of a plot that sustains the suspense right to the end, and a whammy of a finale that hits you like a cartoon piano falling onto a rabbit's head. It takes a lot to catch me out, but this one did. It'll get you, too." —Joanne Harris, author of *Chocolat*

"The strongest, most unsettling thriller of the year, with a final twist destined to provoke arguments for years to come. Read it now before someone spoils the ending for you." —John Connolly, #1 *New York Times* bestselling author of the Charlie Parker novels

"A deliciously dark love story that will keep you guessing. Shocking, gleeful, and thrilling, welcome to the world of Sarah Pinborough." —Sarah Langan, three-time Bram Stoker Award–winning novelist

"If *Behind Her Eyes* isn't the thriller of the year, there is no justice. Hugely entertaining, utterly compelling, and the ending will leave you reeling." —Sarah Lotz, author of *The Three*

"Twisty psychological thriller . . . Pinborough will keep even veteran genre readers guessing about which members of the trio, if any, are providing trustworthy accounts of their pasts and presents." —*Publishers Weekly*

BEHIND
HER EYES

SARAH PINBOROUGH

FLATIRON
BOOKS
NEW YORK

This is a work of fiction. All of the characters, organizations, and events portrayed in this novel are either products of the author's imagination or are used fictitiously.

www.flatironbooks.com

Designed by Omar Chapa

The Library of Congress has cataloged the hardcover edition as follows:

Names: Pinborough, Sarah, 1972– author.
Title: Behind her eyes : a novel / Sarah Pinborough.
Description: First Edition. | New York : Flatiron Books, 2017.
Identifiers: LCCN 2016037630 | ISBN 9781250111173 (hardcover) |
    ISBN 9781250111180 (ebook)
Subjects: LCSH: Psychological fiction. | BISAC: FICTION / Mystery &
    Detective / General. | FICTION / Psychological. | GSAFD: Suspense fiction.
Classification: LCC PR6116.I665 B44 2017 | DDC 823'.92—dc23
LC record available at https://lccn.loc.gov/2016037630

ISBN 978-1-250-11119-7 (trade paperback)

Our books may be purchased in bulk for promotional, educational, or business use. Please contact your local bookseller or the Macmillan Corporate and Premium Sales Department at 1-800-221-7945, extension 5442, or by email at MacmillanSpecialMarkets@macmillan.com.

First Flatiron Books Paperback Edition: January 2018

For Tasha.
Words just don't cover it. All I can say is thanks
for everything and the drinks are on me.

Three can keep a secret if two are dead.

—BENJAMIN FRANKLIN

PART ONE

1
THEN

Pinch myself and say I AM AWAKE once an hour.
Look at my hands. Count my fingers.
Look at clock (or watch), look away, look back.
Stay calm and focused.
Think of a door.

2
LATER

It was nearly light when it was finally done. A streaky gray wash across the canvas of sky. Dry leaves and mud clung to his jeans, and his weak body ached as his sweat cooled in the damp, chill air. A thing had been done that could not be undone. A terrible necessary act. An ending and a beginning now knotted up forever. He expected the hues of the world to change to reflect that, but the earth and heavens remained the same muted shades, and there was no tremble of anger from the trees. No weeping whisper of wind. No siren wailed in the distance. The woods were just the woods, and the dirt was just the dirt. He let out a long breath and it felt surprisingly good. Clean. A new dawn. A new day.

He walked in silence toward the remains of the house in the distance. He didn't look back.

3

NOW

ADELE

There's still mud under my fingernails when David finally comes home. I can feel it stinging against my raw skin, deep under the beds. My stomach twists, wringing fresh nerves out as the front door shuts, and for a moment we just look at each other from opposite ends of the long corridor of our new Victorian house, a tract of perfectly polished wood between us, before he turns, swaying slightly, toward the sitting room. I take a deep breath and join him, flinching at each of the hard beats of my heels against the floorboards. I must not be afraid. I need to repair this. *We* need to repair this.

"I've cooked dinner," I say, trying not to sound too needy. "Only a stroganoff. It can keep until tomorrow if you've already eaten."

He's facing away from me, staring at our bookshelves that the unpackers have filled from the boxes. I try not to think about how long he's been gone. I've cleaned up the broken glass, swept and scrubbed the floor, and dealt with the garden. All evidence of earlier rage has been removed. I rinsed my mouth out after every glass of wine I drank in his absence so he won't smell it on me. He doesn't like me to drink. Only ever a glass or two in company. Never alone. But tonight I couldn't help it.

Even if I haven't entirely got the dirt out from under my nails,

I've showered and changed into a powder-blue dress and matching heels and put makeup on. No trace of tears and fighting. I want us to wash it all away. This is our fresh start. Our new beginning. It has to be.

"I'm not hungry." He turns to face me then, and I can see a quiet loathing in his eyes and I bite back a sudden urge to cry. I think this emptiness is worse than his anger. Everything I've worked so hard to build really is crumbling. I don't care that he's drunk again. I only want him to love me like he used to. He doesn't even notice the effort I've made since he stormed out. How busy I've been. How I look. How I've *tried*.

"I'm going to bed," he says. He doesn't meet my eyes and I know that he means the spare room. Two days into our fresh start, and he won't be sleeping with me. I feel the cracks between us widen once more. Soon we won't be able to reach each other across them. He walks carefully around me and I want to touch his arm but am too afraid of how he will react. He seems disgusted by me. Or perhaps it's his disgust at himself radiating in my direction.

"I love you," I say softly. I hate myself for it and he doesn't answer but unsteadily clambers up the stairs as if I'm not there. I hear his footsteps recede and then a door closing.

After a moment of staring at the space where he no longer is, listening to my patchwork heart breaking, I go back to the kitchen and turn the oven off. I won't keep it for tomorrow. It would taste sour on the memory of today. Dinner's ruined. We're ruined. I sometimes wonder if he wants to kill me and be done with it all. Get rid of the albatross around his neck. Perhaps some part of me wants to kill him, too.

I'm tempted to have another glass of forbidden wine, but I resist. I'm tearful enough already and I can't face another fight. Perhaps in the morning we'll be fine again. I'll replace the bottle and he'll never know I've been drinking at all.

I gaze out into the garden before finally flicking the outside lights off and facing my reflection in the window. I'm a beautiful woman. I look after myself. Why can't he still love me? Why can't our life have been as I'd hoped, as I'd wanted, after everything I've done for him? We have plenty of money. He has the career he dreamed of. I have only ever tried to be the perfect wife and give him the perfect life. Why can't he let the past go?

I allow myself a few minutes' more self-pity as I wipe down and polish the granite surfaces, and then I take a deep breath and pull myself together. I need to sleep. To properly sleep. I'll take a pill and knock myself out. Tomorrow will be different. It has to be. I'll forgive him. I always do.

I love my husband. I have since the moment I set eyes on him, and I will never fall out of love with him. I won't give that up. I can't.

4

LOUISE

No names, okay? No jobs. No dull life talk. Let's talk about real things.

"You really said that?"

"Yes. Well, no," I say. "He did."

My face burns. It sounded romantic at four thirty in the afternoon two days ago with the first illicit negroni, but now it's like something from a cheap tragi-romcom. Thirty-four-year-old woman walks into a bar and is sweet-talked by the man of her dreams, who turns out to be her new boss. Oh god, I want to die from the awfulness of it all. What a mess.

"Of course *he* did." Sophie laughs and immediately tries to stop herself. "*No dull life talk.* Like, oh, I don't know, the small fact I'm married." She sees my face. "Sorry. I know it's not technically funny, but it sort of is. And I know you're out of practice with the whole men thing, but how could you not have known from *that* he was married? The new boss bit I'll let you off with. That is simply bloody bad luck."

"It's *really* not funny," I say, but I smile. "Anyway, married men are your forte, not mine."

"True."

I knew Sophie would make me feel better. We are funny together. We laugh. She's an actress by trade—although we never discuss how she hasn't worked outside of two TV corpses in years—and, despite her affairs, has been married to a music exec forever. We met at our NCT classes, and although our lives are very different, we bonded. Seven years on and we're still drinking wine.

"But now you're like me," she says, with a cheery wink. "Sleeping with a married man. I feel less bad about myself already."

"I *didn't* sleep with him. And I didn't know he was married." That last part isn't quite true. By the end of the night, I'd had a pretty good idea. The urgent press of his body against mine as we kissed, our heads spinning from gin. The sudden break away. The guilt in his eyes. The apology. *I can't do this.* All the tells were there.

"Okay, Snow White. I'm just excited that you nearly got laid. How long's it been now?"

"I *really* don't want to think about that. Depressing me further won't help with my current predicament," I say, before drinking more of my wine. I need another cigarette. Adam is tucked up and fast asleep and won't move until breakfast and school. I can relax. He doesn't have nightmares. He doesn't sleepwalk. Thank god for small mercies.

"And this is all Michaela's fault anyway," I continue. "If she'd canceled *before* I got there, none of this would have happened."

Sophie's got a point, though. It's been a long time since I've even flirted with a man, let alone got drunk and kissed one. Her life is different. Always surrounded by new and interesting people. Creative types who live more freely, drink until late, and behave like teenagers. Being a single mum in London eking out a living as a psychiatrist's part-time secretary doesn't exactly give me a huge amount of opportunities to throw caution to the wind and go out every night in the hope of meeting anyone, let alone "Mr. Right," and I can't face Tinder or Match or any of those other sites. I've kind of got used to being on my own. Putting all that on hold for a while. A while that is turning into an inadvertent lifestyle choice.

"This will cheer you up." She pulls a joint out of the top pocket of her red corduroy jacket. "Trust me, you'll find everything funnier once we're baked." She sees the reluctance on my face and grins. "Come on, Lou. It's a special occasion. You've excelled yourself.

Snogged your new married boss. This is genius. I should get someone to write the film. I could play you."

"Good," I say. "I'll need the money when I'm fired." I can't fight Sophie, and I don't want to, and soon we're sitting out on the small balcony of my tiny flat, wine, crisps, and cigarettes at our feet, passing the weed between us, giggling.

Unlike Sophie, who somehow remains half-teenager, getting high is not in any way part of my normal routine—there isn't the time or the money when you're on your own—but laughter beats crying any time and I suck in a lungful of sweet, forbidden smoke.

"It could only happen to you," she says. "You hid?"

I nod, smiling at the comedy of the memory imagined through someone else's eyes. "I couldn't think of anything else to do. I dove into the toilet and stayed there. When I came out, he'd gone. He doesn't start until tomorrow. He was getting the full tour from Dr. Sykes."

"With his wife."

"Yep, with his wife." I remember how good they looked together in that brief, awful moment of realization. A beautiful couple.

"How long did you stay in the toilet for?"

"Twenty minutes."

"Oh, Lou."

There's a pause and then we both have the giggles, wine and weed buzzing our heads, and for a little while we can't stop.

"I wish I could have seen your face," Sophie says.

"Yeah, well, I'm not looking forward to seeing *his* face when he sees my face."

Sophie shrugs. "He's the married one. It's his shame. He can't say anything to you."

She absolves me of my guilt, but I can still feel it clinging along with the shock. The gut punch of the woman I'd glimpsed by his side before I dashed into hiding. His beautiful wife. Elegant. Dark-haired and olive-skinned in an Angelina Jolie way. That kind of mystery about her. Exceptionally slim. The opposite of me. The snapshot of her is burned into my brain. I couldn't imagine her ever panicking and hiding in a toilet from *anyone*. It stung in a way it shouldn't have, not after one drunken afternoon, and not only because my confidence has reached rock bottom.

The thing is, I'd liked him—*really* liked him. I can't tell Sophie about that. How I hadn't talked to anyone like that in a long time. How happy I'd felt to be flirting with someone who was flirting back, and how I'd forgotten how great that excitement of something potentially *new* was. My life is, as a rule, a blur of endless routine. I get Adam up and get him to school. If I'm working and want to get in early, he goes to breakfast club. If I'm not working, I may spend an hour or so browsing charity shops for designer castoffs that will fit the clinic's subtly expensive look. Then it's just cooking, cleaning, shopping until Adam comes home and then it's homework, tea, bath, story, bed for him, and wine and bad sleep for me. When he goes to his dad's for a weekend I'm too tired to do anything much other than lie in and then watch crap TV. The idea that this could be my life until Adam's at least fifteen or so quietly terrifies me so I don't think about it. But then meeting *the-man-in-the-bar* made me remember how good it was to *feel* something. As a woman. It made me feel alive. I'd even thought about going back to that bar and seeing if he'd turned up to find me. But, of course, life isn't a rom-com. And he's married. And I've been an idiot. I'm not bitter, merely sad. I can't tell Sophie any of these things because then she'd feel sorry for me and I don't want that and it's just easier to find it all funny. It *is* funny. And it's not like I sit at home bemoaning my singledom every night, as if no one could ever be complete without a man. In the main, I'm pretty happy. I'm a grown-up. I could have it way worse. This was one mistake. I have to deal with it.

I scoop up a handful of Doritos and Sophie does the same.

"Curves are the new thin," we say in unison, before cramming the crisps into our mouths and nearly choking as we laugh again. I think about me hiding in the toilet from him, full of panic and disbelief. It *is* funny. Everything is funny. It might be less funny tomorrow morning when I have to face the music, but for now I can laugh. If you can't laugh at your own fuck-ups, what can you laugh at?

"Why do you do it?" I say later when the bottle of wine is empty between us and the evening is drawing to a close. "Have affairs? Aren't you happy with Jay?"

"Of course I am," Sophie says. "I love him. It's not like I'm out doing it *all* the time."

This is probably true. She's an actress; she exaggerates for the sake of a story sometimes.

"But why do it at all?" Strangely, it's not something we've really talked about that much. She knows I'm uncomfortable with it, not because she does it—that's her business—but because I know and like Jay. He's good for her. Without him, she'd be screwed. As it were.

"I have a higher sex drive than he does," she says eventually. "And sex isn't what marriage is about anyway. It's about being with your best friend. Jay's my best friend. But we've been together fifteen years. Lust can't maintain itself. I mean, we still do it, sometimes, but it's not like it was. And having a child changes things. You spend so many years seeing each other as parents rather than lovers, it's hard to get that passion back."

I think back to my own short-lived marriage. The lust didn't die with us. But that didn't stop him leaving after four years to be with someone else when our son was barely two years old. Maybe she has a point. I don't think I ever saw my ex, Ian, as my best friend.

"It just seems a bit sad to me." And it does.

"That's because you believe in true love and happy ever after in a fairy-tale way. That's not how life is."

"Do you think he's ever cheated on you?" I ask.

"He's definitely had his flirtations," she says. "There was a singer he worked with a long time ago. I think maybe they had a thing for a while. But whatever it was, it didn't affect us. Not really."

She makes it sound so reasonable. All I can think of is the pain of betrayal I felt when Ian left. How what he did affected how I saw myself. How worthless I felt in those early days. How ugly. The short-lived romance he left me for didn't last either, but that didn't make me feel better.

"I don't think I'll ever understand it," I say.

"Everyone has secrets, Lou," she says. "Everyone should be

allowed their secrets. You can never know everything about a person. You'd go mad trying to."

I wonder, after she's left and I'm cleaning up the debris of our evening, if maybe Jay was the one who cheated first. Maybe that's the secret at the heart of Sophie's hotel room trysts. Maybe it's all done to make herself feel better or to quietly get even. Who knows. I'm probably overthinking it. Overthinking is my specialty. Each to their own, I remind myself. She seems happy and that's good enough for me.

It's only a little past ten thirty, but I'm exhausted, and I peer in at Adam for a minute, a soothing comfort to be found in watching his peaceful sleep, curled up tiny on his side under his Star Wars duvet, Paddington tucked under one arm, and then close the door and leave him to it.

It's dark when I wake up in the bathroom, standing in front of the mirror, and before I've really registered where I am, I feel the sharp throb in my shin where I've walked into the small laundry box in the corner. My heart races and sweat clings to my hairline. As reality settles around me, the night terror shatters, leaving only fragments in my head. I know what it was, though. Always the same dream.

A vast building, like an old hospital or orphanage. Abandoned. Adam is trapped somewhere inside it, and I know, I *just know,* that if I can't get to him, then he's going to die. He's calling out for me, afraid. Something bad is coming for him. I'm running through corridors trying to reach him, and from the walls and ceilings, the shadows reach out in tendrils, as if they're part of some terrible evil alive in the building, and wrap themselves around me, trapping me. All I can hear is Adam crying as I try to escape the dark, sticky strands determined to keep me from him, to choke me and drag me into the endless darkness. It's a horrible dream. It clings to me like the shadows do in the nightmare itself. The details may change slightly from night to night, but the narrative is always the same. However many times I have it, I'll never get used to it.

The night terrors didn't start when Adam was born—I've always had them, but before him I would be fighting for my own survival in them. Looking back, that was better even if I didn't know it at the time. They're the bane of my life. They kill my chances of a decent night's sleep when being a single mum tires me out enough.

This time I've walked more than I've done in a while. Normally I wake up, confused, standing either by my own bed or by Adam's, often in the middle of a nonsensical, terrified sentence. It happens so often it doesn't even bother him if he wakes up anymore. But then he's got his father's practicality. Thankfully, he got my sense of humor.

I put the light on, look into the mirror, and groan. Dark circles drag the skin under my eyes down and I know foundation isn't going to cover them. Not in full daylight. Oh, good. I remind myself that it doesn't matter what *the-man-from-the-bar* aka *oh-crap-he's-my-new-married-boss* thinks of me. Hopefully, he'll be feeling embarrassed enough to ignore me all day. My stomach still clenches, though, and my head thumps from too much wine and too many cigarettes. *Woman up,* I tell myself. *It'll all be forgotten in a day or so. Just go in and do your job.*

It's only four in the morning and I drink some water then turn the light out and creep back to my own bed hoping to at least doze until the alarm goes off at six. I refuse to think about the way his mouth felt on mine and how good it was, if only briefly, to have that surge of desire. To feel that connection with someone. I stare at the wall and contemplate counting sheep and then I realize that under my nerves I'm also excited to see him again. I grit my teeth and curse myself as an idiot. I am *not* that woman.

5

ADELE

I wave him off with a smile as he leaves for his first proper day at the clinic, and the elderly lady next door looks on approvingly as she takes her small, equally frail dog out for his walk. We always appear such a perfect couple, David and I. I like that.

Still, I let out a sigh of relief when I close the door and have the house to myself, even though that exhalation feels like a small betrayal. I love having David here with me, but we're not yet back on whatever even ground we've created for ourselves and the atmosphere is full of everything unsaid. Thankfully, the new house is big enough that he can hide in his study and we can pretend everything is fine as we cautiously move around each other.

I *do,* however, feel slightly better than I did when he came home drunk. We didn't discuss it the next morning, of course; discussion is not something we do these days. Instead, I left him to his papers and went to sign us both up at the local health club, which is suitably expensive, and then walked around our new chic area, absorbing it all. I like to lock locations in place. To be able to *see* them. It makes me feel more comfortable. It helps me relax.

I walked for nearly two hours, mentally logging shops and bars and restaurants until I had them safely stored in my head, their images summonable at will, and then I bought some bread from the local artisan bakery and some olives, sliced ham, hummus, and sun-dried tomatoes from the deli—all of which were decadently expensive and drained my housekeeping cash—and made us an indoor picnic for lunch, even though it was warm enough to sit outside. I don't think he wants to go into the garden yet.

Yesterday we went to the clinic and I charmed the senior partner, Dr. Sykes, and the various other doctors and nurses we met. People respond to beauty. It sounds vain, but it's true. David once told me that jurors were far more likely to believe good-looking people in the dock than average or ugly ones. It's only the luck of skin and bones but I've learned that it does have a magic. You don't even have to say very much but simply listen and smile and people bend over backward for you. I have enjoyed being beautiful. To say anything else would be a lie. I work hard to keep myself beautiful for David. Everything I do is for him.

David's new office is the second largest in the building from what I could see, the sort I would expect him to have if he'd ever take up a position in Harley Street. The carpet is cream and plush, the large desk is suitably ostentatious, and outside is a very luxurious reception area. The blond and attractive—if you like that sort of thing—woman behind *that* desk scurried away before we could be introduced, which annoyed me—but Dr. Sykes barely seemed to notice as he talked at me and blushed when I laughed at his terrible half-jokes. I think I did very well given how much my heart was aching. David must have been pleased too, because he softened a little after that.

We are having dinner at Dr. Sykes's house tonight as an informal welcome. I already have my dress picked out and know how I will do my hair. I fully intend to make David proud of me. I can be the good wife. The new partner's wife. Despite my present worries. I feel calmer than I have since we moved.

I look up at the clock, whose tick cuts through the vast silence in the house. It's still only 8 A.M. He's probably just getting to the office now. He won't make his first call home until eleven thirty. I have time. I go up to our bedroom and lie on top of the covers. I'm not going to sleep. But I do close my eyes. I think about the clinic. David's office. That plush cream carpet. The polished mahogany of his desk. The tiny scratch on the corner. The two slim couches. Firm seats. The details. I take a deep breath.

6

LOUISE

"You look lovely today," Sue says, almost surprised, as I take off my coat and hang it in the staff room. Adam said the same thing—in the same tone—his small face mildly confused by my silk blouse, new to me from the charity shop, and straightened hair as I shoved toast into his hand before we left for school this morning. Oh god, I've made an obvious effort, and I know it. But it's not *for* him. If anything it's *against* him. War paint. Something to hide behind. Also, I couldn't get back to sleep and I needed something to do.

Normally, on mornings like this, I'd take Adam to breakfast club and then be first at the clinic and have everyone's coffee on before they got in. But today was, of course, one of those days when Adam woke up grumpy and whining about everything, and then couldn't find his left shoe, and then even though I'd been ready for ages, it was still an irritated rush to get to the school gates on time.

My palms are sweating and I feel a bit sick as I smile. I also smoked three cigarettes on the walk from the school to the clinic. Normally I try not to have any until coffee-break time. Well, I say normally. In my head I don't have any until coffee, in reality I've usually smoked one on my way in.

"Thanks. Adam's at his dad's this weekend so I might go for a drink after work." I might *need* a drink after work. I make a note to text Sophie and see if she wants to meet. Of course she will. She'll be itching to see how this comedy of errors turns out. I try to make it sound casual but my voice sounds funny to me. I need to pull myself together. I'm being ridiculous. It's going to be way worse for him than it is for me. I'm not the married one. The pep talk sentences may be true but they don't change the fact that I don't *do* these things. This is not normal for me like maybe it is for Sophie, and I feel totally sick. I'm a mess of jittering emotions that can't settle on one thing. This situation may not be my fault but I feel cheap and stupid and guilty and angry. The first moment of potential romance I've had in what feels like forever and it was fool's gold. And yet, despite all that, *and* the memory of his beautiful wife, I also have a nugget of excitement at the prospect of seeing him again. I'm like a ditzy, dithering teenager.

"They're all in a meeting until ten thirty, or so Elaine upstairs tells me," she says. "We can relax." She opens her bag. "And I didn't forget it was my turn." She pulls out two greasy paper bags. "Friday bacon sandwiches."

I'm so relieved that I've got a couple of hours' reprieve that I take it happily, even though it's an indication of how mind-numbing my life routine is that this Friday breakfast is a highlight of my week. But still, it *is* bacon. Some parts of a routine are less demoralizing than others. I take a large bite, enjoying the buttery warm bread and salty meat. I'm a nervous eater. Actually, I'm an eater whatever my mood. Nervous eating, comfort eating, happy eating. It's all the same. Other people get divorced and lose a stone. It worked the other way for me.

We don't officially start work for another twenty minutes so we sit at the small table with mugs of tea, and Sue tells me about her husband's arthritis and the gay couple next door to their house who seem to be constantly having sex and I smile and let it wash over me and try not to jump every time I see someone's shadow fall across the doorway from the corridor.

I don't see the ketchup drop until it's too late and there's a bright-red dollop on my cream blouse right on my chest. Sue is there immediately, fussing and dabbing at it with tissues and then a damp cloth, but all she achieves is to make a great chunk of the material see-through and there's still a pale outline of washed-out red. My face is overheating and the silk clings to my back. This is the precursor for the rest of the day. I can feel it.

I laugh away her well-meaning attempts to clean me up and go to the toilet and try and get as much of my shirt under the hand dryer as possible. It doesn't dry it totally, but at least the lace trim of my bra—slightly gray from the wash—is no longer visible. Small mercies.

I have to laugh at myself. Who am I kidding? I can't do this. I'm more at home discussing the latest story line of *Rescue Bots* or *Horrid Henry* with Adam than trying to look like a modern, sophisticated woman. My feet are already aching in my two-inch heels. I always thought it was something you grew into, that ability to walk perfectly in high heels and always dress well. As it turns out—for me anyway—there's a small phase of that in the nightclubbing years of your twenties and then it's mainly jeans and jumpers and Converse with a ponytail, accessorized with life-envy of those who can still be bothered to make the effort. Life-envy of those with a reason to make the effort.

I bet she wears high heels, I think as I adjust my clothes. More fool me for not sticking with trousers and flats.

The phones are quiet this morning and I distract myself from the clock ticking steadily round to ten thirty by highlighting the case files on the system for Monday's appointments and making a list of those coming in the rest of the week. For some—the more complex cases—he already has copies of their notes, but I want to be seen as efficient so make sure the full list is found. Then I print out the various emails that I think might be valuable or important or forgotten by the management, and then also print out and laminate a list of contact numbers for the hospital and police and various other organizations that he might need. It's actually quite calming. *The-man-from-the-bar* is fading in my head and being replaced with *my-boss,* even if his face is mashing up rather alarmingly with old Dr. Cadigan, whom he's replaced.

At ten, I go and put the printouts on his desk and turn the coffee machine in the corner on so there will be a fresh pot waiting. I check that the cleaners have put milk in the small fridge hidden in a cabinet like a hotel mini-bar and that there's sugar in the bowl. After that, I can't help but look at the silver-framed photos on his desk. There are three. Two of his wife standing alone and an old one of them together. This one draws me in and I pick it up. He looks so different. So young. He can only be maybe early twenties at most. They're sitting on a large kitchen table and have their arms wrapped round each other and are laughing at something. They look so happy, both so young and carefree. His eyes are locked on her as if she's the most important thing on the whole planet. Her hair is long, but not pulled back in a bun as it is in the other pictures, and even in jeans and a T-shirt she's effortlessly beautiful. My stomach knots. I bet she never drops ketchup on her top.

"Hello?"

I'm so startled when I hear the slight Scottish brogue that I almost drop the photo and I struggle to straighten it on the desk, nearly unbalancing the neat pile of papers and sending them tumbling to the floor. He's standing in the doorway and I immediately want to throw up my bacon roll. Oh god, I'd forgotten how good-looking he is. Almost-blond hair with a shine I'd kill for in my own. Long enough at the front to be able to run your fingers through it, but still smart. Blue eyes that go right through you. Skin you just want to touch. I swallow hard. He's one of those men. A breathtaking man. My face is burning.

"You're supposed to be in a meeting until ten thirty," I say, wishing a hole would open in the carpet and suck me down to shame hell. I'm in his office looking at pictures of his wife like some kind of stalker. Oh god.

"Oh god," he says, stealing the words right out from my head. The color drains from his face and his eyes widen. He looks shocked and stunned and terrified all rolled into one. "It's you."

"Look," I say, "it was really nothing and we were drunk and got carried away and it was only a kiss, and, trust me, I have no intention of telling anyone about it, and I think if we both do our best to forget it ever happened then there's no reason we can't just get along and no one will ever know . . ." The words are coming out in a gibbering rush and I can't stop them. I can feel sweat trapped under my foundation as I overheat.

"But—" He's looking somewhere between confused and alarmed as he quickly closes the door behind him and I can't blame him. "—What are you doing here?"

"Oh." In all my rambling, I've forgotten to say the obvious. "I'm your secretary and receptionist. Three days a week, anyway. Tuesdays, Thursdays, and Fridays. I was putting some things on your desk and I saw . . ." I nod to the pictures. "I, well . . ." The sentence drains away. I can hardly say *I was having a really close look at you and your beautiful wife like a crazy lady would.*

"You're my secretary?" He looks like he's been punched hard in the guts. "*You* are?" Maybe not his guts. Maybe somewhere lower. I actually feel a bit sorry for him.

"I know." I shrug and pull some no doubt god-awful comedy face. "What are the odds?"

"There was another woman here when I came in last month to talk to Dr. Cadigan. Not you."

"Older, slightly uptight looking? That would be Maria. She does the other two days. She's semiretired now, but she's been here forever and Dr. Sykes loves her."

He hasn't moved much farther into the room. He's clearly having a hard time getting this to sink in.

"I really *am* your secretary," I say more slowly. Calmly. "I'm not a stalker. Trust me, this is not great for me, either. I did see you yesterday when you popped in. Briefly. Then I sort of hid."

"You hid." He pauses. The moment seems endless as he processes all this.

"Yes," I say, before adding to my shame with, "In the toilet."

There's a long pause after that.

"To be fair," he says eventually, "I'd have probably done the same."

"I'm not sure both of us hiding in the loo would have served the right purpose."

He laughs then, a short unexpected sound. "No, I guess not.

You're very funny. I remember that." He comes behind his desk, looking down at everything I've laid out there, and I automatically move out of his way.

"Anyway, that top printout is a list of the files you need to go through for Monday. There's coffee on—"

"I'm really sorry," he says, looking up with those gorgeous blue eyes. "You must think I'm a bastard. *I* think I'm a bastard. I don't normally—well, I wasn't there looking for anything, and I shouldn't have done what I did. I feel terrible. I can't explain it. I really don't do that sort of thing and there are no excuses for my behavior."

"We were drunk, that's all. You didn't do anything. Not really."

I can't do this. I remember the shame in his voice as he pushed away from me and walked away in the street, muttering apologies. Maybe that's why I can't think too badly of him. It was just a kiss after all. It was only in my stupid brain that it was anything more than that. "You stopped, and that counts for something. It's not a thing. Honestly. Let's forget it. Start from today. I really don't want to feel awkward any more than you do."

"You hid in the toilet." His blue eyes are sharp and warm.

"Yes, and one way to stop making me feel awkward would be to never mention that again." I grin. I still like him. He made a stupid in-the-moment mistake. It could have been worse. He could have come home with me. I think about that for a second. Okay, that would have been great in the short term, but definitely worse in the long.

"Okay, so friends it is," he says.

"Friends it is." We don't shake on it. It's way too soon for physical contact. "I'm Louise."

"David. Nice to meet you. Properly." We have another moment of awkward embarrassment and then he rubs his hands together and glances back down at the desk. "Looks like you mean to keep me busy. Are you local by any chance?"

"Yes. Well, I've lived here for over ten years if that counts as local."

"You think you could talk me through the area? Problems and hot spots? Social divides, that sort of thing? I wanted to take a drive around but that's going to have to wait. I've got another meeting this afternoon with someone from the hospital, then early dinner with the other partners tonight."

"I can certainly give you a rough outline," I say. "Layman's view as it were."

"Good. That's what I want. I'm thinking of doing voluntary outreach work on some weekends so it would be good to have a resident's perspective on possible causes of addiction issues that are specific to here. It's my specialism."

I'm a bit taken aback. I don't know any of the other doctors in here who do outreach. This is an expensive private clinic. Whatever problems our clients have, they don't tend to suffer from under-privilege, and the partners are all experts in their fields. They take referrals, of course, but they don't go out into the wider commu-nity and work for nothing.

"Well, it's North London, so in the main it's a very middle-class area," I say. "But south of where I live there's a big estate. There are definite issues there. High youth unemployment. Drugs. That kind of thing."

He reaches under his desk and pulls up his briefcase, opening it and taking out a local map. "You pour the coffee while I make space for this. We can mark out places I need to see."

We talk for nearly an hour, as I point out the schools and surgeries, and the roughest pubs and the underpass where there have been three stabbings in a year and where everyone knows not to let their kids walk because junkies deal drugs and shoot up in there. I'm surprised at how much I actually know about where I live, and I'm surprised about how much of my life comes out while I talk him through it. By the time he looks at the clock and stops me, not only does he know that I'm divorced, he knows I have Adam and where he goes to school and that my friend Sophie lives in one of the mansion blocks around the corner from the nicest secondary school. I'm still talking when he looks at the clock and then stiffens slightly.

"Sorry, I need to stop there," he says. "It's been fascinating, though." The map is covered in Biro marks and he's jotted down notes on a piece of paper. His writing is terrible. A true doctor's scribble.

"Well, I hope it's useful." I pick up my mug and move away. I hadn't realized how close together we'd been standing. The awkwardness settles back in.

"It's great. Thank you." He glances at the clock again. "I just need to call my . . ." He hesitates. "I need to call home."

"You can say the word 'wife,' you know." I smile. "I won't spontaneously combust."

"Sorry." He's more uncomfortable than me. And he should be, really. "And thank you. For not thinking I'm a shit. Or at least not showing that you think I'm a shit."

"You're welcome," I say.

"Do you think I'm a shit?"

I grin. "I'll be at my desk if you need me."

"I deserve that."

As things go, I think as I get back to my desk and wait for my face to cool, *that could have been a whole lot worse.* And I'm not at work again until Tuesday. Everything will be normal by then, our small moment brushed under the carpet of life. I make a pact with my brain not to think about it at all. I'm going to have a decadent weekend of *me*. I'll lie in. Eat cheap pizza and ice cream and maybe watch a whole series of something on Netflix.

Next week is the last week of school and then the long summer holidays lie ahead and my days will be mainly awful playdates, using my salary for my share of the childcare and trying to find new ways to occupy Adam that aren't giving him an iPad or phone to play endless games on and feeling like a bad parent while I try and get everything else done. But at least Adam is a good kid. He makes me laugh every day, and even in his tantrums I love him so much my heart hurts.

Adam's the man in my life, I think, glancing up at David's office door and idly wondering what sweet nothings he's whispering to his wife, *I don't need another one.*

7

THEN

The building, in many ways, reminds Adele of home. Of her home as it was *before* at any rate. The way it sits like an island in the ocean of land around them. She wonders if any of them thought of that—the doctors, her dead parents' lawyers, even David—before packing her off here for the month, to this remote house in the middle of the Highlands. Did any one of them even consider how much it would make her think of the home that was lost to her?

It's old, this place, she's not sure how old, but built in solid gray Scottish brick that defies time's attempts to weary it. Someone must have donated it to the Westland trust, or maybe it belongs to someone on the board or whatever. She hasn't asked and she doesn't really care. She can't imagine a single family ever living in it. They'd probably end up only using a few rooms like her family did in theirs. Big dreams, little lives. No one needs a huge house. What can you fill it with? A home needs to be filled with love, and some houses—her own, as it had been, included—don't have enough heat in their love to warm them. A therapy center at least gave these rooms a purpose. She pushes the childhood memories of running free through corridors and stairways playing hide and seek, and laughing wildly, a half-forgotten child, from her mind. It's better to think that her home was just too big. Better to think of imagined truths than real memories.

It's been three weeks and she's still in a daze. They all tell her she needs to grieve. But that's not why she's here. She needs to sleep. She *refuses* to sleep. She was dragging herself through days and nights filled with coffee and Red Bull and whatever other stimulants she could find to avoid sleeping before they sent her here. They said she wasn't "behaving normally" for someone who'd recently lost her parents. Not sleeping was the least of it. She still wonders how they were so sure what "normal behavior" was in these situations. What made them experts? But still, yes, they want her to sleep. But how can she explain?

Sleep is the release that has turned on her, a biting snake in the night.

She's here for her own good, apparently, but it still feels like a betrayal. She only came because David wanted her to. She hates seeing him worried and she owes him at least this month after what he did. Her hero.

She hasn't made any effort to fit in, even though she promises David and the lawyers that she's trying. She does use the activities rooms, and she does talk—or mainly listen—to the counselors, although she's not sure just how professional they really are. It all seems a bit hippie to her. *Touchy-feely,* as her dad would have said. He didn't like that stuff in her first round of therapy all those years ago, and to go along with it now feels like she would be letting him down. She'd rather be in a proper hospital, but her solicitors thought that was a bad idea, as did David. Westlands can be considered a "retreat" but for her to be sent to an institution could be harmful for her father's businesses. So here she is, whether her father would have approved or not.

After breakfast, most of the residents or patients or whatever are going on a hike. It's a beautiful day for it, not too hot, not too cold, and the sky is clear and the air is fresh and for a moment she's tempted to go along and hang out alone at the back, but then she sees the excited faces of the group gathered at the front steps and she changes her mind. She doesn't deserve to be happy. Where has all her happiness led? Also, the exercise will make her tired and she doesn't want to sleep any more than she has to. Sleep comes too easily to her as it is.

She waits to see the look of disappointment on the ponytailed group leader, Mark, *"We're all first names here, Adele,"* as she shakes her head, and then she leaves them to it and turns and walks to the back of the house, where the lake is.

She's done half a circuit of a slow stroll when she sees him, maybe twenty feet away. He's sitting under a tree, making a daisy chain. She smiles instinctively at how odd the sight is, this gangly teenager in a geeky T-shirt and jeans, dark hair flopping over his face, concentrating so hard on something you only ever see little girls do, and then feels bad for smiling. She shouldn't ever smile. For a moment she hesitates and thinks of turning to go back the other way, and then he looks up and sees her. After a pause, he waves. She's got no choice but to go over, and she doesn't mind. He's the only one here who interests her. She's heard him in the night. The screams and raving words that mainly make no sense. Clattering as he walks into things. The rush of the nurses to get him back to bed. These are familiar to her. She remembers it all herself. Night terrors.

"You didn't fancy group hugging on the moors then?" she says.

His face is all angles like he hasn't quite grown into it yet, but he's about her age, maybe a year older, eighteen or so, though he still has train-track braces on his teeth.

"Nope. Not your thing either, I take it?" His words come out with the hint of a wet lisp.

She shakes her head, awkward. She hasn't started a conversation, simply for the sake of talking, with anyone since she got here.

"I don't blame you. I wouldn't want to get too close to Mark. His ponytail must have lice growing in it. He wore the same shirt for three days last week. That is not a clean man."

She smiles then and lets it stay on her face. She hasn't planned to linger, but she finds herself sitting down.

"You're the girl who paints fires," he says. "I've seen you in the art room." He looks at her, and she thinks his eyes are bluer than David's, but maybe that's because his skin is so pale and his hair nearly black. He loops another daisy into the chain. "I've been thinking about that. Maybe you should paint water instead. It might be more therapeutic. You could tell them that the fire paintings represent your grief and what happened and the water paintings are you putting it all out. Washing it away." He talks fast. His brain must think fast. Hers feels like treacle.

"Why would I want to do that?" she asks. She can't imagine washing it all away.

"So they stop hassling you to *open up*." He grins and winks at her. "Give them something and they'll leave you alone."

"You sound like an expert."

"I've been to places like this before. Here, hold out your arm."

She does as she's told and he slips the daisy chain bracelet over her hand. There's no weight to it, unlike David's heavy watch, which hangs on her other wrist. It's a sweet gesture, and for a brief second she forgets all her guilt and fear.

"Thank you."

They sit in silence for a moment.

"I read about you in the paper," he says. "I'm sorry about your parents."

"Me too," she says, and then wants to change the subject. "You're the boy with the night terrors who sleepwalks."

He chuckles. "Yeah, sorry about that. I know I keep waking people up."

"Is it a new thing?" she asks. She wonders if he's like her. She would like to meet someone like her. Someone who'd understand.

"No, I've always done it. As long as I can remember. That's not why I'm here, though." He pulls up his sleeve. Faded track marks. "Bad habits."

He leans back on his elbows on the grass, his legs stretched out in front of him, and she does the same. The sun is warm on her skin and for the first time it doesn't make her think of flames.

"They think the drugs and my weird sleeping are connected," he says. "They keep asking me about my dreams. It's so dull. I'm going to start making stuff up."

"A filthy sex dream about Mark," she says. "Maybe with that fat woman in the canteen who never smiles." He laughs and she joins in and it feels good to be talking *normally* to someone. Someone who isn't *worried* about her. Someone who isn't trying to unpick her.

"They say you don't want to sleep," he says, squinting over at her. "Because you were asleep when it happened and didn't wake up." His tone is light. They could be talking about anything at all. TV shows. Music. Not the fire that killed her parents. The fire that finally put some heat into their house.

"I thought they weren't supposed to talk about us." She looks out at the glittering water. It's beautiful. Mesmeric. It's making her feel sleepy. "They don't understand," she says.

He chuckles again, a short snort. "That comes as no surprise. They strike me as thick as pigshit; one narrative for all. But what exactly in this instance don't they understand?"

A bird skims across the water, its slim beak cutting a slice through the surface. She wonders what it's so keen to catch.

"Sleep is different for me," she says eventually.

"How do you mean?"

She sits up then, and looks at him. She thinks she likes him. Maybe there is a different way to deal with all this crap. A way that will help him, too. She doesn't say so, but this isn't the first time she's been in a place like this either. Sleep keeps bringing her back to therapy. First it was her sleepwalking and night terrors when she was eight and now it's her not wanting to sleep at all.

Sleep, always sleep. Faux sleep, real sleep. The appearance of sleep.

And at the center of it all is the thing she can never tell them about. They would lock her up forever if she did. She's sure of it.

"You make stuff up for them and keep them happy. And I'll help you with your night terrors. I can help you way more than they can."

"Okay," he says. He's intrigued. "But in return you have to paint some water pictures you don't mean. It'll be entertaining seeing them getting all gushy over themselves for *saving* you."

"Deal," she says.

"Deal."

They shake on it, and in the sunlight the daisy centers glow gold. She leans back on the grass, enjoying the tickle of it on her arms, and they lie side by side in silence for a while, just enjoying the day with no one judging them.

She's made a friend. She can't wait to tell David.

8

ADELE

I've been awake since dawn, but haven't moved. We're both lying on our sides and his arm has flopped over me and, despite my heartache, it feels good. The weight of it is protective. It reminds me of the early days. His skin is shiny smooth and hair-free where his scars run up his forearm. He keeps them hidden, but I like to see them. They remind me of who he really is, underneath everything. The man who braved fire to rescue the girl he loved.

Through the gaps in the blinds, the sun has been cutting rough lines across the wooden floor since before six and I know already that it's going to be another beautiful day. Outside, at least. Under the weight of David's arm, I mull yesterday over. Last night's dinner at Dr. Sykes's was a success. In the main I find psychiatrists dull and predictable, but I was charming and witty and I know that they all loved me. Even the wives told David how lucky he was to have me.

I'm proud of myself. Even though it had been hard to muster—I'd had to run five miles on the gym treadmill in the afternoon and then hit the weights hard to calm myself down—I was in a visibly good mood when David had got home from work and the exercise had added to that glow. The evening in company went triumphantly without a hitch and our pretense at glorious happiness led us to both believe in it again for a short while. Last night we had sex for the first time in months, and even though it wasn't quite the way I would like it, I made all the right noises and did my best to be warm and pliant. It felt so good to have him so close, to have him inside me, even if he didn't meet my eyes once and was really quite drunk.

I'd stuck to the rule of one or two glasses, but David hadn't, although he had stayed just to the right side of acceptably merry, until we got home, where he'd poured himself a very large brandy and drank it quickly, probably hoping I wouldn't notice. I did, but of course I didn't say anything even though I'd have been well within my rights to do so.

He was supposed to cut down on that as part of our "fresh start." Even he knows that you can't be a psychiatrist who specializes in addictions and obsessions if you have a drink problem yourself. But then, I guess only one of us was really trying with our fresh start.

David is always in control in our marriage. He looks after me. Some, if they saw closely enough, would say he smothers me and they'd be right, but there are times when I think I may be cleverer than he is.

He's hard in my back and I move carefully, pressing against it, teasing myself, almost sliding him between my buttocks, squeezing him there and nudging him toward the illicit place where I like him best. Maybe sleeping he'll be more conducive. It's not to be, however, and he rolls away, onto his back, taking half the covers with him. He murmurs, soft and sweet, the fading echoes of his dream as he returns to the waking world, and I resist the urge to straddle him and kiss him and let all my passion out, and demand that he love me again.

Instead, I close my eyes and pretend to be asleep until he gets up and pads out to the corridor and to the bathroom. After a moment the boiler cranks into life as the shower starts running. This hurts a bit. I can't help it, however much I have a new resolve to be strong. We have an en-suite with a power shower in our bedroom but he's chosen to be farther away from me and I have a good idea why. What he's doing in there. I teased him awake and now, rather than having sex with me, he's "taking care of himself." It's a stupid phrase but I've never liked the word "masturbation." So clinical. Wanking is better, but language of that ilk doesn't suit me apparently so I trained myself out of crudeness long ago and now it just sounds odd in my head.

By the time he comes downstairs I have a pot of coffee made and there are croissants warming. We smother each other in our own ways and I know he'll need something to soak up the dregs of the hangover he has. I turn away and fuss around the sink so he can get some ibuprofen from the cupboard without any silent judgment.

"I've set the outside table," I say, all breezy and light, transferring the pastries to a plate. "It seems silly to waste such a beautiful morning." The back door is open and the air is warm even though it's only just past nine thirty.

He looks warily out through the window and I can see he's trying to spot where in the flower beds I buried the cat after he left me to deal with it and went out to get drunk and whatever else. He's still thinking about it. I'm trying to put it in the past. He clings to things he can't change but what's done is done whether we like it or not.

"Okay," he says, and gives me a half-smile. "The fresh air will wake me up." He's meeting me in the middle, perhaps as a reward for how well I did last night.

We don't say very much, but I enjoy our for once amiable quiet. I let my silk dressing gown slip so that the sun beats on a bare leg as I sip my coffee and eat my croissants and then tilt my face back. At points I can feel him looking at me, and I know that he's still drawn by my beauty. We are almost content in this instant. It won't last—it *can't* last—but for now I savor it. Perhaps all the more because of what might be to come.

When we're done I go and shower, taking my time and luxuriating in the hot water. The day is an empty landscape but it has its own unspoken routine. David will work for a few hours and then maybe we'll both go to the gym—an activity that we can pretend is something we do together, but of course is done alone—before home, dinner, TV, and probably an early night.

When I come downstairs he's already in his study, and he calls me in. It's a surprise. Normally, he wants to be left alone while he's working and I don't mind that. He has patients' information in there and although he might drink too much, he is in all other regards consummately professional.

"I've got some things for you," he says.

"Oh." This is a divergence from our expected routine and I'm surprised. My heart sinks and hardens a little when the first thing he hands over is a packet of pills.

"For your anxiety," he says. "I think these might be better than the others. One three times a day. No side effects to worry about."

I take them. The name on the front means nothing to me, simply another word I can't pronounce. "Of course," I say, dismayed. More pills. Always with the pills.

"But I also got you these." He sounds hopeful and I look up.

A credit card and a mobile phone.

"The card is linked to mine, but I thought it was time you had one again. The same with the phone."

It's an old handset, no internet I imagine and only basic functions, but my heart leaps. No more relying on David giving me a housekeeping allowance. No more sitting in the house for each scheduled phone call. My grin is one hundred percent real.

"Are you sure?" I say, not ready to believe my luck. I can almost forget the first blow of the medication.

"I'm sure." He smiles, for now glad to have made me happy. "A fresh start, remember?"

"Fresh start," I repeat, and then before I know it, I've run to the other side of the desk and wrapped my arms, my hands still full, around his neck. Maybe he does mean it. Maybe he will try harder from now on.

"Thank you, David," I whisper. I suck in the scent of him as he hugs me back. His warmth. The feel of his arms. The broadness of his slim chest beneath his soft thin sweater. My heart could explode at his closeness.

When we break apart, I see the scribbled-on map he's been looking at and the sheet of notes beside it. "What's that?" I ask, feign-

ing interest. Continuing to be the good wife in this wonderful
moment.

"Oh, I'm thinking of doing some outreach work. Voluntary
stuff. With a charity or something. I'm not sure yet. Part of why I
thought you might need the phone." His eyes dart sideways at me
but I smile.

"That's a lovely idea," I say. "It really is."

"It means I might be out more. At the weekends and evenings.
I'll try to keep it to a minimum."

He's talking in short phrases and I know from that he's uncomfortable. You learn little tells in a long marriage.

"It's fine," I say. "I think it's a very kind thing."

"You mean that?"

Now it's his turn to be surprised. I've always liked him working
as much as possible in the private sector. There's a soothing sophisti-
cation about it, away from the grime and grit of hard living. I've
pushed him for a Harley Street practice, where he belongs. Where
there will be more time for us. He is brilliant. Everyone says so. He
always has been and he should be at the very top. But this suits me. It
will suit both of us.

"I was thinking of doing some redecorating anyway. It will be
easier without you under my feet." I smile, making sure he knows
I'm teasing. I don't suggest that I get a job. Where would I start anyway? I haven't had one in years and I certainly wouldn't get a reference from there.

"You're a good man, David," I say, even though it's hard and
feels like a lie. "You really are."

The atmosphere stills then, a momentary heaviness in the room,
and we both feel the past cement itself between us once more.

"I'll go and take one of these then," I say. "Leave you to it." I
keep my smile up as I leave, pretending not to notice the sudden
awkwardness, but even with the pills I have no intention of taking
in one hand, there is a renewed spring in my step. A phone and a
credit card. Today is like Christmas.

9

LOUISE

By Sunday afternoon I've given up all hope of my "liberating *me me me* weekend" and am just clock-watching until Adam comes home. I had a drink with Sophie after work on Friday and made her laugh some more over *bossgate,* as she calls it, although I could see she was relieved that nothing more had happened. *Don't shit on your own doorstep,* is what she'd said. I almost pointed out that she was *always* sleeping with Jay's friends or clients, but decided against it. Anyway, she couldn't stay out for long and after two glasses of wine I was happy to say good-bye. Her amusement at my situation was becoming tiring.

The thing with couples is that even if they're not as smug as singles think they are, they do fall into that groove in life where they only really do things with other couples. No one wants a spare wheel hanging around and upsetting the even numbers. I remember it. Ian and I used to be like that. And as you get older everyone is married anyway, and those who aren't are frantically dating in order to fit back into the mold. Sometimes it seems like everyone *but* me is paired up.

On Saturday I did the housework, playing the radio loud and trying to make it feel like fun rather than drudgery, and then watched TV, ordered in a pizza, drank wine and smoked too much, and then hated myself for my excesses. What had sounded so decadent when I had planned it felt pathetic living it out.

My resolve to not think about David had failed too. What had they done this weekend? Played tennis? Sat in their no doubt perfect garden sipping cocktails and laughing together? Had he thought about me at all? Was there any reason to? Maybe he was having problems in his marriage. The thoughts had been going round and round while I half-watched TV and drank too much wine. I needed to forget about him, but it was easier said than done. I sleepwalked on both nights, finding myself standing in the kitchen with the cold tap running in the sink, scarily close to the balcony door, at 4 A.M. on Sunday morning. I end up laying in until ten, eating the last dregs of leftover pizza for breakfast and then forcing myself to Morrison's for the weekly shop before sitting and waiting for Adam to get home and fill the flat with life.

Adam finally gets back at just gone seven. I have to stop myself from running to the door and when he races in like a whirlwind, past me, my heart leaps at the noise and the energy. He exhausts me at times, but he's my perfect boy.

"No playing," I say as he wraps round my legs. "Go and run your bath, it's nearly bedtime." He rolls his eyes and groans but trudges off toward the bathroom.

"Bye, son."

"Thanks, Dad," Adam shouts, his backpack barely across his shoulder but holding a plastic dinosaur high. "See you next week!"

"Next week?" I'm confused, and Ian looks down, giving me a brief glimpse of his growing bald spot. He waits until our son is out of earshot.

"Yeah, I wanted to talk to you about that. You see, Lisa's got the offer of a house in the south of France for a month. It seems stupid not to take it."

"What about work?" I feel like I've been slapped in the face.

"I can work from there for a couple of weeks and then take the rest as holiday." His face prickles with color like it did when he told me he was leaving. "Lisa's pregnant," he blurts out. "She—*we*—think this would be a good way for her to bond properly with

Adam before the baby comes. She can't really get to know him properly seeing him only every other weekend. For his sake too. She doesn't want him to feel left out. Neither do I."

I've heard nothing but white noise since the word "pregnant." Lisa is relatively new, a vague name in my head rather than a whole person who is destined to be part of my life forever. She's only been around for nine months or so. I'd presumed, if Ian's track record since our divorce is anything to go by, that her time was nearly up. I have a partial recollection of him telling me that this one was different but I didn't take him seriously. I was wrong. It is.

They're going to be a proper family.

The thought is a knife in my suddenly bitter and black heart. They'll live in a proper house. Lisa will reap the rewards of Ian's steady climb up the corporate ladder. My little flat feels suffocating. I'm being unfair, I know. Ian pays my mortgage and has never argued over money once. Still, the hurt is overwhelming my rational brain, and the thought of them taking Adam from me for the summer to add to their little picture of perfect bliss makes me see red as if my heart has burst and all the blood has flooded to my eyes.

"No," I say, spitting the word out. "He's not going." I don't congratulate him. I don't care about their new baby. I only care about my already growing one.

"Oh, come on, Lou, this isn't like you." He leans on the doorframe and all I see for a moment is his potbelly. How can he have found someone new, someone properly new, and I haven't? Why am I the one left alone, passing my days in some dull *Groundhog Day* remake? "He'll have a great time," Ian continues, "you know it. And you'll get some time to yourself."

I think about the past forty-eight hours. Time to myself is not what I need right now.

"No. And you should have spoken to me first." I'm almost stamping my foot and I sound like a child but I can't help it.

"I know, I'm sorry, but it just sort of came out. At least think about it?" He looks pained. "It's the school holidays. I know they're tricky for you. You won't have to worry about childcare while you're working and it will give you a break. You can go out whenever you want. Meet some new people."

He means a man. Oh, good. Exactly what my weekend needed. Pity from my cheating ex-husband. It's the final straw. I don't even say no again, but close the door on him hard, making him jump back before it hits him.

He rings the doorbell twice after that but I ignore him. I feel sick. I feel angry. I feel lost. And worse than all of that is the feeling that I have no right to any of it. Lisa is probably perfectly nice. Ian doesn't deserve to be unhappy. I hadn't even thought I was unhappy before the stupid drunken kiss. I rest my head against the door, resisting the urge to bang my head hard against the wood to knock some sense into it.

"Mummy?"

I turn. Adam peers through from the sitting room, awkward.

"Can I go to France then?"

"I told you to run your bath," I snap, all my anger resurfacing. Ian had no right to mention the holiday to Adam before talking to me. Why do I always have to be the bad parent?

"But . . ."

"Bath. And no, you can't go to France, and that's final."

He glares at me then, a little ball of fury, my words bursting the bubble of his excitement. "Why?"

"Because I said so."

"That's not a reason. I want to go!"

"It's reason enough. And no arguments."

"That's a stupid reason! You're stupid!"

"Don't talk to me like that, Adam. Now run your bath or no story for you tonight." I don't like him when he's like this. I don't like me when I'm like this.

"I don't want a story! I want to go to France! Daddy wants me to go! You're mean! I hate you!"

He's carrying the plastic dinosaur and he throws it at me before storming off to the bathroom. I hear the door slam. It's not only me who can do that with effect. I pick it up and see the Natural History Museum sticker on the foot.

That only makes me feel worse. I've been promising him we'll go for ages and not got round to it. When you're the full-time parent there's a lot of things you don't get round to.

His bath is short and no fun for either of us. He ignores any attempt I make to explain why I don't think the holiday is a good idea, just glowering at me from under his damp hair. It's as if even at six he can see through my bullshit. It's not that he's never been away for a month. It's not that I think maybe a week would be better in case he got homesick. It's not that maybe Daddy and Lisa need their space now that a baby is coming—it's simply that I don't want to lose the only thing I have left. *Him*. Ian doesn't get to take Adam, too.

"You hate Daddy and Lisa," he growls as I wrap his perfect little body in a large towel. "You hate them and you want me to hate them." He stomps off to his bedroom, leaving me kneeling on the bathroom floor, clothes damp and staring after him, shocked. Is that what he really thinks? I wish he had proper tantrums more often. I wish he'd cry and scream and rage rather than sulk and then spit out these barbed truths. *From the mouths of babes . . .*

"Do you want Harry Potter?" I ask once he's got his pajamas on and the towel is hanging in the bathroom to dry.

"No."

"Are you sure?"

He doesn't look at me, but clutches Paddington tight. Too tight. All that contained rage and hurt. His face is still thunderous. He might as well stick his bottom lip out and be done with it.

"I want to go to France with Daddy. I want to eat snails. And swim in the sea. I don't want to stay here and go to holiday school while you're at work all the time."

"I'm not at work all the time." His anger stings me and so do his words, because there is some truth in them. I can't take the time off to spend with him like some other mums can.

"Lots of the time you are." He huffs slightly and turns onto his side, facing away from me. Paddington, still clutched tight, peers over his small shoulder at me, almost apologetically. "You don't want me to go because you're mean."

I stare at him for a moment, my heart suddenly heavy. It's true. It's all true. Adam would have a great time in France. And it would only be four weeks and in a lot of ways it would make my life easier. But the thought remains like a knife in my guts. Easier, yes, but also *emptier*.

Despite the frigid coldness of his back being to me, I lean over and kiss his head, ignoring his clenched tension as I do so. I suck in the wonderful clean smell that is distinctly his own. I will always be his mother, I remind myself. Lisa can never replace me.

"I'll think about it," I say very quietly from the doorway, before I turn the light out. Letting him go would be the right thing. I know it would, but I still want to cry as I pour a glass of wine and slump onto the sofa. A whole month. So much can change in that time. Adam will be taller for sure. There'll be less of this wonderful time when he still wants to cuddle and hold hands and be happy to be my baby. In the blink of an eye he'll be a teenager, tonight's behavior a precursor of that. Then he'll be grown and gone and having his own life and I'll probably still be in this shitty flat scratching out a living in a city I can't afford with barely a handful of part-time friends. I know I'm exaggerating everything in my self-pity and that really I'm still trying to process the word "pregnant" and the effect that's going to have on my life. I didn't think that Ian would have more children. He was never that interested the first time round.

I was his practice wife, I realize. *Adam and I were his practice family. When the story of his life is spun, we will simply be the early threads. We will not be the color.*

It's a strange and sad thought, and I don't like strange and sad thoughts so I drink more wine, and then make plans to fill those weeks with fun. I could take myself away for a weekend. I could start jogging. Lose this extra half-stone that has settled on my tummy and thighs. Wear high heels. Become someone new. It's a lot to fit into a month but I'm willing to try. Or at least I'm willing to try while I have half a bottle of Sauvignon Blanc in me. Before I can change my mind I text Ian and tell him the holiday is okay. Adam can go. I regret it almost instantly, but I don't really have any choice. Adam will resent me if I say no, and I can't stop him being part of that family too. Trying to keep him all to myself will only drive him away. I feel stronger while tipsy. It all seems a good idea right now.

Later, I wake up in the dark beside Adam's bed. My breath comes in rabid pants as the world settles around me. He is fast asleep, one arm still wrapped around his battered, worn Paddington Bear. I watch him for a moment, letting his calm become mine. How do I seem to him on those occasions when he does wake up? Some crazy stranger who looks like his mum? For a boy who's never had bad dreams it must be unsettling no matter how much he says it's not.

Maybe I should have some proper therapy for my night terrors. One day, maybe. *Shall I lie on the couch, doctor? Care to come and join me? Oh, no, of course, you're married. Maybe we should talk about your problems.*

I can't even make myself smile. Adam's going away for a month. Lisa is pregnant. I'm getting left behind by the world. I crawl between my slightly sweat-damp sheets and tell myself to buck up. There are way worse positions to be in. At least the thing that happened with David proves that there are still men I can find attractive. And, more important, men who still find *me* attractive. Silver linings and all that.

Despite my middle-of-the-night pep talk, and the joy and love in Adam's face when I told him his France trip was on, I'm still miserable as I watch him run through the melee at the school gates without even a glance back. Normally, this makes me happy. I like that he's a confident child. But today that immediate forgetting of me seems symbolic, representing my entire future. Everyone running forward, and me on the other side of the gates, waving at people who are no longer looking back, left behind alone. I think about that for a second and it's so pretentious I have to laugh at myself. Adam's gone to school the same as he does every other day. So what that Ian's happy? Ian being happy doesn't mean that I have to be unhappy. Still, the "pregnant" word sits like a lead weight in my heart

I can't shift, and my eyes itch with tiredness. I hadn't got back to sleep.

Surrounded by shrieks and laughter of children and the chatter of North London mums I wish that, even with the "David situation," I was going to work today. I run through the list of mundane things I need to get done before the end of school and I'm not surprised to find that the idea of scrubbing the bath doesn't really cheer my mood. Maybe I should buy Adam some new swimming trunks and summer clothes to take with him. I'm sure Ian has it covered, but I want some input into this family holiday I'm not part of.

I think about buying Lisa a gift of some baby clothes but that really is too much too soon. Their new baby is nothing to do with me. Why would she want anything from the ex-wife anyway? The first child's mother? The imperfect relationship. What has Ian told her about me? How much has he made my fault?

Once Adam has disappeared inside, I keep my head down as I storm away, not wanting to get drawn into any summer holiday conversation with the other mothers, and I'm desperate for a cigarette and want to be round the corner before I light up. My clothes probably smell of smoke anyway, but I can live without the school-gate judgment.

I feel the collision before I know I've had it. A sudden jolt to my head, the thump of a body against mine, a shocked yelp, and then I'm stumbling backward. I stay upright although the other woman doesn't. I see her shoes first, her feet tangled on the ground. Delicate cream kitten heels. No scuffs. I go into autopilot, and grab at her, trying to help her to her feet.

"I'm so sorry, I wasn't looking where I was going," I say.

"No, it's my fault," she murmurs, a voice like spun brown sugar in the air. "I wasn't looking."

"Well, we're both idiots then," I say, and smile. It's only when she's standing, willowy slim and tall, do I realize, in horror, who she is. It's *her*.

"It's you," I say. The words are out before I can stop them. My morning has gone dramatically from bad to worse and my face burns. She looks at me, confused.

"I'm sorry, I don't think we've met?"

I take advantage of a small herd of prams coming past from the school to cover my embarrassment, and by the time they've passed, I manage what I hope is a genuine smile. "No, no we haven't. But I work for your husband. Part-time, anyway. I've seen your picture on his desk."

"You work with David?"

I nod. I like the way she says "with" and not "for."

"I just left him there. Fancied a morning walk," she says. "Small world, I guess."

She smiles then and she really is oh-so-beautiful. The glimpse of her I'd had before didn't do her justice—although I had been flee-ing in panic to the toilet at the time—and I'd hoped that she just photographed well. But no. I feel like a solid clumsy lump of lard next to her, and I tuck one curl behind my ear as if that's going to suddenly make me presentable.

I'm wearing an old pair of jeans and a hoodie with a tea stain on the sleeve and I haven't even waved a mascara brush at my face before leaving the flat. She looks effortlessly chic with her loose bun and thin green sweater above a pair of pale-green linen trousers. A vision in pastel that should look twee, but doesn't. She belongs in the south of France somewhere on a yacht. She's younger than me, maybe not even quite thirty yet, but she looks like a grown-up. I look like a slob. She and David must make such a beautiful couple together.

"I'm Adele," she says. Even her name is exotic.

"Louise. Excuse the state of me. Mornings are always a rush, and when I'm not working I tend to prefer the extra half an hour in bed."

"Don't be silly," she says. "You look fine." She hesitates for a second and I'm about to preempt what I think is her looking for a way to say good-bye and get on with her day when she adds, "Look, I don't suppose you fancy going for a coffee? I'm sure I saw a café on that corner."

This is not a good idea. I know that. But she's looking at me so hopefully and my curiosity is overwhelming. This is *the-man-from-the-bar*'s wife. David is married to this beautiful creature and yet he still kissed me. My sensible brain tells me to make my excuses and leave, but of course that's not what I do.

"A coffee would be great. But not that place. It'll be filled with the school mums within ten minutes and I can live without that. Unless you're keen on a babies' crying chorus and lactated milk with your coffee."

"No, I don't think so," she laughs. "You lead, I'll follow."

We end up in the Costa Coffee courtyard with cappuccinos and slices of carrot cake that Adele insisted on buying. The morning chill is fading now that it's nearly ten and the sun is warm and I squint a bit as it shines low and bright over her shoulder. I light a cigarette and offer her one, but she doesn't smoke. Of course she doesn't. Why would she? She doesn't seem to mind that I do, and we make polite conversation as I ask her how she's settling in. She says that their new house is beautiful but she's thinking of redecorating some of the rooms to brighten them up and was going to go and pick out some paint samples this morning. She tells me their cat died, which wasn't a great start, but now that David's at work they're settling into a routine. She says she's still finding her way around. Getting used to a new area. Everything she says is charming, with a hint of disarming shyness. She's lovely. I so wanted her to be horrible or bitchy but she isn't. I feel utterly dreadful about David, and I should want to be a hundred miles away from her, but she's fascinating. The kind of person you can't stop looking at. A bit like David.

"Do you have friends in London?" I ask. I think it's a safe bet. Nearly everyone has some old friends lurking in the capital—leftovers from school or college who added you on Facebook. Even if it's not your hometown, it's somewhere people always end up.

"No." She shakes her head and shrugs slightly, nibbling momentarily on her bottom lip as she glances away. "I've never really had a lot of friends. I had a best friend once . . ." Her voice trails away and for a moment I don't even think she remembers I'm here and then her eyes are back on mine and she carries on, leaving that story untold. "But you know. Life." She shrugs. I think of my own scraps of friendships and understand what she means. Circles grow small as we grow older.

"I've met the partners' wives and they seem very nice," she continues, "but they're mainly quite a lot older than me. I've had lots of offers to help them with charity work."

"I'm all for charity," I say, "but that's hardly like a good night out down the pub." I talk as if my life is filled with good nights out rather than quiet nights in alone and I try not to think about my last good night out. *You've kissed her husband,* I remind myself. *You cannot be her friend.*

"Thank god I've met you," she says, and smiles before biting into her cake. She eats it with relish and I feel less bad about tucking into mine.

"Do you think you'll get a job?" I ask. It's partly selfish. If she wants to work with her husband then I'm screwed.

She shakes her head. "You know, other than a few weeks' work in a florist years ago that went terribly, I've never had a job. Which probably sounds a bit stupid to you, and it *is* odd and a bit embarrassing, but, well . . ." She hesitates for a moment. "Well, I had some problems when I was younger, things happened I had to get over and that took a while, and now I wouldn't know where to start with anything close to a career. David's always looked after me. We have money, and even if I got a job I'd feel like I was stealing it from someone who *needs* it and could probably do it better than me. I thought maybe we'd have children, but that hasn't happened. Not yet, anyway."

Hearing his name from her lips is odd. It shouldn't be, but it is. I hope she isn't about to tell me how hard they're trying for a family because that might send me over the edge this morning, but she changes the subject, instead asking me about my life and Adam, and, relieved to be talking about something non-David-related, non-pregnancy-related, I'm soon giving her my potted and not-so-potted history in the way that I do—all the openness, all too quickly—and making the worst parts sound funny and the best parts even funnier, and Adele laughs while I smoke more and gesticulate as I race through my marriage and my divorce and my sleepwalking and night terrors and the fun of being a single mother, all told through the medium of comedy anecdotes.

At eleven thirty, nearly two hours somehow having raced by, we're interrupted by the sound of an old Nokia ringtone, and Adele hastily pulls the phone from her bag.

"Hi," she says, mouthing *sorry* at me. "Yes, I'm fine. I'm out looking for some paint samples. I thought I'd grab a quick coffee. Yes, I'll pick some up too. Yes, I'll be home by then."

It's David, it must be. Who else could she be speaking to? She keeps the conversation short, her head tilted down as she talks quietly into the phone as if she were on a train and everyone could hear her. Only after it's over do I realize she hasn't mentioned me, which seems a little odd.

"That's not a phone," I say, looking at the small black brick. "That's a museum relic. How old is it?"

Adele flushes then, no blotches for her, just a rich rose-red bloom on her olive skin. "It does what it needs to do. Hey, we should swap numbers. It would be nice to do something like this again."

She's being polite, of course, so I recite my number and she carefully taps it in. We'll never do this again. We're too different. After the phone call she's quieter, and we start to gather our things together to leave. I can't stop looking at her. She's like some fragile, ethereal creature. Her movements are delicate and precise. Even after falling over in the street she looks impeccable.

"Well, it was lovely to meet you," I say. "I'll try not to knock you down next time. Good luck with the decorating." Our moment of closeness has passed and now we're semi-awkward semi-strangers.

"It really was lovely," she says, one hand suddenly touching mine. "Really." A sharp breath of hesitation. "And this is going to sound silly . . ." She looks nervous, a fluttering injured bird. "But I'd rather you didn't mention to David that we did this. The coffee. In fact, it's probably easier if you don't mention meeting me at all. He can be a bit funny about mixing work life and home life. He . . ."—she hunts for the word—"*compartmentalizes*. I wouldn't want him to—well, it would just be easier if it wasn't mentioned."

"Of course," I say, although I am surprised. She's right, it does sound silly—not silly, in fact, but peculiar. David's so relaxed and charming. Why would he care? And if he does, then what kind of marriage is that? I'd have thought he'd be happy she'd made a friend. In a strange way, though, I'm relieved. It's probably better for me, too, if he doesn't know. He might think I'm some kind of crazy stalker if I breeze into work tomorrow and say I had coffee with his wife. It's what I'd think.

She smiles and I can see the relief flood through her as her shoulders relax and drop an inch, languid once more.

Once she's gone and I'm heading back to the flat to face scrubbing the bathroom, I think it's a good thing that I met her. I *like* her. I'm pretty sure I do anyway. She's sweet without being sickly. She seems natural. Not at all as haughty as I expected from her photos. Maybe now that I know her I won't find her husband so hot. Maybe I'll be able to stop thinking about that kiss. I feel guilty all over again. She's a nice woman. But I couldn't exactly tell her, could I? Their marriage isn't my business. I'll probably never hear from her again anyway.

10

ADELE

I had forgotten what happiness feels like. For so long everything has been about David's happiness—how to stop his dark moods, how to stop him drinking, how to make him love me—that somewhere in all that my own happiness dulled. Even having David has not been making me happy. And that is something I never thought was possible.

But now there are fireworks inside me. Bursts of colorful joy. Now I have Louise. A new secret. She's funny and sharp. A breath of fresh air after the arid winds of endless doctors' wives' limited company. She's prettier than she thinks and for the sake of half a stone she'd have a wonderful figure. Not lean and boyish like me, but curvy and feminine. She's tough, too, laughing at events in her life that other people would want sympathy or pity for. She really is quite wonderful.

I only half-look at the daubs of paint bar-coding the bedroom wall—various shades of green with suitably expensive names. *Pale Eau de Nil, Vert de Terre, Tunsgate Green, Olive Smoke.* None whose color you could ever guess from the name alone. I like them all. Together in a line they could be leaves from trees in a wood. I can't choose a winner, though, my brain is too busy buzzing with all the things that Louise and I can do together to focus on decor.

Louise only works three days a week. That leaves plenty of time for girl things. The gym perhaps. Definitely. I can help her lose that little bit of extra flesh and tone up. Maybe get her to give up smoking. That would be good and I can't afford my hair and clothes to smell of cigarette smoke. That would betray us. David would know I had a new friend and he wouldn't like that.

We can drink wine in the garden together, or perhaps outside one of the little bistros on the Broadway and talk and laugh like we did today. I want to know everything about her. I'm already fascinated by her. I'm lost in the imagined fun we're going to have together.

I leave my tiny tins of paint and go and make a pot of peppermint tea. I push one of David's pills down the kitchen sink plughole and run the tap to make sure it washes entirely away.

I take my tea out into the garden and the sunshine. It's not long past lunchtime. I have some time before David's next call and I want to enjoy having nothing to do but savor this wonderful feeling and think and plan. I know Louise won't tell David about our meeting. She isn't like that. And she knows it wouldn't do either of us any good.

It was so easy to meet her, thanks to the map David brought home from work, clearly marked up with her help and local knowledge. I navigated while we drove around the area on Sunday afternoon, visiting each of the locations marked down, seeing how the boutiques petered out into pound shops and boarded-up fronts within the turn of a few streets. The underpasses that no one in their right mind but junkies would walk through. The cluster of tatty estate blocks only a mile or two away from our wonderful house. I also saw the primary school with the brightly colored flowers painted on the walls. I read David's scrawled note alongside the location.

After that, it was simple.

Two strangers colliding.

She didn't suspect a thing.

11
THEN

David had been waiting on the line for at least ten minutes by the time they find her, high up in the tree by the lake, laughing with Rob. Nurse Marjorie's doughy face is aghast at their carefree balancing between branches as she shouts at them to come down *right now*. Adele doesn't need any encouragement—her heart is leaping at the thought of speaking to David—and Rob mutters something wryly about insurance and clients falling to their deaths, before faux slipping from the thick rough bark and causing Marjorie to shriek in a way that is very much against the calm of the Westlands ethos.

They laugh at her like naughty schoolkids, but Adele is already shimmying eagerly down, not caring where her stomach is getting grazed as her T-shirt rides up. She runs fast across the grass and into the house, not slowing in the corridors. Her face is flushed and her eyes sparkle. David is waiting. It feels like forever since his last call.

No mobile phones are allowed at the center; contact with the outside world must be controlled, and there's probably no signal anyway, but David is good at calling regularly. This week, however, he's been in hospital again for his arm. As she reaches the small office and grabs for the old handset attached to the wall, the watch he can't wear dangles on her wrist like a thick bracelet. It's too big and manly for her, but she doesn't care. Wearing his watch makes her feel like he's with her.

"Hi!" she says, breathless, pushing her wild hair out of her face.

"Where were you?" he asks. It's a bad line and he sounds so distant. "I was getting worried that you'd run away or something." He's making it sound like a joke but there's concern bubbling underneath. She laughs and hears his quiet breathy surprise at the other end. She hasn't laughed with him since it happened.

"Don't be silly," she says. "Where would I run to out here? It's all moors. And we've seen *American Werewolf in London,* remember? I'm not wandering across that endless heath on my own. Anything could be out there. How was the hospital?" she asks. "Are they going to give you a skin graft?"

"So they say. It doesn't really hurt anyway. It was worst at the edges and that's calmed down a lot. Don't worry about me. Concentrate on getting better and coming home. I miss you. We can have a fresh start. Away from it all if you want."

"And married," she says, smiling. "Let's do it as soon as we can." As Rob says, why shouldn't she be happy? Why should she feel so bad about being happy? *You can't get engaged at seventeen,* her father had said. *You don't know what you want at seventeen. And he's too old. What kind of twenty-two-year-old wants to be carrying on with a teenager?*

Her dad had been wrong, though. She'd wanted David for as long as she could remember. Everything had been there in his blue eyes from the moment she'd first looked into them. Her mum had never said very much, only commenting that his farm was *on the edge of repossession thanks to his drunk father who'd managed to make a pig's ear of everything and an absent mother and he wouldn't have a penny to his name. He came from "bad stock."* There were so many ways to say *not suitable for our perfect girl* without actually saying them. Maybe all of what her mother had said was true, but Adele knows it had nothing to do with who David really was. It never did.

She'd loved him when she'd been a girl of eight playing in the fields and watching him work, and she loves him now. He's going to be a doctor. He doesn't need to worry about his student debts anymore. He's going to be her husband and she's inherited everything. Her parents' disapproval no longer matters and she won't let herself feel guilty. Her parents are gone, and, as Rob says, wishing herself away with them isn't going to change that. The only way to move is forward.

"You sound good. Better." He's quizzical. Slightly wary, as if he doesn't quite trust this apparent upsurge in mood, and that's not surprising. She barely spoke at all the last time he called, but that was ten days ago and a lot has changed for her since then.

"I *am* feeling better," she says. "I think you were right. This place will be good for me. Oh, and," she adds, almost as if it is an afterthought, "I've made a friend. His name's Rob. He's my age. He's very funny, he makes me laugh at the people here all the time. I think we're helping each other." She's gushing but she can't help it. She's also a little bit nervous. As if, after everything that's happened, Rob is a betrayal of David somehow. Which is stupid, because it's entirely different. Just because she loves David doesn't mean she can't like Rob. "You'll have to meet him someday. I think you'll really like him too."

12

ADELE

I have more energy after his afternoon call. He says he's going to be home late. He's meeting two charity organizations apparently, through which he can help with some community recovery patients.

I murmur all the right things in response to his awkward broken sentences, but inside I'm thinking about exactly what those poverty-stricken junkies in shit-filled tower blocks will think when David—the faux middle-class exterior he worked so hard on during his medical training now soaked through his skin like a teak stain—turns up to talk through their problems. I can only imagine the laughs they'll have at his expense when he's gone. Still, it's his personal flagellation and it suits my plans. I have plans now. That realization makes my stomach fizz.

For a moment I almost feel sorry for him, but then remember that it might not even be true. He could be going to get drunk, or going to meet someone, or anything. It wouldn't be the first time, fresh starts or not. He's had his secrets before. I have no time to check up on him. Not today anyway. My mind is too excited, too fixed on other things.

I tell him I've picked some colors for the bedroom and that I think he'll like them. He pretends to care. I tell him I've taken my pills to save him having to ask. I think, if he could, he'd come home to watch me swallow them, but instead he has to accept my lie as truth. He wants me pliable. I've enjoyed our few days of almost contentment but it can't last. Not if I'm to save our love. But for now, I play along. I'm taking care of things. I just need to be brave. I've done it before. I can do it again.

Once the call is over, I go back up to the bedroom and paint the lines of color thicker and longer on the wall. Sunlight dapples them and from the other side of the room it looks like all the colors of a forest. Leaves, definitely. I should maybe have got some pale browns, too, and yellows, but it's too late now. The greens will suffice. I look at the wall and think of leaves and trees and so will he. I think maybe it's all he thinks about. *Can't see the wood for the trees.*

I wash my hands, cleaning away irritating dried drips that cling to my skin, and then go down to the cellar. The movers, under David's guidance, brought several boxes straight down here. He didn't ask me where I wanted them, but then he knows that I wouldn't care. Not really. The past is the past. Why unearth graves all the time? I haven't looked in these boxes in years.

It's chilly under the ground, away from the windows and sunlight, and a single yellow bulb shines on me as I peer at the boxes, trying to find the right one. No one cares what cellars look like. The grime and grit of bare walls is in some ways more honest about the soul of a house.

I tread cautiously, not wanting to get dust on my clothes. A paint spot is fine, but dust could be questionable. David knows I don't like a dirty house. I don't want him to ask where any dust came from. I don't want to lie to him any more than I have to. I love him.

I find what I'm looking for against the farthest damp wall where the pale light struggles to reach it. A stack of four cartons, wearier than the brighter brown of others we've stored down here—extra books, old files, that sort of thing—with far more age in their creased, sagging sides. These boxes themselves are old, nothing in them ever unpacked, and the cardboard is thicker and more sturdy. Solid boxes for hiding the remnants of lives in. All that was rescued from the burned-out wing of a house.

I move the top one carefully to the ground and peer in. Silver candlesticks I think. Some crockery. A delicate jewelry box. I move on. It takes me a while to find what I'm looking for. It's hidden among the odds and ends of photographs and picture albums and books that avoided the flames but still smell of charring. They don't smell of smoke. Smoke is a pleasant smell. These smell of something destroyed; blackened and bitter. I push past the loose photos that flutter through my hands, but in one I catch a glimpse of my face; fuller, glowing with youth, and smiling. Fifteen maybe. It's the face of a stranger. I ignore it and focus on my search. It's in here somewhere. I hid it where I knew David wouldn't look, among these relics that he knows are mine alone.

It's right down at the bottom, under all the junk, but unharmed. The old notebook. The tricks of the trade as it were. It's thin—I tore the last few pages out years ago because some things should stay secret—but it's held together. I'm holding my breath as I open it and the remaining pages are cool and warped slightly from years in the dark and damp, giving them a crisp, autumn-leafy texture. The writing on the first page is careful—neat and underlined. Instructions from another life.

Pinch myself and say *I AM AWAKE* once an hour.

As I look at them it feels as if those words were written only moments ago, and I can see us sitting under the tree and the breeze is wonderful and the lake ripples. It's vivid and *present,* not a memory from a decade ago, and a strange sharp pain stabs in my stomach. I take a deep breath and suppress it.

I replace the boxes exactly as I found them and take the notebook upstairs, holding it like some fragile ancient text that might crumble in my hands when light hits it, rather than a cheap exercise book scavenged from Westlands all those years ago. I hide it in the zipped-up outer section of my gym bag, where it won't be seen.

It's what Louise needs. I can't wait to share it with her. She is my secret and soon we'll have our secret.

He isn't too late home after all, coming through the door at five past seven. With the kitchen filled with cooking smells—I've spent my time waiting for him making a delicious Thai curry—I drag him upstairs to look at the colors in the bedroom.

"What do you think?" I ask. "I can't decide between the *Summer Leaf Green* on the left or the *Forest Haze* on the right." Neither of them is a real name but he'll never know. I've made them up on the spur of the moment. Perhaps it's overkill or overexcitement. I'm not even sure he hears me anyway. He's staring at the strips that shine in the dying sunlight. He can see everything in them that I saw.

"Why these colors?" he asks. His voice is flat. Level. Dead. He turns to look at me and I see it all in his cold eyes. Everything that sits between us.

Good, I think, steeling myself against the rage or silence to come, preparing bitter barbs to battle with.

And now it begins.

13

LOUISE

David is in his office before I even get to work, and as I go to hang my coat up, Sue raises her eyebrows and shakes her head. "Someone got out of bed on the wrong side this morning." For a moment I think she means me, because I must look tired and grumpy. My night terrors woke me, and then I lay in bed thinking of Lisa's pregnancy—I can't think of it as Ian's new baby yet—and Adam's month away and by the time 7 A.M. rolled around I'd had three coffees and two cigarettes and was moody as hell. Somehow this pregnancy of Lisa's has brought back all those terrible emotions I went through when Ian left me, and his happiness feels like a fresh betrayal, which I know is stupid, but I still feel it. Sue doesn't mean me, though, she means David.

"He didn't even say good morning," she continues, pouring me a tea. "And I thought he was quite charming until now."

"We all have off days," I say. "Maybe he's not a morning person."

"Then he shouldn't get here so early. He seems to have taken your place as the early bird."

She has a point. I shrug and smile, but my heart is racing. Has Adele told him about her coffee with me? Is he sitting in there diagnosing me as some obsessive stalker and getting ready to fire me?

I'm almost squirming with guilt. Regardless of whether *she's* told him or not, I should. I've got too much other shit going on in my life to keep a secret for his wife. It's not like I really know her, and he *is* my boss. And I didn't really have any choice but to go for coffee with her. She *asked* me. What was I supposed to say? I remember her face, worried and awkward, asking me not to say anything about our meeting, and I have a moment of doubt. She was so *vulnerable*. But I have to tell him. I *have* to. He'll understand. Of course he will.

I need to face the music and get it off my chest, so rather than scan Maria's notes left from yesterday, neatly typed and printed as always, I go and knock on his door, my heart in my mouth. I open it without waiting for a reply and breeze in. Confidence. That's the way to tackle this.

"There's something I need to . . ."

"Shit!" he barks, cutting me off. He's tugging the thick foil lid from a can of expensive coffee—not the clinic standard but brought in from home—and as he turns, a spray of brown hits the surface of the coffee cabinet.

"Jesus fucking hell, couldn't you knock?"

I'm not sure I've ever seen someone *glower* before, but I have now. I feel like I've been slapped with the aggression and anger in his tone.

"I did," I mutter. "Sorry. I'll get a cloth."

"I'll do it," he snaps at me, pulling some tissues from the box on his desk. "A wet cloth will make it worse."

"At least it didn't get on the carpet." I try to sound cheery. "No use crying over spilt coffee."

"Did you want something?" He stares at me then, and he's like a stranger. Cold. Distant. None of that natural charm and warmth of before. My nerves jangle and my throat tightens. There's no way I'm telling him about the coffee with Adele now. Not while he's in this mood. I can't remember the last time I made someone so angry by doing nothing at all. Is this another side to him? A worm of a thought slithers into my brain. Is this why Adele keeps her friends secret?

"I was going to see if you wanted me to put the coffee on," I say, trying to stand tall. "But I see you've got that all under control." I turn and walk stiffly out, closing the door quietly behind me. It's as close to storming out on him as I can do and keep my job, but by the time I sit down I'm trembling with anger. I haven't done anything wrong. How dare he talk to me like that? Intimidate me like that?

Whatever guilt I've felt over having had coffee with Adele fades as I fume. What really went on with David anyway? A stupid kiss? That was all, and with each day it becomes more like a dream of something that never happened. A fantasy. And Adele and I would probably meet at some point. At the Christmas party or something. So what does it matter if I've accidentally met her already?

"I told you," Sue says as she comes past my desk and puts my forgotten tea down. "Don't take it personally. You know what men are like. They're all grumpy babies at heart." She leans in. "Especially the posh spoilt ones." I laugh, although I'm still hurt at his treatment of me.

Head down, Louise, I tell myself as I fire up the computer and start the day. *And get on with your job. You're never going to hear from Adele again anyway and David is just your boss.*

The Hawkins family arrive in the afternoon, and it's obvious that the patient, twenty-one-year-old Anthony Hawkins, doesn't want to be here. His parents are stoic middle to upper class, in their mid- to late fifties, a cloud of scents accompanying them in; expensive face powder, cologne, perfume. They are well dressed; he's in a suit and she's wearing pearls with her designer blouse and skirt but I can see the tiredness around her eyes. I take them into the waiting room, which is like the drawing room of an exclusive club, and she sits in a wing-backed chair, perching on the edge. Her husband stands, his hands in his pockets, and thanks me loudly. For all his overconfident geniality, he doesn't want to be here any more than his son.

Anthony Hawkins is thin, too thin, and he twitches and tics, and his eyes, full of some primal defensive anger, seem unsteady in his head. They're like those jiggly eyes you get on some children's toys, shaking slightly while not seeming to focus, at least not on anything the rest of us can see. He doesn't look at me at all. Even if I didn't already know he was a heroin user it wouldn't take a genius to guess. Anthony Hawkins could be the poster child for addiction. He looks ready to explode but I can tell it's mainly fear. I keep my distance, though. Fear is no barrier to violence, and I'm always more wary with a court-referred patient.

"I don't want to do this," he mutters, when David comes out to call him into his office. "I haven't got a fucking problem." Anthony Hawkins's accent is pure public school.

"Your parents can wait out here," David says. He's gentle but firm. No sign of his earlier foul mood, but still, he doesn't look at me at all. "It's only an hour. It's not going to hurt you." He shrugs a little and gives Anthony his disarming, charming smile. "And hopefully it will keep you out of jail." Anthony focuses on him then, his wary, trembling junkie eyes suspicious, but like a condemned man to the gallows, he follows him.

As the door closes behind them, I see Mrs. Hawkins's shoulders sag as her facade of false strength falls away, and I feel sorry for her. Whatever Anthony has or hasn't done it's taken its toll on his parents, and not so long ago he was just a little boy like Adam. In his mother's eyes, he probably still is. I make them both a cup of tea—in clients' china, not staff mugs—and tell them that Dr. Martin is very well respected. I don't go as far as to say he'll help their son—we can't give promises—but I wanted to say something, and I can see the gratitude in the other woman's eyes as if she were hugging my words to her chest for reassurance.

The uncertainty of the world makes me think of Adam, and in a moment of maternal paranoia, suddenly worried that perhaps there's been a problem at school or at after-school club and the clinic lines have been busy, I rummage in my bag and check my mobile, but there are no missed calls—all is, of course, routinely well—but I do have a text. It's from Adele. Oh, shit. Why didn't I tell him?

If you're not working tomorrow, do you want to do something? Thought we could go to the gym? They have a sauna and pool so might be relaxing. I can get you a day pass. Be nice to have the company! A x

I stare at it. Shit. What the fuck do I do now? I didn't expect her to ever get in touch. My fingers hover over the keys. Maybe I should ignore it. I probably *should* ignore it. But that would be rude, and then I'd feel awkward around *both* of them. Shit, shit, shit. I almost text Sophie to ask her advice and then don't. I know what she'll say and if I tell her about being friends with Adele I can't untell her and she's going to want to know what happens next. I don't want my life to be entertainment for hers.

I reread the text. I should answer it. I should say yes. I mean, the David thing was only one drunken fumble, over and done with. A stupid mistake on both parts. Maybe Adele could be a new friend. I feel like she needs me. She's definitely lonely. That was coming off her in waves yesterday. And she's not the only one, even though I hate to admit it. I'm lonely too—and terrified that this is *it* for the foreseeable future of my life. The weeks all melting into one.

Adele and I are *both* lonely, and however glamorous and charismatic she is, god knows what their marriage is like if he goes out, gets drunk, and snogs other women. He said it wasn't what he normally does, but they all say that, don't they? And what else could he say? We've got to work together, which is something neither of us was expecting at the time. And yeah, he was lovely the other day, but he's been horrible today. Maybe he was being nice to get me to stay quiet about everything with Dr. Sykes? Thinking about it, I should be on Adele's side in this. I know how it feels to live with a cheating man. I know how that revelation broke me, and I hate that now I've been the potential cause of a pain like that.

I may not know her well, but Adele is sweet. I like her. And it's nice to have someone texting me to do something rather than the other way round. I should meet her. It's polite. And if we get on, then I'll tell David afterward. I'll say I was going to tell him we'd met but he was so snappy that I didn't. It's a good solution. I feel better already.

I only have one reservation. Why couldn't she have suggested lunch and a glass of wine somewhere? The thought of the gym makes me want to hide. I haven't done any exercise in ages other than run around after Adam and he's six now so there's not even so much of that anymore. Adele is so obviously in shape I can only shame my-self next to her. I'm not even sure I've got any good gym clothes. None that fit anyway.

I'm about to make up some flimsy excuse and chicken out, but then I pause. I remember my tipsy self-pitying resolve at the week-end to lose the pounds while Adam is away. To get myself a life. I'm texting before I have time to stop myself.

Sure, but I'm very unfit so don't laugh at me!

I feel quite pleased with myself. Sod David. I'm not doing any-thing wrong. The answer comes back straight away.

Great! Give me your address and I'll pick you up. Around midday?

The idea of gorgeous Adele in my flat makes my stomach clench almost more than the thought of the gym.

I can meet you there? I respond.

Don't be silly! I'll have the car.

With no way out, I wearily type in my address, and make a mental note to tidy up and hoover tonight. It's stupid of course. I'm a single mother living in London—Adele must know I don't live in a mansion—but I know I'll feel embarrassed. Probably not as em-barrassed as I will at the gym, but hey, it'll all be a test of whether this new friendship has legs, and it will also serve as a final nail in the coffin of this *not-thing* that is me and David. It's one day. It'll be fine, I tell myself. What can really go wrong?

The Hawkins meeting overruns by half an hour, but when Anthony finally comes out of the office, he is calmer. He's still twitchy, but there's a definite *relaxing* about him. As David talks to his family and sees them out, Anthony keeps glancing up at him. Awkward admi-ration shines from his face even though he's trying to hide it in front of his parents. I wonder what David said to him to make him open up so quickly. But then I remind myself, bristling a bit, of how I felt in that bar. He makes you feel special. I've been there. I get it. An-thony and I are both suckers for it, by the looks of things.

I pretend to be typing a letter when he comes to the desk and although he seems calmer too, as if a day of dealing with other people's problems has smoothed out his own, I keep my expression cool. I don't know why I've let him rile me. And I wish he didn't still make me feel nervous and tingly. I'm so clumsy when he's close to me.

"I've booked Anthony Hawkins in for another session on Friday," he says. "The same time, three forty-five. It's on the system."

I nod. "Shall I charge for the extra half an hour he's had today?"

"No, that's my fault. I didn't want to stop him once he started talking."

What would Dr. Sykes make of that? David might want to do some charity work, but this is far from a charity business. I let it go. It's a nice thing he's done, and that confuses me slightly more. He's a man of contradictions.

He starts to go back to his office and then turns and strides back quickly.

"Look, Louise, I'm really sorry about being so rude this morning," he says. "I was in a shitty mood and I shouldn't have taken it out on you."

He looks so earnest. I try to stay aloof.

"No, you shouldn't have," I say. "But I'm just your secretary so it really doesn't matter."

The words come out colder than I intended, and he recoils slightly. I drop my gaze to my work as my heart thrums against my chest. Uncomfortable sweat prickles in my palms.

"Well, I wanted to apologize." The softness has gone from his voice and then he's heading away from me. I almost call him back, immediately regretting my surliness, and thinking how stupid it is when we should be friends, and then I remember I'm meeting Adele tomorrow, and I'm trapped in that secret that I haven't told him yet. Should I tell him now? I stare at his closed door. No, I think. I'll stick to my plan. If it looks like Adele's friendship is going to be a regular thing, then I'll tell him.

I need a coffee. I *need* something stronger but a coffee will have to do for now. How has my life got so complicated?

14

ADELE

"Oh god, this feels good. I could stay in here forever." Beside me, Louise rests her head back against the wood and lets out a contented sigh. We're sitting on the top step of the steam room, engulfed in scented mist, our skin slick with drops of water and sweat.

"I can never manage more than ten minutes or so," I say. "You must like the heat." It is lovely, though, all the tension melting away as my body has no choice but to relax. It's been a great couple of hours. Louise was sweetly awkward when I got to her flat, and I could tell she didn't really want me to come in—she had her bag ready by the door—but I insisted on a guided tour. She could hardly refuse, and she's many things, but rude isn't one of them. Which is good, because I wanted to see inside.

"This is the closest I'm getting to a holiday this year," she murmurs with a half-laugh.

I've closed my eyes too, mentally checking my catalogue of the rooms of her home. The sitting room: one TV, a cream sofa with a beige throw covering the old cushions, a small cigarette burn on the left arm. Blue carpet. Hard-wearing. Child-proof. The main bedroom. Small, but enough space for a double bed. Feature wallpaper behind the bed. White built-in wardrobe. White chest of drawers with a cluttered surface of makeup. A tangle of cheap jewelry overflowing from a small bag—the kind that probably came free with a face cream or in a gift set. A dressing gown hooked on the back of the door—once a fluffy white, now rough and tired from too many washes and with coffee or tea stains on the sleeves.

I've learned to be good at taking in the details. The details are important when you need to *see* a place. It's a compact flat. Adam's room—I didn't study that one so hard—is much smaller and more colorfully crowded, but it's certainly homely. Lived in.

"Also," Louise continues, and I pay attention now I'm sure I have everything securely logged in my head, "this sitting-still business is always preferable to the gym. I'm going to ache tomorrow."

"You'll feel better for it, though," I add.

"I do already, I think," she says. "Thanks for helping me. And not laughing." I feel a surge of affection for her. She did quite well, all things considered. She tried, at any rate. I hadn't run as fast or as long as usual but I didn't want to put her off. Today was about getting Louise into the idea of the gym rather than my own workout, and after spending nearly all day lying on my bed yesterday my joints were stiff and it was good to be moving, even if it wasn't that strenuous. We did some light cardio and then I showed her around the various weight machines and she valiantly tried them all as I designed a few circuits for her that would keep her muscles curious.

"You know, I'd like a regular gym buddy," I say, as if it's the first time the thought has occurred to me. "Why don't you come with me on the days you're not working?" I pause and drop my head and my voice. "And on a weekend if I come on my own. You know, without David."

She glances at me then, a mixture of concern and curiosity, but she doesn't ask why the secrecy. I know she won't. We're not close enough for that.

"That would be nice," she says after a moment. "It's going to be a long month. Adam's going to France with his father. I know it will be great for him and everything, and it probably sounds stupid because he exhausts me most of the time and I should want to kill for the chance of a month to myself, but I'm feeling a bit lost already." It comes out in a rush. "It's the end of term at lunchtime tomorrow and then his father is picking him up at five thirty. It's all been organized so fast, I haven't really got my head round it." She sits up suddenly then, eyes wide with a realization. "Oh, crap. I meant to ask for a day's holiday and I totally forgot. I'll have to call them and beg."

"Relax," I say. Of course she forgot. She's had other things on her mind. "Call in sick. Why lose a day's pay?"

Her face clouds over. "I'm not sure." She glances at me. "Your husband was in a foul mood yesterday, I don't want to add to it."

I look down at my knees. "He can be that way," I say, almost awkwardly, before lifting my head and giving her a soft smile. "But you calling in sick isn't going to change that. And it's one day. It means a lot to you but it won't mean anything to them."

"True," she says. "Maybe I will."

We sit quietly for a moment and then she asks, "How long have you been married?"

It's an innocuous question. In an ordinary friendship she'd have asked it before now, but of course what Louise and I have isn't ordinary.

"Ten years," I say. "Since I was eighteen. I loved him from the moment I set eyes on him. He was the one. I knew it."

"That's very young," she says.

"Maybe. I guess. You know he saved my life?"

"He did what?" Despite the drowsy heat, she's fully attentive now. "Are you talking literally or metaphorically?"

"Literally. It was the night my parents died."

"Oh god, I'm so sorry." She looks very young, her wet blond curls pushed out of her face and dripping onto her shoulders, and I think when she's lost half a stone or so, her bone structure is going to be to die for.

"It's fine, it was a long time ago."

"What happened?"

"I don't actually remember anything about that night at all. I was seventeen, nearly eighteen. I was asleep at my parents' house on their estate in Perthshire."

"Your parents had an estate? Like a proper country estate?"

"Yep. Fairdale House it was called." I can feel myself becoming even more fascinating to Louise: a beautiful, damaged princess. "I did say I didn't really need to get a job. Anyway"—I shrug as if embarrassed—"my bedroom wasn't too close to theirs. We liked our own space. At least, *they* did. They loved me, but they weren't exactly *loving,* if that makes any sense. And once I was old enough the space between us was good. It meant I could play music as loudly as I wanted and I could sneak David into the house at night without them knowing, so it worked."

"And?" She's listening, rapt, but I know she wants to get to the meat of the story—*David.* I'm happy with that. I don't have any details of the fire anyway. It's all secondhand.

"The long and short of it is that my parents had had some people over, and the investigators think they were both quite drunk after their guests left. At some point in the night, a fire started and really took hold. By the time David broke in at about 2 A.M., got to my bedroom, and dragged me out, it had spread throughout one half of the building. The half we mainly lived in. I was unconscious. My lungs were smoke-damaged and David had third-degree burns on his arm and shoulder. He had to have skin grafts. I think that was partly why he went into psychiatry rather than surgery. His nerves are damaged. Despite the burns, he still tried to go back for my parents but it was impossible. If it wasn't for him, I'd be dead too."

"Wow," she says. "That's amazing. I mean terrible, obviously, but also kind of amazing." She pauses. "What was he doing there in the middle of the night?"

"He couldn't sleep and wanted to see me. He was going back to uni in a couple of days. Just lucky, I guess. Anyway, I try not to think of all that too often."

She's lost in the story still, and I think it must sting a bit. Make her feel second-best. Perhaps she's used to feeling second-best. Even if she doesn't know it, she has a natural shine and people always like to dampen that. I fully intend to polish it back up.

"I'm going to go and cool off in the pool for a minute," I say. All this talk of fire has made the steam unbearable. "How about we grab a salad from the restaurant afterward? They're lovely. Healthy *and* tasty."

"Sure," she says. "At this rate you'll have me back in my size-ten jeans before I know it."

"And why not?"

"Yeah, why not?"

She gives me an enthusiastic grin as I head out into the blissfully cool air and I feel happy. I like her. I really do.

I kick hard and fast in the water, which is deliciously cold on my skin, and as my stroke slices through in long, lean lengths, I get some of the workout I've missed. I need the rush that comes with it. I love the rush.

We're headed to the café, fresh-faced and hair dried, when I glance up at the clock on the wall. It's two o'clock.

"Is that the time? Hang on," I say, in a sudden panic, and squat to rummage through my bag.

"You okay?" Louise asks. "Did you leave something in the changing room?"

"No, it's not that." I frown, distracted. "My phone. I forgot my phone. I'm not used to having one, you see, but it's two o'clock and if I don't answer . . ." It's my turn for words to come out in a rush. I look up and force a smile. It's not very convincing. "Look, why don't we go to my place for lunch? The salads here are good but I've got some great deli stuff in the fridge and we can sit in the garden."

"Well, I don't—" she starts, clearly not keen on being in my house—David's house—but I cut her off.

"I'll drop you home after." I smile again, trying to be dazzling and brilliant and beautiful. "It'll be fun."

"Okay," she says, after a moment, even though she's still perplexed. "Let's do that then. But I can't stay long."

I do like her. Strong, warm, funny.

And also easily led.

15

LOUISE

I try to make conversation in the car, telling her I can only stay an hour or so because Adam gets dropped home from after-school games at five and so I need to be back by four thirty, latest, but she's not listening. She mutters the right sounds but she keeps looking at the clock on the dashboard while driving too fast for the tight London roads. Why is she in such a hurry? What important call is she going to miss? Her brow is tight furrows of worry. Only when we're through the front door does she relax. Which is ironic, because the act of stepping over the threshold makes me feel slightly sick. I shouldn't be here. Not at all.

"Ten minutes to spare," she says, smiling. "Come through."

It's a beautiful home. Absolutely gorgeous. Wooden floors—thick, rich oak slabs, not cheap laminate—stretch the length of the hallway and the stairs rise elegantly to one side. It's a house you can breathe in. The air is cool, the brick walls old and solid. This house has stood for over a century and will easily stand for a century more.

I peer into one room and see it's a study. A desk by the window. A filing cabinet. A wing-backed chair. Books lining the shelves, all thick hardbacks, no holiday reads there. Then there's a beautiful sitting room, stylish but not cluttered. Light and airy. And everything is pristine. My heart is thumping so hard it makes my head

throb. I feel like an interloper. What would David think if he knew
I'd been here? It's one thing having coffee with his wife, but another to be in his house. Maybe he'd think both were equally crazy.
Adele would too if she knew about what happened with David. She'd
hate herself for inviting me into her home. She'd hate me. The worst
part is that here, where I feel most out of place, I have a pang for
the-man-in-the-bar. I don't want him to hate me. I'm going to have
to tell him. I'm going to have to come clean.

God, I'm such an idiot. I should never have let things get this
far with Adele. But what am I supposed to do about it now? I can't
just walk out. I need to stay for lunch as agreed. And I like her. She's
sweet. Not aloof or stuck-up at all.

"Here it is!"

I follow her into the kitchen, which is about as big as my entire
flat, and probably costs as much. The granite surfaces have a polished
gleam and I can't see a single ring or stain from a coffee drip. Adele
holds up the little black Nokia. It looks so wrong in this luxurious
house. Why does she have such a crappy old phone? And why the
panic to get home?

"Are you okay?" I ask. "What's the big deal about missing a call?
Is it something important?"

"Oh, it'll sound stupid." Her shoulders hunch in a little, and
she focuses on filling the kettle from the filter jug to avoid looking
at me. "It's David. He worries if I don't answer when he rings."

I'm confused. "How do you know he's going to ring?"

"Because he calls at the same times every day. He worries,
that's all."

My discomfort at being in their home, my pang of feelings for
David, both evaporate as I stare at her. This beautiful, elegant young
woman, rushing home in a panic to take a call from her husband?
"You have to be at home when he calls you? How often is that?"

"It's not how it sounds," she says, her eyes pleading with me.
"Just a couple of times a day. And I have the mobile, so now I don't
have to be at home."

Is it panic she's feeling or fear? It's like a slap in the face. What
do I really know about David anyway? One drunken evening and

from that I built a whole character for him. A fantasy. I remember his bad mood yesterday. That wasn't part of how I imagined him either. But then neither was being married.

"Good," I say, folding my arms. "Because it sounds more than a little bit crazy and controlling."

She flushes and puts some peppermint tea bags in a china pot. "He likes to know I'm okay, that's all."

"Why?" I ask. "You're a grown woman." The phone peals out and we both start slightly. "Maybe you should ignore it. Call him back later."

She looks at me then, a glare full of jittery nerves, and I feel bad. It's not my business. I smile. "I'm only kidding. I'll stay quiet."

She rushes out into the corridor, the handset already pressed to her ear, and when the kettle finishes boiling I pour the water into the pot. I can't hear every word, but if I listen hard I can get some of it. Now I really do feel like an intruder but I can't help it. I'm too curious. It's so weird. David may be a few years older than her, but not enough to turn him into some kind of father figure. Her voice drifts in to me.

"I didn't forget. I'll take it now. I only just got back from the gym, that's all. No, everything's fine. I'm making tea. I love you."

What's in that voice? Is she fearful? Fine? Awkward? It's so hard to tell. Maybe it's the way they normally speak to each other. I'm contemplating opening the back door and going for a quick smoke when she comes back in. I haven't heard one laugh while she's been on the phone but she looks more relaxed.

"I filled the pot," I say.

"Great." She's not going to talk any more about the call and I don't ask. "Grab some plates from that cupboard there and there's a bunch of hummus and cold meats and some wonderful stuffed peppers in the fridge."

While I'm distracted by the wealth of deliciousness stacked in their huge stainless-steel Smeg, she gets some pita breads from the bread bin and then furtively opens the cupboard above. I glance over my shoulder and then stop.

"Wow, that's some pill cupboard."

"Oh, I have some anxiety issues." She shuts it quickly. "Naturally nervous, I guess. That's why I like the gym so much. It helps me burn it all out."

"How many do you take a day?" There were a lot of pill packets stacked up and I can't help but think that much medication doesn't do anyone any good.

"Only one or two. Whatever David prescribes. I'll take them later. After some food."

I'm making her feel uncomfortable, but my face has always been an open book. She seems pretty normal to me. What doesn't seem normal are the phone calls and the pills. And prescribed by her husband? I'm not even sure what the ethics of that are. Suddenly I don't want to be here at all. None of this has been a good idea. I'd imagined they lived in some wonderful perfect marriage, but now, even after seeing this beautiful home, I'm not envious. I'm not even envious of Adele with all her beauty and elegance. Not really. The house feels like a gilded cage. What can she possibly find to do all day? My life might be an exhausting round of routines, but at least I'm busy.

"Let's take this all outside and enjoy the sunshine," she says, and I figure the subject is closed for now.

The food is delicious and I'm starving after the gym, and what's even better is to see that Adele doesn't eat as I'd imagined. I thought she'd be one of those "Oh, I'm full" after three mouthfuls of salad women, but instead she tucks in as heartily as I do. It doesn't take long until we've demolished most of what we brought out and Adele has to go in for more bread.

"Why don't you have children?" I blurt the question out. I can't see why they wouldn't. They've got money, she doesn't work, and they've been together a long time.

Adele sips her tea before answering. "We haven't wanted them at the same time, I guess. David did, early on, and I wasn't ready. Now it's the other way round."

"The body clock kicking in?" I ask.

"Maybe. A little." She shrugs. "But we're very focused on his career."

"He might be, but you must get bored." I don't know why I'm asking all this. I don't know why I want to help her, but I do. There's something vulnerable about her.

"I cook. I clean the house myself. I hate the idea of someone coming in and doing that. I like to be a traditional wife, I suppose. I just like to make him happy."

I really don't know what to say about that, and I feel sweat prickle under my thighs. While she's at home cooking, cleaning, and going to the gym to keep herself perfect, he's out getting drunk and snogging chubby single mums with baggage.

"Oh god, I forgot!" She's up on her feet and darting inside, gazelle-swift, and I wonder, *What now?* Some other David-instilled regime she's missed? What the hell goes on in this house? But then she's back outside, beaming and clutching an old exercise book. "I meant to give it to you at the gym and then with the phone thing it slipped my mind. It's to help with your night terrors."

How the hell did she remember those? I mentioned them over coffee, sure, but only in passing.

"I used to get them as well. Terrible ones. David tried to help in his own way; he gave me a book from a charity shop on the power of dreaming, but I ended up having to have therapy and everything."

"When your parents died?" An awful prickle of understanding comes to me.

"No, before that. When I was very young. After my parents died I had other sleep issues but that's a whole different story. How long have you had them? Did you see anyone about it?"

I feel a bit gut-punched. God, look at me and Adele. Same night terrors. Same poor taste in men.

"Since I was little," I say, forcing myself to be airy. "Like you, I guess. My mum took me to the doctor but apparently I was supposed to grow out of them. Instead, I just got used to them. Was a killer with boyfriends. I'd be wandering around with my eyes open like a crazy person from a horror film and then when they tried to wake me up, I'd hit them and then burst into terrible bouts of tears." I smile, although the memories aren't that funny. Ian found it so tiresome. I still think maybe that's part of why we broke up. "I did go back to a doctor, but they said they couldn't be proper night terrors because I remembered them, so I was left to kind of get on with it. Sleeping pills help a bit, but they make me feel like shit the next day, and I don't like taking them if I've had some wine."

I don't add *and I have some wine every night*. She doesn't need to know that. It's not as if I get *drunk* every night. There's no real harm in one or two glasses, whatever they say. It works for the French. I don't want to think about France. *Pregnant*.

"That doctor was wrong," Adele says. "Some people do remember their night terrors. People like you and me. Do you know how rare we are?"

I've never seen her this animated. She's focused on me. Intent. Her back straight. I shake my head. I've never really given it much thought. It's just part of who I am.

"Less than one percent of adults have night terrors, and only a tiny percent of those remember them. People like you and me." She smiles, pure happiness. "How remarkable that two people in that tiny amount have found each other!"

She looks so joyful that I have another wave of guilt. I should get home. Back to my own life and out of hers. I don't want her help. But I am curious. She said she had problems with anxiety, not sleep. If she's like me, then I'd have thought sleep would be top of her list. I look at the thin notebook on the table between us.

"So how will this help?"

"You need to learn to control your dreams."

I laugh then, I can't help myself. It sounds like new-age meditation shit and I'm a born cynic. "Control them?"

"It's what I did. I know it sounds silly, but it changed my life. Take the notebook. Read it. Trust me, if you put the effort in then no more night terrors and just amazingly vivid dreams *of your choosing*. Lucid dreaming."

I pick up the book and glance at the first page. The words are neatly printed and underlined.

Pinch myself and say I AM AWAKE once an hour.

Look at my hands. Count my fingers.

Look at clock (or watch), look away, look back.

Stay calm and focused.

Think of a door.

"Is this yours?" I flick through. There are some pages of scrawled writing, the neatness obviously lost after that first page, and then toward the back lots of sheets of paper have been torn out. It's not exactly well loved.

"No," she says. "It belonged to someone I used to know. But it's part me. I was there when he learned how to do it."

16
THEN

"Pinch myself and say I'm awake? Every hour? You want me to go around this place doing *that*? Like we don't have enough people thinking we're crazy."

"Then it won't matter."

"If you say so."

"And what's with the fingers?"

The spot by the river under the tree has become theirs and while the spell of weather holds they spend their free time there, happily lazing under the branches in the warmth.

"Your hands look different when you're dreaming. I learned all about it in a book David gave me when I was little. My parents took it away from me—they said it was rubbish, I think David did too a little bit—but it wasn't. It taught me everything I'm going to teach you." She's almost content and although the moments like this are fleeting and she's still filled with grief and guilt that she hasn't dealt with yet, they are definitely more frequent. Becoming friends with Rob has saved her from herself. He's bringing her back to life.

"They're right about you," Rob says. "You are crazy."

She swats at him and laughs. "It's true. You'll see. Same with the time. Time is never consistent in a dream. Clocks change faster."

"I am awake." He smiles at her. "See? I'm doing it." He wiggles his fingers and stares at them.

"You don't have to do it all at the same time."

"If I'm going to look like a mental," Rob says, "then I intend to look like a proper mental."

Adele looks at her own hands, dried blue paint under her nails, David's watch face glinting in the sunlight. Rob was right and the nurses are pleased with her new water art—if it can be called that—but it's not helping her lay her family to rest. Instead, she's found she imagines the old disused well in the woods at the back of her parents' house. She sees herself standing beside it and pouring her past into it. Maybe one day she'll find it metaphorically full and she can cover it over and move on. Maybe then she'll sleep. Like she used to. She's missing that time behind her own eyes. It's a part of her and guilt isn't enough to shut it off completely.

"Just do it, Rob," she says. "You'll thank me."

"Okay, okay. Only for you, though." He winks at her and they smile at each other and the warmth isn't only from the sunshine, but from within her for a moment too.

17

LOUISE

My guilt over taking a fake sickie is totally washed away by the tidal wave of sadness when Adam leaves for the month, racing out of the flat causing the casual hurt that only children can inflict in their excitement. As soon as the door is closed behind him, our tiny flat feels too big and too empty. Like everyone's moved out and left me behind. I don't know what to do with myself. I prowl around the flat until I can no longer ignore the lure of the wine bottle. As I reach for the bottle opener I see where I threw the notebook Adele gave me into the drawer. I stare at it for a long moment before taking it out.

On the inside cover of the book, high up in the corner, a name is carefully printed, ROBERT DOMINIC HOYLE, and those words interest me more than the list of instructions on the opposing page. *Pinch myself and say I AM AWAKE once an hour.* I ignore these for now—but at least they can be done at home—and stare at the stranger's name. I've always loved books with names handwritten in them, like those you pick up in charity shops that were once gifts and have notes scribbled on the inside, whole stories hidden behind a few words, and this one is no different. Who is this boy? Are Adele and David still friends with him? Did he think that this whole thing was as stupid as I do when Adele first tried to help him?

I turn the page and expect it to be more instructions, but the scribbles, tight spiky writing in Biro that doesn't entirely stay within the lines, are more than that. A record of attempts, I think. I open the wine, pour a large glass, and settle back, curious at this time capsule of writing, this snippet of Adele's past, and start to read.

If I keep pinching myself like a twat then my arm's going to be so bruised the nurses will think I'm using again (I fucking wish) but at least it's marking off the hours in this shit place. Two days of counting my fingers and looking at clocks and pinching the shit out of myself and nothing. Adele says I have to be patient. At least she says it with a smile. I'm not good at patience. I am good at making her laugh, though. She makes me laugh too. Thank fuck for Adele. Without her this do-goody up-its-own-arse place would be enough to make me throw myself in the lake with boredom. I did fucking rehab. Don't know why they had to send me here and punish me twice. So typical of fucking Ailsa. It's free so do it. I'm sure she talked the doctor into referring me so I wouldn't clutter up the flat and she could shag whoever whenever.

Adele is different. I'm only trying this shit for her. The dreams don't really bother me, I like them sometimes in a twisted way. They make me feel more alive than I do in my real life. Sometimes that feels like walking through water. Everyone's dull. Everyone's predictable. Everyone's out for themselves. Me included, but then what do people expect? Have they seen where I fucking live? People are inevitably shit and deserve to be treated as such. Not Adele, though. Adele is properly beautiful inside and out. Of course now I've written that she can never see this book. I don't want her laughing at me. I may be funny and clever but I know I'm also skinny and spotty and have these stupid braces on my teeth. She wouldn't get it. She'd think I wanted to fuck her (which I really don't). I guess I just don't like most people. Most people don't even exist to me, not in any real way, but I like Adele. I like being around her. I'm happy around her and my skin doesn't itch to get high so much when I'm with her. We're friends. I reckon we're probably best friends. I can't remember the last time I had a best friend. Adele Rutherford-Campbell is my first best friend. It's actually—weirdly—a pretty good feeling.

When the doorbell goes, I get up so fast I nearly knock over whatever's left in the bottle of wine by my feet. The notebook is instantly forgotten as I race out of the sitting room. It's Adam, it's got to be. He's changed his mind. He doesn't want to go away for a month after all and, crying and kicking, he's demanded Ian bring him home. To me. His mother. Mummy. The center of his universe. Despite the overexcited squeals he was making when he left at five thirty, Paddington clutched under his arm, I've so convinced my tipsy brain that it's going to be him coming home that when I open the door, all I can do is stare, confused.

"Oh," I say. "It's you."

"Hey."

It's not Adam. It's David. David is at my front door, leaning against the frame as if it's holding him up. My eyes are seeing him but my brain is struggling to believe it. David is here.

"You called in sick. I thought I'd check on you." He looks awkward but that somehow makes him better looking and I'm suddenly very, very aware of the glass of wine in my hand. What the hell is he doing here? Why would he come here? Why haven't I got makeup on? Why is my hair a mess? And why, like an idiot, do I care?

"It was a headache. I'm feeling better now."

"Can I come in?"

My heart races and I'm blushing. I look like shit. Not that it should matter. It doesn't matter. I also feel like I've been caught out with my lie to work, and under all of that is the stupid secret I've got myself trapped in. *Hey, I'm friends with your wife!*

"Sure." I step aside, and only then do I realize that he's not exactly sober himself. He's not steaming drunk, but there's a vagueness in his eyes and he's not as sure on his feet as he should be. He loiters in the kitchen and I send him through to the sitting room while I get another glass and a fresh bottle from the fridge and then join him. The notebook Adele gave me yesterday is on the side table by the sofa, and as I sit down I quickly slip it onto the floor where he can't see it. I feel a bit sick. What the hell is he doing anyway? Am I getting fired? What mood is he in?

He's sitting on the edge of the sofa, out of place in the mess of my life, and I remember the space and neatness of his home and shrivel a bit. There's dust on the TV where I haven't wiped it down in forever, and the constant whirlwind of Adam is still evident in the abandoned toys and tangled games console in one corner. I hand him the glass and fresh bottle while filling up my glass with the dregs of the one I've already nearly finished. I'm going to have a hangover at work tomorrow, but I suspect I'm not going to be the only one. And it will be Friday and at least I don't have to worry about getting Adam up for school. That makes me feel empty and I drink some more.

"How did you know where I lived?" It feels weird sitting next to him like this. My whole body feels electrified, betraying me even as I try and stay cool.

"I was worried it was my fault that you didn't come in." He doesn't look at me. "You know, because I was so shitty to you. They said you never take sick days."

That part's true. It's a good job and close to home. I'd rather drag myself in with flu than risk losing it and it's a wonderful break from school mums and children. Adult company three days a week. I feel guilty for pulling a sickie. I should have been honest, but Adele made it seem so reasonable and to be fair it's not like everyone else in the country doesn't do it sometimes.

"I got your address and phone number from your file, but I thought if I called you'd hang up." He looks at me sideways; defensive, sad, and drunk. *Gorgeous*. The kind of man you want to heal. The kind of man you want to heal you. Who is he anyway? Why does he even care about my day off? And why would I hang up on my boss? I think of the pill cupboard and the phone calls and Adele's sweet smile. Is he trying to control me, too? Or is that just my mind seeing suspicious behavior in all men because I'm angry with Ian for being happy with someone else? Ugh, I hate my overthinking.

"You should probably go home," I say.

He frowns and looks around, as if he's suddenly noticed something missing. "Is your son in bed?"

"No. He's away with his father for a month. They left today." I take another long swallow of wine even though my head is already swimming slightly despite the surge of adrenaline at David's arrival.

"Ah," he says. He might be a bit drunk but he's not stupid and I can see the penny of my sick day dropping. Still, not much he can really do about it now, unless he wants to tell Dr. Sykes that he was in my flat and drinking and that would definitely sound odd.

"It must be nice to have a family."

"I *had* a family," I say, and I sound more bitter than I intend. *Lisa's pregnant.* "Now I'm a single mum in London, where it's always *so* easy to make new friends in your thirties. Or not." I hold my glass up. "Living the rock 'n' roll lifestyle. Anyway," I add. "You could have children. You're both young enough." I say this almost aggressively—a firm reminder that he's married. A reminder to me as much as to him. To my body that can't settle while so close to him.

He drains his wine fast and pours himself some more and even in my own far-from-sober state I think he's a little too expert about it. Is this part of their problems? His drinking? How often does he get like this?

"I wonder if it was fate," he says. "Us meeting in that bar."

I almost laugh out loud, but instead it's a weary giggle. "I think it was simply bad luck."

He looks at me then, properly looks at me, right in the eyes, and he doesn't seem to notice that my hair is a mess and I've got no makeup on and I basically look like shit.

"Is that how you see it?"

My stomach fizzes slightly. I can't help it. He *does* something to me. It's like my brain gets put in a box and my body takes control. "Well, all things considered, it didn't turn out great for me. I finally meet a man I actually like and he's married." It's flirtatious. A half-drunk half-opening of the door. I could have said it was a mistake and it would never happen again. I should have. But I didn't.

"I hadn't felt that relaxed with someone in a long time," he says. "We really laughed, didn't we? People should be able to make each other laugh. That should always last whatever else happens."

It makes me think about what Sophie said about being best friends with your husband and I feel sad and lost. What does he want from me?

"This flat is so cozy. It feels lived in." He catches sight of my embarrassment. "You know what I mean. A family lives here."

"I think the word you're looking for is 'messy.'"

"I keep thinking about you."

He says it with such regret but my heart still leaps. He thinks about me. I immediately wonder how often and when and what it is he thinks and all the time my conscience is whispering, *You know his wife, you like his wife,* and *He has strange mood swings and his marriage is weird.* But still my stomach tightens and I feel a rush of warmth and longing.

"I'm nothing to write home about," I say as every nerve tingles and I feel awkward beside him. "Your wife is very beautiful."

"Yes," he says. "Yes, she is." He drinks more wine and so do I. Where is this leading? Is this leading where I think it's leading? I should make him leave, I know I should, but instead I sit there and swallow hard, my whole body a fluttering of nerves. "But you are . . ." He looks at me then and I want to melt. "But you are *lovely.*"

"How long have you been together?" I need to calm this down. I need to calm *me* down. I should tell him that I know her. I should but I don't. That would be the end of it, whatever *it* is, and I just can't do that yet. It's not as if anything's *happening.*

"A long time," he says, and stares at his feet. "Forever really."

I think about how she told their story. How he saved her from the fire. Why aren't I seeing that love for her here? But then, why would he show that to me? "Is she a doctor too?" I ask. Lies and truths and tests.

"No. No, she's not. I'm not sure what she is. But she doesn't work." He still doesn't look at me, but swirls his wine around in his glass before taking another long drink. "And she hasn't made me laugh in a long time." He looks at me then and his face is so close to mine I think my heart is going to burst out of my chest.

"Then why stay?" The words are such a betrayal of Adele, but I want to push him. To see if he'll snap or be filled with remorse and leave or something. Whatever resolve I had is crumbling. If he stays here much longer I'm going to make a fool of myself again. "If you're unhappy then maybe you should separate," I say. "It's not so hard once you do it."

He barks out a short laugh as if that's the craziest thing he's heard all day, in a day filled with listening to crazy thoughts, and then he's silent for a while, staring into his glass. Who is this man he hides beneath the charm and wit? Why this drunk moroseness?

"I don't want to talk about my marriage," he says eventually. "I don't want to think about my marriage." He touches my hair then, a loose strand wrapping itself around his finger, and I feel as if someone has set me on fire. The wine, Adam leaving, the loneliness, and the awful feeling of victory that he's in my house are all touchpaper to my lust. I want him. I can't help it. And he wants me too. He leans forward and then his lips are drifting across mine, butterfly light in their exquisite teasing, and I can no longer breathe.

"I need to . . ." I nod, embarrassed, toward the corridor, and then get up and go to the bathroom.

I use the toilet and splash water on my face. I can't do this. I can't. Even as I'm thinking that, I quickly wash myself and thank god that I shaved my legs and waxed my bikini line before the gym trip with Adele. I'm drunk. I'm not thinking straight. I will hate myself in the morning. I'm thinking all these things, but there's a rush of white noise and drunken lust drowning them out. Adam's gone for a month. Lisa's pregnant. Why can't I have this one thing? My face is flushed in the mirror.

Just tonight, I tell myself. It will never happen again. He might even have gone home already. Realized the error of coming here and gone back to his perfect house and perfect wife. That would be good, I think even as my body calls that thought out as a lie. I can't do this. I shouldn't do this.

When I open the door he's standing outside waiting for me and before I can say anything, he's pulling me close and his mouth is on mine and electricity rushes from my toes to my scalp. I think I mutter that we should stop but at the same time I'm tugging at his clothes and we're stumbling, drunk, toward the bedroom. I need to do this once. And then it'll be out of my system. It has to be.

Afterward, when we've got our breath back and we don't know quite how to be with each other, he goes for a quick shower while I pull on my tatty dressing gown and go and clear up the wineglasses and bottles in the sitting room. I don't know how I feel. I don't know how I should feel. My head hurts and the sex and wine have combined to make me drunker than I should be. *He's washing me off.*

I try not to think of Adele waiting for him at home with something home-cooked in the oven. My skin still tingles even though my heart feels hollow. It's been so long it's like my body's just woken up. It wasn't great sex—we were both too drunk for that—but it was close and warm and he watched me while we fucked, really looked at me, and he was *the-man-from-the-bar,* not *my-boss-Adele's-husband,* and I didn't let my eyes or hands linger on the scars he got saving his wife from a fire.

When he comes into the kitchen, he's dressed and he can't quite meet my eyes. I feel cheap. I deserve to. He's showered without getting his hair wet, the condom flushed down my toilet, all evidence of infidelity washed away.

"I should go," he says. I nod and try to smile but it's more of a grimace.

"I'll see you at work tomorrow." I expect him to open the door and rush out, and for a moment it looks like he will, and then he turns back and kisses me.

"I'm sorry," he says. "I know this is shit."

I think of Adele's sweet smile and I want to tell him I'm as guilty as he is of betraying her, but I can't.

"Forget about it. It's done. We can't undo it."

"I don't want to undo it. But things are . . ." He hesitates. "Difficult. I can't explain."

It's not that difficult, I want to say. People cheat all the time. The reasons are always selfish and base, it's the excuses we make that are complicated. I stay quiet, though. My head is throbbing and my feelings are all over the place.

"You need to go," I say, giving him a shove toward the door. I don't want him to say anything else that's going to make me feel worse than I already do. "And don't worry, I won't bring this to work."

He looks relieved. "Good. Sometimes she . . . I don't know

how . . ." He's not making any sense, but I let him carry on. "I don't like to . . . things should stay out of the office."

He compartmentalizes. That's what Adele had said. If only she knew how much.

"Go," I repeat, and this time he does.

Well, I think as the door closes, leaving me suddenly alone and terribly lonely, *that's that then.* A new low reached. Even Sophie wouldn't have done this. After all my concerns for how he treats Adele I've still had sex with him the first chance I've had.

I pour a glass of water and get some ibuprofen and shuffle back to my bed. I don't want to think about it. I don't want to think about them. I don't want to think about *me.* I just want to sleep it away.

I wake up in the kitchen with the tap running and my arms waving round my face, beating my dreams away. I'm gasping, my head full of heat. It's light already, and I blink and pant rapidly, for a moment thinking the stream of early sunlight is flames around me, and then I slowly settle back into the world, but the dream is still clear. The same one as ever. Adam lost. The darkness coming alive to trap me. This time was slightly different, though. Every time I got close to Adam's voice and opened a door in the abandoned building, I found Adele or David in a burning room, both shouting something at me I couldn't hear.

It's 6 A.M. and I feel like shit and my stomach is churning with hangover and guilt and the embers of the dream, and I'm exhausted. It's too late to go back to sleep and for a brief second I think about calling in sick for a second day, but I'm not going to be that person. Sue will already have noticed that I'm not getting in as early every day as I used to, and another sick day will make her worry. Also, I want to get things back to normal. To pretend last night never happened. I am such a shit person but even as I think that, I'm tingling a little with the memory of the sex. I didn't come—I never do first time—but he woke my body up and it's going to take a while before it settles back into my sexless life.

I make coffee and go into the sitting room and see the notebook sitting on the floor. It makes me feel guilty all over again. Adele's been trying to help me and I've slept with her husband. How have I let this happen?

I need to put what happened with David in a box in my head, separate from Adele, because otherwise I might do something stupid like tell her just to make myself feel better. And I won't feel better, but she'll feel worse. I think about Sophie and her affairs and how no one ever tells the wife and how everyone's life is probably a mess of secrets and lies when you boil them right down. We can never see who someone really is underneath the skin. In some kind of solidarity with Adele I pinch myself.

"I am awake," I say, and feel stupid hearing my words aloud in an empty flat. This whole thing is stupid, but I persevere. I look at my hands and count my fingers. I can't be arsed to get up and look at the clock in the kitchen. I figure I can do that bit at work. This is no real penance, though. Not for what I've done. Being a good student hardly makes up for this betrayal. God, my head hurts. David and Adele—I don't really know what they each are to me. A lover now? A new friend? Neither? I am fascinated by them—individually and as a pair, but maybe that's all it is really. Other than a mess waiting to happen. I can't keep both of them. I can't. I need to choose.

My phone, still in the bedroom, starts ringing, and my heart races.

"Bonjour, Maman," Adam says, and then giggles. "Hello, Mummy! I'm in France and I haven't eaten snails yet but Daddy said I should call you before you go to work . . ."

In that moment, listening to his excited, breathless morning babble that makes my tired eyes well up a bit, I could kiss Ian. He knows, deep down, how much this has cost me, to let my baby go away with them, especially now, especially now the *pregnancy* is among us. He knows how important it is for me to hear from him without having to be the one to call. He knows I don't want to feel needy, even though Adam is my baby and always will be. He knows I'm proud and capable of biting off my nose to spite my face when I'm hurt. He knows me. I might hate how he treated me, and I might hate that he's happy, but he *knows* me. After last night with David, it's a strange comfort.

I laugh along with my little boy for a couple of minutes and then he's racing off somewhere, and Ian tells me that everything's fine, the weather's good and there were no delays. It's the usual polite conversation but it makes me feel better about things. This is my real life, even if I'm now feeling insecure on the edges of it. This is the life I have to make my peace with.

If and when this terrible mess I'm making explodes, at least I will still have Adam and Ian in our own way. We're tied together by our child.

By the time we hang up, I'm feeling better, and the shower clears away the worst of my hangover. I look down at my hands under the water spray and count my fingers. I pinch myself and say that I'm awake. I try not to think about the sex I had with David even as I wash it away. I'll wear trousers and minimal makeup today. Whatever happened last night can't be repeated. It really can't. I need to do the right thing. And that isn't choosing David.

18

ADELE

I bought it on the credit card mixed in among the supermarket shopping. I normally keep all my shopping receipts just in case he asks for them, but he hasn't done that in a couple of years, and even if he starts again now, I'll pretend I lost that one. I won't be able to buy everything I'm going to need that way, but for now, the credit card has its uses. I can't cut back on any more housekeeping petty cash money because I've used enough of that to buy Louise a month pass at the gym and will have to adjust my spending accordingly—to use David's favorite phrase.

Still, all it means is I have to make a few sacrifices on my food tastes. A supermarket corn-fed chicken for Sunday instead of one from the organic butcher. David wouldn't notice the difference anyway, even though he's still a farm boy at heart, under all the layers he hides behind. He can tell a fresh farm egg from a free-range supermarket one, but that's about it. I'm the one who enjoys decadence in food and he allows me that.

I look at the e-cigarette and the spare battery and extra cartridges. She's probably in no emotional state to try going cold turkey right now, but she'll try this. I know she will. She's a people pleaser. I feel another surge of bitterness. A *fat* little people pleaser. I fight the urge to throw the expensive device against the wall.

Thinking of her makes me cry once more as I sit in the kitchen, sunlight streaming through the back door and snot streaming from my nose. I dread to think what I look like. Terrible, I imagine. I haven't even looked in a mirror today. I don't want to look at the beautiful face that's failed me. My coffee sits on the table, cold and untouched, and I stare down through blurred vision at the mobile phone clutched in my hands. I take a deep breath and contain myself before quickly typing out the text prepared in my head.

I hope you're okay and coping without Adam :-(. I've got a present for you to cheer you up! Shall we do the gym on Monday? And then lunch? Let's get bikini body ready even if we're not having holidays! A x

I don't mention the fight I had with David last night, or how he stormed out, or how I'd pretended to be asleep when he finally crept in and went to the spare room. I don't tell her how in the middle of the night he came into my room and stood over me, silently staring at me, and as I lay there with my eyes squeezed shut I could feel all his hate and anger radiating out at me from his tense, clenched body and I could barely breathe until he left. I don't tell her that I didn't even get up to see him off to work but instead lay crying into my pillow and trying not to throw up and that I'm still trying not to throw up.

I don't tell her any of these things because, angry as I am, I don't want her to feel any worse than she does already. I don't want to lose my new friend even if she's betrayed me and I'm filled with rage and envy of her. I need to crush that. It won't do me any good and it won't make David love me.

It's just come as a surprise. I hadn't expected their relationship to escalate quite so quickly. I'd forced the argument last night, but it hadn't been difficult. We have too much simmering under the surface; the forest-green bedroom walls, the cat, the thing that happened before we moved, and always, always, the secret in our past that binds us too tightly. I thought he would go out and get drunk somewhere, but I hadn't expected him to go from a bar to Louise's door. Not yet. Not last night.

Tears spill fresh. A bottomless well of them inside me and I try deep breathing to get them under control. I knew this would be hard. I need to squash it. At least Louise tried to say no. She has a good heart. She's a good person. She mentioned me and she tried to send him home. And she was drunk herself. It's easy to lose control when you're drunk; we're all guilty of that. I hate that she slept with him, and I hate how it hurts me, but I can't even blame her for that. She met him before she met me and her lust had already been ignited. At least she hadn't tried to take it further at work even though that first night in the bar must have made her feel special in her sad little life. I like her for that. Of course she's smitten with him. How can I be angry with her for finding him fascinating when I love him so much?

It's been quicker than I expected. He likes her more than I thought and it's knocked the wind out of me.

I need to be strong. I've got soft over the years. Louise makes David happy and that's all that matters even though I want to go to the clinic and drag her into the street by her hair and scream at her for being so weak—for spreading her legs so easily for my faithless husband. I remind myself that I *need* her to make him happy and I need to pull myself together and make a plan.

I sip my cold coffee and force myself out into the sunshine. The fresh air feels good on my burning face. It's still early and the dawn chill is lingering in the sunshine. I hope I haven't got it all wrong. I hope my faith in Louise isn't misplaced. I hope she is everything I think she is. If not, this could all get very complicated. I don't let myself linger on that. I have to be positive.

First of all I need to sleep. Properly sleep. I'm tired, emotionally and physically, but every time I close my eyes, they're all I can see. His pathetic sadness sitting on her tatty couch. Their drunken fuck. The tears of self-pity in the shower after he flushed away the condom. The way he scrubbed at his skin with the travel-sized shower gel he'd had in his jacket pocket, one that matches his at home in case I smelled some lingering scent of her from across the hallway. Her guilt and longing. I feel sick all over again.

PART TWO

19

LOUISE

"Why did you become a psychiatrist?" I ask. I can't actually believe that I'm lying in his arms. This is the first time he's stayed and talked to me rather than rushing to shower away his guilt and then leave. Tonight we've really talked, about my divorce, my night terrors, the ridiculous dates Sophie has tried to set me up on over the years. We laughed and it was a good sound to hear from him.

"You really want to know?" he says.

"Yes." I nod against the warmth of his chest. Of course I want to know. I want to know everything about him. Despite having vowed that this would never happen again, this is the third time in ten days he's turned up at my flat. Once was at the weekend—and even though I tell him every time to go home and that we can't keep doing it, I still let him through the front door and into my bed and I can't seem to stop myself. It's like my resolve melts when I see him. Worse than that, I actually long to see him. We drink, we fuck, he looks at me so wistfully that it breaks my heart. It's stupid. It's crazy. But it makes my heart race. It makes me throb. It lets me lose myself for a while. I try and pretend he's *the-man-from-the-bar* so I don't feel so bad, but I know I'm kidding myself. There's something that draws me to them both.

I should have told David about knowing Adele, but the moment to say something passed long ago and if I told him now I'd look crazy. But neither can I bring myself to end the friendship with Adele. She's so vulnerable. And she shows me another side of David that intrigues me almost as much as she herself does. Every day I decide that one or the other of them has to go, and every day I avoid making the decision.

I'm already a bit in love with Adele in a strange way; she's so beautiful and tragic and fascinating and kind to me. And then there's David; a dark mystery. He's gentle and passionate in bed but never talks about his marriage, which I know is toxic on some level. I should give one of them up, but I can't bring myself to. I feel like I'm woven around both of them and they're woven into me. The more I fall for David, the more fascinated I become with Adele. It's a vicious circle.

I've started to try to compartmentalize, like he does. I've separated them. Adele is my friend and David is my lover, *not* her controlling husband. It's not perfect, but for now it's almost working. There are Adele days, and David nights. Maybe I even see more of him than she does. I don't like how that makes me feel. Almost victorious.

"When I was a teenager on the farm there was this little girl who used to follow me around. She was lonely. Her parents were rich—they owned the big estate—and they spoiled her but also ignored her, if you know what I mean. They were busy people. Sometimes too busy to really spend any time with her. Anyway, she'd chatter away while I worked, telling me about her night terrors that kept them all awake," David says. "After I realized she was really quite worried about them, I found a book on sleep and dreaming in a charity shop and gave it to her." I stiffen slightly as I recall Adele mentioning the book and it's obvious that she's the little girl he's talking about. I feel momentary guilt as well as curiosity. Why doesn't he say that his wife used to have bad dreams? It's not like I don't know he's married. Why does he *never* reference her?

"Did it help?"

"I don't think so. It was all very new age if I remember right and full of crazy stuff. It was also way too old for her to understand properly. I think her parents took it away from her in the end, and sent her off for some therapy instead. She was only eight or nine at the time. My father was a farmer. Well, he was a better drinker than he was a farmer and whenever he'd have an accident with the machinery I'd patch him up. I knew I wanted to be a doctor of some kind, even though it felt like a pipe dream at the time, but giving the little girl that dream book was the first time I wanted to help the inside of someone's head. The bits a scalpel can't reach." He pulls me in tighter then, and even though he's really not told me much about himself at all, I feel like this was an effort for him to share.

"And it's an interesting job," he continues. "Getting inside people's heads and seeing what makes them tick." He looks down at me. "Why are you frowning?"

"I'm not," I say.

"You are. Either that or your forehead has aged very suddenly." He wrinkles his own comically, which lightens the moment that shouldn't feel heavy, but somehow does.

"I don't know," I say. "I just think people's heads, in the main, should be left alone. I don't like the idea of anyone playing around in my mind." I do think that, but I'm also frowning because of Adele. How he's telling her story at an angle. A little girl he used to know. It's not a lie, but it's not quite the truth.

He smiles at me, and I can't help but enjoy the strength of his broad chest under my head as I look up. A farmer's son. Maybe he avoids mentioning her to save my feelings but it's not as if I'm some ingénue who doesn't *get* the situation. "Are you sure you're working in the right place?" he asks. "Head-tinkering is what we do."

"That's why I stay behind my desk and don't get on the couch."

"I bet I could persuade you onto my couch."

"Don't get cocky, it doesn't suit you." I poke him in the ribs and we both laugh.

"But seriously," he says after a moment. "If you want help with your night terrors I can promise you I won't give you a dodgy woo-woo book and send you on your way. I'm better trained now."

"That's a relief," I say, trying to sound lighthearted, but I'm thinking of the notebook Adele gave me, and what David would think if he knew. I almost wish he *had* got up and left.

"Maybe you should find that little girl," I murmur. "See if she still needs your help."

He doesn't say anything after that.

20
THEN

The rain hammers hard at the windows and it's making Adele sleepy as she lies on her bed with Rob after his therapy session. She should be in the art room but she's bored of painting. She went to yoga to pacify the nurses—apparently it would help relax her and it did, mainly from the dullness of it—but really she wants to be in the fresh air with Rob. Maybe out on the moors as a change from the lake. Even though they're not supposed to go off the grounds without a "group leader," they could probably sneak away and no one would notice. That's the thing with hippies, as Rob says. They're so full of trust. They don't even lock the gates in the daytime.

"I am awake," Rob says beside her, pinching himself. "Only just, though. This is all so dreary."

She giggles and sighs. She had hoped that the storm would clear the air entirely but instead the fierceness has died down to this constant gray downpour and he's right, "dreary" is the word.

"When is this going to work?" he asks. "I'm so bored of counting my fingers. I half-expect to see eleven one day."

"Good," she says. "If you do, you'll know you're dreaming. And then you can picture the door and open it to take you anywhere you can imagine. Anyway, it's only been a few days. Patience, young Jedi."

"If this is all a piss-take then my revenge will be sweet and terrible."

"Where will you take your dreams," she says, "when you can create the door?" It's comfortable lying here beside him. Not like with David, no heat of that passion, no pounding of her heart, but something different. Something calm and comforting. "Will you go home?"

He laughs then. Not his infectious warm laugh, but the short bark reserved for irony. She knows these things now.

"Fuck no. Although I might dream of some decent food. This place really needs to learn to add some flavor to its lunches. Mmmm."

He's trying to swerve the conversation and she notices. She's always thought he doesn't talk about his family for her sake, because she no longer has one. Suddenly, she feels like a bad friend. So much has been about her, her loss, how to pick herself back up, how to move on, that she realizes he's never really opened up about his own world. He's *entertained* her with tales from his drug-taking, but that's about it. Nothing real. Nothing emotional.

"That bad?" They've been lying on their backs staring up at the ceiling, but now she rolls onto her side and up on one arm. "Is that why you took smack?"

"No." He smiles. "I took smack because it feels good. As for family, well, I mainly live with my sister. Ailsa. She's thirty." He sees her reaction to the age gap. "Yep, I was an afterthought, which is a really polite way of saying 'mistake.' Anyway, I live with her now. And she's a fuck-up, just in a different way to me, but thinks she's god's fucking gift. It's all a bit shitty—you really don't want to know about it."

"You're my friend," she says, poking his skinny ribs. "Probably my only real friend other than David. Of course I want to know about it."

"Well, you, my tragic Sleeping Beauty princess, are far more fascinating than me."

"Obviously." She blushes slightly. She likes it when he calls her that, even though she shouldn't and her parents are dead and it sounds almost mocking of them.

He sighs dramatically. "God, I want to get high."

"I've never taken drugs," she says. "Not even weed."

It's his turn to be surprised. "No shit."

"Yeah, literally no shit. We live—*lived*—in the middle of no-where. Bus into school and bus back, and then when I had my problems I was home-schooled for a while."

"Every layer under your flawless skin gets more interesting. Home-schooled? God, no wonder you fell in love with a country boy."

She lets the small dig slide by. She knows he already thinks she's too dependent on David. It's as much in what he doesn't say as what he does.

"We're probably going to have to rectify that," he says. "You would love it."

She laughs aloud. Rob makes drugs sound like the most normal thing in the world. For him, she guesses, it kind of is. And he's not so bad.

"Some weed at least."

"Okay," she says, playing along. "I'm up for that." And in the moment she is, but she also knows that it's not exactly likely to happen in Westlands. She can feel free and wild like Rob without actually having to do it. But maybe she should do it, she thinks rebelliously. Maybe she should behave like a normal teenager for a while.

What would David think? She tries to squash the question. She knows the answer. David would not be happy. But should her first thought about every decision be to question what David would want her to do? That can't be normal. Maybe she should be a bit more like Rob. Irreverent. Independent. Just thinking it feels like a betrayal. David loves her and she loves him. David saved her life.

Anyway, she thinks. Maybe she could do it and not tell him. It wouldn't be a big secret. It would just be one moment of fun she'd keep to herself. She might not even like it. She looks down at David's watch, dangling loose on her wrist. It's gone two.

"I'm going to hold you to that," Rob says. "We're going to get mashed together. It'll be brilliant." She can already see his mind ticking over wondering how he can make this a reality. She wonders what he'd be like if he'd had her life. Maybe he'd have been at some great university now, on a scholarship. Maybe he'd have been the son her parents really wanted.

"I have to go," she says, and he looks up, surprised.

"Not another session?"

She shakes her head, awkward. She hasn't told him about this. "No, it's my lawyers. They're coming in. I want to talk to them about some stuff. You know, all the inheritance things." She doesn't know why she feels so flustered, but she does. "See how clearing out the damage on the house has gone. Getting security people to set up alarms and stuff around the land."

"They're coming in for that?"

She lets her hair hang over her face as she gets up. "Yeah. It's complicated." Finally, she gives him a dazzling grin. A heart-melting grin. One that says everything is fine. "You concentrate on pinching yourself. If you don't get the hang of this soon, I'm going to think you're faking your nightmares."

He smiles back. "Okay, Yoda. But only for you. I might have a wank first, though."

"Gross."

They're both smiling as she leaves and that makes her happy. She knows Rob worries. She knows he thinks David has too much control over her. And she knows that he absolutely wouldn't be happy with what she is about to do.

21

LOUISE

It's been ten days since Adele gave me the e-cig starter kit and a week since I've smoked a real cigarette and I can't help the feeling of slightly smug pride as I tuck it into my bag and stroll into work. I should have tried it earlier really. I've seen them everywhere, but like everything else on my personal to-do list, giving up smoking always ended up carrying over to the next day. But I could hardly not try it once Adele had spent the money on it, especially given everything. I didn't expect to like it, I didn't expect it to work, but it's nice to wake up and not have my hair reeking of smoke. The same with my clothes. Adam will be happy too, and Ian, not that he really matters, but at the same time I don't want to be the kind of mother who the second wife can judge for smoking even though she has a child. And now I'm not. True, I probably use it too much—it's so easy to use in the flat—but I've made a vow that when Adam is home, I'll treat it like a real cigarette and go out on the balcony when I want it.

There's a spring in my step as I breathe in the summer morning air, and I feel happy. I shouldn't. Everything is, in so many ways, a total mess and all my fault, but somehow I'm managing to ignore that. I'm even guiltily enjoying Adam being away a little bit. I miss him all the time, but there is more freedom in my time now. I can be a woman of my own rather than just *Adam's mum*.

This morning the scales had gone down over a kilo. Not only is it day ten of e-cig, it's also day ten of no pasta, potatoes, or bread, and I can't believe how much better I'm feeling for it already. Adele was right. Carbs are the devil's work. Save them for treat days. It's also so much easier to follow a diet while Adam's not home. Plenty of steak and fish and salads. Eggs for breakfast. I don't even feel all that hungry but that's also partly because my stomach is in knots of lust and guilt for most of the time. Maybe I will drop the half a stone after all. I've even cut down on the wine, and what I do drink, I factor into my calories for the day. Now I need the dream thing to kick in so I can have a decent night's sleep. I need to do the routines every hour today instead of starting well and then letting it slide. I'm determined to try harder. I feel like after everything Adele's help-ing me with, I'm letting her down. I know how crazy that sounds too.

I'm early—for once these days—and rather than going straight in, I decide to stroll round the block and enjoy the beautiful morning. It'll also add to my step count, the new app on my phone quietly insisting I reach my ten thousand. Another Adele idea. She is a good friend to me. And the worst part is that if any of this ever ended up on some tabloid TV–style chat show, I would be seen as such a bitch. Maybe I am one. I'm behaving like one anyway. I know that. But nothing is ever that clear-cut, is it? I do really like Adele. She's the best friend I've had in ages and she's so different from other people. So elegant and fit and sweet and interested in *me*. With So-phie I feel like I'm begging to be fitted into her social calendar. It's not like that with Adele. I've barely texted Sophie since Adele came along. Her friendship should be enough, I know it. But it hasn't been. I may not be eating so much these days but I'm still greedy. Adele and David. I want them both. Another reason I haven't spoken to Sophie. She'd give me an earful over it. I dig out the e-cig and puff on it as I walk.

Anyway, I tell myself as the clinic comes back into view, the sex can't last. Adam's only away for a couple more weeks or so, and I won't be letting David in at night after that. What if Adam ever met Adele? What if he talked about David? And what kind of mother wants to set her son that example? To say that it's okay for a married man to come round, fuck, and then leave? I try to tell myself that's my main concern but I'm kidding myself. My main worry is that Adam is too young to keep secrets and if he ever gets dropped off at the clinic after school for some reason, the last thing I'd need is for him to recognize the man who visits Mummy some nights. It's all so sordid. Worse than that, it's a stupid, selfish thing to be doing. But when David touches me, I come alive. I love the smell of him on me. I love the feel of his skin. I love his smile. I'm like a teenager when he's there. And then when I'm with Adele I feel like I *matter*. I'm important to her.

I can feel the waistband of my trousers moving slightly as I reach for my office keys. I'm definitely getting slimmer. Perhaps between the two of them, David and Adele, they're bringing me back to life.

"I wasn't sure if you wanted one." Sue has the kettle boiling and is holding up a bacon roll. I can see the ketchup grease through the paper. "No problems if you don't, I can always find a home elsewhere for it." She smiles. "Or, of course, eat it myself."

"No thanks," I say, happy to break another routine. "Tomorrow's treat day." I'm hungry after last night's sex but I've got two hard-boiled eggs in a Tupperware pot and I'll have those instead. Preparation is key in a diet, Adele's taught me that, too, and I boil up the eggs six at a time and store them in the fridge. The bacon does smell good, but there's a strange pleasure in refusing it. Like I have control, at least over *something*. The bacon isn't the pleasure I should be saying no to, but it's a start. "Sorry," I say. "I should have texted you and said. I'll give you the money."

"You'll do no such thing." Sue puts my tea in front of me. "You're looking well at the moment. Glowing almost." She looks at me curiously.

"I'm not pregnant if that's what you're asking!" Despite the recent lift in my mood, that *pregnancy* is never far from my mind.

"I was going to ask if there was a new man in your life actually."

"I should be so lucky." I laugh then, and concentrate on peeling my egg.

"Well, carry on as you are and you'll be fighting them off," she says. "A pretty woman like you shouldn't be single. It's time to get back out into the dating game."

"Maybe," I say. "Right now I'm just concentrating on me." I still smile, although I feel a little sick imagining trying to explain it all to Sue with her lifelong marriage and settled ways. Sue would think I'm crazy and wrong, and I am. But I'm also happy for the first time in what feels like forever and is that really so terrible? As long as no one gets hurt? We're all keeping secrets. Adele, me, and David. As long as it stays that way, can't I have this? Can't I have both of them?

Sue's still looking at me, sure I'm hiding something, and I can't blame her for it. I know that my eyes are sparkling and there's a spring in my step that's been missing for a while.

I finish my eggs and look down at my hands, counting my fingers. I hope Adele is okay. Did they fight last night? Is that why he came round? Or did he claim he was at his outreach to get out that way? I think about them more than I think about me sometimes. He'd been drinking but he wasn't drunk when he left. He could probably have covered it. I'm starting to think he's pretty good at covering up his drinking. Maybe I should try and talk to him about it. His drinking. Maybe that's what's wrong in their marriage? Adele doesn't really drink at all. When we've had lunch, I might have a glass of wine, but she doesn't. I need to cut down more too. Less wine will definitely help drop my extra pounds more quickly.

I leave Sue to her second bacon roll and go to David's office and set the coffee machine going. In a stupid way it's like pretending to play house with him. I have butterflies in my stomach and I can't stop the excitement. I've always liked my job, but now there is an added thrill to it. I find myself looking at his hands as he signs off on prescriptions and letters and remembering how they've touched me. Where they've been.

I still sometimes think about how panicked Adele was when she thought she'd miss a phone call, and all those pills in their cupboard, but maybe there's nothing sinister in it really? Maybe she *is* nervy. Even she admitted she had problems in her past. Perhaps David's behavior is protective rather than controlling? Who really knows what goes on behind closed doors? I can't ask him about it anyway, not without letting on that I know Adele, and then he really would think I'm a crazy stalker, *and* I would have betrayed Adele. It's all so messy. I know it is, but that doesn't stop my heart thundering in my chest when he appears in the doorway.

"Morning," I say.

"And a good morning to you." He looks tired but his smile is warm and genuine, and his blue eyes twinkle just for me, and heat rushes in blotches to my face. It's ridiculous. We work together. I should be used to the sight of him by now, but this morning is different. Something shifted last night when we lay in bed and talked. Of course it didn't last—the familiar guilt soon settled in between our cooling bodies. Men are strange. As if the betrayal is in the laughter and the closeness rather than the sex. But then I guess it is. That thought hurt me most when Ian cheated, once I'd stopped obsessing about the sex. Maybe because laughter is harder to compartmentalize.

It's *all* a terrible betrayal, that's what I'd wanted to say to him when he left. All of it. But I couldn't bring myself to speak. How could I? I don't want it to stop. That's the honest, unpleasant truth. I want to have my cake and eat it. I want my lover *and* my new best friend.

"You're in a good mood," I say.

He's about to answer, a half-smile on his open mouth, his hands stuffed into his trouser pockets in a way that totally makes my heart melt for some reason, when Dr. Sykes comes in.

"David? Can I have a word?"

I smile and disappear back to my desk, closing the door on them. The little almost-moment between us is gone and it's probably best that way. I need to get a grip. Whatever this is, it can't last, and I mustn't get attached. It's only lust. It will pass. It can't turn into something more, and I won't let it. The words feel hollow, though. My heart's beating too fast for them to be true.

By lunchtime I'm on my sixth call from Anthony Hawkins, and in each one he's become more agitated and I'm trying very hard to stay calm while getting him off the phone.

"As I said earlier, Mr. Hawkins, I will pass your messages on to Dr. Martin as soon as he's free. If this is an emergency, can I recommend that you—"

"I want to speak to David. I need to talk to him."

"Then I'll make sure he calls you back as soon as he can."

His breathing is fast in my ear. "And you definitely have my mobile number, right? I don't want him ringing the wrong number."

I repeat the number on my screen back to him, and finally he hangs up. I add this final call to my list of messages for David and will him to come out of his practice meeting so he can take Anthony off my hands. I'm a bit concerned, to be honest. As far as I'm aware their sessions have been going well and Anthony's booked in for another on Monday. He's having three or more a week, at his own insistence, and I hope he hasn't had some kind of relapse to cause this sudden need to speak to David before the weekend.

Finally, the doctors emerge and I pass the call list to David. "I know it's lunchtime, but I think you should call him back. He sounded quite agitated."

"Was his speech slurred?" David scans the times of the calls.

"No. No, I don't think so."

"I'll call him now. And can you get me the numbers for his parents and his solicitor? And his medical doctor?"

I nod. We're back to boss and secretary, which isn't at all sexy despite the clichés. "I'll email them to you."

"Thanks."

He's still looking at the note when he goes into his office. I'm kind of hoping he'll glance back at me and smile or something but he doesn't. His mind is fully on Anthony. I like that about him. There are doctors here who—despite being excellent at their job— can fully disassociate themselves from their patients. Maybe that's the best and most professional way to be, but I don't think David is like that. But then I doubt those doctors drink every night either. He's a strange one. I wonder, as I'm always wondering, what demons drive him. How someone so good at listening to others and drawing them out can be so shit at talking himself.

I eat my salad at my desk and then let the Friday-afternoon quiet waft over me. Anthony calls twice more, even though he confirms he has just spoken to David. He says he forgot something and he needs to speak to him again. I politely cut him off, not wanting to get drawn into a conversation I'm not qualified to deal with.

At two thirty I see the light on David's Line 1 telephone button come on. The call only lasts a minute or so, and I know it was to Adele. I've tried not to track his calls like this, but I can't help it. Eleven thirty and two thirty every day. Short calls. Not long enough for the politenesses of a work conversation. Every day it reminds me of Adele's panic to get back from the gym, and I've spent enough time with her now to have seen more of these calls from the other end, even though she always disappears to another room or the hallway to take them. Of all the things wrong with my situation, of all the ways I should be feeling terrible, it's these calls that gnaw at me the most. What is it with these two? What kind of love do they have? Is it even love at all? A stab of envy hits my stomach.

At the end of the day, the last clients gone and the weekend ready to claim us, David comes out of his office, jacket on and briefcase in hand. I don't expect him to linger at the office—he never has and it would be weird—but I still feel a little pang of disappointment.

"Is Anthony okay?" I ask, part concern, part wanting to talk to him. He can't give me details, I know that, but I still ask.

"Keep any calls he makes brief," he says. "I've given him a direct line number for now as a stopgap, but if he can't get through on it, he might ring your line. Don't get into any personal discussions with him."

I nod, a little confused. What the hell has gone on? "All right." My face is full of questions, though, and he can see it.

"He's an obsessive. I imagine the heroin use gave him a release from it but became an obsession in itself. I had hoped he wouldn't get attached so quickly, but I was wrong."

I think about all the calls. "He's got a fixation on you?"

"Possibly. But I don't want it transferring to you if he can't get hold of me. It's not that he thinks I'm particularly special—he's got a history of attaching to new people. I'm part of that pattern."

"I can manage the calls," I say. I want to point out that I'm actually quite good at my job, but I also like that he's worried about me. I'm more concerned for him, though. "Is he dangerous?"

"I don't think so," he says, and smiles. "He's just a bit troubled. But it's not your job to take those chances."

Sue is in the kitchen, and she can see us from where she's rinsing mugs for the dishwasher, and so I can't ask him about his weekend plans—even though I don't really want to know; Adele is always sitting between us even though she's never mentioned—and now that the work chat is done, he awkwardly wishes me a good weekend and heads to the door.

He looks back as he leaves, a quick glance over his shoulder. A last look. It makes my stomach fizz with a surge of happiness, and then it twists in jealousy. He's going home to her for the weekend. Does he think of me at all on those days? I know he must do sometimes because he's turned up at my door on a Saturday before, but *how* does he think of me? Does he consider leaving her for me? I wish I knew what I am to him. Where this is leading, if anywhere at all. Surely he should be talking about that by now? It's not like we're kids. I feel cheap all over again and I slump back in my chair. I should end it. I know I should.

I look at the clock. It's coming up for five. I look away and look back again and the time remains the same. I need to clear out the coffee, finish some admin to leave for Monday, and then it's time to go home myself.

I think about going for a jog this evening, but I'm so tired from my broken sleep that I know it's not going to happen. I pinch myself. "I am awake," I mutter.

22

ADELE

Even though we spent the evening at home like any other couple—dinner, TV, minimal conversation—David still slept in the spare room last night. He blamed it on the warm weather, but this is a big old house and the thick walls keep the airy rooms relatively cool. He didn't look at me as he went up to bed. It wasn't entirely unexpected but I still felt stabbed in the guts with a shard of my own broken heart.

When I heard him moving around this morning, I got up and went to the gym to avoid facing him across the invisible bitter split in our marriage. I had to let out some of my pent-up emotions and I ran hard on the treadmill and then did heavier reps on the machines than I've done before, but I didn't take any pleasure in it. It all feels like a waste of time. What does it matter? What do *I* matter anymore?

I got home in time to make us both a light lunch and then he was gone. Off to his outreach work. Some badly dressed lump of a man picked him up in an old car. They all look the same, do-gooders. That's a thing that hasn't changed since Westlands days. As if dressing badly somehow makes them more worthy. At least the outreach work hasn't been a complete lie, even though I know he's used it as an excuse to go and see Louise at least once.

After he'd left I thought about texting her myself to see if she fancied a coffee somewhere—I suddenly felt lonely in the house—but then decided against it. I don't know where he goes on these days and even though it's a busy area we live in, coincidences do happen. I can't risk everything on him spotting us from a car just because I'm feeling down.

Instead, I cleaned the house for an hour or two, scrubbing the bathrooms until they sparkled and I was breathless, and then I was interrupted by the Saturday post clattering—late as usual—through the letterbox.

When I saw the envelope, the familiar company stamp in the corner and neatly handwritten address, I was glad I hadn't started an argument today. It would have been too much and it isn't needed. This will be enough to unsettle him. In my mind's eye the past is like quicksand and David's stuck in it, slowly, slowly sinking. It makes me sad again.

I open the envelope and stare at the columns of description and expenditure and glance over the cover letter. Nothing unusual or surprising there, but then there never is. We don't go back to Fairdale House and no one has lived there since the one wing burned. I reread the letter. A few repairs done on the main building. Fences maintained. Security cameras all working. No new damage to the property. Gas and electric still connected and fees paid. Drainage is fine. Rents are being paid on the outlying fields. The summer report is always cheaper than the winter one. No need to run the heating so much against the Scottish cold. To be honest, I think most people have forgotten the estate is even there: Sleeping Beauty's castle behind the hedgerows.

I put the letter and the bill down on the kitchen side where David will see it. I place it so it looks as if I've casually tossed it there. That will annoy him too. I shouldn't have opened it. I should have put it on his desk when I saw the company stamp. It's addressed to both of us, but everyone knows he's in charge of the money. I'm only the pretty, tragic puppet wife who needs looking after.

The solicitors have stopped asking us if we're going to sell the estate. We could never sell it. Although, maybe, in the future . . .

My stomach flips with the potential of everything. With the possibility of our secret being out in the open and allowed to crumble to dust and then nothing. To be free. It's dizzying but also strengthens me.

I look at the clock. It's eight thirty. Outside the summer day is beginning to fade. David will be out until ten. He didn't want dinner waiting, so I don't have that to worry about. I do have a place to go, however, and there's no point in putting it off for longer. I need to be prepared. I need to be ready. In some ways I'm actually looking forward to it.

I just have to be very, very careful.

23

LOUISE

"Dude! Are you high or something? I mean, this is a real shitfest you've got yourself into. Even I can see that, and you know how I like a good mess." Sophie's disapproval comes through loud and clear on the phone and I wish I hadn't said anything.

"What have you been thinking? And why didn't you tell me already?"

"I've been busy," I mutter. What gives her the right to be so judgmental? She's in no position to be.

"No shit. The boss thing aside, this is not good. As much as I'm happy you're getting yourself out there, this isn't quite what I had in mind." She's trying to temper her point by being funny, but I still flush as I pace around the house. She's only called me because her plans for the evening fell through and she's stuck at home with Ella. She probably hasn't even noticed that I haven't been texting her.

"I know, I know," I say. "And I will end it."

"End which? Her or him? I feel like you're shagging both." She pauses. "*Are* you shagging both?"

I smile a little at that even though I'm annoyed with her. "No, of course I'm not. It's just . . . I don't know—every time I try to end one or the other, I can't."

"You want my advice?" Sophie says, before a small voice interrupts in the background. "Hang on, Louise." Her voice quiets as she turns away from our call. "What?" she says, irritated. "I told you, Ella, Mummy's on the phone. Go and ask Daddy. Well, ask him again." She comes back into my ear. "Sorry, Lou. Bloody children . . ."

My throat is tight. I'm not sure I do want her advice. What I really want is for her to laugh and tell me it's all fine and isn't it so exciting? I have a feeling that's not coming. I'm right.

"If you want my advice, honey," she continues, "ditch them both. You can't be her friend because you'll always have shagged her husband and that's shit, and you can't be his lover because he's married to a woman you've been friends with and that's also shit. Having an affair is a big enough secret and not one I think you're really cut out for—and that's a compliment. You're better than this, Lou. Get on Tinder or something. There are lots of hot men out there—trust me. Single ones and everything. I swear to god, if you haven't got a profile set up by the next time I see you, there's going to be trouble. Okay?"

"Okay," I say, lying through my teeth to make her happy and get rid of her.

"I've got to go, Lou—Ella's about to go into meltdown. But keep in touch. I'm here if you need me."

She hangs up but I still hear her words echoing in my head. *Ditch them both.* That's easy for her to say with her busy life and her family and her affairs. Sophie is never short of attention or company.

I probably won't even see her before Adam gets back and then I'll have to dump David so it will all be resolved. Not that I need to do anything to please Sophie. When she tells me about her affairs, I listen and nod and keep my judgments to myself. Why couldn't she do the same? She thinks she knows best, but she doesn't. I can't imagine Adele ever telling me what to do like that. Adele would listen and be supportive—like a proper friend.

I realize how crazy that sounds, given the situation, and so I put Sophie firmly out of my head and pour my second glass of wine, adding some ice to make it last longer. I don't feel too bad because I've allowed the calories for it and to be honest I could have been worse

today. Weekends are hard to diet on, but now I'm feeling the difference, it's getting a bit easier. I didn't jog because my sleep screwed me
over and I couldn't face it, but I did go for a long walk, and although
I had a massive craving for bread I just had fish and vegetables for dinner before calling Adam and Ian and hearing about all the delicious
things they'd been eating, which made my stomach rumble more.

So, I'm not going to beat myself up over the wine. You've got to
have some fun and it's not like getting tipsy can lead me down the
dark path to overeating. The cupboards are bare and I'm too lazy to
go out at this time of night. I need the wine to sleep anyway. I'm sure
my night terrors have got worse but then I guess that's not surprising
as I'm fucking my new friend's husband. I say the word harshly in my
head so that I flinch. Yeah, no wonder my sleep is so disturbed.

I flick through the channels looking for some distraction. Some
awful talent show is on, but that's about it. An old episode of *A Touch
of Frost*. Nothing to grab me. I drink more wine, and my mind drifts
back to David and Adele. There's always some part of my brain
thinking about David and Adele. Is he thinking about me? Is *she*
thinking about me? I almost laugh. How fucked up is that? I should
get an early night. At least tomorrow I can lie in if my sleep is shit.

I go to the kitchen and top up my glass. Still just under half a
bottle left if I stop now and that's way better than normal. Is David
drinking at home? Have they gone out for dinner? Are they having
some kind of guilty make-up sex? Does he compare our bodies?
God, I hope not. The questions hum away in my head and I give up
fighting them.

I get the notebook out of the kitchen drawer. It's my link to
them, and if they're going to be in my head, then I may as well dip
back into Adele's past, even if it is a strain to figure out the scribbled, messy words. Also, I've been much better at the routines over
the past couple of days. Maybe this will help me really grasp it.

I switch off the TV and take my wineglass through to the bedroom. I've got a mellow, tired buzz on even though I haven't drunk
all that much. Dieting is turning me into a cheap date. I try not to
think about how cheap I already am, given everything.

I keep my T-shirt on but ditch the rest of my clothes on the floor and get into bed. My eyes are already heavy and I take a big swallow of wine. I haven't brushed my teeth. I'll do it when I finish my drink—mint and wine are not a good mix—but the odds are on I'll probably fall asleep first and then do it when my bad dreams wake me up in a few hours. I'm so rock 'n' roll, I think, half-smiling at how not rock 'n' roll I am, in bed before ten, and then I flick on the bedside lamp and open the notebook. The small spiky writing hurts my eyes at first, but slowly I learn the shapes of it. Adele and David's past. Your sleep, my inner voice tells me. You're reading this to help your sleep. Yeah right, I answer myself. We both know that's a lie.

. . . It starts the same as usual. I'm running and they're all coming after me. The dealers from the estate, my long-gone waste of space mother, Ailsa, that boy I beat up in the alley that time for no other reason than my skin itching, my lack of high, and all my bubbling rage. They're them, I know they're them, but they're also not them. Monstrous versions of themselves, how I see them really; sunken eyes, flabby skin, sharp teeth bloody from sucking me dry of everything with their constant existence. I've got marks in my arms where my mum and Ailsa have caught and bitten me before I've broken free. Don't need a head doctor to tell me what that's about. They'd call it guilt. Guilt about my habit and the effect it has on my family. They have no idea what's in my head. The marks and the biting and the sucking my blood are about them sending me to rehab and making me give up the one thing I actually enjoy in this dreary life.

I'm running through the tower block. Not the one I live in with Ailsa, but the one my mum and "Shanks," her pedo boyfriend, really named Terry, shared before he disappeared. It's old and stinks so badly of piss in the lifts that even when they're working it makes you think fuck that and take the stairs. I'm on the stairs in the dream and I can hear them behind me, calling after me, insulting me. "We know about you! Don't think we don't!" my mum shrieks. The voices are wet, too many sharp teeth in their mouths. I can hear metal clattering against the concrete steps and my legs feel as if they're moving through treacle. I can't get any speed up. I reach a landing and look back.

They're two flights down but moving fast in a crazy half-human, half-beast pack. Their hands have long, sharp knives where their fingers should be, dragging along behind them. They're coming to slice and dice me and then eat me up. I'm too tired to keep running up the stairs and I look toward the door from the stairwell to the line of crappy flats. Hip-hop music booms from somewhere. There's a grimy glass panel in the door and through it I see Shanks, never one to be left out. He glares at me from the other side of the dirty glass and raises a finger-knife and wiggles it as if telling me off.

I'm stuck. They're going to catch me, I know it. Their fingers will tear me apart. This is normally where I freeze in the dream and only when Ailsa reaches me do I wake up. But not this time. This time, dream-me has a moment.

Doors.

Fingers.

I look down at my hands. There's an extra little finger on my right one. I stand there on the landing and almost laugh. I'm dreaming and I know it. The sound of scratching metal fades as I concentrate. I look at the landing door, but I know it's not the door I want. I turn to the wall where some amateur ugly graffiti tags have been lazily sprayed. I mentally rearrange the lines to form a small door with a round handle like on a kid's drawing.

The monsters behind me are closing in, but I ignore them as I reach out to open my new door. I think of a beach. Not the one from the crappy holiday we had in Blackpool, where it rained nearly every day and Ailsa had teenage tantrums all the time because she hadn't been able to bring her spotty twat of a boyfriend, but a really posh beach like in travel agents' windows.

I twist the handle and step through.

My night terror disappears, and I'm on a white beach, warm breeze in my hair, the sand hot between my toes as the warm water laps at them. I'm in shorts and a T-shirt. I'm calm. I want to laugh. I want Adele to see this and then suddenly she appears—a dream-Adele. The water is unnaturally blue but it's how I've always imagined the ocean to be. I add dolphins. I add a waiter

*walking toward us with tall cocktails. They look odd. I've never
had a cocktail, but it tastes of strawberry slush, how I think they
should. I almost add a needle and a high, but I don't. In the dream
I laugh and then the dream-Adele laughs and then I can't hold it
anymore and I wake up.*

*BUT I DID IT. I can't fucking believe I did it. I fucking
did it! I can be the king of my own dreams. The next time will be
better. I know it. I'm too pumped to go back to sleep. It's 4 A.M.
and everyone's asleep but my heart is racing. I haven't felt this
good about anything in forever. It was like magic. Real magic, not
a drug high. I'm itching to go and tell Adele but the girls are in
the other half of the house and I can't risk getting caught in there.
They'd kick me out. When I got here I'd have welcomed that, but
not now. I'm totally buzzing. I'm grinning like a twat just writing this. I won't tell her that I imagined her on the beach with me,
that she appeared straight away as if it were meant to be. As if
I can't imagine being happy without her. That freaks me out
enough, fuck knows how she'd feel about it.*

*Nearly halfway through our stay now. What will happen
when we leave? Can't imagine Doctor-David wanting me around.
Adele says he'll love me, but she doesn't know people like I do and
he seems like a control freak to me.*

*I'm still wondering what that solicitor shit was all about. I
haven't pushed her on it, but she was weird after. She'll tell me eventually. I'm good at getting people to talk. I do more listening than
talking in the sessions now. Everyone wants to talk about themselves.
Fundamental. Maybe I should get a fucking job here. (JOKES.)*

*The birds are waking up outside. I still can't believe I did it.
All that pinching and finger counting paid off. I controlled my
fucking dream. David can't do that. This is something that's hers
and mine . . .*

My eyes are blurring and I find myself reading the last sentence
twice as the wine makes my head fuzzy. I close my eyes. Just for a
second. The book slips from my hand. I need to brush my teeth,
I think, vaguely, and then I'm asleep.

24

ADELE

It's just awful. Awful. There are no other words to describe this morning. The shouting has stopped but this deathly quiet is worse. I feel sick. I'm shaking. I don't actually know what to say, or if there's anything I should say. Or can say. This is all my own doing.

"I'm moving into the spare room. For now. For a while. I think that's for the best. Until we decide what we're going to do." His voice is professionally calm, but he's livid. I know him. All I want to do is cry, but I don't. I keep my face haughtily impassive. I don't want him to know how much he's hurting me.

"Where's the credit card?" he asks, his eyes cold.

The things I've ordered from the shopping channel started arriving at 8 A.M. and were all here by nine. I timed them all perfectly, paying extra for a specific time slot. The buying only took an hour or so of dedicated effort, but David's American Express account is now hyperventilating at the cost of my random purchases. A new coffee machine—the finest model. A new bread maker—the same. Some jewelry. A very expensive camera. A slicer/dicer/steamer with all the accessories. And the pièce de résistance, a top-of-the-range treadmill. Thousands of pounds gone.

Like a child I take my handbag from the back of one of the

kitchen chairs and pass it to him, and then watch as he pulls the precious card from my wallet and cuts it up.

"I thought this was supposed to be a fresh start," he says as he throws the plastic quarters into the bin. He looks so cold. I want to tell him that everything is going to be okay and to trust me, but I can't. I've started down this path, doing things to push him away from me and toward her, and I have to stay on it. I can't be weak. I have to have faith in Louise and me and David to make this work.

"I thought all this was done with a long time ago," he mutters, and stares down the hallway where it looks like we've just moved in again, boxes everywhere. "I'll arrange to have everything sent back." He pauses. "You can keep the treadmill if you want."

I know what he's thinking. He can trap me in the house for more of my time with that. "It can go back," I say. He can't cancel the gym membership anyway. We're paid up for the year. It was cheaper that way and I was trying to please him at the time. Our *fresh start.*

I stare at him. Does he still have even a tiny ember of love left for me? He must do. He must. He goes back into my bag and takes my house keys.

"I have to go to the outreach center. I don't have any choice. They've arranged a clinic, but I'll only be two hours."

Of course he has to go out. Work comes first. He always wants to help people. Except us. Except me. He's given up there. For me it's just pills, pills, and more pills. I don't understand why he's taken my keys until he goes to the kitchen door, locks it, and pockets the key, and then I bark out an unpleasant half-laugh. I can't help it.

"You're locking me in?" I'm incredulous. Our marriage has felt like a prison for some time, but is he now becoming my jailer?

"It's for your own good." At least he has the decency to redden and not meet my eyes. "Only for this morning. I can't be . . . I can't be . . ."—he struggles to find the words—"I can't be distracted." He gestures feebly at the corridor and then at my face. "By all this." He looks away. He can't bear to look at me. "Get some rest. Maybe we need to change your meds again. I'll sort it out tomorrow."

I'm stuck on that word, "distracted." What he means is he can't be distracted by wondering where I am and what I'm doing. Even our little phone call routine isn't enough for him.

Maybe you should cut your distractions by not fucking your fat receptionist, is what I want to scream at him, but I don't. The pills he made me take in front of him are kicking in and I'm starting to feel a bit drowsy. I don't actually mind. Some sleep will do me good.

His phone beeps and his lift is here. He doesn't take *my* phone from me—whether on purpose or because he's still reeling with everything else and has forgotten about it—and I'm relieved. I've hidden it just in case, but I'm taking enough, probably premature, risks already. The phone is for another time.

"We'll talk more later," he says, heading for the door. His words are hollow. Talking is something we really don't do. We don't talk about us and we don't talk about *that*. He pauses and looks back, and I think he's going to say something more but he doesn't.

We stare at each other for a long moment, once lovers, now silent combatants, and then he's gone.

I hear the key turning in the bottom lock and I feel entombed in our house. It's very strange to know I can't get out. I haven't felt so helpless in a long time. What if there's a fire? What if the house starts to burn while I sleep? I'm dozy on medication. What if I put a pan on to boil and forgot about it? Has he considered any of these things? It's not as if a fire hasn't happened before. Perhaps he thinks I'm resourceful enough these days to get out by myself. And to be fair, the windows would be easy enough to break if I put my mind to it.

I stand in the silence and stare at the glass and think of flames and my mind ticks over with ideas, and then the throbbing in my face brings me back to the present. I've taken all *his* pills but what I really need is some ibuprofen.

I take two with water and then go into the downstairs cloakroom and turn on the light, leaning over the sink to examine my face in the mirror. The bruise is quite something, blooming high on my cheekbone. My skin has swelled tight and I flinch when I gently touch it. Last night, it was just a red glare. Today it's staking its claim on my face. My eye isn't closing up, though, which is a relief. The bruise will have gone within a week, I'm sure.

I hate it. His concern at the growing bruise first thing this morning vanished when my shopping started to arrive and that was that. More anger and the same demanding questions of last night that I still wouldn't answer. He wanted to know where I'd been. Why I was out when he got home. What I'd been doing.

I obviously can't tell him where I *really* was—I'd planned to be home before him but my poor timing was another error in last night's fiasco—but perhaps I should give him something. Or not. I'm quite enjoying this moment of quiet power over him. I may be the one locked in, but what he wants to know is locked in my head. I'll take that. Still, I feel exhausted now that I'm alone.

It's not only my face that hurts. My arms and legs ache too. My muscles scream from being strained. Even my ribs hurt a little.

I need a bath. I need to soak it all away and think. I take the stairs slowly, weighed down by my self-loathing and self-pity, and as I start the water running, I move his shirts from our wardrobe to the smaller one in the spare bedroom. I hang them in color order, how he likes it. I touch them with all the gentleness with which I can no longer touch him. Self-doubt grips me and I feel very, very alone.

I take my mobile phone out of the shoebox at the back of the cupboard, hidden under a pair of satin Jimmy Choos, and then peel off my clothes and lower myself into the hot bubbly water. I keep the phone within reach, on the toilet lid. Maybe he'll try ringing me. Maybe he's sorry. Maybe he'll tell me he wants to make everything better. They're idle thoughts. We're too far down this long track for that.

I close my eyes and let the water soothe my muscles. My heartbeat throbs in my face; a steady rhythm pacified by whatever drug he's made me take. It feels quite pleasant in a strange way. I'm about to drift off when the sharp buzz of vibration jolts me upright. It's a text. From Louise. I stare at the screen. She never texts at weekends.

I did it!!!!

I stare at the words, and then I smile, despite the pain in my face. She did it. She actually did it. My heart races, pounding its beat in my chest and cheekbone. I love Louise. I really do. I could burst with pride.

Suddenly, I'm no longer sleepy.

25

THEN

The smoke is strong and sweet and when it hits her lungs it's such a shock that she coughs it back out until her eyes water and then they're both laughing, even though her chest feels like it did in the days after the fire.

Rob takes the joint back and smoothly inhales a deep lungful. He blows out smoke rings. "That, my dear," he says in a faux posh accent, "is how to do it."

"Where did you get this shit?" She tries again, and this time manages to fight the urge to choke. The buzz is pretty instant. A warm, tingling, lightheaded feeling. She likes it.

He wiggles an eyebrow at her. "I have my own irresistible ways."

"No, really. Where?" Rob is pure energy to her. She loves him a little bit, she knows that. He's so *different*. She has never met anyone who gives less of a shit about all the things you're supposed to find important. All the things her parents found important. The things David finds important. Having a plan. A career. Rob is like the wind. Here, there, and everywhere. Destination unknown. It must be wonderful to be like that.

"One of the nurses. I persuaded him to get it for me."

"Which one?" She stares at him. She can't even imagine how she'd start going about that.

"Does it matter? They're all equally dull," he says, looking out into the night. "Just one of them." They're locked in one of the bathrooms. The sash window is pushed up high, and they're squashed together as they lean out, smoking. She had gone to the boys' wing even though Rob had volunteered to come to her. She wanted to do it. She wanted to take a risk. To feel something. And creeping through the corridors to the central staircase, sneaking past the solitary light of the night nurse's station below, and then up to the other, illicit wing of Westlands had been exhilarating. She'd been breathless and giggling when she got there and now with the weed burning her lungs she feels brilliant.

She wonders which of the nurses he got it from and why he won't tell her. Is it because she hasn't told him why the solicitor was here? He hasn't asked, but she knows him well enough to know that isn't because he's not curious. Of course he's curious. He's the cleverest person she knows, except maybe David. She takes the joint from him and inhales. There's a cool breeze that lifts her hair and she feels like she's flying. She laughs a little bit, from nowhere. Flying. Maybe she will tell Rob about the solicitor. They have their own secret now anyway. As if in tune to her thinking, Rob speaks.

"Where do you go when you dream? You know—what's on the other side of the door for you?"

"Different places," she says. It's a deflection. It's harder for her to explain. The first door was a long time ago for her. It's different now and has been for a few years. He's new to all this. "Depends on my mood."

"It's so weird," he says. "Weird, but brilliant."

It's been five nights since Rob first managed it, and since then he's been like a natural. She knows he's not lying—not that she thinks he would—because all the therapists are calling it progress. They're all feeling smug. He's the golden boy at Westlands now that he sleeps without screaming—they think they've cured him. They think they've helped her, too. If only they knew they had nothing to do with it. There are doors in the mind to be opened, but not how they think. Not at all. How would they cope with the truth?

They'd probably need therapy. She giggles aloud at that. She's start-ing to think like Rob.

"It's like having the world at your fingertips," he says.

"Yep." She nods. "And no more nightmares."

"Amen to that," he says, and passes her the spliff. They've nearly finished it, but she doesn't mind. Her head is swimming and she thinks that much more might make her sick, but she's loving the way her skin feels odd and all she wants to do is laugh. Everything is funny. She grins at Rob and he grins back and they don't need to say anything. After a moment, she rests her head on his arm. It's thin and wiry, so different to David's broad shoulder and farm-strengthened bicep. David's watch would hang as loosely on Rob's wrist as it does on hers. It feels good to lean on Rob, though. She feels safe.

She could never have this moment with David, and that makes her a little bit sad. David barely dreams, let alone has night terrors. David didn't listen when she tried to tell him. David would never be able to do what Rob has done and that's a simple fact. But it doesn't stop her feeling wonderful that there is someone who can. A friend who can. Someone she can share it with. Some of it at least.

26

ADELE

He's true to his word and is only out for two hours, and I'm meek when he gets home. Although the text from Louise has lifted my spirits, I'm still haunted by last night's events and my abysmal failure. I was too sure of myself and now my confidence is entirely knocked and I feel terribly alone.

"I've moved your clothes into the spare room," I say softly when he finds me in the kitchen, suitably cowed.

He replaces the kitchen door key in the lock and at least has the decency to look uncomfortable for trapping me in here. He stays facing the door for a moment and then turns. The fight has gone out of both of us. His shoulders are as slumped as mine.

"Why did you paint our bedroom and hall those colors?" he asks. He's asked the question so many times already, but I love that he says *our,* as if we are still somehow a *we.*

"They're just colors, David," I say, repeating the same answer I've given every time. "I like them."

He gives me that look again, as if I'm a stranger from some alien planet that he has no chance of ever understanding. I shrug. It's all I've got.

"Don't paint the spare room."

I nod. "I hope you sleeping there is temporary."

This is us *talking*. This complete noncommunication. Perhaps it's him who needs all the medication, instead of spending his days drinking his brain to dullness. It's not good for him. It's not good for the future. It needs to stop, but I'm hardly in a position to put my foot down now. Maybe he'll stop when this is all over. Maybe he'll let me help him then.

He goes and hides in his study, mumbling something about work, the conversation over for now. I presume that looking at me has made him want a brandy and I don't want to analyze the reasons for that.

I let him go and don't call him on the fact that I know he has several bottles of spirits in his study and that maybe I'm not the only one with secrets in this marriage, however well he thinks he hides them from me. Instead, I do what I do best, and start preparing the roast lamb for dinner. There is something heartwarming about a roast dinner and we both need that.

I season the meat with rosemary and anchovies driven into the fatty skin, and then, as I chop and sauté and simmer my potato and vegetable side dishes, the steam makes my bruise throb. I've covered it with makeup and David no doubt thinks that's to hide it from him, but he'd be wrong. It's to hide it from myself. I'm filled with shame at my own weakness.

I lay the dining room table using our best dinner service and have candles lit and all the dishes laid out between us before calling him in. I've poured him a glass of wine even though my glass is only filled with San Pellegrino. I'm not sure if I've done all this to please him, or to comfort myself after the ugliness of last night. I look for some sign of approval but he barely registers my efforts.

Our plates are full, but neither of us really eats anything. I try and make small talk about his outreach work—as if I care—but he cuts me off.

"What's going on, Adele?"

I look up at him, my stomach in knots. He's not worried, he's cold. It's all part of my plan but it's not what I want. And I certainly don't want it yet. I try to think of something to say but my words have dried up. I only hope I look beautiful in the candlelight, even with the mottled bruise he's trying not to see. He puts his knife and fork down.

"What happened before we moved, that was—"

"That was your fault." I find my voice now, even though it's almost whiny, nails on a chalkboard. "You know it was. You said it was."

"I said it to pacify you. I didn't mean it. You wanted a fresh start and I've tried to give you one."

I can't believe he has the audacity to say that. He's fucking his receptionist. Some fresh start. I lower my own knife and fork, carefully placing them on the edge of my plate. My efforts over dinner are going to be wasted.

"I admit I've made some mistakes," I say. "And I'm so sorry. You know I have problems. I think moving unsettled me."

He shakes his head. "I can't contr—I can't look after you anymore. I'll ask you one more time. Where did you go last night?"

Control. That's what he meant to say. He can't control me anymore.

"I went for a walk," I say. "I lost track of time."

We stare at each other and I try and look innocent, but he's not buying it.

"Honestly," I add, and immediately regret it. It's the word everyone uses when they're lying. *Honestly, she's just a friend.* That's what David had said when we lived in Blackheath.

"This can't go on," he says.

Is he talking about us or me? Does he want me locked up somewhere? Another residential home where people can *help* me, but this time on a long-term basis? While he swans off with my money and his freedom? It makes me want to cry.

"I think I missed a few pills," I say. It's a risk. I don't want him popping back from work to make sure I take them. I need a clear head and my mind is working just fine anyway. "I'll level out. You know that."

This is like the early days all over again, but now he doesn't have the wealth of love for me that sustained him before I got myself together. That well has run dry.

"You know you can never leave me, David," I say. It's good to say his name aloud. "You know that." It's a threat. It's always been a threat.

And there it is, the past sitting between us alongside my untouched roast and creamed leeks and glazed carrots and three types of potato, and I know that, despite everything, I'm doing the right thing to save my marriage.

"I know," he says, pushing his chair back. "I know." He doesn't look at me as he walks toward the door. "I'm going to have a shower and an early night."

"I'll repaint the bedroom," I say, to soften my last words. "If you'll come back to it."

He glances back then and nods almost imperceptibly, but the lie is in his eyes. There's only one bed he wants to share and it isn't mine. I wonder what Louise is doing. I wonder if she's thinking of me or him. I wonder if all my planning is going to go to shit.

Dinner, it would appear, is over. I watch him leave, and then, once I hear the heavy tread on the stairs, I get up and drain his wine. I look at the china. The leftover food. This life I fought so hard for. My bruise throbs hard as I fight tears. I take a deep shaky breath. I never used to cry at all. I don't know what's happened to me. I've changed. I almost let out a weepy laugh at that. At least I still have my sense of humor.

I've got the roasting pan soaking when the doorbell goes. A short, sharp burst. I go into the hall and glance up the stairs, but the shower is running and David hasn't heard. I feel breathless. Who can it be? We don't have passing visitors. We don't have friends. Only Louise. She wouldn't come here. Would she? This is not the time for her to confess. That would complicate everything.

I open the door an inch or two and peer out through the gap. The young man stands nervously on the second step to the front door, as if almost afraid to come right up.

"Can I help you?" I ask quietly, opening the door wider.

"Is Dr. Martin in?" he says. "It's Anthony. Tell him it's Anthony. I'm a patient of his." He's been keeping his eyes down, but then he glances up at me, and I see myself as he must see me. A fragile beauty with a black eye. Suddenly, I find some use for last night. I look over my shoulder, as if nervous, before answering.

"He's gone to bed with a headache. I'm sorry." I keep my voice low. I'm glad I didn't dress up too much this evening. Even with the bruise I would have looked too aloof, out of reach. I'm wearing a long summer dress with shoestring straps and my hair is loose. His eyes have stayed on me, and I know that look. I've seen it on many men before. Surprise and longing and lust. I have that effect on them. I think he's forgotten about David already.

"I'm his wife," I say, and then, for good measure, I add, "I can't talk to you."

The skinny dark-haired boy's hands twitch and one foot taps on the step but he's not aware of it. He's wearing a black T-shirt and I can see the traces of track marks on his arms. I recognize what he is.

"You have to go away," I lean out and whisper, knowing full well that by tilting forward slightly I'm giving him a teasing glance of my breasts. "Please." I lift one hand almost to my face, to where the growing bruise mars my skin. "This isn't a good time."

"Are you all right?" he asks. His accent is so middle class, at odds with his look.

"Please go," I repeat. "I think he's coming." I make sure there's a wonderful hint of urgency in my voice and then close the door. Through the glass I can see that he lingers for a few moments longer and then the dark shape of him disappears.

I lean against the wood. Anthony. His name is like sweet ambrosia to me. My shoulders relax as my shame at last night's failure fades. Maybe it's all going to work out after all.

27

LOUISE

"What the hell happened?" I say, aghast. It's Wednesday and the first time I've seen Adele this week. And now I know why.

I thought I'd definitely hear from her on Monday morning—not only because the gym has kind of become part of a new routine—but also because I'd been so excited about controlling my dreams. More than that, I really thought she would be too. I thought she'd want to hear *everything*. But she was silent. I thought about sending another text but didn't want to be needy and I'm on a guest membership she's paid for at the gym so didn't want to look like I was taking it for granted.

At first I was only a little upset, but by Monday evening, when I was sitting alone at home and David hadn't appeared either, my hurt had turned to worry. Maybe I'd got Adele into trouble with my weekend text? Maybe David had seen it? But if he'd seen it then surely he'd have come round and wanted to know what was going on. It was possible that she had my number logged under a false name. Maybe he did too for that matter. But if so, then why hadn't I heard from her? Had he taken the phone?

Yesterday David was quiet at work, none of the shared smiles and flushes we've had recently, and by the time I went to bed last night after a second evening alone, I felt like I'd been dumped by both of them and it took all my strength not to text him to find out if everything was okay. It was strange how empty my life felt without either of them in it and that made me worry more. I *needed* them. It hurt to see David avoiding me. Not hearing from Adele either set my imagination alight. Had they told each other about me? Them and me. Always them and me, no matter how much I feel inserted between the two of them. Inserted or trapped. One or the other.

But now, Adele in front of me, I can see why she didn't want to meet up sooner. I feel a bit sick. She's tried to cover the fading bruise with makeup but it's still visible. Dark brooding purples and greens on her perfect cheekbone. In some ways, the foundation almost makes it more noticeable, caked and flaking over the color.

"Oh, it's nothing," she says, concentrating on driving—or pretending to concentrate so she doesn't have to look at me. "A silly accident. I opened a cupboard door into my face. Like an idiot."

She's trying to sound lighthearted, but I don't buy it and my legs sweat on the hot car seat. Something's happened. I look at her properly while she indicates and turns. She seems diminished, haunted even. Her hair has lost its luster. For the first time I feel like I'm the one who's glowing, not her. A few good nights' sleep have changed me. I'm refreshed and energized. I haven't felt so well in years, if ever. I feel like a new me and I want to celebrate it with my friend, but now, seeing her so *small,* I feel almost guilty for my joy.

"I thought we could give the gym a miss today," she continues. "I'm not really in the mood for it. And it's a lovely day. Let's have lunch in the garden and you can tell me about the dreams." She smiles then and I see her flinch slightly. A tremor, but enough for me to know that the bruise still hurts.

"Sure," I say. My mind is racing. Who opens a cupboard door into their own face? With that amount of force? Is it even possible? *Phone calls. Pills. Bruises.* All of it makes my stomach clench. All signs I'm so desperate to ignore that there might be something seriously wrong with David. Adele loves the gym. Why doesn't she want to go? Has she got more bruises on her body that she's afraid I'll see in the changing room?

I want to say something, to check she's okay, and then her mobile, sitting in the key well, rings. I don't need to ask who it is.

"I'm just going to the gym," she says after answering it. She sounds almost apologetic. "Yes, that's right. No, I'm going straight home. I promise. Okay, I'll speak to you then. Bye."

"Well that was romantic," I say dryly, and open the window. It's hot in the car and I feel slightly queasy after seeing the bruise and hearing their conversation. I feel awful. Angry. Upset. Confused. David hasn't been avoiding my bed because he's rekindling his marriage, that's for sure.

"Did you two have a row?" I don't use the word "fight." I don't want her to think I'm asking if David hit her, although that's pretty much *exactly* what I'm asking, even though I can't quite imagine it. Not *my* David anyway. Adele's David is a stranger.

"Oh, no," she says, but she doesn't look at me as she parks the car. "No, nothing like that. Just, you know, marriage."

I don't know, I realize. I know nothing about their marriage, but it seems very different to most, to what Ian and I had definitely. Ian and I rubbed along together, before his affair, like everyone else. The odd falling-out but I was never afraid of him. David and Adele's is nothing like that. The phone calls, her nervousness, his moods, the pills, and now this. How much am I supposed to ignore because he seems different with me? I love Adele. She's given me the ability to sleep properly at night, which is the best thing ever. I don't want her to be unhappy and hurt. But my feelings for David are real too. Am I being an idiot? Is he an abuser? Will it be me with a black eye soon? It all feels surreal.

Could he have hit her? I think as I get out of the car. *Really?* Surely not. Maybe Adele is telling the truth and she just had a stupid accident at home. Maybe that's why he hasn't turned up at my door. He's been looking after her. Feeling a bit guilty? The tension seeps out of my stomach a bit as I cling to that explanation and follow Adele to the front door. An accident, that's all.

There's a boxed treadmill in the hallway, and Adele laughs when I see it, a tinkling broken-glass sound. She says David bought it for her as a gift, but they're sending it back. She didn't want to stop going to the gym.

My mood sinks again as my head adds these new pieces to the puzzle. Was it meant to be a nice gift, or was there a more sinister motive? Was David trying to chain her to the house further? If she wasn't going to the gym there was one less reason to go out and meet new people on her own? Maybe that caused a fight. Did she try to assert herself and then he punched her? And now, out of guilt at his own behavior, he's relented and is sending it back? But if he's that jealous of how she spends her time when he's at work, then why has he been sleeping with me? Why isn't he at home with her all the time? And why isn't he jealous of where I am when I'm not with him? Maybe we're too early in our relationship for that. I've seen those films where the men are all charming at first and then the violence comes. It feels weird to even think of David and violence in the same sentence. Maybe he simply doesn't care enough about me to want to know my every move. *Maybe,* I try and tell myself, *he didn't hit her at all.*

"Which cupboard?" I ask, when we're in the kitchen. Part of my brain is telling me to shut up and let it go, but I'm too curious. I can't help myself. She looks at me, confused, as she gets plates out and starts so easily preparing a tapas-style lunch that never seems to include leaving coleslaw or hummus in their tubs and dumping them on the table like normal people.

"Which cupboard? You know . . ." I wave my hand around my own cheek.

"Oh!" she says. "Oh, that." Her eyes frantically run along the row for a moment. "That one. Above the kettle. Silly really. I wanted an ibuprofen and the kettle was boiling and steam got in my eyes so I couldn't see what I was doing. So stupid."

I nod and smile, but my heart is thumping hard and I know she's lying. She picked at random and from where I'm standing I'm pretty sure she'd have to be crouching a little for the corner of the door to hit her cheekbone. I can't see how it could have hit her directly in the face if she was the one opening it. Not with enough force to cause that injury. It's a dying bruise so it must have been there for a few days.

I very nearly ask the question that hums between us—*Did David do it?*—but I chicken out. I don't think I want to know, not here and not now. Not where my own reaction can't be tempered. My guilt would show. I'd end up telling her what I've been doing with him, and I can't do that. I can't. I'd lose them both. And anyway, she's too fragile for that right now. It would probably break her.

Instead, still feeling sick, I grab the bottle of sparkling elderflower water and two glasses and take them out into the fresh air. For the first time in ages I'm craving a real cigarette and I can't get my electronic one out of my bag fast enough.

"So, tell me!" she says, once she joins me with our two full plates that look wonderful even though I don't feel at all like eating. "You actually did it?"

"Yep." I breathe out a long stream of vapor, letting the nicotine calm me slightly. For the first time today I see proper happiness in her face and she claps her hands together with joy like a child would.

"I knew you could do it. I just knew it."

I smile. I can't help myself and I push David from my thoughts, for now. I *compartmentalize*. This is me and Adele. Her marriage is not my business. Also, selfishly, I've been dying to tell her since I woke up on Sunday morning.

"I feel so good," I say. "I never knew how much difference a few good nights' sleep could make to my life. I've got so much more energy."

"Well, come on, tell me! How did you do it?"

"It just happened." I shrug. "It was really easy. I fell asleep reading the notebook you gave me, and in it Rob had found his dream door, so it must have filtered into my subconscious. So, I was in my usual nightmare, Adam lost in this big old abandoned house and calling for me and I'm trying to find him while these dark tendrils were breaking free of the walls and trying to get to my throat—" I feel silly telling it because it sounds so stupid, but Adele is rapt. "And then I stopped running and thought, 'I don't have to be here. This is a dream.' And then there it was on the ground in front of me."

"A door?" she says.

I nod. "The door from my old Wendy house when I was a kid. Pink and with butterflies painted on it. But it was bigger, like it had grown with me. And it was just there, out of nowhere. Seeing it made me think of the house I grew up in before my parents fucked off to Australia to try and save their shitty marriage, and then I crouched down, opened the door, and let myself drop in. I was there. Back in that house. Exactly like it was when I was a child."

"What happened to the door?"

"I looked up and it wasn't there anymore. And then I knew I'd done it."

"And you didn't wake up? When you realized you were controlling everything? It took Rob a couple of times before he could stay in the dream, I think."

"No, I was fine." My stomach is unknotting and I eat a ricotta-stuffed bell pepper before continuing, enjoying sharing the experience. "I wandered through the house, ate some of my mum's apple pie that was in the fridge, and then went up to my old room, got into bed, and went to sleep."

"You went to bed?" She looks at me, halfway between incredulous and laughing. "You could make up anywhere to go and you went to sleep? Oh, Louise." She shakes her head and laughs and this time she doesn't flinch. I've made her feel better too.

"God, though, it was such a good sleep," I say. "The past few nights have been amazing. I think I can honestly say you've changed my life. I didn't realize how tired I was all the time."

She pops a small piece of pita and hummus in her mouth and shakes her head while she chews, still amused. "You went to bed."

"I know." It's my turn to laugh.

"You'll feel equally as rested no matter what you do," she says. "Trust me on that. You can go anywhere with anyone you want. It's your dream. You're in control."

"Hmmm, anywhere with anyone, you say?" I wiggle an eyebrow. "Robert Downey Jr. springs to mind. That would still involve a bed, though." We both laugh then and I feel a surge of affection for her. She's my friend. I'm a bitch. She doesn't have many friends and the one she's helping has been sleeping with her husband, who treats her badly enough as it is. Great. Her helping me makes me think of Rob from the notebook.

"Rob went to a beach in his dream," I say. "He imagined you were there." I'm a bit worried about mentioning the notebook in case she remembers how much detail is in it and wants it back, but I'm doing so much wrong that I want to do at least *one* thing right. I don't want to read any more unless it's okay with her. "Are you sure you don't mind me reading it? It seems quite personal. I feel a bit weird reading about your past from someone else."

"It was a long time ago," she says softly, and for a moment a cloud passes overhead and casts a dark shadow of something sad across her beautiful face, but she brightens quickly. "I knew reading about someone else doing it would be better than me trying to explain. I'm terrible at explaining things."

I remember the first time I saw her before I ran and hid in the loo and I thought she was so elegant and in control, so far from this nervous, self-deprecating woman. It's strange how different we all appear to who we really are. How does she see me? Am I a dumpy, scruffy blonde in her eyes, or am I something else?

"So you don't mind?"

"No." She shakes her head. "Actually you can keep it. I should have thrown it away ages ago. It's a time we try not to think about."

I can understand that. She'd just lost her parents in a fire and it must have been terrible. But I'm still intrigued about the life between those pages.

"Are you still friends with Rob?" I ask. She never mentions him and it seems weird given how close they were at Westlands.

"No," she says, looking down at her plate, no cloud needed to cast a shadow on her face this time. "No. David didn't really like him. I don't know where he is now."

Inside, the doorbell goes, and Adele scurries off apologetically to see who it is, and the moment is broken. *David didn't really like him.* Another sign of David's controlling behavior that I have to figure out a way for my brain to ignore. But then, maybe I don't need to think about it anymore. He hasn't exactly been knocking my door down this week or paying me any attention at work. Perhaps it's over. I hate how much that hurts.

Adele comes back, mumbling something about a tea-towel seller and *aren't they everywhere at the moment, this awful economy,* and I don't push her about Rob. I don't want to say anything that might make her take the notebook back. I understand these two people who've become so important to my life little enough without losing this glimpse into their past. And if Adele doesn't mind then there's no harm in it, surely?

28

ADELE

"Oh, honestly," I say. "Really? Is that a serious question?" My laugh is a delightful tinkle into the telephone and I can almost hear Dr. Sykes relaxing slightly on the other end. "I'm sorry," I continue. "I know it's not a funny subject and I'm not laughing at it, but David? That's funny. Yes, I do have a bruise on my face, but it was my own silly fault. A clumsy moment in the kitchen. Surely David told you that?"

To be honest I do feel quite amused as Dr. Sykes whitters into my ear. How typical of a junkie to exaggerate, and of course Anthony wants to *save* me so he's embellished what he saw. How wonderfully perfect. I told David about him turning up at our door on Sunday evening—of course I did. He was likely to find out anyway if the boy went to a session. But I didn't tell him that I'd given the impression of being afraid. And I haven't told him that Anthony's been back, almost causing an awkward moment when Louise was here. I got rid of him quickly, but not without hinting that I was glad to see him. He was worried about me, apparently. Quite sweet.

Maybe I should start lunching with Louise in town instead of here in case he's loitering at our door and she sees him.

David went into work on Monday and immediately recommended a new therapist for Anthony, quite disturbed that he must have followed David home at some point to know where we lived. Maybe more than once. Perhaps he'd spent several evenings studying our home from the end of the road, trying to pluck up the courage to approach. According to David, Anthony is a junkie only because he's an obsessive, and he'd developed a fixation on him. I could hardly blame the boy for that. I love David madly too, and have done since I first saw him, but it would seem Anthony's obsessions are rather more fickle. One look at my beautiful, bruised face and his fixation shifted to me. And now here I am on the phone defending my poor husband against allegations of wife-battering.

Dr. Sykes, to be fair, at least sounds hugely uncomfortable having to raise this with me. He's got me on speakerphone; I can hear the echo in the call quality. Is David listening? I can only imagine his face when they decided to ring me. Quite panicked. He wouldn't have wanted this to happen. He wouldn't know what I was likely to say. That irritates me slightly. He should trust me more than that. I would never damage his career. Why would I? I want him to be successful. I know how important it is to him.

"To be clear," I say. "There was no fight. And we would never have words in front of a stranger. And certainly not a patient." *Have words.* I sound just the right amount of indignant. We are all very middle class after all, and Dr. Sykes the most. He must be mortified by now. "The young man came to the door and asked for David while I was clearing the kitchen after dinner, and I told him that David had gone to bed with a headache and that was that. He must have seen my bruise and created a story around it. Perhaps he was feeling rejected by my husband and wanted to punish him in some way?" I know exactly how that feels. That is something young Anthony Hawkins and I have in common.

"That's what I thought," Dr. Sykes says. "But obviously when he told his parents that he'd seen . . . well, what he *said* he'd seen, they felt a moral obligation to follow it up."

He sounds relieved. Maybe he had a few doubts. It wouldn't surprise me. It's so easy to sow those seeds in people. None of us really knows each other, after all.

"Of course," I say. "And please do thank them for their con-

BEHIND HER EYES   143

cern, but there really is nothing to worry about here. Except perhaps my clumsiness." I laugh a little again then, as if the whole thing
is still amusing me. "Poor David," I say. "He's the last man alive who
would ever hit a woman. Please tell the boy's family that I hope he
gets the help he needs."

This can work well for me, I think as we say our good-byes
and hang up. David will be relieved at how well I've handled it and
hopefully will give me a little more space and go back to his seedy
evenings with duplicitous Louise. If he continues to suffocate me I
can always threaten to tell Dr. Sykes I was lying and that he *did* hit
me. It would be an empty threat—compared with others I can
make—even if David wouldn't realize it. Why would I ruin him?
Yes, we have wealth, but David has always needed more than that
and I can't take his career from him. Of all things, that would destroy him.

More important, however, I can use this with Anthony. He'll
feel terrible that his parents went to the clinic to report it. His guilt
at potentially placing me in harm's way with my violent husband is
something I can use to make him get me what I want, and the icing
on the cake is that even if he tells anyone, it will be dismissed as
another fantasy. No one will listen to him.

I quickly send David a text.

Are you okay? That boy needs help!! xx

I know they're probably all still in the same room and it's likely
Sykes will see it. A further proof of innocence should it be required.
And also a reminder to my husband that when the shit hits the fan
we are a team and always will be. It won't repair our marriage for
him—even I know he's too far gone for that—but it will soften him
toward me.

The doorbell goes, three sharp rings. Frantic. The poor boy
come to grovel, I imagine.

Everything is going so well.

29

LOUISE

I've got a glass of wine poured before I've even put my handbag down. My nerves jangle and I feel as if there are ants trapped in my head. I don't know what to think.

I'd gone out at lunchtime for a walk to stretch my aching legs from last night's jog and clear my thoughts a bit, tired of staring at David's door and willing him to call me in to explain what the hell is going on. I've been on edge all day. He's been ignoring me as if we were teenagers rather than grown adults, and I don't understand why he can't *say* if he doesn't want to see me anymore. He started all this, after all. Not me. Why can't he just *talk* to me? My stomach is in such a tight knot I couldn't eat even if I wanted to.

I decided that after my walk I was going to go and have it out with him—professional or not—but when I got back he wasn't at his desk and Sue, all aglow with excitement, told me that Anthony Hawkins's parents had come in, and they and David were in with Dr. Sykes.

"Anthony says he saw Dr. Martin hit his wife. Right in the face!" Sue had said it with such whispered glee that I felt like I'd been punched myself. Gossip for her, more head-fuckery for me. I didn't see David after that. I sat at my desk, my mind a blur of half-formed thoughts and worries, wanting to get out of there, which I did, bang on five. I wanted a glass of wine. I wanted to think.

And yet I don't know *what* to think. The wine is cool and crisp and I take my e-cig and go and sit on the balcony, letting fresh air into the stuffy flat. Adele says she walked into a cupboard but Anthony says David hit her. Why would Anthony lie? If it's true, though, how did Anthony see it? Was he peering through windows? David referred Anthony to a new doctor on Monday and I figured that was because he'd got too attached. But maybe it was because Anthony had seen something David didn't want him to.

I feel sick and drink more wine, my head already buzzing slightly. I haven't eaten much today and now my appetite is totally gone.

The doorbell goes twice before I hear it, I'm so lost in my own thoughts, and I scurry back inside.

"Hey."

It's him. Barely 6 P.M. and he's at my door for the first time this week. I'd thought he was never coming back and I'm too surprised to say anything as I let him in. He's brought wine and immediately opens it and gets another glass out of the cupboard.

"Make yourself at home," I mutter, a whirl of conflicting emotions.

"I wish I could," he says with a sorrowful—or self-pitying, I can't decide which—half-laugh. He drains his glass and then refills it. "What a fucking day," he says, tilting his head back and letting out a sigh. "What a fucking life."

He drinks a lot; I'm realizing now that I've cut back so much myself. Is he a mean drunk? Is that what happens? I look at him. A fight, a fist, a face.

"I can't stay long," he says, and then reaches for me, pulling me into his chest. "But I had to see you. I keep telling myself to stop, *promising* myself I'll stop, but I can't."

"You see me all day." I'm stiff in his arms. Is that brandy I can smell? A terrible thought strikes me. Does he drink in the office? He kisses the top of my head, and under the booze and the aftershave I catch the scent of him, and I can't help but like it. I crave it if I'm honest, when I'm alone at night. But if he thinks we're going straight to bed now, or to bed at all, then he's wrong. He's hardly looked at me in days and now he just breezes in. I pull back and take my drink. Screw him. I look at his hand on his wineglass. Strong. Big. I see the bruise on Adele's face. For once, I'm going to be the friend she thinks I am.

"But not like this," he says. "Not when we can be us."

"Us." The word sounds dead as I repeat it. "There's hardly an us, is there?" I lean against the kitchen counter rather than leading him into the sitting room or bedroom like usual. I haven't spoken to Adam today and I won't miss that, not for a cheating, maybe-wife-beating man. I suddenly feel tired. Adam's home in about a week, so all this craziness is going to have to stop anyway. Maybe it will be a relief.

He frowns slightly, realizing my bad mood. "Are you okay?"

I shrug. My heart races. I hate conflict. I'm shit at it. I tend to revert to being a sullen, silent teenager rather than spitting out what's wrong. I gulp my wine and then take a deep breath. Fuck it. This is the only chance I'm going to get to talk about their marriage. This is something I can *legitimately* know.

"Sue told me what happened. With Anthony Hawkins's parents. What they said?"

"Thank god that's cleared up," he says. "I didn't need that today." He looks at me then, sees my questioning suspicion, and his face falls. "Wow, Louise."

"What?" I sound defensive and I feel it too. Now that he's here in front of me I feel stupid for half-believing he could do that. Even Adele didn't say that he'd hit her. But there's so much going on that doesn't make sense and I can't figure any of it out.

"You seriously don't think I hit my wife?"

"I don't know what I think," I say. "You never talk about your marriage. Your wife. You're doing *this*." I gesture around my pathetic little flat as if he's fucking it and not me. "When it suits you at least. We talk but you never talk about your marriage. You close down every time I try and ask you anything, and you always seem so fucking unhappy that I can't understand why you're still there. With *her*. Just get a fucking divorce!"

It's pouring out of me, all my pent-up confusion and hurt, bubbling in hot rage from my lips. I've seen Adele's bruise. I know how fragile she is. I know about the phone calls. I can say none of these things, however much I want him to explain them to me, so all I can do is bring it back to the mess that is us. The mess he only knows half of.

He's staring at me like I've stabbed him, but I keep going. "I mean, this isn't exactly fair on her, either, is it? What you're doing?"

"You really have to ask me if I hit her?" He cuts through all my bullshit. "Do you know me at all?"

I almost laugh at that. "Know you? How could I possibly know you? You know me—I'm an open book. You know just about everything about me. We talk about *me*. But you? I don't know what I'm supposed to make of you."

"Of course I didn't bloody hit her." He slumps, the life gone out of him. "She says she opened a kitchen cupboard onto her face. I don't even know if that is true, but I know I didn't hit her."

I tingle with a flood of relief. At least they're both giving me the same explanation.

"Anthony came to see me on Sunday night," he continues, "but I was in the shower. He must have seen her face and made up the story to get my attention or hurt me or whatever."

Maybe it's true. It sounds true. And now I feel terrible for doubting him, for doubting her, but what am I supposed to do when there are all these questions trapped inside me? About them, about us, about where all this is going?

"Why don't you ever talk to me?" I ask. "Properly talk to me. About your life."

He stares into his wineglass. "I really wouldn't know where to start," he says. "And it's not your business. I don't want it to be your business. I don't want to . . ." He hesitates, looking for the right word. "I don't want to *taint* you with it all."

"What does that even mean?" I ask. "Look, I don't expect you to leave her for me. I know I'm not important to you—"

"Not important to me?" He cuts me off. "You're the only good thing I have. That's why I have to be so careful. That's why I don't want to talk to you about my marriage or my life. I don't want any of that to be *inside* us."

He drains his glass, several long mouthfuls. How can anyone

drink like that and not want to throw up? Glass after glass, so fast. His self-pity isn't attractive, but my neediness loves that he thinks I'm important. It makes me feel stronger.

"Take me out of the picture for a minute," I say. "You're obviously unhappy at home. So leave. That's what my husband did and it didn't kill me. It hurt but I got over it. Life moves on." *And now Ian's having a baby with my replacement and I'm like a ghost in my own life.* I keep that thought to myself. "I don't see what the problem is."

"You can't possibly see what the problem is. You'd have to know us. Really know us for that. And I'm not even sure we know each other anymore." He's bitter. His words are sharp with it as he stares into his glass. "But something has to change," he says eventually. His words slur slightly. "But I need to figure out how to do it. To get rid of her *safely.*"

"Maybe talk to her," I say, trying to be as loyal as I can to Adele in this completely disloyal moment. "She's your wife. She must love you."

He laughs then, at first with sudden humor, but then the sound sours. "Oh, she loves me. For what that's worth."

I think of my fragile friend, running to answer calls and take pills and cook dinners, and I'm angry. How can he treat her like this? With such contempt? If he doesn't love her then he should set her free to love someone else. Someone who'd treat her as well as she deserves.

"Go home," I say, cold. "Go home and sort your shit out with your wife. I can't deal with this right now." He doesn't say a word, but stares at me, his eyes starting to glaze with alcohol. Is he driving? I don't care, I decide. That's his problem. Right now, I just want him gone. "Go," I repeat. "And stop drinking. You're a fucking mess." I want to cry, for him, for Adele, and for me. Mainly for me. I don't want to fight with him. I want to understand him.

I don't look at him as he leaves and I don't return the squeeze he gives my hand as he passes.

"I'll fix it," he mumbles from the doorway. "Somehow. I promise."

I don't look up. I give him nothing. I may be a bitch and duplicitous, but enough is enough. I want him, but not like this. I can't do this anymore. I really can't. He and Adele are tearing me in two.

*   *   *

After he's gone, I pour another glass of wine and fight the stupid urge to cry by calling Adam. Even his bubbly joy can't lift my spirits and as he tells me about their day at the water park and the slides he went on with Ian, part of my mind is playing back the conversation with David. I make all the right sounds, and it's lovely to hear my baby boy, but I'm also relieved when he says he has to go. I need the quiet. I feel empty and exhausted and sad and a whole heap of other stuff I don't want to examine. It's our first argument and maybe our last. I also realize, too late, that I don't think he hit Adele. Not deep down. Not anymore.

Even though it's not yet nine o'clock, I take my wine and crawl under the duvet. I want to forget about it all for a while. Sleep it away. Maybe in the morning everything will somehow be better. I feel numb, but still part of me hates myself for sending him away when we could be in bed together. In bed with *my* David, not Adele's. I keep seeing the look in his face when he realized I was wondering if he'd hit his wife. That awful disappointment. But then I also keep seeing the bruise on Adele's face. All her fear and secrecy on display in those sickly greens and muted blues. Whether he hit her or not, something isn't normal in their marriage. But then nothing about this is normal and I'm probably the worst of the three of us.

I feel trapped. I don't know what I'm supposed to do. I do the only thing I can and drain my wineglass, my head buzzing with the alcohol, and then close my eyes. Adam will be home soon and then I can cocoon myself in him, in the safety of us. I focus on thoughts of my boy. The one person I can love without guilt or recrimination. I sleep.

This time, as the sticky shadow tendrils reach for me and I open the Wendy house door, I don't go to my childhood home, but instead to the house that Ian and I lived in when we were first married. When we were both still happy. I'm in the garden and it's a perfect sunny day—not too hot but beautifully warm, and I'm playing with Adam. He's six, though, my Adam as he is now, not the tiny baby he was when we lived here, and we're at the pond and trying to catch tadpoles. Our feet are muddy and wet, but we're both laughing as we dip our nets and jam jars into the slimy surface of the water.

The smell of meat cooking on a barbecue drifts on the air, and even before I've consciously thought of him, I hear David calling out that the burgers are ready. We turn and smile and Adam runs to him. I'm about to follow when I see something glitter in the pond from the corner of my eye. A shape under the surface. It shimmers at the edges as it forms, almost silver beneath the dark water. I frown, confused. This is my dream—I'm controlling it—and yet I don't know what this is. I step out, onto the pond's surface, and walk across it like Jesus—and almost laugh at that, I am the God of my dreams—until I can crouch beside it. I dip my hand into the liquid, rippling it, but the glowing shape beneath stays in place. It's another door, I realize, and the edges glow brighter as if to confirm my thoughts. I look for the handle but there isn't one. A door without a handle that I haven't purposely imagined. I don't know why it's here.

I stare for a moment longer and then David calls for me again, and Adam too. They're waiting for me before they start eating and I want to be with them. The shining door fades and then there's nothing but pond beneath me.

I wake up early, just after five, dehydrated from the wine, and I'm disappointed with myself. The dream I created had been so perfect, the three of us playing happy families, and despite the thirst, I do feel rested, like Adele said I would. My self-disgust bites a little. I should have imagined Adele in the dream. My loyalty should lie with her. She's been nothing but kind to me, whereas David is a cheating, unreliable drunk and god knows what else, but still, if my dream is anything to go by, I want him madly. I might not have let him fuck me in my bed, but I certainly did in my head. Not just fuck me, either. In my dream I made him love me and I loved him and we were a family, no sign of Adele anywhere. I wiped her out of existence.

I groan and then get up for water and put the kettle on. I'm wide awake after my early night and there's no point in trying to go back to sleep just for an hour or so. As the kettle boils and I try and shake the vividness of my dream life away, I look into Adam's bedroom and get a pang of excitement that he'll be home soon, after which maybe I should ease myself out of my friendship with Adele.

Take Sophie's advice. Be free of both Adele and David and this stupid stupid mess I've got myself into.

I have a shower to wash away the dregs of my mild hangover, and then get dressed and ready for work, but by the time I sit down with a second cup of tea it's still only 7 A.M. Sunlight glints on the dusty TV screen, and the second door in my dream, the shimmering one I saw in the pond, comes to mind. I get the notebook from its home in the kitchen drawer. Maybe Rob saw one too. My heart races. After last night I shouldn't read any more. I'm doing enough damage here without delving into their pasts. But I can't help it. I want to know about them. And the second door is my excuse.

> . . . It's so easy. I can go wherever I want. Mainly I go to imagined places because I've never been fucking anywhere and there's no fucking way I'd choose to go home. Wherever I am, Adele's always there, though. I don't even really imagine her there but she just appears. Maybe that's cos I'm always thinking about her. Not in a want-to-fuck-her way, something way better than that. Something purer. We get high a lot in my dreams. It's kind of what I like best. I can get off my face as much as I want with no comedowns and no fallout.
>
> Adele's sleeping properly again. Everyone at Westlands fucking loves us now as if they had something to do with our recoveries— we're like their wet dream patients. I'm happy about it, though. That she's sleeping. I know she's not lying because I sneak to her room and watch her for a few minutes most nights. Man, I sound creepy reading that back. But she's like Sleeping Beauty and I'm watching over her. It's sort of peaceful and I don't need to sleep so much now that I'm clean and what sleep I'm getting isn't full of night terrors. Only at the beginning before I control them. Sometimes I choose to stay for a while for the thrill. Like going on a roller coaster. I know they can't harm me because I'm in charge.
>
> Yeah, it's good that she's sleeping properly. She's got a lot to catch up on after weeks of trying to stay awake and she needs to put all that shit behind her. It's weird worrying about someone. I worry about Adele and I've never worried about anyone before. Not my shitty family, and barely myself. Everyone's been gray

before Adele. No one mattered. I never actually thought it was possible for someone to matter before. Is this what love is? Maybe I do love Adele in my own way.

Does she imagine me in her dreams, or is it always the legendary bore that is David? I worry most about David. I don't know why she's so caught up in him. I don't think she can see what he's really like. She TRUSTS him, she says. Yeah right. I bet he loves that. She trusts him so much that she's signed control over all her money and stuff to him. A fucking fortune and he's in charge of it all. That's what her solicitor was doing here. Finally she told me. I knew she would. She doesn't like secrets. But what the actual fuck? So David's off at unifuckingversity getting his endless degrees and living the high life while she's in this mental home, and she's given him control of all the estate and money and everything.

I can't believe it. I nearly shouted at her but she looked so uncomfortable telling me that I couldn't. And it's done now. She said it was temporary because she didn't want to think about it and they were getting married anyway, but who the hell gives all their money away to someone else? Even for a little while. I mean, why would she do that? There's love and there's stupidity. She doesn't get people like I do. She's been protected all her life. What she hasn't figured out is that everyone's out for themselves. I don't even really blame David for taking the money—at least it's something less DULL that he's done, but I hate that she's let him. Money fucks people over, and David's one of those people who nearly had quite a bit of money from the farm—and then his dad pissed it all up the wall. Funny how now he's got a lot of money anyway. Thanks to Adele.

I bet he won't sign it back to her when we get out of here. I bet he'll come up with excuses. David, the poor farmer's boy who now has a fortune at his fingertips. It actually makes me want to laugh because it's so crazy. I get so angry that it stops me getting back to sleep when I wake up at night. It's got me thinking, too— what really happened to Adele's parents? I mean, how was he driving by in time to save her in the middle of the night? Was he driving by in time to start the fire too?

This has worked out pretty well for him from where I'm sit-

ting. Our time here is nearly done, but if Adele thinks that I'm going to forget her and all this, that's not going to happen. I'm going to look out for her. Because I don't for one fucking second think that David is . . .

"I'm sorry," he says.

We're in his office, separated by his desk. I'm trembling. I've been trembling since putting the notebook down this morning.

"I know I'd been drinking but I meant it when I said I'll sort things out," he continues. He's quiet. Thoughtful. Probably hungover. "I know my marriage is bad. I know it. And I shouldn't be messing you around like this. What you said last night—"

"I didn't come in here to talk about last night." I'm cold with him, cutting him off. I feel like I've been dunked in freezing water. I'm burning to see Adele and find out if my suspicions are true. "I need the afternoon off. My boiler's playing up and the plumber just rang and said he could come out between two and six. Sue says she's got a light afternoon so she can check your clients in and work at my desk." He's got four appointments booked and I'm glad about that. I won't have to worry about him coming home and seeing us together.

I texted Adele as soon as he got to work this morning, knowing she'd be alone and safe. I didn't say what it was really about, I didn't want her to feel defensive or worried, so I sent: *There was a weird second door in my dream last night. No handle? Couldn't open it? You ever had that? I've got the afternoon off if you fancy lunch?* All light and easy, despite how my hands shook as I typed. She answered straight away with a yes, suggesting a little bistro place with outdoor seats not too close to the clinic and also slightly off the main roads in a more residential area. She doesn't want to get caught either.

"Sure," he says. My palms sweat as he looks at me, and for the first time he's like a stranger. Not my David, not Adele's David, but maybe *David's David,* the one who always gets what he wants. I silently say my thousandth thanks that Adele has agreed to lunch. I couldn't wait until Monday. I need to know, and she's the only one who can tell me. I'm starting to complete the jigsaw of their crazy marriage and I don't like the picture it's revealing.

"I hope it's nothing too serious," he says. "Boilers can be expensive." He looks up then. "If you need any—"

"I've got an insurance package." I cut him off again. Was he really going to offer me money? Whose? His, or Adele's?

"Okay." He's short, my constant coolness hitting a nerve. He looks hurt, but I'm not sure how much I care.

"Thanks." I head for the door, my limbs moving awkwardly, knowing he's watching me leave.

"Louise."

I turn and look at him. He's stuffed his hands in his pockets and it reminds me of the first time we spoke in this room, the electric tension between us. It's still there, pulling me toward him, but now it's shrouded in doubt and suspicion. It's bruised like Adele's face.

"I really care about you, you know," he says. "Properly. I think about you all the time. I can't help myself. It's like I lead a separate life with you in my head." The words are spilling out of him and all I can think is that I don't need this, not now, not until I *know*.

"I think . . . I think I'm falling in love with you. And I know I have to get my life straight. I have to get this mess straight. It's keeping me awake all night trying to figure out how and I know you don't understand that, and I'm not helping you understand that, but this is something I have to get sorted on my own. But I'm going to start. Today. And I know you're right to be pissed off with me. I wanted to say that. That's all."

Blood rushes to my face and to my feet and to everywhere in between as if it's racing around my veins trying to find a way flee my body. Now? He says this now? My head is already fucked and he's throwing this at me. Falling in love with me? Oh god. I don't know what to think. I don't know what to feel. But Adele is waiting and I need to know at least some truth from her before I can even contemplate this. I need to know what kind of man he is, he *really* is, under the skin. In his head.

I nod and swallow hard and then leave him standing there, grabbing my bag from under my desk and rushing out into the fresh air without even telling Sue I'm going.

30

ADELE

I sit in the sunshine and sip a glass of cold forbidden Sancerre and wait for Louise. Louise. It's amazing how much this wonderful woman can affect my mood. Last night, when David went to her grubby little flat straight after work, I was so hurt I wanted to kill her, even if she had done her pathetic best to defend me and send him home. It was too little too late if I'm honest and worse than that was David's choice to go straight to her instead of me, after all I'd done for him on the phone with Dr. Sykes. I could have *ruined* him, but he didn't take that into account. There was no gratitude. Then he came home and got drunk in his study before stumbling to bed. Not so much as a thank-you.

I love David. Truly, madly, deeply, however cheesy that may sound, but I'm stronger than he is. Yes, things have to change, but it's me who will have to get my hands dirty doing it. I swallowed my hurt last night, though. Pushed it deep down inside where it can't touch me because we can't afford another argument. Not just yet. And then, like a miracle, I got Louise's text. The second door. I smile as I sip my wine, even though I'm alone and probably look slightly mad to anyone passing. She's seen the second door. Already. This changes everything. It all has to be in place before she opens it. Before she knows.

I tingle with excitement as I see her turn the corner and come down the street. She's looking good, really good, and I feel very proud of her. She's even walking taller now that she's slimmer and fitter and her cheekbones—while they'll never be feline sharp as mine—are soft highlights on her pretty face. My own muscles ache from lack of exercise and my back is stiff from tension. I'm fading as she blooms. No wonder David is falling in love with her. The thought stings. The thought will always sting.

"Wine?" she says, and smiles. She's flustered, and her bag slips to the ground as she tries to hang it on the back of her chair.

"Why not? It's a lovely day and this is a nice surprise." I see her eyes on my face where the dregs of the bruise remain. It's healing quickly now, as if it's somehow aware that its work here is done. I signal to the waiter to bring another glass.

"How come you've got time off?"

"Oh, a problem with my boiler," she says airily. "The plumber is coming later but I figured I'd take the afternoon. Be a devil."

She's a terrible liar. It's really quite endearing given how she's been fucking my husband for our entire friendship. The waiter appears quickly with her drink and two menus and we both pretend to scan them as she takes several quick sips of the wine.

"So you saw another door?" I ask, leaning in conspiratorially even though we're the only al fresco diners. I want her to feel close to me. "Where? What was it like?"

"In the pond of my old house. I was there"—she flushes slightly—"with Adam, playing, and then as I was turning to go back, it appeared under the surface. It was glowing."

She's not telling me the whole truth of her dream—David must have been there, I can see that in the blush—but I don't give a shit. If she'd imagined three Davids gangbanging her I wouldn't care. It's the door. That's what matters.

"Like a shimmering silver," she adds. "And then it vanished. You ever have that?"

I shake my head, puzzled. "No. How weird. I wonder what it's for."

She shrugs. "Maybe it was my brain having a glitch."

"Maybe." My heart is racing, though. Already thinking ahead to what I have to get done before she opens it.

The waiter comes back to take our orders and I make a big fuss about not being hungry, I just wanted to get out of the house, and then I see her face, the thoughtful worry in it, and I know how far she's got in the notebook. I know what this lunch is really about. I have to concentrate hard not to smile and laugh at the brilliant perfection of today and how well I've planned everything.

"You've got to eat something, Adele. You're getting too skinny. Anyway," she adds, too nonchalantly, "it's my treat."

"Oh, thank you," I gush. "I'm so awfully embarrassed, but when I got here I realized I've come out without my wallet. I'm such a scatterbrain."

She orders us two plates of mushroom ravioli—taking the lead in a way she never would have done when we first met—and then waits until the waiter has gone before speaking.

"Did you really come out without money, or does David control what you spend?"

She's blunt, Louise, I'll give her that. I act flustered, as if trying to cover something, murmuring how ridiculous that suggestion is, until she reaches across and takes one of my flapping hands in hers. A gesture of solidarity, of friendship, of love. I do believe she loves me. Not as much as she wants my husband, but she does love me.

"I read something in the notebook that worried me slightly," she continues. "And feel free to tell me to bugger off and it's not my business and everything, but did you really sign over all your inheritance to him? After the fire? And if you did, please, for the love of god, tell me that it was only temporary."

"Oh, don't worry about that," I say, and I know I look like a wounded deer staring into a marksman's rifle sight. The classic victim defending her abuser. "David's much better with money than me, and it was such a lot to manage, and oh god, this is so embarrassing . . ."

She squeezes my hand. "Don't be silly. Don't be embarrassed. I worry about you. He signed it back over, though, right? After you got out of Westlands and were back on your feet?"

Her hand is clammy. She has a vested interest here and I know it.

"He was going to," I mumble. "He really was. But then I had another little breakdown a few months later, and he decided—*we* decided—that it was better if he just stayed in charge of everything. And then we got married and so it was *our* money anyway."

"Wow." She sits back in her chair and takes a long swallow of wine as it sinks in and her suspicions are confirmed.

"It sounds worse than it is," I say, soft and protective. "He gives me an allowance and a food budget and I've never really cared for money that much anyway."

"A food budget?" Her eyes are wide. "An allowance? What is this, nineteen fifty-something?" She pauses. "Now the shitty phone makes sense."

"I don't care about phones, either. Really, Louise, it doesn't matter. I'm happy. I want David to be happy." It might be a step too far into the pathetic, but the truth is always believable, and I *have* been pathetic in my wanting to keep him happy.

"You don't even have joint accounts or anything?"

"It's fine. If I want something he gets it for me. It's the way our marriage has turned out. Don't worry. He's always looked after me." I push a strand of hair out of my face and let my fingers linger momentarily over my bruise. A tiny gesture, but enough for her to register it and file the bruise and the money together in her head.

"Like you're a child," she says. And I know her head is filled with our secret friendship, the phone calls, the pills, the bruise, and now the money locking it all into place. Right now she loves me far more than David. Right now I think she hates David. I could never hate David. Maybe that's the biggest difference between us.

"Please, just leave it. It's fine. When does Adam get back?" I ask, using her comment on children to change the subject. "You must be so looking forward to seeing him. He's probably grown a little. They grow fast at that age, don't they?"

Our food comes and she orders us a second glass of wine each as she silently adds my regret at not having a child of my own to her list of David's shortcomings. Fuel for her growing fire. The ravioli is perfect but she pushes it around her plate, not touching it. I should probably do the same to maintain my nervous appearance but I'm tired of good food going to waste and so I eat it—delicately, but still eat it all the same—as she tells me about Adam's holiday and how glorious a time it sounds like he's had.

Neither of us is really paying attention to the stories. Her head is filled with rage and disappointment and mine with excitement at her discovery of the second door. I make the right noises and smile and she forces words out, but I want this lunch over now. I have things to do.

"Is that . . . ?" She pauses midsentence and frowns, staring somewhere over my shoulder.

"What?" I turn.

"It is." She's still staring and half-risen out of her chair. "It's Anthony Hawkins."

Now I see him, and as useful as he's been, my irritation rises. He's following me. Of course he is. "Maybe he lives around here," I say.

"Or maybe he's following you." There she is, my great protector. My husband's lover.

"Oh, I doubt it." I laugh it off, but my eyes are fierce on Anthony and, realizing that he's making me uncomfortable, he has the brains to turn and go into a small corner shop. "He's probably buying cigarettes." His adoration of me has been useful, but following me is simply not acceptable.

"Maybe," she says, unconvinced. We both watch the doorway until he comes out, and I hope Louise doesn't see the glance back of *longing* he gives me as he walks away, but she's squinting in the sun and so I'm probably safe. Not that it matters. By tomorrow the last thing she'll be worrying about is Anthony.

Once our lunch is over and I've hurried her back to her fictional broken boiler, I go to the gym. I'm there just before David makes his next call, but I'm not working out as I claim to be; I'm putting the next wheels of my plan in motion. David says he's coming straight home after work because we *have to talk,* and then I speak to the receptionist about what I need and claim to be too busy to wait, but tell them to call us at home after six to confirm my request. I don't doubt they will. This is a very exclusive health club, we pay for the full package, and more than that I'm always polite and sweet. Polite and sweet is what I *do* when I'm not at home, and it always pays to be nice to service staff. Some of the other members here could learn that.

I'm breathless with excitement and my nerves are jangling with what's to come. By the time I'm home and preparing dinner, my hands are trembling and I can barely focus. My face is hot like I've got the start of a fever. I try to take deep breaths, but they're shallow and shaky. I keep focused on that second door and remind myself that I will probably never get a chance like this again in my entire life.

My sweaty fingers slide on the onion I'm attempting to dice and I nearly cut myself. I don't know why I'm taking so much care with this dish. It's all going to end up in the bin anyway, but I have to make things look as normal as possible, and cooking has become a surprising area of pride for me since I've been married. Careless onion slices could be a possible clue that I *know* what's coming, and David is nothing if not suspicious of me these days.

I hear his key in the lock and my whole body fizzes with tension and the kitchen lights are suddenly almost too bright. This time I do manage a deep breath. I see my mobile phone on the counter by the sink, sitting in no man's land between where I am and the landline phone holstered on the wall. I look at the clock. Just touching six. Perfect.

"Hi," I say. He's in the hallway and I know he wants to go and hide in his study. "I bought you a bottle of Châteauneuf-du-Pape. Come and open it so it can breathe."

He walks toward the kitchen like a reluctant wild dog being offered scraps of meat. How has our love come to this?

"So, we're still pretending everything is fine," he says wearily.

"No," I answer, wounded. "But we can at least be civil. We can be friends, surely, while we work on our problems? We owe each other that, don't we?"

"Look . . ."

The phone rings and although it's expected I still nearly jump and my hand tightens around the chopping knife. I step toward the phone, but David blocks me as I knew he would.

"It'll be the clinic," he says. "I'll get it."

I keep my eyes down, chopping at the onion, my skin burning with nerves as I listen. It's time for his blissful little secret relationship to get as fucked up as this marriage.

"Hello? Yes, this is David Martin. Oh, hi . . . You wanted to confirm what? I'm sorry, I'm not sure I'm following. An extended guest membership?"

I turn to face him then, I have to, my face all innocent worry that he'll be angry at my spending, that I have a friend I haven't told him about. He's not looking at me. Not yet.

"For whom?" He's frowning.

Then I see it. The shock as he tries to take it in. The confusion.

"Sorry, did you say Louise Barnsley?" Then he looks at me, but he's still trying to put everything in place in his head. His world just turned upside down and then got shaken all over again. "And this is an extension on a guest membership my wife arranged?"

I shrug at him, pleading, and mouth, *She's a friend I made.*

"Okay, yes, thank you. That's fine." His eyes fall to my mobile phone and he's reaching for it as he hangs up and before I can even make the pretense of going for it myself.

"I'm sorry," I say. "She's someone I met. That's all. Just a friend. I didn't want to say anything. I was lonely. She was nice to me."

He's not listening to me, but scanning through the texts in the phone, his face like thunder. I've kept most of them. Of course I have. In preparation for this.

He stares at me then, for a long moment, and he's gripping my phone so tightly I think he might crush it. Whose windpipe would he like to crush most right now, mine or Louise's?

"I'm sorry," I say again.

He's pale, his jaw clenched tight, his whole body trembling with pent-up emotion he's fighting to contain. I've only seen him like this once before and that was so long ago. I want to hold him. To tell him everything's going to be okay. That I'm making everything better for him. But I can't. I have to be strong.

"I'm going out." The words are forced out between his teeth. I don't think he's even seeing me.

He storms toward the front door and I call after him but he doesn't even pause in his stride, a whirlwind of rage and confusion.

The door slams and I'm alone. I hear the clock tick in the silence. I stare after him for a moment and then pour a glass of the opened red wine. It should breathe for longer, but I don't care.

I let out a long sigh after the first sip and then roll my head around my shoulders, releasing the tension. Poor Louise, I think. I'm exhausted, but I try to shake it away. I still have things to do. See if Anthony has left the package where I asked him to, for one thing. And then *see* what David is doing. My tiredness is going to have to wait.

After all, I can sleep when I'm dead.

31
THEN

They leave tomorrow. The month is over and there's no reason for either of them to stay longer, star patients that they are. It's a weird feeling but Adele can't help smiling as she packs. Freedom from Westlands and David to marry at the end of his university term. Despite everything that's happened, her future looks good. Her only worry is Rob. He's making jokes about it, but she can see that he doesn't want to go back to his sister, not at all. It hurts her to see him almost vulnerable. It also hurts to leave him. It's her only sadness as she folds her clothes into her small suitcase, but it's a sharp one.

"Want to go down by the lake?" she asks. He's sitting on her bed, watching her pack, and, for the first time since she's known him, he looks like a little boy rather than an almost-man. His dark hair hangs over his face, but she can see the glint of the braces he hates so much on his teeth. His T-shirt is still ironed, though. She's never known anyone to press a T-shirt or their jeans before. Maybe he even irons his socks. Perhaps it's one small bit of control he has in what seems like a uncontrolled life to Adele. One kink in his wildness.

He pulls something from his top pocket and grins. A neatly

rolled joint. "The last of the weed. We might as well. Maybe they'll catch us toking and we'll have to stay longer."

She knows he kind of hopes for it. She knows he'd love for them to have to stay longer and part of her wishes for the same, because she can't imagine not seeing Rob every day. But she's missed David so much and she's fizzing with the excitement of seeing him and kissing him and marrying him with no parents around to disapprove.

Rob suspects that this is the end of their friendship, but she knows it isn't. Maybe Rob can come and live with them at some point when they're married. David will like him, she's sure of that. How could he not? Rob is too fabulous for anyone not to like.

She grabs his hand. It feels good in hers. She's almost forgotten what holding David's hand feels like and that feels like a betrayal, but David isn't here and Rob is and they do love each other in their own way.

"What are we waiting for?" she says.

It's not so warm today, the wind on the water carrying a chill that bites every now and then, but they don't care as they sit under the tree where they first met and pass the spliff between them. She'll miss this, too. She can't imagine David ever wanting to get high. She can't tell him she's done drugs here. He'd be horrified. Another secret that's hers and Rob's.

"Maybe I'll burn the notebook now," Rob says. "A ceremonial farewell." As ever his tone is light and his eyes sparkle, but she knows he's down. She squeezes his hand tightly.

"No, keep it. You never know, your dreams might hold more surprises." She inhales, enjoying the relaxing buzz, and then passes the joint back to him. "And when you come to visit you can tell me about them. Where you've been, who you've seen." She smiles at him. "You'd better include me in some of those dreams."

"Back at ya," he says. "You're going to be seeing enough of dreary David. You don't need to dream about him too."

She gives him a playful punch on the arm and he laughs even though he means it. It'll be different when they meet. How could she love them both if they can't love each other? It's not possible.

"You okay about going back to your house?" he asks.

"I think so." She's not sure, but it's part of her therapy plan. Face the music, as it were. Go back to the source of the trauma. Spend some time there. "There are plenty of rooms that aren't damaged and the burnt-out ones have been cleaned up and temporary repairs done. David's organized it."

"I guess he can now you've given him all your money," Rob says dryly.

"No I haven't," she says, exasperated. "I keep telling you that. It's only for now. It's easier. His uni fees and everything, and the stuff with the house, I couldn't do that from in here. And on top of that, it's too much to think about. I'm *happy* he's taken it on. Let it go, Rob. And don't tell anyone. It's been difficult enough for David since the fire without this in the newspapers."

"Okay, okay. I just worry about you." This is no time for their first argument and she knows he knows that. He pauses. "I'll worry about you even more in that big old house by yourself."

"I'll be fine. It's only for a few weeks. People will be checking in on me. Some of the locals, my solicitors, and of course a doctor. Someone's even coming in to bring food and clean for me when needed. David says he'll come at weekends when he can."

"A whole new life ahead for you," he says wistfully. "Think of me back on the shitty estate still trapped with my fucking awful sister."

"Is it that bad?" she asks. He's still never opened up about his life, even though she has tried gently prodding him to over the past week or so.

"It is what it is." He tries to blow smoke rings but the wind breaks them up before they're half-formed and he gives up. "I don't want to think about it until tomorrow."

"You can call me, you know," she says. "I'll give you my mobile number. If things are shit, call me. Come and stay for a few days."

"Oh, I'm sure David would love that."

"David's at university," she says, and then in a moment of rebellion adds, "and it's my bloody house."

They grin at each other then and she can see that he loves her and it makes her feel warm inside, if a little complicated. David is everything to her, but now there is also Rob in her heart. She would never have felt so much better by now without him. She'd probably have been locked up for good.

"I mean it," she says, a rush of affection enveloping her. "Whenever."

"Okay," he says. "Maybe I will."

She hopes he will. She hopes he'd call her rather than be miserable. But he's proud, Rob, she knows that. As proud as David in a different way.

"You promise?" she says, leaning forward so their faces are close and her hair is brushing his cheek.

"I promise, my beautiful Sleeping Beauty princess. I promise."

"Good." She kisses him on the nose. "That's settled then."

32

LOUISE

I shouldn't have let him in, I shouldn't have let him in, is all I can think as the horror of the whole mess now collapsing around me sinks in. If I hadn't let him in, I wouldn't have had to face it. Not yet. I want to be sick. I don't know what to say.

He's shaking with rage as he stands in my sitting room, waving Adele's crappy mobile phone at me, shouting something about having read all the texts. I'm crying, and I don't even know when I started, maybe when he first stepped through the door and I instantly *knew* he knew, but I wish I wasn't. My stomach has turned to water and I feel as if I've been caught in an affair and I'm trying to explain it away. I hate myself.

"The *whole* time?" He's incredulous, still struggling to get his head round it. "All this time you've been friends with *my wife* and you didn't tell me?" His Scottish accent is stronger in his anger, country rough, and it surprises me. A stranger's voice.

"I didn't know how to!" I wail at him, my hands gesticulating with no meaning at all except to maybe try and wave it all away. "I didn't . . . I literally bumped into her in the street and she fell over and then we went for coffee! I didn't mean to be her friend but then she texted me and I didn't know what to do!"

"And you didn't think to mention to her that you worked for me? You didn't think that would be *normal*?"

I'm shocked into momentary silence that must look like more guilt. I thought he knew everything. Maybe he found Adele's phone and then came straight here? Maybe he hasn't spoken to her yet? Or maybe she didn't tell him that part. *Maybe she was too afraid.* I don't know what to say. Should I tell him that of course she knew? That she asked me to keep it a secret? But then that gets her into more trouble. And of *all* of us, Adele is the one who hasn't done anything wrong here. I say nothing.

"How fucking crazy are you?" Spit flies out with his words. "Jesus, I thought you were so honest. So straightforward. Have you been stalking me?"

"I felt sorry for her!" I scream at him, even though the walls are thin and Laura next door will definitely hear. "She was lonely!"

"Jesus fuck, Louise. You know how crazy this is, don't you?"

"I didn't want to be her friend. I didn't." The words are snotty through my tears. "I got roped in and at the start I thought what we'd done in the bar was a one-off."

"But why didn't you tell me? All these fucking lies, Louise? Who *are* you?"

"I didn't lie, I just didn't—" I shrug, helpless. *I just didn't tell you.* It's feeble and I know it even before he cuts me off.

"What was it you said to me? You're an open book?" He sneers and I barely recognize him. "You're full of shit. I thought I could trust you." He turns away and runs his hand through his hair but it looks like he's on the verge of tearing it out by the roots. "I can't get my head round this. I can't."

"What are you really worried about, David?" I take the moment. The best form of defense is attack and if he thought he could trust me then why didn't he ever tell me anything? Maybe he's the one full of shit. "That maybe I know things I shouldn't? That maybe I'll make Adele grow a spine and sort you out? Kick you out? Get her life back?"

"What?" He turns and looks at me, properly looks at me, for

the first time since he's stormed inside. He frowns. His voice lowers. "What has she said to you about me?"

"Oh, she never says anything other than she loves you." It's my turn to sneer. "But I *see* things. I know how you treat her. How nervous of you she is. I see how you've been playing around with her head."

He stares at me long and hard. "Don't for a second think you know anything about my marriage."

"I know you have all her money. Is that why you won't leave? The poor little farmer's boy saves the wealthy heiress and then gets her to sign over her inheritance and never gives it back? You're a walking Agatha fucking Christie plot." Now I'm angry. Yes, maybe he is right to be so upset with me and I don't know how I'd feel in his position—violated and cheated maybe—but he was sleeping with me behind his wife's back so I'm claiming that as a get-out-of-jail-free card, for now, anyway.

"You really think nothing of me at all, do you?" He's pale and shaking but his eyes are all fire.

"No, that's not true," I say, hating the way fresh tears spring from my eyes. "I have feelings for you. I thought maybe I loved you. Was partway there, at any rate. But there is all this *other* stuff, David. Stuff you don't tell me. Stuff your poor wife is too afraid to talk about."

"What the fuck is it that you think you know, Louise?" His words are cold and clipped and a terrible stillness has settled on him. Contained rage. Is that a threat or a question? I'm more afraid now than I was when he was shouting. I think about how he treats Adele and I think of his burn scars and how he rescued her from the blaze. I think of the money. Were his heroics for her or for him?

"What really happened to Adele's parents?" My arms fold across my chest as my quiet voice hurls the implied accusation. "A fire in the middle of the night and you happened to be passing. She *told* me about that. Her hero." I make a *pfft* sound to finish showing exactly what I think of that, even if I don't really know what I think of that.

"I fucking saved her life," he growls as he jabs a finger at me, almost stabbing me with it. I take a step back.

"Yeah, you did. But not her parents. They died. That worked out well for you, didn't it?"

He recoils, his eyes wide. "You fucking bitch. You think I . . . ?"

"I don't know what to think!" I'm shouting, ranting. "I'm tired of thinking about it. The pills, the phone calls, all that shit! Adele's controlling David, my kind but fucked-up David, trying to figure the real you out in the mess of it all. I never wanted to have to think about it! I never wanted to be her friend, but I am and I like her and I feel shit about everything!" I'm so upset I can hardly get a breath, sobbing and panting and fighting for air. "I feel like shit!"

"For fuck's sake, calm down, Louise." He takes a step forward, trying to grab my arms, but I shake him off as I gasp and cry. He's shocked by my torrent of emotion; I can just about see that.

"I'm her only friend." I'm on a roll to destruction and I can't stop it. I'm tired of having all the questions eating me up inside. "Her *only* friend. Why is that?"

"Louise, listen—"

"What happened to Rob, David?"

He freezes then, and I can almost feel the whole world hold a breath between us. My own breathing levels. "Why aren't they friends anymore?" I ask. "What did you do?"

He stares at me. "How do you know about Rob?" The words are barely more than a whisper.

"What did you do?" I ask again, but something in his face makes me wonder if I really want to know. He doesn't seem to hear me. For a long moment he says nothing and I realize he's not staring at me, but at something beyond me, something only he can see.

"You're fired," he says eventually.

The words, cold and clinical, are so not what I'm expecting that I don't make any sense of them.

"What?" It's my turn to frown, confused.

"Hand in your immediate notice tomorrow. By email. I don't care what reason you give—make something up. You should manage that easily enough."

I'm stunned. My job? He's taking my job?

"And if you think about telling Dr. Sykes about our tawdry little affair, then I will show him this." He holds up Adele's phone. "And then you're going to look as obsessive as Anthony Hawkins." He leans in close to me, threateningly controlled and quiet. "Because only a fucking crazy person would start a secret friendship with the wife of the man they're fucking." He pulls back slightly. "And Dr. Sykes is a man's man. He won't care that I fucked you. But he won't respect you for fucking me. He'll find a way to get rid of you himself."

I'm losing my job. Suddenly, this is all very real. David hates me, I don't know if Adele's okay, and now I've lost my job. I think back to that first night in the bar where we laughed and drank and he made me feel so alive and then the tears come thick and fast and fresh and full of self-pity. It's my mess and I should own it, but knowing that makes me feel worse.

"You said you loved me." I'm pathetic in my mouselike quiet.

He says nothing to that but his face is twisted and sour and not *my* David at all.

I want to cry some more, and what's worse is that even now, even after it's all out in the open, I'm still none the wiser about anything. For all my accusations he hasn't given me any answers.

"David, just tell me—" I start, hating the pleading in my voice, the need to repair *something.*

"Stay away from me." He cuts me off, his voice like ice. "Stay away from Adele. Trust me on this, Louise, if you know what's good for you, you'll stay away from both of us. We are not your business, you understand?"

I nod, a cowed child, the fight gone out of me. What am I fighting for anyway? I can't undo the things I've said and I'm not entirely sure I want to. I just want answers, and those he won't give me.

"I never want to see you again," he says. The words are soft but brutal. A kick in the kidneys that leaves me breathless as he turns to go.

And then there is the click of the front door and I'm alone.

I dissolve, crumpling to the floor, curling in on myself, weeping like a child, long, hard, uncontrollable sobs.

David is so angry. And I can't even text Adele to warn her.

33

ADELE

He goes for a drink before he comes home. Always the need for a drink with David, but this time I don't mind. I'd rather he gave himself time to calm down. I make sure that when I hear the front door open I'm sitting at the kitchen table, evidence of tears on my face. I'm not crying, though. He's had enough of crying women for one night, I imagine.

I maintain my confusion about Louise. I apologize, over and over, for not telling him about my new friend, but I was lonely and I was worried he'd stop me seeing her and that I was trying to be normal. I thought she'd be good for me. I ask where he went. I ask who she is to him, and why her name made him storm off like that. Of course he doesn't tell me the truth, although he should really know better by now.

He says she's one of his patients and watches me carefully for my reaction, testing me. He doesn't quite buy my innocence here, he knows me too well for that. I let my mouth fall open into a slightly confused "Oh." To be honest, I'm mildly disappointed in him. Even if I *didn't* already know he'd been fucking Louise and she was his secretary, surely this would make me suspicious. Much as I adore David, having one obsessive patient is believable, but two somewhat stretches the bounds of credibility. Still, all I have to do is play along, so I do.

I ask all the right questions, and he bats answers at me. He doesn't give me the phone back, but his own guilt reeks from his lack of inquisition over our friendship. I feel sorry for Louise—he clearly took most of his anger out on her. But then he's not used to being angry with her. I'm a whole different story. He doesn't have the energy to stay in a rage with me anymore. It would exhaust him.

"We should maybe go away for a couple of weeks," he says. His shoulders slump as he looks down at the floor. He's tired. So very, very tired. Of everything. Of me.

"We can't do that," I say. And, to be frank, we can't. That doesn't fit in with my plans *at all*. "You've only been at the practice for a few weeks. How would that look? Just move this Louise patient on like you did with that boy."

"Maybe for a few days then. So we can talk properly." He glances at me then. Suspicion. Nerves. All in that brief look. "Decide what we're going to do."

Good little Louise has kept our secret, but she mentioned the pills and the phone calls and he's wondering how much of that was accidental or whether I orchestrated it somehow.

"We can't keep running away," I say, all soft reason. "Whatever our problems we should stay and face them."

He nods, but he's watching me, thoughtful. It's Louise who deceived him but he doesn't trust me one little bit. Constantly trying to analyze my mood, my thinking, my actions. He's not convinced I didn't know who Louise was, but with her lack of confirmation, he can't prove anything. I can feel the battle lines being firmly marked out between us on our expensive kitchen tiles.

He's a man on the edge and he'll do something soon. Divorce me at the very least regardless of my threats to destroy him. I think he's almost past caring about that, and I've known for some time that my hold over him was waning. He'd be relieved it was all over and done with. For a while at least, before the realization that he'd totally fucked up his otherwise perfect life for something that happened a long time ago kicked in.

I'll act quicker than him, though. I'm braver that way. I've always been one step ahead. My resolve hardens. David will never be happy until he's free of the past and I can never be happy until David's happy.

When we finally leave the kitchen, him first, to his study for a while to avoid the awkwardness of our walk to separate bedrooms, and then me heading upstairs to our big empty bed, I lay awake awhile staring into the darkness and thinking about it all. More precisely, thinking about them, us, him.

The course of true love never did run smooth.

34

LOUISE

From having felt so refreshed, I'm now exhausted. I've barely slept in two days, the fight with David playing round and round on a loop in my head, and I've only left the flat to shuffle to the local shop for wine and bad food, my hair pulled up in a ponytail as a poor disguise for the fact I haven't even showered. Sophie sent me a "how's it going?" text, which I deleted without answering. I don't need any smug "I told you so" coming from her right now.

I nearly threw up when I sent my resignation email. I typed it out four times through tears of self-pity before I finally pressed send. I cc'd David into it and seeing his name there in the email made me want to cry some more. Dr. Sykes rang straight away, full of concern, and that made me cry again, which backed up my "personal family business" story.

I didn't give details and he didn't press for any. He told me to reconsider in a month and he'd consider it a hiatus. They could get a temp in to cover my days. I didn't fight that. Maybe in a month things will be different. Maybe David would have calmed down. Maybe they'll leave and move away. I don't really understand either of them, so I don't know what they'll do. The polite and courteous email I got from David—with Dr. Sykes cc'd in—was as if from a stranger, not a man who'd raged at me in my sitting room the night before. I was right. I don't know him at all. Adele is the only one who has been my friend. He's damaged us both.

I'm worried about Adele, though. I'd half-hoped that she'd show up at my door at some point, but so far she hasn't and I'm not surprised. She's so scared of upsetting David, she probably wouldn't take the risk. I've seen him angry now. I've felt that awful loathing coming off him. I can't imagine being on the receiving end of that for years. Maybe he's even working from home and claiming illness or something. When I'm not completely absorbed in my pity party for one, my mind is on fire with it, imagining him as some Hannibal Lecter–type monster. Mainly I need to know Adele's okay. I promised to stay away from her but how can I? David was so cold at the end of our fight. What did she face when he got home? I can still see that bruise on her cheek and despite his insistence he didn't hit her, don't all abusive husbands deny their actions?

I'm so tired and emotional all logical thinking has gone out the window. All I know is that I have to check on Adele and I'm running out of time to do it. Adam comes back the day after tomorrow and then who knows what spare time I'll have? It'll definitely be more limited and I don't want Adam dragged into this mess. I need to close a door on it. It still feels surreal, the thought of no David and no Adele. And no *job*. I bite back more tears. Even I'm getting bored of my crying. *It's your mess,* I keep telling myself. *Suck it up.*

Tomorrow. I'll see her tomorrow if I can, but how, without risking more trouble for both of us? I pour a glass of wine, not caring that it's barely two in the afternoon—these are exceptional circumstances—and slump on the sofa. I also need to clean my house. I don't need Ian judging me when he gets back. I take in the disarray and my eyes fall on my laptop, discarded on the floor by the TV where I tossed it after sending my email to Dr. Sykes, and then the thought comes to me.

Dr. Sykes told me to take a month. This isn't like I've been fired—even though you wanted to fire me, thank you very much, *Mr.-bastard-from-the-bar*—and so they won't have deleted my remote log-in.

I sit cross-legged on the carpet, my wine beside me, and, with my heart racing as if somehow they can see me, I log in to the clinic server. My palms are sweating and even though I'm not technically breaking any rules I feel like I'm going through a lover's emails and text messages. I bring up David's diary for tomorrow. His afternoon is pretty fully booked. He won't be leaving work until at least five. Even if he goes home for lunch he'll have to be back by one thirty. I log out and sip my wine, making my plan.

In the morning I'll double-check his diary and make sure he hasn't canceled any appointments last minute. I'll go to Carphone Warehouse on the Broadway and buy a cheap prepaid phone. Adele needs to have a phone and I don't know if David's kept that crappy one she had. At least if I give her one to hide somewhere I'll know that if she's in serious trouble she can call me. I'll feel more relaxed about letting them both go then. I have to be. I have no choice.

I feel better for having a plan, and as I take my wine out to the balcony and the afternoon sunshine, I realize I also feel better for defying David. *Screw you,* I think. *Who the hell do you think you are, anyway?*

I try not to think about how it felt having him in my bed and how I miss that closeness even though I hate myself for it. I don't think about how he's always there in my constructed dreams playing happy families through that first door. Instead, I think about how hurt I feel and how he's to blame and I'm fucked if he's going to tell me what to do like I'm a little nervous Adele.

Tomorrow. I can put it all behind me tomorrow.

35

ADELE

It takes several rings before I even realize it's the doorbell. At first, in my blissful haze, I think some exotic bird has got into the house, and then I wonder if I'm even in the house at all, and then I hear it again. The doorbell. Definitely the doorbell. It irritates me, and my head feels heavy as I sit up straight on the sofa.

"Adele?" The disembodied voice drifts into the room and I frown. Is that really her? I've been thinking about her so much I don't know if I'm really hearing her or if she's in my head. It's so hard to focus and she feels so constantly entwined with me that right now, in this state, I don't know where I end and she begins.

"Adele, it's me. Louise! Please let me in. I'll only stay a moment. I just want to know you're okay."

Louise. It *is* her. My savior. I smile, although it feels like I'm gurning and I probably am. There's some drool on my chin and I clumsily wipe it away before hauling myself to my unsteady feet. I knew she'd be back but I wasn't expecting her so soon.

I take a deep breath to try and clear my head a little while I decide whether to answer the door. It may be a risk, but still I hide the things I need to in the ornate little teak box on the side table. I don't know where I bought it from or why, but at least it finally has a use.

She calls my name once more and I catch my reflection in the mirror. I look like a mess. I'm sweaty pale and my pupils are so dilated that my eyes are almost black. My lips twitch. I don't recognize myself. That makes me giggle, a sudden sound that almost spooks me. To let her in, or not to let her in, that is the question. But then, in the part of my brain that's functioning properly, I realize how I can work this to my advantage. I was going to have to fake this behavior at some point, but now I don't. My plan marches on. But then my plans always do.

I shamble toward the front door and open it, flinching in the bright sunlight. An hour ago I wouldn't have been able to move, but now that I'm concentrating my limbs are doing what I tell them. I'm feeling quite proud of myself, but Louise looks shocked. It takes a second before I realize I'm the one who's swaying slightly, not her and the pavement outside.

"Shit, Adele," she says, quickly coming inside and gently taking my arm. "You're in a right state." She leads me toward the kitchen. "Are you drunk? Let's get some coffee on. I've been so worried about you."

"I'm so sorry about my phone," I slur. "So sorry." She lowers me into a chair. It's a relief to be sitting down. One less thing to concentrate on.

"You have nothing to be sorry about," she says as she fills the kettle and searches for mugs and instant coffee. I'm glad there's a small "in case of emergencies" jar in the cupboard. I may be semifocused now but I don't have the energy to explain the coffee machine.

"You're allowed to have friends, Adele. Everyone's allowed to have friends." Her eyes scan the room for evidence of booze, but she sees nothing. "What's the matter with you? Are you sick? Has he done something?"

I shake my head slowly, keeping the world in place. "The pills. I maybe took more than I should."

She goes to the cupboard and as she opens it I know she's calculating whether it would be possible to give yourself a black eye when doing so.

"Really, don't worry, it's fine, they're prescription," I mutter. She doesn't stop, though, of course not. She ignores the little defensive line of ibuprofen and antacid tablets and reaches to the packets beyond, spreading them out on the counter. The kettle clicks off but she doesn't move. She's studying the labels. All neatly printed with my name and dosage instructions, as prescribed by my husband.

"Fuck," she says eventually. "David prescribed these for you?"

I nod. "For my nerves."

"These aren't for your nerves, Adele. These are strong antipsychotics. I mean, really strong. All of them to one degree or another."

"No, you must be wrong, they're for my nerves," I repeat.

She doesn't say anything to that, but continues to stare at the packets, many with half-empty strips of blisters hanging out where I've washed down the sink. She rummages inside one box.

"No information sheet. Does David bring these prescriptions home for you or do you collect them yourself?"

"He brings them," I say quietly. "Can I have some coffee, please? I feel so tired." Actually, I'm surprised at how quickly I'm straightening out, given that this is only my second time practicing this.

She finally makes the coffee and comes to sit opposite me. There's nothing ditzy about chubby little Louise anymore. In fact, there's nothing chubby about Louise anymore. These past couple of days of heartache have knocked the last difficult pounds off.

"How long has he been making you take these?" she asks.

I shrug. "For a while. But he's always trying different ones." I stare into my coffee, enjoying the burning sensation of the hot mug on my oversensitive fingers. "I don't always take them. But sometimes he watches me."

I lean my head against the wall behind me, tired of holding it up. My mind might be straightening out, but the rest of me has a way to go. "I said I wanted control of my money back," I mumble, as if this seed of information isn't important. "Before we moved. After what happened in Blackheath. But he said no. He said I had to take the pills for a while first to calm me down, then we'd talk about it. He'd been trying to get me to take them for a while and I'd always said no, but then I thought after all that, I'd try. For him. For us."

"What happened at Blackheath?" Her self-pity is gone now and she's drawn back into our story. I pause for a long moment before speaking.

"I think he had an affair." The words are barely a whisper but she leans back slightly when she hears them and her face flushes. *Yeah, that hurts, doesn't it? Now you know how it feels.*

"Are you sure?" she asks.

I shrug. "I think so. The woman who owned the little café round the corner from the clinic of all people. Marianne, her name was." The pretty name is still bitter on my tongue.

"Wow."

Yeah, wow, Louise. Suck that up. You don't feel so special now, do you? I want to giggle and for a horrifying moment I think I will, so instead I cover my mouth and look away as if I'm fighting back tears.

"This was supposed to be our fresh start. This house. This job. I asked for my money back again, just to be in control of it more, and he went mad. He . . . he . . ." My breath hitches and Louise's eyes widen.

"He what, Adele?"

"You know I said our cat died after we moved in?" I pause. "Well, he kicked it. Really hard. And then, when she was dazed, he stamped on her." I stare toward the back door and the garden beyond, where I buried it. "He killed her."

Louise says nothing. What is there to say? She's too horrified to speak.

"That's the thing with David," I continue, tired and still slurring slightly. "He can be so charming. So wonderfully funny and kind. But then when he's angry he's like a different person. I always seem to make him angry these days. I don't understand why he doesn't leave me if he's so unhappy," I say. "I wish he'd love me again." And I do. I really, really do.

"If he divorces you, he'll have to give your estate back," she says. Her face hardens as the jigsaw puzzle pieces I've carefully laid out for her fall into place, and then she rummages in her bag and pulls out a mobile phone.

"It's prepaid and my number is in it. Hide it somewhere. But if you need me just text or call, okay?"

I nod.

"You promise?"

"I promise." I sip my cooling coffee, my hand still trembling.

"And stop taking those pills if you can. They're no good for you. You're not sick. Fuck knows what they're doing to your brain chemistry. Now let's get you to bed. You can sleep this off before he gets home."

"What are you going to do, Louise?" I ask, my arm draped round her shoulder as she helps me upstairs. "Don't do anything silly, will you? Don't confront David, will you?"

She laughs, slightly bitterly. "Unlikely, given that he's fired me."

"He what?" I feign surprise. "Oh, Louise, this is all my fault. I'm so sorry."

"It's not your fault. Don't ever think that. You haven't done anything wrong."

Her body feels strong, firmer and tighter than when we first met. I've *created* this new Louise, and I feel a moment of pride as I sink down onto my comfortable bed.

"Oh, Louise," I say sleepily, as if it's an afterthought. "The plant pot at the front door. The right side."

"What about it?"

"I hid a spare key in it in case I locked myself out. I want you to know that." I pause. "He locked me in once. I was scared."

"If he does that again, call me straight away." She's almost growling, this fierce tiger of a woman.

"I don't know what I'd do without you," I murmur as she covers me with a blanket and then gently pushes my hair out of my face. "I really don't."

And it's the truth.

36

LOUISE

He's a little brown nut, my baby boy. Maybe not so little. He's grown. Even though it's late and he's barely awake I can see how tanned and healthy he is, and I very nearly cry as he runs into my arms and hugs me tight. My one good thing.

"I got you this, Mummy." He holds up a key ring with a small shell trapped in clear resin adorning it. It's a cheap seaside souvenir, but I love it. I love that he chose it for me.

"Oh my gosh, thank you! It's beautiful. I'll put my keys on it first thing in the morning. Now why don't you take your bag into your bedroom while I say good night to Daddy?"

"See you soon, soldier," Ian says, and then, when Adam's wheeled his little Buzz Lightyear suitcase away, he smiles at me. "You're looking good, Lou. Have you lost some weight?"

"A bit." I'm glad he's noticed but although I may be looking slimmer, I'm not sure "good" is a word I'd have chosen for how I appear today. A night of no sleep while tossing and turning and thinking about David and Adele's fucked-up life, my own hurt heart and my self-pity, and my lack of a job has left me looking washed out.

"Ah, I probably shouldn't have brought you these then." He holds up a bag. Two bottles of French red wine and several cheeses.

"Always welcome," I say with a tired grin and take them. I don't tell him I've lost my job. That can wait for a while, and I'm going to have to make up some lie to cover it. There's no way I can tell him the truth. I don't want to make him think we're now on some even moral ground. He cheated on me, and now I've slept with a married man. I'm definitely not giving him that. I'll say my new boss had his own secretary or something. That's the thing I'm learning about affairs. They breed lies.

"You'd better get off, shouldn't you?" I say. "Lisa must be knackered in the car." Their delayed Eurostar has meant it's nearly midnight. They should have been home by nine.

"Yeah, she is." He looks momentarily awkward and then adds, "Thanks for this, Louise. I know it's not easy."

"It's fine, honestly," I say, waving him away. "I'm happy for you. Really." I can't decide if that's a lie or not and I find that it's part-lie, part-truth. It's complicated. I do want him to leave, though. After the intensity of the past few weeks and days I don't really have small talk in me and this invading return of normality feels surreal.

When he's gone, I get Adam into his pajamas and squeeze him tight, relishing the gorgeous smell of him while he sleepily mumbles tales of his time away, most of which I've heard on the phone. I don't mind. I feel like I could listen to his chatter all night. I put a big plastic cup of water by his bed and we talk for a little while as he gets drowsier and drowsier.

"I missed you, Mummy," he says. "I'm glad I'm home."

My heart melts then. I *do* have a life of my own. It might all be wrapped up in the package of this little boy, but I love him with all my heart and that love is pure and clean and perfect.

"I missed you too," I say. Those words don't cover how I feel. "Let's go up to Highgate Wood tomorrow if the weather's nice. Get some ice creams. Have some pretend adventures. Would you like that?"

He smiles and nods, but he's drifting off to his own world of sleep. I kiss him good night and watch him for a moment or two longer before turning the light out and leaving him.

I feel utterly exhausted. Having Adam back has calmed me, and now there's just tiredness weighing me down. I pour a glass of the rich red wine Ian brought and it eases the final dregs of my tension until I can't stop yawning. I try and let Adele and David float away. Adele has a phone. If she's in any real trouble she can call. Unless, of course, she's too smashed off her face on whatever concoction of pills David has given her. But there's nothing I can really do. I've thought about calling Dr. Sykes, but who's he going to believe? And I'm pretty sure that Adele would lie to protect David—and herself. I can't understand why she still loves him, which she clearly does, when it seems obvious to me that he's only there for her money. How much is she worth? How much has he spent? Maybe they've been together so long Adele is mistaking dependency for love.

It stings, too, that Adele said David had a *thing* with someone where they used to live. So much for all his *I don't do this* angst. It hurts and I keep replaying how he was that awful night, so cold in what he said. A stranger. The other side to him, like Adele said.

I let out a long sigh as if I can somehow expel them both from me. Adam is home now. I have to focus on him. Him and trying to get another job. Whatever Dr. Sykes says, I can't go back to the clinic. Even if David left, the place is too full of him now—too full of all this—for me to ever want to work there anymore. It wouldn't be the same. I do a halfhearted job search on the net but there's nothing suitable for me, and it makes me more miserable. Thank god I've got some savings in the bank to give me a few months' breathing space, but they won't last forever and then I'll be back on Ian's charity. I want to curl up in a ball until it's all gone away. Instead, I drain the glass and then head to bed. Adam's back and there'll be no more lie-ins for me.

I fall asleep quickly. These days the night terrors are barely there, I'm in for a second or two, check my fingers, and then the Wendy door appears and I'm gone. As has become habit, I'm in the garden by the pond and Adam is there with me, and although we're trying to have fun it's a gray, drizzly day, as if, even in the dream I'm controlling, my emotional mood has a say. I know the dream is all only a fantasy, and the fantasy isn't living up to much with just the two of us here. David is not barbecuing tonight. I don't want him here. Not with his *if you know what's good for you, you'll stay away from both of us* so clear in my head.

I'm by the pond but Adam has got distracted from the abundance of tadpoles and fish by the toy cars and trucks that are strewn over the lawn, and he barely looks up. I know that I'm putting him there—if I want Adam by the pond with me fishing for treasure then I only have to will it—but this also isn't the real Adam, merely an imaginary creation of him, and tonight that's not enough.

The real Adam is fast asleep in his own bed, tucked up under his duvet and cuddling Paddington. I think of him, sleeping so close to me, and picturing him there back in his room makes my heart glow and I want to see him and hug him until he can barely breathe. I feel it with a mother's ferocity, and then, suddenly, there it is again.

The second door.

It's glowing under the pond's surface like before, but this time it moves, rising up to stand vertical, and although the edges are shimmering mercurial silver, the door itself is made of water. I stay still and it comes quickly toward me, and for a second I think I can see tadpoles and goldfish swimming in the surface, and then I'm touching the liquid warmth and passing through it and then I'm—

—standing by Adam's bed. I feel momentarily dizzy with the change, but then the world settles. I'm in his bedroom. I can hear him breathing, slow and steady, the breathing of the very old or the deeply sleeping. One arm is over his face and I think about moving it but don't want to disturb him. His duvet is half–kicked off and at some point he must have knocked his water over and it's spilled all over poor Paddington, who's fallen out of bed. I'm glad it's a dream. Adam would hate that Paddington needs drying out. He won't even let me put him in the washing machine.

I bend over to pick the bear up, but my hand can't grasp it. More than that, I can't see my hand. I look at where they should be. *I have no hands.* There's nothing there. Confused, I try three times to touch the bear with my invisible fingers, but with each attempt I have the sensation of passing right through the soft, wet fur, as if I'm not there at all, as if I'm a ghost, and then I'm horribly unsettled and I feel an enormous tug from behind as I'm yanked backward, and for a brief moment I'm terribly afraid and then—

—I wake up with a gasp, upright in my own bed, sucking in deep breaths of air. I feel jolted awake, like in those almost-dreams of falling you get when on the cusp of sleep. My eyes dart around in the gloom, trying to shake my complete disorientation. I look down at my hands and count my fingers. Ten. I do it twice before I'm sure that this time I truly am awake.

My lungs feel raw, as if I've been out and smoked twenty cigarettes in the pub like in the days of old, but I don't feel tired. If anything, I feel weirdly energized, given how emotionally battered I am and how tired I was when I went to bed. I'm thirsty, though. Desperately thirsty. Wine before bed. I'll never learn.

I get up and creep to the kitchen and drain two glasses from the tap and then splash my face. My lungs return to normal, the rawness fading. Maybe it was just some echo of the dream.

It's only 3 A.M. and so I head back to bed, even though I'm not sure I'll go back to sleep, and I pause at Adam's door and look in and smile. He's definitely home. That part wasn't a dream. I'm about to close the door when the bear on the floor catches my eye. Paddington. Fallen out of bed. I frown and come in closer. The plastic cup on the bedside table is on its side and empty. The bear is soaked. This time I *can* pick Paddington up and he's heavily sodden. I look at Adam, my heart starting to thump faster. One arm is over his face and his legs are sticking out from the half-kicked-off duvet.

It's like a moment of déjà vu. Everything is exactly as I saw it in my dream when I went through the second door. But that can't be right. I can't have seen it. I was in a dream. But I couldn't have known that he'd spilled his water and soaked his bear and that his arm was over his face. I wouldn't have imagined those things. Adam is the soundest sleeper I know. He normally barely even moves, but stays curled up on his side all night. None of this is anything I would have pictured if I was thinking of Adam sleeping.

I don't know what to think. I can't make any sense of it. And then it strikes me. I must have sleepwalked. It's a small moment of relief, of logic, and I cling to it even though it doesn't feel true. I haven't done that once since I started the lucid dreaming. But that must be what happened. Maybe I was sleepwalking and half–woke up or something. Saw the room then went back to sleep and carried it into my dream.

When I realize there's no point in standing there staring any longer, I go back to bed and look up at the ceiling for a while. The whole thing has unsettled me, although I'm not sure why. The way I couldn't touch the bear. My invisibility. That never happens in my "new" dreams. I can eat, drink, fuck, whatever. How come I couldn't pick up Paddington? How come I didn't have hands? It's weird. And it wasn't like the other dreams. Despite my lack of body, the dream itself felt more solid. More real.

I must have been sleepwalking, I tell myself over and over. *I mean, what other explanation can there be?*

PART THREE

37

ADELE

We are two strangers in the house now, circling each other warily, and—at least on David's part—there is very little pretense at anything else. We're barely even civil. He grunts answers to my questions like he's devolved into some Neanderthal beast no longer capable of full sentences, and he avoids looking me in the eye. Maybe he doesn't want me to see that he's drunk most of the time. I think he's saving all his "normality" for work and doesn't have the energy for it at home.

He seems smaller—diminished. If *I* were the shrink I'd say he was a man on the edge of a nervous breakdown. My friendship with Louise has completely knocked him. No, that's not quite right. Louise's friendship with me has knocked him. She was *his* special secret thing and that's been ruined. He's been fooled.

Now that the initial shock of the discovery has passed, I know he blames me.

"Are you sure you didn't know who she was?" he asked me last night, hovering in the doorway of my bedroom, not wanting to cross the threshold. "When you met her?"

"How could I have possibly known she was a patient of yours?" I answered, all wide-eyed innocence. A *patient*. His lie, not mine. He might have been drunk, but he didn't buy my answer. He can't put his finger on how I knew about her, but he knows I did. My behavior's confused him, though—this isn't my "form." In Blackheath I was far more direct in my approach, but Marianne was nothing but a potential threat to my marriage. Louise is—well, Louise is the great white hope of our happiness. Louise is wonderful.

I hate acknowledging mistakes but I have to admit I was probably too obvious in Blackheath. I shouldn't have let my rage get the better of me—at least not so dramatically—but that was different. And anyway, it's all in the past. I never care about the past unless I can use it for something in the present, and perhaps Blackheath will turn out to be useful, in which case it won't have been a mistake at all. The past is as ephemeral as the future—it's all perspective and smoke and mirrors. You can't pin it down, can you? Let's say two people experience exactly the same thing—ask them to recount the event later and although their versions might be similar there will always be differences. The truth is different to different people.

Poor David, though. He's consumed by the past. It's concrete boots on him, weighing him down, drowning us. That one moment in the past has shaped him into this broken man. One night has led to the drink, the worry, the inability to let himself love me, the guilt. It's been so fucking tiring living with it and trying to make it all right for both of us. Trying to make him see that it doesn't matter. No one knows. No one was ever going to know. So in many ways, as no one knows, then it never even really happened. If a tree falls in the woods and no one's around to hear it, blah, blah, blah.

Soon, however, our terrible guilty secret will be dragged out into the light and we shall be free of it. David is on the verge of telling, I know that. I imagine that prison seems a better option to him than this continued hell. It doesn't hurt as much as it should, to think that the man I love so very, very much considers life with me to be hellish, but then, this has been no picnic for me either of late.

Telling, though, will only be a momentary relief. He hasn't grasped that yet. Telling won't win him Louise. Telling won't bring him trust and absolution. David deserves both. Some secrets need to be excavated, not just told, and our little sin is one of those.

I could have done all this much more easily. I could have left them well alone and maybe David would have eventually told Louise the truth of our marriage, and the event that has shaped it, and she'd have believed him, but he'd always wonder if she had a little doubt. He'd be constantly looking in her eyes for suspicion. There is nothing solid in a telling.

It all comes down to Louise. She has to uncover our sordid past herself. She needs to set us both free with her complete belief. I'm working hard for that. Even if he can't bear to look at me, I'm doing it all for David.

I make a pot of peppermint tea and then, while it's brewing, I fetch the little handset from the wardrobe, turn it on, and text Louise, my little pretty puppet on a string.

Wanted to let you know all okay here. I'm trying to be normal. Emptied out capsule pills so just taking empty cases when he's here. Not swallowing others, putting them under my tongue and spitting out. Looked in his study to see if he has a file on me but can't find one :(Glad u know where spare key is. Feel crazy being worried about D—he's always looked after me—but ur right, not enough that I love him. Maybe i'll contact lawyer about divorce. Oh, I imagined us in my dream—on the Orient Express—great girls' holiday—we should do that one day!! A xx

It's a long text but it shows how much I need her and miss her. I don't bother putting the phone back yet—Louise always replies fast, and this time is no exception.

So glad ur ok and good work with the pills! I've been worrying bout u. I had a dream and I went thru that second door I told you about. I ended up in Adam's bedroom. Stuff was moved around. When I woke up and went in to check on him, it was all exactly like in my dream. Weird, huh? You really never get the second door? I think maybe I was sleepwalking. And YES TO ORIENT EXPRESS!

I reply how odd that is and that no, I don't ever have a second door and I guess her brain must work differently to mine, but my hands are shaking with elation as I type. I can barely sit still with the sudden rush of adrenaline. She's doing it already! She hasn't figured out quite what she's doing yet, but she's so fast at this. Faster than I ever was. A natural. I have to get things moving more quickly now that it's not entirely in my control.

Will check his study again for a file on me. Where can it be? Anyway, have to go. Take care. A xx

I can't be bothered to get into a long chat with her now. I'm too excited. I've nudged her, though, in that last text. Another little seed planted to get her synapses firing, even though the answer is so fucking obvious she'd have to be a retard not to have the solution. What must she really think of my intellectual capacities? Poor little Adele. So sweet and kind, and yet so simple and stupid. That's what she must make of me.

If only she knew.

38

LOUISE

It's been a great day out in the woods and then to the adventure playground and then a late lunch at the café, and both Adam and I are glowing from the fresh air and giggling when we get back to the flat. I'm glad Adele texted this morning to let me know that at least things aren't any worse and I thank god she's trying not to take those pills. Fuck knows what they'd do to a healthy mind.

Having a few hours worry-free has done me a world of good and I'm still smiling as I rummage in my bag for the keys. It might not have been France and snails and swimming pools, but I still know how to make my little boy laugh. We'd played Doctor Who among the trees. Adam was the Doctor, of course, and me his trusty companion. Apparently the trees were an alien race and at first they wanted to kill us, but somewhere along the way—I'm sure it made sense to Adam—we saved them and then peace was restored and we were ready to take our Tardis off to another adventure. After an ice-cream fuel stop, obviously. Adam was convinced that ice cream was what the Doctor and his companion ate when traveling and I didn't argue. It totally broke my diet, but with the stress of everything that's been going on while my baby's been away, the pounds have been melting off. And god, it tasted good. My real life feels good.

"Where's my key ring?" Adam asks, slightly put out. "You said you were going to use it today."

"Silly Mummy forgot," I say. It's still on the coffee table where I left it last night. After the distraction of the weird dream it had slipped from my mind. "I'll do it as soon as we're inside." I ruffle his hair and smile, but I'm annoyed at myself. How could I have forgotten that? His present to me. A gift from the one person who loves me unconditionally and I forgot about it.

Only when he's settled in front of some games on his dad's old iPad, with cartoons playing in the background, and I start transferring my bundle over do I realize that I still have my keys to the clinic. My heart thumps faster. If David did have some kind of file on Adele then he wouldn't keep it at home. It would be at work, where she couldn't inadvertently find it.

But somewhere I could. If I dared.

I stare at the keys. I could get in without anyone knowing. I know the alarm code. I could do it tonight. I feel slightly sick at what I'm suggesting to myself but I also have a surge of adrenaline. I need to know. Adele needs to know. And I owe it to her after everything I've done, even if she's blissfully unaware of what a truly shit friend I am.

Adam is absorbed in the film, watching dozily, still tired out after his holiday and then a day at the woods, and I sneak out and knock for Laura next door.

"Hey," she says, all smiles, the sound from her huge TV wafting out to me. "Louise. What can I do for you? Do you want to come in?" I like Laura, even though I haven't seen much of her recently, and I have a moment of embarrassment at the thought that she probably heard David and me fighting the other night.

"I can't stop, I've left Adam. I was wondering, and I know it's really short notice, but could you maybe babysit him tonight? I'm really sorry, it's a last-minute thing."

"A date?" she asks, grinning.

I nod, which is stupid. Now I'm going to have to get dressed up for a night out just to break into my old office. Thinking about it, the reality of actually doing it, I suddenly will her to say no.

"Of course I can," she says, and I curse my impetuousness. "I'll never stand in the way of potential true love or a good shag. What time?"

"About eight?" I'm going to have time to kill, but any later would sound odd. "Is that okay? He'll be in bed by then, and you know what he's like, he'll never wake up."

"It's no problem, honestly," she says. "I didn't have anything planned."

"Thanks, Laura. You're a star."

That's that then. I'm doing it.

I get more tense as the afternoon stretches into the evening, my mind filled with worries. What if they've changed the alarm code, is my main one, but I can't see it. The code's been the same for as long as I've worked there and other members of staff have come and gone in that time. And as far as Dr. Sykes is concerned I might come back to my job. Why would he worry about me having access? But still, by eight fifteen when Laura's settled and I'm out of the flat, I'm dithering as to whether I should go through with it. If anyone was to find out, I could get in serious trouble. I think about the pills. The state Adele was in at her house. She could be in worse trouble if I don't do it.

I can't go straight to the clinic, it's way too early, so instead I go to an Italian restaurant on the Broadway, ensconce myself in a corner, and order a dinner I really don't want to eat. My stomach's fist-tight with anxiety, but I force half of the risotto down. I do, however, drink a large glass of red wine to steady me. It barely touches the sides and I feel stone cold sober.

By ten I've stayed as long as I can and I wander through the town for an hour, puffing constantly on my e-cig until my mouth and throat are dry. I try to focus. I think about Adele. I know I *have* to do this. It's important. And it's not like I'm breaking in anyway. Not technically. I have keys. If anyone turns up—*oh please fuck god don't let anyone turn up*—I can claim to be picking up something I've left there. *Yeah right, Louise, because after eleven is always the time people innocently do stuff like that in business premises.*

The road feels oppressively dark as I turn down it, and my

footsteps are the sole ones disturbing the peace of the empty pavement. Most of the buildings here are solicitors' or accountants' offices and although some of the higher floors are flats, barely any light filters out from under their heavy, wealthy curtains or designer blinds. I should be happy that I can't be seen, but the hairs on the back of my neck still prickle as if *something* in the darkness is watching me. I glance back over my shoulder, momentarily convinced that someone is right there, but the road is clear.

My shaking hand pulls the keys from my bag. *In and out. It'll be easy. Pretend you're James Bond.* I don't feel very much like James Bond as the keys slip from my fingers and clatter loudly on the top step, but within a moment I've got the door unlocked and am inside. My heart is in my mouth as I flick on the light and race to the alarm box, which is beeping out its thirty seconds before all hell breaks loose.

I've done this a hundred times and, my face flushing hot, I'm sure that this time I'll punch in the wrong code, but my fingers fall into habit and fly over the keypad and then the beeps fall gloriously silent. I stand there, in the strange, gloomy emptiness, taking a few deep breaths and forcing my racing heart to slow. I'm in. I'm safe.

I head toward David's office, leaving as many lights off as possible. I've been here alone before, and in the dark on early winter mornings, but the building feels different tonight. Unwelcoming, as if I've woken it from sleep and it knows I should no longer be here.

The doctors rarely lock their offices—the cleaners need to get in and there's an air of middle-class complacency that hangs over the clinic; an old-school trust. Plus, on a more practical level, it's not as if they have cabinets full of morphine to steal from, and as for information, most of the patients' files are stored in password-protected computer systems that only the doctors can access. If David has a file on Adele here, though, it won't be in the system. He won't want it where any of the other practice partners could see it, even if they couldn't access it. Questions would be raised, ethical ones if nothing else.

His door is indeed unlocked and I flick on his desk light and start searching through the old filing cabinet in the corner, but it's mainly filled with pamphlets from pharmaceutical companies and self-help guides to give out to patients. A lot of this crap must have been left over from Dr. Cadigan. It's all dry and bland. I take everything out and go through it but there's nothing hidden at the bottom of any of the drawers.

It's been twenty minutes by the time I've got everything back in, hopefully in the right order, but my disappointment has made me more determined than ever to find what I'm looking for. I won't have the nerve to come back again but I also need to be home by one at the latest so that Laura doesn't ask too many questions. I look around. Where else can it be? He must at least have notes somewhere—he's prescribing for her. He'd need *something* to cover himself.

His desk is the only place left to go in the uncluttered room and I tackle it feverishly. The top drawer is notebooks, pens, and stationery—surprisingly untidy given how spotless his home is—and then I yank at the larger bottom drawer. It's locked. I try it again, but nothing gives. One locked drawer. *Secrets.*

I search the top drawer for the key, but it's not there. He must keep it with him. *Shit, shit, shit, shit, shit.* What can I do? I stare for a long moment and then my curiosity overwhelms me. I have to get inside. Screw the consequences. He might know someone's broken into it, but he won't know for sure it was me. I get a knife from the kitchen and jam it into the small gap at the drawer edge, trying to get some leverage to force it open. At first I don't think I'm going to manage it, and then with a spat-out mutter of "Come on, you fucker," I give one big shove and the wood splinters. The drawer slides open an inch. I've done it.

The first things I see are the brandy bottles. Two; one half-empty. I should be shocked, or at least surprised, but I'm not. David's drinking is perhaps the least well kept of his secrets, from me and Adele anyway. There are also multiple packs of extra-strong mints. How much does he drink in the day? I can almost picture him—a sip here, a sip there, not too much but just enough. Why does he drink? Guilt? Unhappiness? *Who cares,* I decide. *I'm not here for him.*

I'm tempted to go and empty the bottles down the sink but I

don't, instead just taking them out and rummaging underneath. I'm on my knees and sweating beneath the makeup I've had to put on for Laura's benefit as I paw through envelopes and folders of receipts and copies of medical articles he's written.

Finally, right at the bottom, I see a large manila envelope. Inside is a buff A4 folder. It's lost that firm, crisp newness, now soft to the touch, and the various pages inside are held together with treasury tags, a random collection of sheets of notes, not like a proper medical file at all. It's what I'm looking for, though. Her name is there, right on the front, in thick black marker. *Adele Rutherford-Campbell/Martin.*

I sit in his chair and run my fingers over the surface for a moment, before turning to the first page. It's not a conventional medical file, that's for certain, more a collection of random notes. Scratched-out scribbles in his poor doctor's handwriting on various types of paper—seemingly whatever he had at hand at the time. I'd thought that whatever I found would go back a year or so, from whenever he'd started hatching this plan. Maybe when he met Marianne from the café in Blackheath, a thought that still stings my pride. But no, the first entry is from six years ago and it talks about things going back a decade. He's infuriating in his lack of detail.

I pull the chair closer to the desk so the file can sit directly under the soft yellow glow of the desk light while I try and make some sense of his scribbles.

A minor breakdown three months after leaving Westlands during which time she had an abortion.

What was it Adele had said? At the start of their marriage he wanted kids and she didn't. How would her choosing to have an abortion have made him feel? Must have hurt. The start of his resentment maybe? I flick through, further forward.

Suspicions of paranoia and extreme jealousy. She knows things she shouldn't. Is she spying on me? How?

"Now who sounds paranoid, David?" is what I want to scribble under his jottings.

> *Adele claims incident at florist with Julia was not her fault, but too many similarities to the past? No action taken—no proof. Julia upset/afraid. Friendship over. Job over. Agreed no more work. Did she do it so she could stay at home?*

The job Adele mentioned she once had. This must be it. But what happened? I think of the daily phone calls. Did David sabotage her work to make sure she stayed at home? But what was the incident? What actually happened? This file would never work to get her sectioned. There's no detail and no official evaluations or sessions recorded. Maybe he's relying on his reputation to be able to use this against her. A subtle damning of her rather than going big guns so he can appear almost reluctant. I scan forward to the most recent entries, my eyes picking up on phrases that chill me.

> *Psychotic break. Sociopathic tendencies.*

I see where he's jotted down prescriptions, but everything is vague. Just alluded to. It's all notes as if a private record, but I still feel like he's talking about a stranger—this isn't Adele.

> *Marianne not pressing charges. No proof. Have agreed to move. Again.*

Marianne was the name Adele gave of the woman in Blackheath. What really happened there? Adele obviously found out he was seeing her, and maybe there was a confrontation? I feel a wave of nausea imagining myself in that situation. It could easily have been me. I hate the thought of Adele ever finding out what I did, and not because I think she's crazy, whatever David wants the world to believe, but because she's my friend. I would hate for her to know how I betrayed her.

I look at that note. The *again* after moving. How many times have they moved? Adele hasn't said and there are no clues here. Maybe when he finally presents all this shit to someone—Dr. Sykes maybe—he wants it to look like he was protecting her but can't any longer. I study the most recent pages, but his writing is indecipherable. I pick out a couple of words that make my heart almost stop— *parents*; *Estate*—and my eyes strain trying to make sense of the paragraph of broken sentences around them but I can't. This was written drunk, I'm pretty sure of it. I feel like I'm looking into the mind of a mad person rather than reading a file on one.

The last two pages are virtually bare, but what's written on them makes me freeze.

> *Rage out of the blue after the move. Kicked the cat. Stamped on it. Killed it. Too many coincidences.*

Then, farther down the page—

> *Was it a threat? Making a point? Medication changed. How many accidents can there be?? Have there ever actually been any?*

There's only one line used on the last page but I stare at it for a long time.

> *Louise. What to do about her?*

39

THEN

She's been at home alone for two days before David arrives and she's surprised at how much at peace she feels. The solitude has been strange after the constant company of Westlands, but it's also been soothing to her soul. Even at night, in the silence of the countryside, where it would be easy to believe she was the last person on earth, she's felt calm. Not that she ever feels isolated from people and places. Not really. Not with what she can do.

But still, she thinks maybe they were all right, in a way. The young do heal fast. And Fairdale House now feels like a facsimile of her home. The same but so different without her parents here. She's even felt strong enough to look inside the charred remains of their rooms and box up some bits and pieces—her mother's filigree jewelry box, the silver candlesticks that had been her grandmother's, other odds and ends that each hold memories for her. Some photographs that were in a box in her bottom drawer that somehow survived the blaze. All taken with her father's expensive camera and developed in his own darkroom. One of the many hobbies he preferred to being a father. There's one of her at around fifteen. One of her and David sitting on the kitchen table taken not so long ago. That had been a good evening. Her parents had been drinking and were less disapproving of him that night, a rare time they all spent together. She puts the first picture in one of the boxes but keeps the second.

She gives it to David when they're walking through the estate, the air fresh and damp but invigorating. "I found this," she says, her arm linked through his. He's been quiet since he arrived and their reunion was almost awkward to start. They'd thrown themselves at each other and kissed, both overjoyed to be reunited, but the month apart and the fire still sit between them, and after an hour of polite and stilted conversation about Westlands and whether she had everything she needed—even though it was clear she had, and anyway, being David he'd also brought a boot full of food with him—she suggested the walk.

It was the right thing. He was relaxing with every step, and she was annoyed at herself for not thinking that being at the house might affect him, too. He'd been there that night. He had the slowly healing scars to prove it. And unlike her, he could remember the fire. She leans her head on his arm as they leave the path behind and trudge into the woods. It's been raining and the ground is muddy and covered in moss and leaves, but there's something earthy and wonderful about it.

"I'll take it back to uni and frame it," he says. "That was a good day."

"And we're going to have loads more," she says, grinning up at him. "A lifetime of them. Once we're married. Let's do it at Christmas. Once you break up for the holidays and I'm eighteen and no one can frown at us." She pauses. "Not that there's anyone left to frown at us."

He squeezes her arm. He always gets tongue-tied when it comes to talking about the deep things and she doesn't mind that.

"I was thinking maybe I should drop out of uni for a while," he says. "To look after you. You know, while you have to stay here."

She laughs, and she still finds it strange that she can laugh, and she has an ache of missing Rob. She loves David with all her heart but it's Rob who gave her laughter back. "That would somewhat negate the point of me spending time alone here, wouldn't it? And anyway, you can't do that. This is what you've always dreamed of. And I'm so proud of you. I'm going to be a doctor's wife."

"If I pass all the exams," he says.

"Oh, you will. Because you're brilliant." And he is. He has the most quietly brilliant mind of anyone she's ever met.

They stop and kiss for a while and his arms feel good around her and she feels safe and settled and thinks that maybe their hearts are building solid foundations for their future.

When they've walked a bit farther, she realizes that they've come as far as the old well. It's barely visible against the greens and browns of the wood, the brick covered in moss, a relic from a time long ago. A forgotten thing.

She leans on the side and looks down into the darkness, a dry and empty pit. "I imagined this well when I was at Westlands," she says. "I imagined crying all my sadness into it and then sealing it up." It's close to the truth. "Imagined" isn't the right word, but it's the best she can tell David.

He comes up behind her and wraps his arms around her waist. "I wish I could make it better."

"You make everything better." And it's true, he does. He may not have the wildness of Rob, who makes her feel young and free, but he is solid. And that's what she really needs. Even though she misses Rob, David's who she really wants. Her rock. His watch still hangs on her wrist, and she holds it up. "Can you wear your watch yet?"

"I could, but you keep it. You wearing it makes me feel like I'm with you."

"You're always with me, David Martin. Always. I love you." She's glad to keep the watch. She knows he'll visit at weekends when he can, but the watch is like him—reliable. Strong. There's a weight to it she can feel. She needs an anchor. Maybe one day she'll even tell him why. Explain about the night of the fire. Maybe. Maybe when they're old and gray and he sees more mystery in the world than he does now.

A chill has crept into the afternoon air and suddenly there's the quiet patter of rain on the leaves overhead. A gentle steady shower, rather than the force of a downpour, but they head back and make a picnic of all kinds of food and drink a bottle of wine that David has brought with him, before tumbling into bed in one of the spare rooms. She's not ready for her bedroom yet. It belongs in the past. So much belongs in the past.

"We should sell this place," she says when they've made love and are lying sleepily in the dark. Her fingers gently run along the new smoothness of scars up his arm. She wonders how much they still hurt. David would never say. "Once we're married."

"New beginnings," he says. He doesn't want to linger here any more than she does, and what do they need this enormous place for anyway? Her father only needed it for his ego.

"New beginnings," she answers, before they both drift into sleep. No swift summoning of a second door for her tonight. She's not ready for that. Just the first door for a change. She intends to dream of their future together. How perfect it will be.

40

LOUISE

"Since you've been ignoring my texts, I decided to pop in to your office to surprise you for lunch," Sophie says, breezing into the flat, little Ella trailing in her wake. "But I was the one who got the surprise when Sue said you'd quit. What the fuck is going on?"

I really don't need this now. I've barely slept after last night's adventure and my nerves are on edge. I texted Adele this morning to say I needed to see her, but she hasn't answered and I'm freaking out that maybe David's found the phone. Why else hasn't she got back to me if he's at work?

She takes off her jacket and flings it onto the sofa. "Tell me you haven't quit over *him*. Tell me you took my advice and dumped them both? Please tell me that."

"Auntie Sophie!" Adam tears in from his room and wraps himself around her legs. "Ella!" Ella is a quirky, ethereal child who never seems to repeat a single word of either of her parents' colorful language—unlike Adam, who I try not to swear around but who somehow manages to pick up on it anyway. If a six-year-old is capable of being hopelessly in love, then I'm sure that Adam is in love with Ella.

"I've been to France for a month! And I'm going to have a brother or sister! Lisa's making a baby!"

It's the first he's mentioned the pregnancy in front of me—I wasn't even sure he knew—but his *what-might-upset-Mummy* caution has gone in the rush of his excitement.

"Ian's having another baby? You didn't mention that," Sophie says. She sounds a bit stung. I shrug.

"You were too busy lecturing me." The mention of the impending baby is still a barb in my side, but I don't want her to see that. We usher the children off to Adam's room to play, clutching bags of sweets that Sophie's brought with her, and we go out to the balcony with wine.

She lights a cigarette and offers me one, but I wave my e-cig at her. "I sort of quit," I say.

"Wow, well done. I keep meaning to get me and Jay onto those. Maybe one day. So"—she looks at me, wine in one hand and cigarette in the other—"talk to me. What's happened? You've got thinner. Is that stress or intentional?"

"Both," I say. And then, despite myself, I tell her. I'm bursting with the anxiety of it all, and sharing it seems like such a relief. She lets me talk and talk, barely interjecting, but I know I've made a mistake when I see her face darken and the lines she tries hard to hide with her fringe furrow deep in her forehead. She's looking at me like she can't believe what she's hearing.

"Well, it's no wonder you lost your job," she says when I finally finish. "What did you expect him to do? You'd made friends with his wife and didn't tell him." She's frustrated with me. "Who does that? I told you on the phone you couldn't keep it up."

"I didn't mean to carry it all on," I say. "It just happened."

"What, like letting him in and fucking him repeatedly once you were friends with her *just happened*? Like this crazy breaking into his office *just happened*?"

"Of course that didn't just happen!" I snap. She's speaking to me as if I'm some kind of teenager. With her track record I expected more understanding.

"But anyway, all that isn't the point. I'm worried about her. What if he's trying to get rid of her? Their marriage is totally weird and this stuff with the pills and controlling the money—"

"You don't know what their marriage is like." She cuts me off. "You're not in it. And Jay looks after all our money and I'm pretty sure he has no dastardly motives."

"You're not worth a fortune," I mutter, biting back the urge to remind her that all their money *is* Jay's money because she doesn't exactly bring the big bucks in. "This is different."

She sucks hard on her cigarette, thoughtful. "You've been shagging this bloke, and you've not shagged anyone in ages, so you must really have liked him. How come you're on her side in all this? You sure you're not feeling guilty and somehow trying to redeem yourself?"

She does know me, I'll give her that. "Maybe it's partly that, but there's so much evidence, Sophie. And if you met her, you'd think the same. He's so moody. Properly dark moods. And she's so nervous of him. She's so sweet and fragile."

"Fragile?" She arches a perfectly shaped eyebrow. "Or crazy?"

"What do you mean?"

"Well, you're wanging on about these pills and everything and seeing it as something sinister that he's doing to her—but what if she *does* have a screw loose? Have you thought about that?"

"These are serious pills."

She shrugs. "It might be a seriously loose screw."

I shake my head, adamant. "If she was crazy I'd know. It would show. We've spent a lot of time together."

"Yeah, because crazy always shows. Tell that to the people who knew Ted Bundy or just about any other serial killer. All I'm saying is that maybe you're overthinking all this. Seeing something that isn't there."

"Maybe," I say. I don't believe that for a second, but there's no point in talking to her about it anymore. I know I can overthink things, but I'm not overthinking this. I wish she hadn't come over. Looking at her, I think maybe she's wishing the same. She's pitying me a little, I can see that, as if she's sad that I can't even get the fun of an affair right.

"Maybe this is about Ian really," she says cautiously. "You know, with the new baby coming. It can't be easy for you."

"You think I'm inventing problems in David and Adele's marriage because my ex has got his bimbo girlfriend knocked up?" I snap back at her. More of a growl really. *Fuck off,* I think with a surge of anger. *Fuck off back to your shallow affairs. I'm not giving up on Adele. I'm not.* "You think I made up that file I found? The pills?" We stare at each other for a long moment, neither speaking.

"No, of course not," she says eventually. "I'm worried about you, that's all. Anyway"—she makes some pretense of looking at her watch—"I've got to go. My mum's coming round this evening for my sins, and I've got to figure out what the fuck to cook." There's still half a bottle of wine sitting at our feet and I'm pretty sure she's lying. I don't know how that makes me feel. Lonely. Friendless. Empty. Angry at her.

"I love you, Lou," she says when Ella's gathered up and they're at the front door. "But stay out of their business. No good comes from getting in the middle of a marriage. You've totally crossed all the lines. You know that. Step away. Leave them to it. Move on."

"I'll think about it," I say. "I will. I promise."

"Good," she says, and gives me a half-smile. I can almost hear her telling Jay about this. *Oh my god, guess what Louise has done! It's crazy! Poor cow!*

I smile back as she and Ella leave, but my teeth are gritted.

I save the rest of the bottle of wine until Adam is in bed, even though I've been smarting all afternoon over Sophie's derision of my concerns about Adele and David. I should have kept my mouth shut. The story of my life, always blurting things out that I should keep to myself. She hasn't even texted since she left, not even to joke about it by way of apology, which would be her normal thing. Sophie hates confrontation and although we didn't technically argue, there was no denying the heavy cloud of disagreement and disapproval over our whole conversation. She'd made her mind up as soon as she knew I hadn't taken her advice and ended it with both of them. Everything after that was white noise in her head. So much for all her free-thinking, free-living stoner mentality.

When the doorbell goes at seven I've poured myself the last of the Sauvignon Blanc in a failed attempt to settle my mood, and I nearly drop the glass when I open the door. I don't know who I'm expecting. Laura, maybe. Sophie even, come to make peace.

But no. It's him. David.

The long summer evenings are fading and the sky has turned gray. It feels like a metaphor for everything that's happened between us. Blood rushes to my face and I know even my chest is blotching. I feel sick. I feel afraid. I feel a whole host of things I can't pin down. My ears buzz.

"I don't want to come in," he says. He looks like an untidy mess, his shirt not quite tucked in right. His shoulders are slumped. I feel like a vampire. As I've grown stronger from getting better sleep, they've both grown weaker.

"I wasn't going to invite you," I retort, pulling the door slightly closed behind me in case Adam gets up. Also, I feel safer outside.

"The office keys. I want them back."

"What?" I say, although I've heard him clearly and my mouth has instantly dried with guilt.

"I know it was you, Louise. I haven't told anyone what you did. I just want the keys back. I think that's fair, don't you?"

"I don't know what you're talking about." I stick to my guns as my stomach roils once more.

"You're a terrible liar." He stares at the ground as if he can't bear to look at me. "Give me the keys."

"I don't need them anyway." I keep my chin up, defiant, but my hands are trembling as I take them from my shell key ring. His fingers brush mine as he takes them and my body betrays me with an urgent *longing*. Does he feel it too? What a head fuck all this is. How can I still have these feelings even though he part terrifies me?

"Stay away, Louise. I told you before and I meant it."

"And I told you, I don't know what you're talking about. And I have stayed away. I've had enough of the pair of you." I deliver it fiercely, but it's all lies, lies, lies. He can see through me. I hate that.

He looks at me for a long moment, and I wish I could read him better. His blue eyes have dulled to match the dying sky and I can't see what's going on behind them. What he's thinking.

"Stay away from us. If you don't want to end up hurt."

"Is that a threat?" I want to cry and I don't even know why. What have I got myself into? And after everything, why do I find it so hard to hate him when he's right in front of me like this? *My* David.

He glares at me. That cold David is back. The stranger. "Yes, it's a threat. Believe me, it's a threat. You know what you forgot last night?"

I'm silent, just staring. What? What did I forget?

"There's a security camera outside the clinic."

Oh god, he's right. I can see where he's going with this before he says it. He knows, but he says it anyway.

"One word from me to get last night's recording looked at and at best all that will happen to you is that your chances of future employment are screwed. *At best.*"

He jabs a finger at me and I flinch. The pills. The file with all the notes on Adele. *Psychotic break. Sociopathic tendencies.* Maybe it's he who has them. Maybe he's not only a mercenary after his wife's money. Maybe he's the madman. But still, although he has me over a barrel, none of this would look good on him if I got to have my say. I'm a threat to him, too.

"Stay out of my marriage," he finishes. Each word is spat out as if he wishes he could spit right at me.

"Says the man who fucked me. Maybe you should worry about yourself rather than whatever I'm doing or not doing."

"Oh, I do, Louise," he says. "Trust me, I do." He turns to walk away and then pauses. "There's one thing I'd like to know. One thing I need to know."

"What?"

"How *exactly* did you meet my wife?"

"I told you. I bumped into her. I wasn't stalking her or you or anything." *Don't flatter yourself,* I want to add.

"I know that. I mean when and where."

I stare at him, hesitant. "Why does it matter?"

"Humor me, Louise. I want to know."

"It was a morning. I'd just dropped Adam off at school. She was on her way back from walking with you to the clinic and I bumped into her and knocked her down." It feels like yesterday and yet so far away. So much has happened since then. My head starts to throb. Ensnared as I am, as much as I'm determined to help Adele, right now I wish I'd never met either of them.

David shakes his head and half-smiles. "Of course," he says.

"What?"

He looks at me then, directly at me, but his face is in shadow, his eyes glints of glass in the gloom, his words disembodied. "My wife has never walked to work with me in the mornings."

"I don't believe you," I say. "I don't believe anything you say anymore."

He's still standing there, a darkening figure, when I close the door, shutting him out, reclaiming my small world, my private space. I press my ear against the door to see if I can hear his footsteps on the concrete outside but my head is filled with my heartbeat throbbing in my ears.

Oh god, oh god, oh god. What am I doing? Maybe Sophie is right. Maybe I should walk away. How much of my life do I want to fuck up for this? David could make me look like a crazy person to Dr. Sykes. To everyone. I could be screwed for work forever. I could probably go to prison. It's all my own fault. My curiosity's fault. If I hadn't been curious about Adele I would have made my excuses and not gone for coffee that morning. And what did he mean, "she never walks to work with me"? She must have done. What's he trying to make me think?

Don't trust him, I tell myself. *Don't listen to him. Go with what you know. You know about the pills. You know about the calls. You know about his drinking and the money and the file in the office. These things are solid things. And he just threatened you.*

Adele still hasn't texted me back, but even if I do decide to walk away from it all, she needs to know about what I found in the office.

She needs to make her own decisions based on that. I'll go and see her tomorrow and then I'll leave it all alone. I've said that before but this time I mean it. I have to mean it.

My head is pounding and I sit on the sofa and let my skull rest against the back cushions. I need to calm down. I inhale through my nose and breathe out through my mouth, letting the air get deeper and slower and forcing the tense muscles of my scalp, face, and neck to relax. I empty my thoughts, imagining them being blown away on a night breeze. I don't want to think about *them*. I don't want to think about my mess. I don't want to think about anything. I want to leave myself behind, just for a while.

It happens so suddenly. Almost between breaths.

The silvery edges of the second door appear in the darkness behind my eyes, shining so brightly that I almost flinch, and then, before I even see the shimmering watery surface, I'm through it and—

—I'm standing over myself. But I can't be, because I can see me sitting on the sofa, my head lolling back. My eyes are closed, my mouth half-open. The wineglass sits, empty, on the table beside me. I don't remember bringing it in. How am I seeing myself? What is happening? I panic and I feel a massive tug at the very core of me— *exactly like the tug in my dream of Adam's room*—and then my eyes open and I'm back on the sofa.

There's nothing calm about my breathing now, and I'm wide-awake and alert. What the fuck was that? I look to the side table and see the wineglass there where I must have absently put it down after David left. What the fuck just happened?

41

ADELE

Watching, waiting, learning, practicing. My days are fuller than they've been in as long as I can remember and it's wonderful. I've got heels on when David finally gets home, ones that match my outfit. It's nice to get dressed up and to be beautiful. The skin between my toes on my right foot is sore and scabby but the irritation with each step is worth it, just like the increasing *itching* is worth it. It's a reminder that I'm in control. It keeps me in control. Anyway, I've mastered that now. I'm ready for that part of my plan and I'm glad that I can now shake adoring Anthony off.

Things are starting to move apace. Louise is my little terrier and she's gripped the bone I've given her and I know she won't let go. I'm curious to see where she takes it, how she'll play out my game. I can't entirely control how everyone will behave in this set of circumstances, but that somehow only makes it all the more interesting. I'm playing the odds with their personalities, and thus far neither David nor Louise has let me down. David might be the head doctor, but I know how people tick. And I adapt.

The kitchen smells delicious as he comes and stands in the doorway. I've made a fresh pasta carbonara and a peppery rocket salad, which I fully intend to eat even if he doesn't. He stays on the other side of the threshold to me, leaning against the doorframe. He looks a mess. He won't keep his reputation at the clinic if this goes on much longer.

"Still playing Stepford Wife, I see." He smiles as he speaks, a twisted humor. He's laughing at me; at my clothes and my cooking and all my effort. I look hurt. I *am* hurt. He's not even pretending to love me anymore.

"You should eat something," I say. *Instead of drinking all your calories.*

"What is it you want, Adele? Really?" He looks at me with blurred contempt. "What is all this for? This prison we live in?" He's definitely drunk and for the first time in a long time I see true, naked aggression in him.

"I want to be with you." It's the truth. It's my eternal truth.

He stares at me for a long time, as if trying to figure out what's going on inside me, who I really am, and what new label he can apply to make sense of it—schizophrenic, sociopath, obsessive, plain batshit crazy—and then his shoulders slump with the effort and the lack of an answer.

"I want a divorce," he says. "I want this over. All of it."

There's no need to elaborate on the last point. We both know what he means. The past needs digging up and laying to rest properly. The past. The *body*. He's said this before, but this time I'm not so sure he'll change his mind when he sobers up, regardless of what I might do. Regardless of how I could ruin him if I tell.

"Dinner will be ready in ten minutes if you want to freshen up," is all I say. My normality unsettles him more than any verbal threat.

"You knew who she was, didn't you?" He loathes me. It drips from him even more heavily than his self-pity. "Louise. You knew when you met her?"

I frown, puzzled. "Where's this coming from, David? How could I possibly have known she was your patient?" His lie used against him again.

"You always know things. How is that?" He's bitter but he still sounds weak. Pathetic. Not my David at all.

"You're not making any sense." I frame my face into a picture

BEHIND HER EYES   217

of worried concern. "Have you been drinking? You're supposed to be cutting down. You said you would."

"Play your games, Adele. Play your games. I'm done. I don't care anymore. And I don't want any fucking dinner."

He calls out the last line as he disappears upstairs and I wonder what's happened to the person I fell in love with. How far hidden is he inside that shambling embarrassment of a man? I know he's been to see her. To warn her. He really does love her, which of course pleases me in one way, but in another I want to take one of our Sabatier knives and go upstairs and cut out his ungrateful fucking heart. I squash that urge. I could never hurt David and I know it. That's the cross I have to bear.

And anyway, Louise heard his warning as a threat, because she belongs to me. She sees *my* truths. For now, at any rate. I haven't answered her text yet and I won't. I need her to come here tomorrow. I need her to find me. Another thing she has to *understand* before she can put all the pieces of our tale of woe together. Show, don't tell; that's what they say, isn't it? And that's what I'm doing. Tomorrow will be another breadcrumb in the trail I'm leaving for her. She's my little wind-up doll, walking in whatever direction I point her.

God, I love Louise. I love her almost as much as I love David. And after I've shared my story with her, she's going to hate him. I can't help but think he deserves that.

42

LOUISE

It's pouring with rain, proper sheets of it falling from the sky, and the gray is thick overhead as I drop Adam off at Day Play. The dry spell is over, and although it's not cold and there's no autumn wind to drive the rain into me, it feels like the death knell of summer. Nearly September already. He kisses me good-bye and runs inside, my confident friendly boy, used to this routine. I haven't told him I'm not going to work. Instead, I told him I'd taken a couple of days off to spend with him and now we're back to normal. It doesn't really register with him. He's six, the days are all a blur, but he'll be seeing his dad soon and I'm not ready for the "Oh, Mummy hasn't been to work" fallout.

I stop at Costa Coffee and stand at the window bench, staring out through the steamy glass at people hurrying along the Broadway in the downpour, heads down, umbrellas clashing like antelope horns. My mouth burns with the hot drink and I impatiently clock watch until I think it's probably safe to go. I have no idea if David is in work at his usual time. I tried to check his diary, but my log-in no longer works. The bastard must have canceled it. I'm going to the house anyway. I need to see Adele and she still hasn't answered my text and I'm worried about her. Screw him, if he's at home.

Maybe I'll tell her what we did. Maybe that will prompt her to do what she needs to do. I'll lose her, too, but at least she'll be free.

At ten, I gird my loins and head over. Her car's there, so she's not left for the gym yet, if she's even still going, and with my heart in my mouth, I press on the doorbell. I hear it ring out on the other side, heavy and dependable. I stand and wait, peering through the glass for any shadow of movement, but the house is still. I press it again, for longer this time. Still nothing. Where is she? She can't be in the garden in this weather and I know she can hear the bell from there anyway. I give it a third go, holding the button down for nearly ten seconds. At least I know David's not home. He'd have been shouting at me on the doorstep by now if he were.

The door stays firmly shut in front of me. Maybe she's popped down to the shops. But in this rain? She'd take the car and go to the big Sainsbury's if she needed anything, surely? I leave my umbrella at the door and come down the few steps to cross to the big bay window; I frame my eyes with my hands and peer in. It's David's study, so I'm not expecting to see anything, but Adele is sitting in a wingback chair in the corner by the bookshelves. One arm is hanging down and she's slid sideways, only the jutting edges of the old-fashioned leather chair holding her in. I bang on the glass. "Adele! It's me! Wake up!"

She doesn't move. Not even a twitch. How can she not hear me? I bang harder and repeat her name, one eye out for nosy neighbors who might mention seeing me to *that lovely doctor next door*. Still nothing. He must have made her take those pills before he went to work, it's all I can think. Maybe she's taken too many. Maybe she's had an adverse reaction. *Shit, shit, shit.*

I look back at the front door, my hair now slick against my face, and drips of water running cold under the collar of my jacket making me flinch and shiver. I see the big planters. *The keys.* I rummage in the damp dirt until I find them, inches down, flashes of silver. The bottom lock is off, so at least David hasn't locked her in, which was my first thought, and I slide the Yale key in and twist. I'm in.

My shoes leave wet footprints on their perfect floorboards as

I rush through to the study, but I don't care. I don't care if David figures out that I've been here. I'm done with him.

"Adele," I say, shaking her shoulder gently. "Adele, wake up. It's me." Her head lolls forward and for an awful gut-wrenching moment I think she's dead, and then I see the very gentle rise of breath in her chest. I grab her hand—her fingers are cold. How long has she been sitting here?

"Adele!" I bark her name out. "Wake up!" Still nothing. I'm rubbing warmth into her hand and I think I might have to slap her round the face or something drastic. Should I call an ambulance? Try and get her to throw up? I shake her again, much harder this time, and for a moment I think it's not going to work, and then she sits up ramrod straight in the chair, her hands gripping the arms. She gasps loudly, as if she's been drowning, and her eyes fly open.

It's so dramatic that I stumble backward. "Shit, Adele."

She stares at me as if I'm a stranger, and then she blinks. The tension goes out of her spine and she looks around as she pants, her breath still ragged. "What are you doing here, Louise?"

"I let myself in. You weren't answering the doorbell and I could see you through the window. Are you okay?"

"You're soaked," she says, still disoriented. "You need a towel."

"I'm fine. It's you I'm worried about. How many pills did you take this morning?"

"Just one. I was . . ." She frowns, collecting her thoughts. "I thought I'd look in here again, for, I don't know, something. Anything. Then I felt really tired so I sat down."

"I thought you were flipping dead," I say, and then laugh, my nerves needing a release. "Anyway, his file on you isn't in here." She focuses then.

"What?"

"It's in his office. I went and looked. But first"—I take her arm and help her out of the chair—"you need coffee."

We stay in the kitchen, clutching mugs of coffee, the continuing downpour outside pattering against the windows as I tell her what I found, talking quietly and slowly so she can take it all in.

"The thing is," I say, in a long pause after I've finished, "these notes he's been keeping go back pretty much ten years. I thought maybe he was trying to get you sectioned to keep your money, but that would be a more recent thing, surely? He couldn't have been planning that all this time. I mean, could he? It doesn't make any sense."

Adele stares straight ahead, her face filled with sadness. "It makes sense to me," she says eventually. "It's an insurance policy."

"What do you mean?"

"I did have some problems when I was younger, after my parents, after Westlands, but that's not it. That's not why he's got this file. It's about Rob."

I frown, confused. "What about Rob?"

"It's insurance in case I decide to voice my suspicions about what happened to him. Who would anyone believe? The respectable doctor or his crazy-lady wife?"

"I don't get it." This is a new twist in their crazy marriage. "What happened to Rob?"

"Rob's our unspoken secret," she says, and then lets out a long sigh. She looks small in the chair, narrower with her shoulders hunched, as if she's trying to fold in on herself and disappear. She's thinner, too. Vanishing.

"I want to show you something," she says. She gets up and I follow her as she leads me up the stairs.

My heart is racing. Am I finally going to learn what's at the core of this marriage that I'm so entangled in? I follow her into the large master bedroom, high-ceilinged and airy, with an en-suite in the corner. Everything in it is elegant, from the metal-framed bed, sturdy and wide and clearly from somewhere like Liberty's rather than some lightweight chain-brand copy, to the Egyptian cotton duvet set, a deep brown offsetting the olive green of the walls and the rich worn wood of the floor. On a feature wall behind the chest of drawers, three thick stripes of varied greens run from floor to ceiling. I could never be this stylish.

"It was all magnolia when we moved in," she says. "Some off-white shade anyway." She's looking at the walls, thoughtful and reflective. "I chose these colors to test him. They're the colors of the woods on my parents' estate. We never go back there. Not since I was there after Westlands. Not since Rob came to visit." She brushes her fingers across the walls as if feeling the bark of a tree rather than cool plaster.

"He refuses to sell it even though it's just sitting there, empty and forgotten." She's talking softly, as much to herself as to me. "I think that's part of the reason he'd be reluctant to give control of my money back. He knows I'll get rid of it. And that's too much of a risk."

"What happened to Rob?" I ask as my heart races. She turns to me then, wide-eyed and beautiful, and spills out her answer as if it were the most ordinary thing in the world to say.

"I think David killed him."

Hearing it out loud, rather than some almost-suspicion in my own head, makes me reel. David. A killer? Is that even possible? I step backward and find the bed, sitting down heavily.

I think David killed him. I feel like I did when Ian told me Lisa was pregnant, but everything is amplified.

"Rob came to stay," Adele continues. "He was so unhappy with his awful sister and he texted me, and I insisted he come to Perth. He'd been so good to me. He'd brought me back to life. I wanted to help him in return. Maybe give him some money to set himself up somewhere away from that awful place he lived. I was happy to have him around. He did that for you, Rob. He made you happy. He made you feel special. I suggested to David that he could live with us for a bit when we were married. Just until he got himself sorted. David didn't like the idea. He was jealous of Rob. David had always looked after me, but at Westlands Rob had taken on his role. He was suspicious that there was more than friendship going on even though I kept telling him it wasn't like that. I loved Rob, but not in that way. I don't think he loved me in that way either. We were like brother and sister."

I'm hanging on her every word with both anticipation and dread. "What happened?" My mouth is tinder dry and I can barely get the words out.

"David came for a weekend while Rob was staying. I thought

that once they got to know each other they'd be fine. I thought that because I loved them both it would be enough for them to love each other even though they were very different. Looking back, I was so naïve. Rob was determined to make an effort—on his best behavior for such a wild thing—but David was off with him. On the Saturday David seemed to thaw a bit, so Rob told me to go to bed and leave them to it. He thought they could use some man-to-man time." She looks back at the walls, the forest colors, her eyes drifting over them as if the past were written there.

"When I woke up, Rob was gone," she continues. "David said he'd decided to leave, and at first I thought maybe David had paid him off. But that didn't make sense. I'd already offered Rob money, and he wouldn't have taken a bribe not to be my friend. He wasn't like that. He'd have laughed at that. Sometimes, when I play it over in my mind, I wonder if he decided to have it out with David about my money. Maybe he told him he had to give it back. He said he wouldn't mention it, but who knows? Perhaps he did. Maybe that sent David over the edge into one of his terrible moods. Maybe they fought and it got out of hand. The one thing I do know is that Rob would never have left without saying good-bye."

"Are you sure?" I ask, trying to find something rational here that doesn't involve my married ex-lover having killed a rival. "I mean, maybe they had an argument or a fight, and Rob thought it was best to leave. That's possible, isn't it?"

She shakes her head. "Rob had hidden his stash of drugs and the notebook in the barn. I didn't find them until after David and I were married, but Rob wouldn't have left the drugs behind. Not if he was angry. He'd have wanted to get high."

"Did you ever confront David about it? Ask him?"

"No. We got married very quickly, maybe a month or so after I last saw Rob, and David had changed by then. He was more reserved. Cooler with me. Then I found out I was pregnant." Her eyes fill with tears that don't quite spill as I sink into the awfulness of it all with her.

"I was so happy. *So* happy. But David made me have an abortion. He said he couldn't be sure it was his. After that I had a little breakdown—I think I couldn't face my fears about Rob, and I was still recovering from my parents' deaths, and then the abortion on top of it all was too much. We moved down to England, and that was that. David softened and looked after me, but he refused to sell the estate."

"You think Rob's still there, don't you?" I say, lost in their past and terrified by our present. "Somewhere in the grounds?"

She stays very still for a long moment and then nods. "Rob would never have up and vanished on me like that. Never. I was all he had. He'd have got in touch." She sits on the bed beside me. "If he was still alive."

Neither of us says anything for a long time after that.

43

ADELE

She insists on staying for a while and talking about it more, obviously. She's shaken, I can see that, but her mind is whirring. That curious, busy head of hers. Tick tick tick. Always ticking over. When she asks why I never looked for Rob, I give my pathetic shrug and say I didn't want to know. I loved David and I'd married him. I was young. He was my safe place. I'm impressed she doesn't slap me hard round the face and tell me to pull myself together and face the music. I'd want to do it if I were her, listening to my spineless drivel. I tell her I'm tired and don't want to talk about it and I see her pity then. She quiets.

It doesn't take much to get her to leave. I mention that David will call and then I'm going to lie down for a while, and she nods and hugs me, squeezing me so tightly in those slimmer, firmer arms, but I can see she's already thinking about what to do next. How she can help me, or help herself, or whichever. As long as the outcome is the same, who cares?

David doesn't call at our agreed time; another clue that he meant what he said last night. He's washing his hands of me. Maybe even challenging me to make good on my threat. Poor thing. He's at his wits' end.

I make a peppermint tea and go upstairs and lie on the cool duvet cover and stare at the ceiling. I'm remarkably calm, given the situation. There are still some wild cards out there and I'm entirely reliant on Louise to find and put together the pieces of the puzzle I'm laying out in front of her. At the right moment she needs to grasp the significance of this morning. If she doesn't I'll need to find another way to show her. Still, life is better when it's interesting. I feel quite content.

Being *told* a thing is never enough. I've *told* Louise what I think David did all those years ago, but words really don't carry any weight. Momentary sounds on air have no solidity. Written words, slightly more perhaps, but even then, people don't ever really trust each other enough to not have doubts. No one ever truly thinks the best of anyone else.

To trust the truth of a thing, you have to suffer the thing. You have to get mud on your hands and dirt under your fingernails. You have to dig for it. A truth like David's and mine anyway. That can't be understood by telling. I need to take Louise into the fire before she can come out the other side pure and clean and trusting. If David is to finally be free and unburdened, she needs to carry the burden first. The truth has to be *hers*. She needs to take the truth to him.

And then let it unravel them.

44

LOUISE

. . . I'll wait till Ailsa's asleep or passed out drunk with gimpy Gary and then I'll go. Fuck them and their shitty little flat and their shitty little lives on this shitty little estate. Pissy Pilton. Like it's the whole fucking world. Maybe it is for them. It's not going to be like that for me. No wonder I wanted to get off my face as soon as I was back here. What did they think, that after rehab and everything, wanky Westlands would miraculously work? They're idiots. They're scum. They're all scum and I can feel their dirt trying to stick to me. They won't even care when I'm gone. They'll be relieved. And they'll be relieved of whatever cash is in the flat too, ha ha! I need something to take to Adele's with me and it was benefits day today. Their loss, my benefit.

I can't believe I'm going to see her so soon. It's like there's color in the gray world again. I almost didn't text her. I didn't want to risk her saying no. How that would feel. I'm not used to caring about someone like this and wanting them to like me. I'm not used to caring about anyone. If I hadn't had the dream door and been able to see a made-up her that way I think I'd have gone mental by now. I laughed and joked when we said good-bye but she could see it was hurting me. It was hurting her, too, but even though she tried to hide it from me she was excited to be getting out. She's got *a life, she's got money, she's got David. I've got my bitchy sister's box room that needs repainting in a shite Edinburgh schemey flat.*

But now I'm free! I'll hitch or jump the train to Perth and then she said to get a taxi and she'll pay. She's missed me, I can tell. That's what makes me the happiest. I make her laugh. She's different with me. She says I'll get to meet David because he visits some weekends from university. She reckons we're going to get on, but I think the one thing that me and dull David have in common is that neither of us is convinced about that. He's not going to want me around. I wouldn't want me around. I'll try for her sake, though. It's not like he's going to be there all the time anyway. I can pretend to like him for a couple of days at a time if it keeps Adele happy. I may even try not getting stoned when he's there. I'm not going to let the thought of David bring me down. Tomorrow I'll be back with Adele! Fuck off, old life; hello, new! Adele, Adele, Adele! The gateway to my happy future.

There's no more in the notebook; whatever else Rob wrote has been torn out. Did David do that? Did those pages say things that could incriminate him? My mind is on fire, working so hard my scalp is almost burning. Could David really have killed Rob? Maybe it was an accident. Maybe they fought and things got out of hand and he hit his head falling down or something?

Or maybe Rob isn't dead at all. Maybe Adele is worrying over nothing and he *did* just leave. She says he wouldn't have been bought off, but he stole his sister's dole money, so who knows? It's clear from the notebook that he loved her but he was from a poor home and maybe the promise of several thousand pounds in hand was too much to say no to? But why won't David sell the estate if there's nothing to hide there?

Questions, questions, questions. It seems that ever since David and Adele came into my life I've been filled with questions. They're like weeds in water. Every time I think I can swim away another one tangles around my legs to drag me back down.

I need to know what happened to Rob. I need to find him. It's not about Adele and David anymore, I need to know for *me*. I can't have this *not knowing* in my head forever. I don't have to pick Adam up until five fifteen so I make a strong coffee—even though my nerves are jittery enough—and open my laptop. Everyone's findable these days. If Rob was only a few months older than Adele then he's still under thirty. Surely, even if he's a junkie somewhere, there'll be some trace of him? I flick back to the first page of the notebook to where his whole name is printed so neatly, and type it into Google: *Robert Dominic Hoyle.*

A list of results comes up; various LinkedIn accounts, a few Facebook ones, and some news reports. With my heart racing, I work my way through them, but none match. They're too old, American, too young, and the only one whose Facebook profile picture looks about the right age says that he's from Bradford and there's a list of schools he's attended, none of which are in Scotland. I try searching the name with "missing or dead" added, but I get the same set of results. I try "Robert Dominic Hoyle Edinburgh" and still nothing.

My coffee sits untouched and cold beside me, and I'm not even puffing on my e-cig. Why are there no results at all for him? If David *had* bought him off, then for a little while at least he would have been on his feet. Surely he'd have got a laptop and the internet? I thought everyone had Facebook? But then, it didn't sound in the notebook like he had a lot of friends or any real desire for them. Only Adele and probably some junkies. Facebook might not be his thing.

Maybe he's living in some squat somewhere and all his money is going on drugs? That doesn't feel right. Junkies are devious—all addicts are, the condition makes them that way. If Rob needed money, he'd have found his way back into Adele's life and got some— either from her or David. Maybe he has. Maybe David's still paying him off occasionally and not telling Adele. But why would he bother? And that still leaves the big question—why hasn't he sold the estate? Or rented it out? Why is it still sitting there empty when it could be earning money?

I stare at the screen, willing an answer to appear there, and then decide to try another tack. Rob's sister, Ailsa. I type her name in and start to sort the wheat from the chaff. As with Rob, there are several people with her name across the country and globe and then an electoral register site gives me a list of seven Ailsas, only one of whom lives in Edinburgh.

Bingo.

I can't get a further address on that site without paying, which I'm prepared to do if it comes to it, unemployment be damned, but on the next search page I find a small news article about a Lothian Arts Festival. It mentions some local shops that were set up by grant initiatives and that have stalls there. One is called Candlewick, and the owner is mentioned—Ailsa Hoyle. Candlewick has a website and a Facebook page. I've found her. At least I hope it's her. I stare at the phone number, which almost throbs its presence through the screen. I have to call it. But what will I say? How do I even go about starting this conversation without looking like a crazy person? I need to lie, I know that, but what lie to tell?

I look at the old notebook and it comes to me. Westlands. That's how I'll ask her. I use the landline to block the caller ID but still I pace the room for a few minutes, sucking on my e-cig, before I brave pressing the dial button. *Okay,* I think eventually, my whole body tingling hot. *Just do it. Call. She's probably not even there.*

She is there. My heart leaps to my mouth as the shop assistant calls her to the phone.

"This is Ailsa, how can I help?" Her accent is strong. I can imagine that voice, unleashed from the telephone middle-class politeness, screaming at Rob.

"Hello," I say, deepening my own voice and smoothing it, just as I'd do when taking calls at the clinic. "I'm sorry to bother you at work, but I wondered if I could have a few moments of your time. I'm writing a paper on the effectiveness of the Westlands Clinic"—I suddenly realize I have no idea where the clinic was or any of the doctors' names and that I'm woefully underprepared to carry this deception through if she starts to question me—"and I believe your brother was there for a time. Robert Dominic Hoyle? I've been trying to locate him, but he's not appearing on any records anywhere. I wondered if perhaps you had a contact number for him, or could pass mine on."

"Westlands?" She barks out a laugh. "Aye, I remember it. Complete waste of time. Robbie was back on the gear within days of getting out of there. Then he stole money from my purse and fucked off in the night. Sorry about the language." She pauses, perhaps lost in angry memories of her own. "But I cannae help you, I'm afraid. I never heard from him again. He's probably dead or close to it in an alleyway somewhere."

"I'm sorry to hear that." My heart is in my mouth.

"Don't be," she says. "It was a long time ago. And he was a wee shite, he really was. You can't cure them all."

I apologize for disturbing her day and mutter a polite good-bye, but she's already hung up. I throw away my cold coffee and make a new one, just for the sake of doing something as it all sinks in. It's actually possible. What Adele suspects could well be true. I'm only just beginning to see that. For all my questions I was pretty certain, deep down, that Rob must be still alive. These things don't happen in real life. Murder. Hidden bodies. Only on the news and in films and books. Not in my mundane, dull existence. I ignore the coffee and find a forgotten bottle of gin left over from Christmas at the back of the cupboard. I've got no tonic but I add Diet Coke to a generous measure and take a long swallow to calm down before grabbing some of Adam's drawing paper and getting a pen. I need to think this through. I start with a list.

David—Wants the money or protecting himself against Adele? Both?

Rob—Vanished. Still on the estate somewhere? What happened in the torn-out pages? Evidence of a fight? Offer of money?

The notebook makes me remember one of Rob's suspicions and I add that.

Adele's parents. Was it really an accident? Who benefited most— DAVID.

Adele's parents. Of course—why haven't I thought of that before? There must be stuff about that on the internet. The fire would have been big news. I look at the clock—quarter to five. I have to go and pick Adam up, and that almost makes me scream with frustration and then I hate myself. All the times I wanted him back from his holiday and now I'm ditching him at daycare when I don't have to and resenting him getting in the way of my . . . of my what? *Murder* investigation? I nearly laugh out loud at the awful absurdity of admitting it to myself. Because that's what I'm doing. I'm trying to piece a murder together.

I'm going to need to buy a bottle of wine.

"But I don't want to go to bed yet."

I love my boy but I hate it when he whines and he's definitely been more whiny since France.

"I'm not tired."

"It's bedtime and that's that. Now get your pajamas on."

"One more game."

"I said now, Adam!" He storms off to his bedroom, huffing and puffing and whinging all the way, but one look at my face tells him this isn't open for discussion. I've done his Day Play coloring home-work with him, he's had his tea and played some games, and now I'm desperate to get him to sleep so I can get back to mining the internet for treasure. I can't do it while he's up—he'd be looking over my shoulder the whole time and asking questions. "And brush your teeth!" I shout after him. A second later, the bathroom door slams. This is what the teenage years are going to be like, I realize. Sulky, rebellious moods, interspersed with tiny nuggets that make it all worthwhile.

That thought saddens me and I get up to go and read with him and cajole him back into being my happy boy. The internet can wait ten minutes longer.

By seven thirty he's asleep, and I'm back at my laptop, a large glass of white beside me.

This search is easy. I have Adele's maiden name from Rob's notebook and "Rutherford-Campbell fire" brings up streams of information, mainly newspaper articles from the aftermath, both national and local. There's pages of it here. Faced with so much information, I can't believe I haven't looked all this up before, when she first told me. When she gave me the notebook.

At first, I'm entirely distracted by the photographs. It's hard not to be as I open link after link, leaving about fifteen tabs on my browser. There are aerial before and after shots of the estate, and Adele hadn't been joking when she said it was a big place. In the second picture I can see where one part of the building is blackened and charred, but what's left is still the size of maybe three or four normal houses. It's built from thick pale stone and looks like it's been there for a couple of hundred years or more. Built in a time of landed gentry. There are woods and fields surrounding it, creating a sanctuary for the building away from prying eyes. I try and imagine it now. Does someone keep up the grounds? Or is it now overgrown and forgotten?

There's a photo of Adele's parents, and seeing her mother is like looking at a reflection of her face on unsettled water. Almost the same but slightly different. Adele is more beautiful, her features more aligned, but her mother had the same dark hair and olive skin. Her father, originally an investment banker, and with a personal fortune of several million as well as a portfolio of high-profile investments according to these articles—looks gray and serious in one picture—obviously from his time in The City—but there is another of him in a Barbour and wellies smiling straight at the camera. His skin has reddened from time in the fresh air or maybe from too much good wine and good food, and he looks happy.

There are pictures of Adele, too—the tragic beautiful daughter left behind. A face slightly plumper with the glow of youth, but still the Adele I know. The *heiress,* one paper calls her. How much money is she actually worth? A fortune, it would appear. Her eyes sparkle with carefree laughter in a photo of the three of them one Christmas.

In another, blurry and taken from a distance in that way that tabloid journalists do, her head is down, one hand covering her face, and she's thinner, her jeans hanging loosely on her hips as she walks through the grounds of the damaged house. Grieving. There's a man beside her, one hand on the small of her back, his face turned almost directly to the long-lens camera as if he can somehow sense it's there. His other arm is bandaged and in a sling. David. His face is blurry but it's him. He looks wary and protective and tired. They both look so *young.* Them but not them. I stare at the picture for a long time and then lose myself in the myriad news articles, piecing the story together from all the different angles.

There's talk of Adele's parents' partying, of their wealth and their move from London after their daughter was born. All the usual gossip from neighbors feigning shocked grief but actually giving snippets of judgment. Adele was a lonely child, apparently. Her parents didn't have much time for her. A lot of space is given to the romance of the poor farm boy and the beautiful daughter, and how he saved her from the blaze. There's mention that some sources say Adele had been in therapy as a child.

Then I find something that stops my heart aching at their story that I'm not a part of, at David's obvious love for her in that moment, of how intertwined they are in ways that make my entanglement with them seem like gossamer threads, not weeds at all. Three words that stamp themselves into my head. Heavy boots on my sentimentality. A reminder of why I'm doing this before I get sucked down the rabbit hole of digging into their relationship.

Suspicion of arson.

There, in the later reports, once the emotional tabloid feast is done, the words slip in, insidiously. A policeman, Angus Wignall, is pictured studying the fire damage. A thickset man in his thirties maybe. A comment on the speed at which the fire spread. The mention of petrol kept in canisters in the barn for the quad bikes. Arson can't be ruled out.

> *Detective Inspector Angus Wignall was seen leaving the Perth Royal Infirmary, where David Martin is being treated for third-degree burns to his arms. Sources say that the inspector, accompanied by a sergeant, spent two hours talking to the student, who has been hailed as a hero after rescuing his girlfriend, Adele Rutherford-Campbell, 17, from the blaze in which both her parents died. Inspector Wignall has refused to comment on the nature of his visit other than to say it was part of an ongoing investigation . . .*

I scan the reports, my eyes darting to and fro across the lines to find out more. There's talk of a disgruntled estate manager, and also a later mention of David's father's financial troubles. Talk of how Adele's parents disapproved of their relationship. It all stays the right side of outright accusation, but there is a definite shift in mentions of David from hero to something *other*.

Then on the third page of search results, where the internet starts drifting into other vaguer territories, I see a report on their wedding. A quiet ceremony in the village of Aberfeld. There are no pictures in this one, and I think of Adele's suspicions and the fact that maybe between those earlier reports and this one a terrible crime has been committed and a boy has lost his life. The thought strikes me that maybe that wasn't in fact the *first* terrible crime. How much did David want to change his life from poor farmer's boy to wealthy doctor? Enough to set a house on fire in the middle of the night?

I drink my wine and stare into space for a while, letting it all soak in. I can't just go to the police with my suspicions about Rob— I'd look like a crazy jilted lover if I tried to explain it. But if there was someone who already had suspicions about David—this Angus Wignall, for example—then maybe they'd pay attention to an anonymous letter and at least search the estate?

I Google him and find that he's still in Perthshire and is now a detective chief inspector based at Perth Police Station. I scribble down the address. Would he take an anonymous letter seriously? Or would it go in the crackpot file? I guess it depends on how suspicious he was of David all those years ago. If he really thought David had something to do with the fire but couldn't prove it, then this might pique his interest. It's better than doing nothing. It's better than letting all these questions fester inside me forever.

Maybe there'll be no body. Maybe Ailsa's right and Rob's just a junkie somewhere living off the grid. Maybe David is innocent— of this, at any rate—but at least it will bring it all out into the open and free Adele of her doubts. Should I tell Adele what I'm thinking of doing? I decide against it. She'd try and talk me out of it, I'm sure. For all her fears and worries, she'd be afraid of rocking the boat. She's too subservient to David and has been for far too long. She wouldn't like me letting all her suspicions out into the world.

And anyway, this isn't about them anymore. It's not about them or me or any combination of the three of us. This is about Rob. This is about justice for him. Although I feel slightly queasy at the thought of it, I'm going to write the letter now and send it before I can change my mind. Enough's enough. Then I'm done.

45
THEN

It's a warmth, that's the best way she can describe it. Rob is here and she feels warm inside. Glowing. He's her friend and he's back. As much as the time alone has been good for her—surprisingly good for her—there is a joy in Rob being here. The house feels alive again. Rob has no memories of this place like she and David do. There's nothing to weigh him down and that frees her. She doesn't have to be *sad* with Rob here.

He laughs over and over as she shows him the house. She'd already told him it was about the size of Westlands if not bigger, but it's clear he hadn't believed her, and by the end of the tour, even she's smiling at the ridiculousness of one family owning so much. The only pause for quiet was when she showed him the charred rooms where her parents died. His eyes were wide then, and they stood in hushed silence for a moment until he said, "Let's get the fuck out of here. It stinks." She loved him for that. The lack of need to explore her feelings or make sure she was okay. Rob makes her feel strong because he thinks she is strong.

He hasn't brought much with him, some clothes, his notebook, some beers, and a bag of drugs. They take some of the weed out and then Adele makes him hide the rest in one of the barns.

"People do come to the house," she tells him. "A woman comes and cleans a couple of times a week and brings food. My solicitor sometimes pops in. He worries about me being here on my own. Says he thinks this is inappropriate therapy. He says I'm too young." She rolls her eyes. Her life has been so pampered compared to Rob's.

"Yeah right," he says. "Like you're going to set the place on fire or something."

Her eyes widen with shock at what he's said, and then she bursts into laughter.

"God, you're a dick." She links her arm in his.

"Yeah, but I make you laugh." There's a pause. "So be honest, is it really those people you're worried about finding my stash, or your precious David?"

She says nothing for a moment and then sighs. "Yes, maybe David most. He's not anti-drugs as such—" She sees the cynical disbelief in Rob's face. "He's really not, but I doubt he'd think getting high would be good for me right now. He'd think I was using it as a crutch."

"It must be so hard to breathe with all these people worrying about you all the time," Rob says. "If only they could see you how I do."

"And how is that?" she asks.

"A phoenix rising from the ashes, of course."

She likes that. She likes it a lot. It reminds her that the world is her oyster now. They stay arm in arm as they walk through the grounds and out to the well, where they make silent wishes even though Adele isn't sure a dry well can work for wishes.

In the evening they cook frozen pizzas and drink cans of the cheap strong beer Rob's brought with him and then they get high in front of a fire in the drawing room. They sit on cushions on the floor and talk and laugh about everything and nothing. Adele sucks deep on the grass joint, loving the mellow, giggly buzz of it. She's missed it. Like she's missed Rob.

She's seen his stash bag and she knows he's got some heroin with him too, but he doesn't mention it and neither does she. That's his business. She doesn't want him to take it, but neither does she want to sound like one of the therapists at Westlands. She wants Rob to be happy and if that's what it takes to see him through for a while, then she's not going to fight him over it. He's clearly not a total addict. If he were he'd be wasted, not sharp as a tack, and anyway, she can't see any fresh track marks on his arms. Maybe he snorts it sometimes or however else people take that stuff. Maybe he's brought it just in case of a dark day. Hopefully, they've both already had their share of dark days.

There are two spare bedrooms neatly made up, but they end up in her bed, stripped to their T-shirts and underwear, lying side by side and staring up at the ceiling. She wonders if David would see this as a betrayal, having another man in her bed, but close as she and Rob are, there's nothing sexual happening. This is almost something purer.

"I'm so glad you came," she says. "I've missed you."

"I'm glad you let me." He pauses. "It's so quiet here. And so dark outside. It's like we're the last people on earth."

"Maybe we are. Maybe there's been an apocalypse."

"As long as it's not a fucking zombie one." Rob snorts. "People are dull enough when they're alive."

"Do you think it's wrong that I don't miss my parents ever so much?" she asks. It's a thought that she worries about. What it says about her. If there's something bad about her.

"Nope," Rob answers. "There's no right and wrong with feelings. There is only what there is."

She thinks about that for a while. There is only what there is. That makes her feel better.

"What do you want to do with your life?" she asks.

"You sound like a Westlands therapist."

"No, really." Rob is so good at answering questions with something funny but this time she wants to get past the deflections. "There must be something."

"Don't know." He stares up at the ceiling. "Never really thought about it. I don't really come from a *career* family. Sign on and chill out was more their style. What about you? Other than marry dull David and make baby Davids."

She slaps him and laughs, but inside she wonders if that's so bad. That *is* what she wants to do. It's what she's always wanted to do.

"You should stay with us for a while. As long as you like. While you figure out your future."

"It's a nice idea, but I don't think David's going to want me hanging around once you're married up."

"You shouldn't judge him before you've met him. He's training to be a doctor. Helping people is what he *does*."

"Hmmm."

Their voices are disembodied in the darkness, but she takes Rob's hand and squeezes it. "Anyway, I'm rich now and I'm going to help you."

"I hate to remind you, darling, but unless you've got it all signed back over, technically it's David who's rich."

"Oh, shut up." She needs to get that sorted, but she's not worried about it. David's not out buying fast cars or living the high life at uni. The thought alone makes her laugh, and if she's honest, he'll probably be better at managing her—*their*—money than she could be. He's had to watch his pennies all his life whereas she's never had to think about it.

She'll talk to him about it when he comes back in a couple of weeks. Tomorrow, she'll tell him about Rob being here. She's sure he won't mind that she's not following through the therapy plan like she's supposed to, and anyway, Rob's been the best therapy she's had.

"I love you, Rob," she whispers, when their chatter falls into sleepy silence. "You're my best friend."

"I love you too, Adele," he replies. "My tragic Sleeping Beauty turned phoenix. I really do."

46

ADELE

The days drag by, each one feeling like a week, even though it's only been forty-eight hours since my *grand revelation* to Louise. I ache from so much lying still, but watch and learn is all I can do. I hide in my room when David gets home, pleading headaches or tiredness, and he barely speaks, instead nodding with thinly veiled relief. I leave him food in the fridge that he sometimes nibbles on but doesn't eat, as if he thinks maybe it's poisoned or contaminated in some way. I should care more that he's not interested in spending time with me, but I'm so much in Louise's life that if he did it would be a hindrance.

I wish he'd work later, which is something I've never wanted before. But I'm waiting for one moment. *The* moment when I can turn everything on its head. I can't miss it.

What if David decides he wants my attention at the moment when I need to be *there*? What then? I want to know when all the pieces of the puzzle have been thrown up in the air.

I lock the bedroom door just in case, but he doesn't knock. He hasn't been back to her either, which is a relief. I've needed them apart and that has worked. I doubt that right now Louise would even open the door to him. Not now that she's sent that letter. And now, after our sneaky texts of late last night, she has filled me with joy even though she doesn't realize it. I know she's feeling guilty about the letter she doesn't know I know she's sent. Her accusations about David. When I texted her that he was being very attentive and maybe I was overthinking it all and we should forget it, she changed the subject. People always change the subject when they feel bad about something. But this time she changed the subject to mention her dreams. She told me about the *weird second door* and how she found herself floating above her body in the sitting room for a moment. How she hadn't been asleep, but trying to shift a headache with some deep breathing and it just happened.

Although that left me bursting with excitement, I replied that it had never happened to me, but I've been taking sleeping pills so I'm not even going through the first door at the moment. I tell her I'm enjoying the oblivion. The feeling of nothingness. Of nonexistence. I text her that sometimes I think I'd like to be nothing. I wonder how she felt reading those words. A hint of what's possibly to come. Words to haunt her later.

She ended our text chat after that when I mentioned David again. She feels like she's betrayed me twice now, I imagine. She knows poor, fragile Adele wouldn't want her secrets aired to the world. Not when dangerous David is in the house. But still, she thinks she's strong enough for both of us. She thinks she knows best. I wonder whether the police will come before or after her doubts set in, or if they'll come at all. I half-expect the doorbell to go at any moment, even though I know it will take the police longer than the time passed to get their shit together if they decide to take her letter seriously. Perhaps they will just dismiss it. Perhaps I should send a letter of my own. It's a deliciously dark thought but I decide against it for now. I'll see how things play out.

Secrets, secrets, secrets. People are filled to the brim with them if you look closely. Louise is collecting several of her own, this letter being the most recent. I feel a slight betrayal that she hasn't told me about it. That she hasn't considered my feelings in her actions when she's supposed to be my best friend, but I keep my irritation in check. She's doing exactly what I want from her, after all.

My feelings don't really matter anymore, just like maintaining my figure and fitness don't matter anymore.

After all, what's the point? I'm going to be dead soon.

47

LOUISE

I don't know why I feel so nervy; it's not exactly like the police are going to turn up at my door waving the letter at me and asking me to explain myself. I even went to Crouch End to post it despite the fact they probably use the same sorting office as here. I wanted some distance between me and it. The envelope was damp from my clammy hands when I finally slipped it into the box.

Still, I constantly feel sick, and then David texted me last night. He said he wanted to meet up and talk. I stared at the words for an hour or so, my head pounding, but in the end I ignored it. What did he mean by talk? Threaten me some more? He was drunk anyway; even autocorrect had given up on some of his spelling. I don't want to talk to either of them, if I'm honest. Adele texted with some simpering stuff about David being different and maybe she was over-thinking. I bet she's regretting telling me everything about Rob. Sharing a secret always feels great in the moment, but then becomes a burden in itself. That gnawing in the pit of your stomach that something has been set free and you can't call it back and now some-one else has that power over your future. It's why I've always hated secrets. They're impossible to keep. I hate knowing Sophie's secrets, always worrying that one day I'll be wine-happy and something will slip out in front of Jay. Now, I'm in a mess of secrets and I've taken

Adele's into my own hands. She'd hate that I've sent that letter and I can't blame her for that. But what else could I do? In the end, I changed the subject of our texts to my dreams. I told her about the weirdness of feeling like I'd left my body by going through the second door. It seemed a safer subject than the weirdness of their marriage and the very real possibility that David is a murderer.

My head still aches, a constant throb I can't ignore, and even going out in the fresh air to collect Adam from a birthday party at the community center doesn't shake away the nausea. I haven't even really slept. I lie in bed exhausted, but as soon as the light goes off the lights in my brain come on. I think maybe I preferred the night terrors to the complete insomnia. Back when life was simple. Back before *the-man-in-the-bar*.

Adam is stuffed with sandwiches and sweets so we put his wrapped piece of birthday cake in the fridge for later, and he runs off to his room to examine the contents of his ridiculously expensive party bag. I don't even want to see what's in it—Adam's birthday is coming round fast and it'll be my turn to spend money I can't afford on expensive rubbish for children who don't need it. It's an unfair thought. Ian will help out. He's nothing if not generous where Adam is concerned, but I'm tired and stressed and need everything to slow down.

"I've got a headache," I say, popping my head round his bedroom door. "I'm going to lie down for a bit. Is that okay?" He nods and smiles, today my perfect boy, and I remember how lucky I am to have him.

"Wake me up if you need anything."

I don't think for a second that I'm going to sleep, I just want to close the curtains and lie in a darkened room and wish this headache away. I take a couple of pills and go to my room, relishing the cool pillow under my head, and let out a long sigh. A quiet half an hour is what I need. The headache is too invasive to even think much, and I focus on taking deep relaxing breaths. My heartbeat and the headache throb in unison like mad lovers. I try to let the tension out of my shoulders, hands, and feet like they make you do in those endlessly dull yoga videos. I empty my body of breath and empty my mind of more clutter with each exhale. The pain lessens a fraction as I relax and my arms feel heavy by my sides as if they're sinking into the bed beneath me. To escape for a while. That's what I need.

I barely see the door this time, it comes so quickly. A flash of silver. Streaks of light and then—

—I'm looking down at myself. My mouth is half-open. My eyes are closed. If I'm still taking deep breaths it doesn't show. I look dead. Empty.

I am empty. The thought is like cold water running through me, whatever *me* is, right now. *I'm up here. That's just . . . a body. A machine. My machine. But no one's at the controls. No one's home.*

I hover for a moment, resisting my panic of last time. I have no headache. I have no sense of any feeling; no arms, no legs, no tension, no breath. Maybe this is a dream. A different kind of dream. It's *something* anyway. I move back toward my body and feel the immediate tug from it and then I force myself to stop. I can go back if I want to—but do I want to?

I can see the line of dust on the top rim of the light shade, gray and thick. I pull back slightly, toward the door, even though I'm terrified of losing sight of my body, as if I will somehow lose my way back completely. In the mirror I can see my frighteningly still figure behind me on the bed, but *I* have no reflection. *Call me Count Dracula.* I should be petrified but it's all so surreal I'm strangely entertained.

Now that my fear is fading, I feel something else. Free. Released. I have no weight. I almost go to Adam's room, but worry that somehow he will *see* me. Where can I go? How far can I go?

Next door. Laura's flat. I somehow expect to be there in a flash, as if I'm some kind of fairy godmother waving a magic wand, but nothing happens. I focus harder. I *feel* for Laura's flat. The wholeness of it. The oversized TV that takes up most of one wall. Her awful pink faux-leather sofa that I should hate but makes me smile. Her cream carpet, the kind you can only have when you don't have small children. The sofa, the carpet, her marshmallow color scheme. I *will* myself into it. And then, as if propelled on a gust of wind, I'm there.

Laura's sitting on the sofa, in jeans and a baggy green fleece, watching TV. A rerun of *Friends* is on. Laura breaks off a chunk of Fruit & Nut chocolate and puts it in her mouth. She has a mug of

coffee beside her—a mug with little pretty flowers on it. I wait for
her to notice me, to look up in shock and ask me how the hell I got
into her sitting room, but she doesn't. I even stand—for want of a
better word—right in front of her, but nothing. I want to laugh.
This is crazy. Maybe I am crazy. Maybe David should be giving me
some of those pills he's trying to fill Adele up with.

David and Adele. Their kitchen. Could I go as far as that? I focus,
and for a moment, as I picture their granite surfaces and expensive tiles,
the unused calendar discreetly hung on the far side of the fridge so it
doesn't disturb the lines of the room, I feel something change, the
breath of wind rising to carry me there, but nothing happens.

At the core of this strange invisible me I feel as if I'm at the end
of a stretched elastic band. I try again, but I can go no farther, as if my
body is tugging me back like a toddler. I move more carefully this
time, out into Laura's kitchen, where I take note of the unwashed
dishes on the side, not too many but enough to prove she's having
a lazy day, and then I go through the door to the external walkway
between our flats. I feel no temperature change even though it
was chilly outside when I collected Adam from the party.

You can't feel it because you're not actually here, I tell myself. *You
just walked through a door.*

I feel wonderful, as if all the stresses and strains have been left
behind and I am entirely liberated. No hormones, no tiredness, no
chemicals adjusting my mood; I'm simply *me,* whatever that is.

I try once more to get to Adele's house, to check that she's okay,
and although I find myself at the far end of the walkway this time,
that's it. The elastic feels stretched to the breaking point and it's
slowly pulling me back, despite my resistance. I move back, enjoying the height, the almost *flying* of it, toward my own front door,
and then I'm inside my home.

"Mummy!" I hear him before I see him.

In my bedroom, Adam is beside the bed, tugging at my arm,
my mobile phone in one hand.

"Wake up, Mummy! Wake up!" He's almost in tears as he shakes
me. My head has lolled sideways, and my hand is dead in his. How
long has he been here? How long have I been gone? Ten minutes at

most, but enough to worry my baby boy trying to wake me. I'm alarmed to see him so upset and I panic and I—

—sit bolt upright with a huge gasp of breath and my eyes fly open. I feel the sudden weight of every cell of my being and my heart goes like a jackhammer with the shock. Adam has stumbled backward, and I reach for him, my hands cold against his warmth.

"Mummy's here," I say, over and over, when the world and my body have settled back around me. "Mummy's here."

"I couldn't wake you up," he says into my shoulder. A tremor has run through his safe world, an almost-death he doesn't understand. "You wouldn't wake up. Your phone was ringing. A lady."

"It's okay," I mutter. "Mummy's here." I don't know who I'm trying to convince; him or me. My head is spinning slightly as I settle back into the weight of my limbs, and although his bottom lip is still wobbling slightly, he holds out the phone to me. I take it.

"Hello?"

"Louise?"

It's Adele. Her voice is soft in my ear but it brings me back to the moment. Adele never calls.

Adam is still watching me, almost distrustful that I'm actually alive and well, and I smile at him and mouth to get some juice and put some cartoons on. He's a good boy and he does what he's told, even though he's unsure.

"Are you okay?" I ask Adele. I shiver, cold from lack of movement.

"I wanted—well, I wanted you to forget about all the stuff I told you the other day. It was stupid. Just ridiculous thoughts. Put them out of your head." She sounds cooler, the tone of someone who's regretting sharing a secret and now wants some distance.

"It didn't sound stupid to me." I think of the letter slipping from my fingers into the post box and my stomach squirms with guilt. I can't tell her about that now.

"Well it was." Sharp. I've never heard her sound like this before. "I'm sorry I involved you in my marital problems. But really, we're fine. I'd appreciate it if you never mentioned it again."

"Has something happened?" This isn't like her. It doesn't even sound like her. She's always been so gentle. Have they fought? Has he threatened her?

"Nothing's happened. I can just be prone to overimagination."

"I didn't overimagine that file he's got on you." I almost snap the sentence out. I'm still vague from whatever it was that just happened, and for the first time she's coming across as a bit pathetic. "And what about Rob?"

"Forget about Rob," she says. "Forget about all of it." She doesn't even say good-bye but hangs up. That's me told, then. I should feel hurt or angry but I'm not. If anything, I'm confused. Has David done something to her?

I stare at the phone for a moment. What would I have seen if I could have got to her house rather than only next door? A fight? Threats? Tears? Sitting here, the thought of invisibly transporting myself there sounds crazy. Did I really go to Laura's? While still in my bed? How is that even possible?

I find Adam in his room, looking tiny and woeful sitting on his bed halfheartedly playing with his plastic dinosaurs.

"Why didn't you wake up?" he says. "I was shaking you for ages."

"I'm awake now!" I grin and make light of it, but vow that this—whatever *this* is—will never happen again while he's in the house. My headache has gone, I notice as I go to get him some juice and tell him we'll watch some cartoons on the sofa together. The tension has left me, even after that call from Adele. I've sent the letter. I can't unsend it. I actually feel a relief that she's been cool with me. Maybe this is the break I need from them in order to get my life back on track, and this way, if the one-in-a-thousand chance comes off and the police do search the estate, I can feel slightly less guilty about it. I feel awake and alert for the first time in days, as if exiting my body has given it time to repair itself without worrying about the inhabitant.

Is that what I did? Really? Leave my body? The thought alone is insane. But this isn't the first time it's happened. I know that now. There was Adam's bedroom. And the time I floated above myself. And now this. All through the silver door. But is it real or was I dreaming?

When the cartoons are on, I slip out the front door and go to Laura's. I'm shaking as I knock on the door. This is crazy. I'm crazy.

"Hey." She's wearing jeans and a green fleece. "What's up?" I stare at her for a moment, and she frowns. "You okay?"

"Yes!" I force a smile. "I wondered if I could have a look at your TV? I've been promising Adam for ages that we'll get a bigger one and I'm looking at Argos online but I'm rubbish at picturing sizes in the room. I'll only be a second. Sorry to disturb you."

"Not a problem, just ignore the mess." She lets me in and I follow her through the flat. There are plates on the kitchen side, just as I saw them, the remnants of toast or a bacon sandwich littering one.

"This is too big for the room really," she says, "but I love it. It's a forty-six-inch screen, which at least means I can see it without my glasses on." She laughs and I laugh with her but I'm not really listening. The bar of Fruit & Nut chocolate is on the arm of the sofa. The flowery coffee cup is on the table. *Friends* is on the TV.

"Thanks," I mutter. "That's a great help."

"No problem, anytime." She tries to talk to me about dating and if there is any sign of true love in the cards, but I can't wait to get out of there. My head is buzzing, Adele's call virtually forgotten. I *had* been there. I *had* seen her. Just as I *had* been in Adam's room that night when he'd spilt his water.

I go back to my own sofa, where Adam snuggles into my chest, still feeling the echoes of his fear when he couldn't wake me, and I stare at the cartoons as he becomes absorbed in them. How is what I did even possible?

It is only later, at night, when I'm alone in my bed in the dark, that a terrible thought strikes me. It curdles my blood with the possibilities.

Adam not able to wake me. Shaking my cold arms. Thinking something was wrong. Me, sitting bolt upright in bed, gasping as I wake. Not a natural wakeup at all.

It's all exactly as it was when I was trying to wake Adele.

She lied about the second door.

48

ADELE

The course of true love never did run smooth. I know that better than anyone. But still, I believe in it, I really do, even after everything. Sometimes true love needs a helping hand. And I've always been good at providing that.

49

LOUISE

By nine thirty on Monday I've dropped Adam off at Day Play and
I'm waiting to catch a train to Blackheath. I should be exhausted—
I've barely slept since Saturday—but my brain is filled with questions and fire ants of doubt. If Adele lied about having the second
door then that changes everything. What else has she lied about?

Two questions burn brightest in my mind as I take a seat by the
window, my back stiff with tension, my fingers picking at the skin
around my nails. If Adele has the second door and can leave her
body, how far can she go and what does she *know*? It sounds like a
poem and it goes round and round in my head in time with the
steady rhythm of the engine lurching me across London Bridge.

Of course the bigger question is what does she know about me
and David. *Does* she know about me and David? If she does, well,
then . . . I feel sick contemplating that. I can't take in that everything
I've believed so readily might be wrong. How stupid I might have
been. What I've *done*. The letter. All the detail I put into it about
Rob and David and Adele—all guilt pointing at him. God, it's so
potentially awful. I think of Sophie sitting on my balcony. What
was it she said? *Fragile? Or crazy? Maybe she does have a screw loose?* Oh
god, oh god, oh god.

Rather than searching for a list of cafés in Blackheath, most of which probably don't have websites anyway, I've looked for psychiatrists instead, and there are only three, which was a tiny wave of relief amid my tsunami of panic. Even if there had been fifty, though, I'm determined to find Marianne and talk to her. I need to know what happened between her and David and her and Adele. The notes in David's file were so vague. *Marianne not pressing charges*—pressing charges against whom? Him or her? And for what?

It's taken all my resolve not to buy a packet of Marlboro Lights at the station. Why should they drive me back to smoking? I'm not giving them that. *Them. They.* I can't trust either of them right now. The tangles around me feel like barbed wire. Maybe my new panic is all for nothing. Maybe David *is* the bad guy here just as Adele has made out. Maybe Adele doesn't have the second door, and even if she does, maybe she still doesn't know anything. Maybe, like me, she can't go very far. She could still be telling the truth.

The thought feels hollow. I remember her cold hand and the gasp of her wakening in the chair in David's study. If she can't go very far, then why would she bother with the second door at all? I can't imagine spending hours watching Laura and not being able to get past the end of our block's walkway. It would be weird. And it would be dull, especially when the first door on its own allows you to dream anything you want.

She was through the second door that day when I found her in David's study. I'm sure of it. But where was she? What was she watching? And why lie to me about it? My foot taps on the floor until we finally reach Blackheath and I rush from the train, as if trying to run from myself.

I walk fast through the streets of the affluent suburb, mumbling the occasional apology as I barge past prams and strolling pedestrians, but not slowing my pace. There are a lot of cafés and restaurants here but I focus on those closest to the clinics. If I'd been able to log in to work then I probably could have checked which clinic David had come from, but he's shut that avenue down, and if anyone ever told me, my brain has forgotten.

In one dead end, I order a bacon roll I don't want and when I find out there's no Marianne there, I leave and dump it in the bin outside. Two take-away coffees follow and still no Marianne. I want to weep with frustration even though I've been here barely an hour. I have no patience left.

Finally, I find it. A small, chintzy, but on the right side of sweet rather than tasteless café and tea shop down a quiet cobbled mews that you'd miss unless you knew it was there. I can see why David would come here. It's homely looking. Welcoming. I know it's the right place before I've even stepped inside. I can feel it. Just like I know when I see the earthy woman behind that counter that the answer to "Are you Marianne?" is going to be yes.

And it is. She's older than me, maybe close to forty, and she has the tanned, toughened skin of someone who holidays in the sun maybe three or four times a year and relishes hours by the pool. She's attractive, but not beautiful, and she has no wedding ring. Her eyes are kind, though. I see that straight away.

"I really need to talk to you," I say, my face flushing. "About David and Adele Martin. I think you knew them?" The café isn't busy, only a well-turned-out older couple enjoying a full breakfast and the newspapers in one corner, and a businessman sipping a coffee and working on his laptop in another. She can't use being too busy as an excuse.

She stiffens. "I have nothing to say about them," she says. The kindness has gone from her eyes. Now I see hurt and defensiveness and anger at someone forcing a memory of something wanted forgotten.

"Please," I say. "I wouldn't have come all this way to find you if it wasn't important." I hope she can see the utter desperation in my own gaze. Woman to woman. Perhaps victim to victim.

She does. After a moment's hesitation, she lets out a long sigh and says, "Take a seat. Tea or coffee?"

I choose a table by the window and she joins me with two mugs of tea. I start to try and explain myself, to tell her something of what's brought me here, why I need to hear her story, but she cuts in, stopping me.

"I'll tell you what happened but I don't want to know anything more about them. About *her*. Okay?"

I nod. *Her. Adele.* Oh god, oh god, oh god.

"There was never anything in it, David and I. He was too young for a start and he was a nice, quiet man. He'd come in early, have a coffee, and sit and stare out of the window. I always thought he looked sad, and I hate to see people sad so I started chatting to him. Not much at first, just in the way I try to make regulars feel at home, but then slowly we started to talk more and he was charming and funny. I was newly divorced and feeling raw and it was like having free therapy." She smiles, almost wistful. "We'd joke about that. How I was paying him in coffee. Anyway, that's how it was. She came in once or twice too, before I knew who she was. Right at the beginning. I was struck by her beauty. She was the kind of woman you remember."

"Like a movie star," I mutter, and she nods.

"Yes, that's it. Almost too beautiful. I didn't know she was his wife. She didn't say. She just drank her peppermint tea and sat and studied the place. It made me feel slightly uncomfortable, as if I was being inspected by the health board. But that was in the early days and she didn't come back after that. Not to here, anyway."

It all sounds so innocent, I can't imagine what went wrong. My heart, despite everything else, thumps in relief that there was no affair. David has not done what he did with me before. Adele was wrong, about this woman at any rate. I trust Marianne. She has no reason to lie to me.

"So what happened?"

"He started to open up to me a little. He might have been the psychiatrist but when you've worked in the service industry as long as I have you develop your own way with people. I say he opened up, but actually it was more that he talked *around* things, if you know what I mean. I told him I thought that under his witty exterior he always seemed slightly unhappy, and we talked about love. He asked me once if it was possible to love someone so much that it makes you completely blind to them for a while. I told him that's what love is at its heart. Only seeing the good in someone. I said love was a kind of madness in itself, because I must have been mad to stay with my John as long as I did."

"I think *you* should be a psychiatrist," I say. We're warming to each other. A support group of two.

"After that he started turning up half an hour or so before I opened and I'd make us both breakfast. I'd probe him a bit more, and eventually, one day he said that he did a thing a long time ago that was wrong. He thought at the time that he was protecting the woman he loved, but it was always there between them and then, after a while, he began to worry that there was something very wrong with her. She wasn't who he thought she was. He wanted to leave but she was holding this thing he'd done against him as a threat. To keep him. She said she'd ruin him."

She's looking out the window rather than at me, and I know she's back in that time, those moments I'm making her relive. "I told him that the truth was always better out than in and he should face this wrong thing he'd done, whatever it was. He said he'd thought about that a lot. It was all he thought about. But he was worried that if he did, and he had to go to prison, then there would be no one to stop her hurting someone else."

My heart races and I barely feel my hands burning as they grip the hot mug. "Did he ever tell you what this wrong thing was?" Rob. It's something to do with Rob. I know it.

She shakes her head. "No, but I got the feeling it was something bad. Maybe he would have told me eventually, but then *she* turned up at my door."

"Adele?"

Her mouth has twisted into a sour pout at the mention of the name, but she nods. "She came to my house. She must have followed me home one day. She told me to stay out of her marriage. She said I couldn't have David and that he belonged to her. I was shocked and tried to tell her that there was nothing going on, and after what happened when my own husband cheated I wouldn't do that to another woman, but she wasn't listening. She was furious. Beyond furious."

I wouldn't do that to another woman. Marianne is a better person than me. It's my turn to look away, even though I'm listening intently, sucking in her every word to savor later.

"She told me to stop talking to him," she continues, oblivious to my sharp pang of guilt. "To stop advising him if I knew what was good for me. She said he wasn't going to leave her and that he loved her and whatever was in their past was their business and theirs alone." She pauses and sips her tea. "I felt awful. Mortified, even though I hadn't done anything wrong. I told her we were friends and that was it. She said I was a miserable old woman with only a cat for company and no man would ever look at me. It was such a childish insult that I actually laughed at it. Shock, I think, but I laughed all the same. That was probably my mistake."

"Did you tell David?"

"No. I was actually surprised when he turned up at the café the next morning, to be honest. I'd presumed he must have told her about our conversations because how else could she have known about them?"

How else indeed. *How far can you go, Adele?* I can just imagine Adele hovering above them, invisible, as they talked. How angry she must have been. The image leads immediately to that of her hovering above my bed watching me fuck her husband. *Oh god.*

"But he acted like nothing had happened. He looked tired, yes. Unhappy, yes. Hungover, probably. But certainly not as if he'd told his wife all about our conversations. I created the opportunity to say he should talk to her about their problems. He said they were beyond that and that she never understood. I was obviously feeling quite uncomfortable about it all, so I told him what I really thought. That he should stop talking to me about it, but if he was that unhappy then he should leave her and hang the consequences. I was angry with her by then, after the shock of her visit had worn off. She was a harpy, I thought. The kind of woman nothing would ever be good enough for. He'd be better off out of it."

I like this woman. She's a straight-talker. I doubt she has secrets or invites them from others or is great at keeping them. I've missed being that person. *Open.*

"What I failed to realize, however," she says softly, "is that I'd be the one facing the consequences. Or, more accurately, Charlie would."

She sees my quizzical expression.

"My old cat. She killed him."

My world spins.

Another dead cat. Coincidence? My thoughts sound like David's notes. David, who Adele claimed killed their cat, and I believed her over him. *Oh, Louise, you stupid fool.* "How?" I croak out.

"He didn't come in one night and I was worried. He was fifteen and his days of hunting mice to bring in for me were over. Mainly he slept on the sofa while I was at work and then slept on me when I got home. As much as I hate to admit it, she was right on one thing—since my divorce Charlie had been my main source of company. It's hard adjusting to being single after being part of a couple."

I know exactly what she means. That left-behind feeling.

"Anyway," she continues, "I think she must have poisoned him first. Not enough to kill him, but enough to subdue him. He was a greedy bugger and very friendly. He'd come to anyone who had a scrap of chicken for him. I couldn't sleep wondering where he was, and then just after dawn I heard a yowl from outside. It was a pathetic sound. Weak. Distressed. But it was definitely my Charlie. I'd had him since he was a kitten, I knew all his noises. I leapt out of bed and went to the window to see, and there she was. Standing in the road holding my limp, sick cat in her arms. At first, I was more confused than alarmed. I had no idea what she was doing there so early, but my initial thought was that he'd been run over and she'd found him. Then I saw her face. I've never seen someone that cold before. That devoid of feeling. 'I warned you.' That's all she said. So quiet. So calm. Before I could react—before I could really grasp what was happening—she'd dropped him to the ground, and as he started to try to crawl to the front door, she . . . she stamped on his head."

As she looks into my wide eyes I can see the remembered horror in hers, and then the slight movement in her throat as she swallows. "She was wearing high heels," she finishes. No more elaboration is needed after that.

"Jesus Christ."

"Yeah." She takes a deep breath and lets it out slowly as if she can sigh it all out of her head. "I'd never seen anything like that before. That level of rage. Of madness. I never want to see it again."

"Did you call the police?"

"Oh, I was going to. But first I wanted David to *see* what she had done. It was nearly time for me to come and open up here, so I thought I'd show him—give him a short, sharp shock—and then call the police. I was angry and heartbroken, but I was also afraid. I was afraid for him and for *me*. I wrapped my poor Charlie up in a blanket and took him with me. I had no intention of working that day, I just wanted to see David and then go home and cry. That probably sounds ridiculous over a cat."

"It really doesn't." I mean it too, as I reach across the table and squeeze her arm. I know how bad it is to be alone, and at least I've always had Adam. I can only imagine how awful she felt.

"David's reaction was interesting." She's thoughtful now the worst of her story is out of the way. Maybe my visit is unexpected therapy for her. "I didn't see it at the time, but when I look back on it, I do," she continues. "He was appalled, that's true. And disgusted and upset. But he wasn't shocked. You can't fake shock. Not well, at any rate. I actually think he was relieved that she'd only hurt the cat. That scared me most of all of it. That relief. What did he think she was really capable of, if killing a cat like that was a cause of relief?"

My hands are shaking so much I have to hide them under the table. *Oh, Adele. What games have you played with me?*

"He persuaded me not to press charges. He said he knew Adele and it would be my word against hers and she could be very convincing. That beauty of hers works for her. But he told me I'd never have to worry about her again. He'd make sure of that. He said he'd make a payment to the Cat Protection League. He basically begged me not to call the police and I was too tired and emotional to argue. I just wanted them both out of my life."

"So you didn't report her?"

She shakes her head. "No. I closed the café for a few days and stayed at home, grieving and also jumping every time the doorbell went in case it was her. But she didn't come back, and I never saw him again."

"And that was it?" I ask. "They vanished?"

"I got a letter from David a few weeks later, sent to the café. He said he'd found a new job and they were moving away. He thanked me for my friendship and said he was sorry that it had been so damaging for me and he would never forgive himself for that. It made me feel sick to look at it. It went straight in the bin. I wanted to forget all about them."

"I'm sorry I've brought it all back up," I say. "And I'm sorry about your cat. But thank you for talking to me. For telling me. You've really helped. More than you can know."

She gets up from the table and I do the same, my legs weak beneath me.

"I don't know how you're involved with them, and I don't want to know," she says. "But get away. As fast as you can. They're damaged goods and they'll hurt you."

I nod and give her a weak smile and then rush out into the fresh air. The world seems too bright, the leaves too green on the trees, their edges too sharp against the sky. I need somewhere to think.

I order a large glass of wine and take it to a corner table, obscured slightly from view of the businessmen and early lunch customers who are slowly filling up the Blackheath pub with laughter and conversation. I barely hear them. Only when I've drunk half my wine does the white noise of panic in my head abate and I'm left to face the stark realization I can no longer avoid.

I believed everything Adele told me so easily. I sucked it all up. And it was all lies. Suddenly I see all my rows with David so differently. There was *fear* in his anger. When he told me to stay away from them, he wasn't threatening me, he was *warning* me. His aggression was to protect me. Does he really care about me after all? Did he mean it when he said he was falling in love with me?

Oh god, I've been a stupid, stupid fool. I want to cry and the wine isn't helping. I've been best friends with a psychopath. Friends? I rethink the word. We haven't been friends, not at all. I'm a fly caught in her web and she's toying with me. But why? If she knows about me and David why didn't she just hurt me?

I need to talk to him. I need to talk to her. But how much does she actually know? Does she know I've come here and spoken to Marianne? And why did she teach me about the dreaming if she knew about me and David? Why help me like that?

With no answers there, I flip my thinking to David. The pills, the phone calls, the money. Is it all containment? Trying to keep the world safe from her? Or is he protecting himself as much as her? I still don't know what happened to Rob. David made a mistake in his past. *No,* I correct myself. That's not what she said. *She said he'd done something wrong thinking he was protecting the woman he loved.* Something *wrong* is bigger than a mistake.

I get my phone out of my bag and find the clinic's number in my contacts and my finger hovers over the dial button. What if he did kill Rob and then I tell him about the letter I've sent to the police, then what? What will he do? Should I trust him and tell him everything? My heart races at the thought. *Fuck it,* I think. *Trust your heart. For once in all this, trust David. Deal with Adele afterward.*

I hit the dial button and press the phone to my ear. Sue answers and I make an attempt to disguise my voice. I tell her my name is Marianne and I must speak to Dr. David Martin as a matter of urgency. She tells me she'll see if he's free and to hold.

He'll agree to meet me. He *has* to.

50

THEN

"Fuck, I'll be glad when this visit is over," Rob says, reluctantly peeling the potatoes and putting them in a pan of cold water. "Polish this, clean that, throw that away, hide this." He looks over to where she's pouring boiling water into the stuffing mix. "He's just a bloke, not the fucking pope." Adele sticks her tongue out at him, and he throws some wet potato skin at her.

"Don't worry, I'll pick it up!" he says, gently mocking her once more.

"I want things to be nice," she says. "For all of us." She's so excited about David coming that she could barely sleep last night even though they'd got pretty stoned. Rob, however, has got more and more moody about the visit, even though he's promised to be nice. She's pretty sure it's nerves. People aren't his thing, and no matter how much she says he'll like David she can see that he's not at all convinced.

"It'll be fine," he says, his dark hair flopping over his face as he returns to his task. "Well, if you don't poison us all with that chicken, anyway. And make sure you rub plenty of butter into the skin."

The past twenty-four hours have kept them busy. They've cleaned up all the debris of their feral lives—no evidence of junk food or joint roaches or spilled tobacco anywhere—and the rooms smell of polish and air freshener. A proper grown-up house. Rob's even promised not to mention drugs or get high or anything over the weekend. Adele doesn't believe for a second that he won't have a joint when he's on his own in his room, but Rob's sharp enough to open a window and the house is certainly big enough that the smell won't carry.

When the chicken is finally stuffed and in the oven, she checks her watch—David's watch that's now hers, a constant link to him—for the thousandth time that day.

"He'll be here soon," she says, grinning. She's glowing and she can't help it. David, David, David. Her head is filled with him. "Ten minutes or so, I think."

"Whoop-de-do," Rob says. "Can we have a drink now?"

She pours them both a glass of wine, feeling very grown-up with her roast dinner on and drinking from her parents' best crystal glasses. They should probably wait for David, but a drink will relax Rob. They lean against the kitchen table together and she links her arm into his.

"David can be a bit quiet and reserved at first," she says. "But don't read anything into it. That's just his way. He's a bit shy. But he's very funny when he relaxes."

"Funny like me?" Rob looks sideways at her and she nudges his ribs.

"Different funny. Anyway, I have every confidence that you'll like him. If you can get past the awful fact that he *worries* about me. I mean, how terrible of him, after everything."

"Okay, okay, point taken. And *you* stop worrying, I've told you I'll be *nice*."

They both smile then, and she feels some of the tension ease out of his wiry arm.

"Come on," she says. "Let's go and wait for him."

They take their wine and go and loiter on the wide stone steps and while Adele impatiently peers up the drive, Rob leans against one of the pillars by the heavy oak doors and drinks. He looks entirely relaxed, which reinforces Adele's suspicion that he's actually a bundle of nerves.

Finally, the purr of an engine cuts through the stillness and Adele lets out a yelp and runs down onto the gravel, jumping up and down.

"He's here! He's here!" She's so excited. It's like her little family will be complete. No missing Rob when she's with David, and no missing David when she's with Rob.

It takes a minute or so for the car to make it down the long drive from the gates, but as soon as he's pulled up, Adele is by the door waiting for him to get out. She looks back at Rob and grins, and from his place, still on the steps, he sends back a half-smile as if suddenly awkward and out of place. He looks small and young standing there, and she wishes he would believe her that it's all going to be okay.

David unfurls himself from the car, tall and broad in jeans and a T-shirt with a thin pale-blue V-neck jumper over the top, and, as it does every time she sees him, the sight of him takes her breath away. He's a grown man. *Her* man.

"Hey," he says, and pulls her in for a kiss. "I've missed you."

"I've missed you too." She can't keep the smile from her face. She grabs his hand. "Come on."

"What about my stuff in the car?"

"That can wait."

She pulls him toward the house, to where Rob is shuffling his feet, his shoulders hunched over, as if he's wishing the ground could open up and swallow him. She understands it. Their whole friendship has always been only him and her. In a sudden wave of sympathy, she lets go of David's hand and runs up the stairs to Rob, linking her arm in his and dragging him out of the shadows.

"David, this is Rob, my best friend. Rob, this is David, my fiancé. I command that you both love each other immediately." She smiles, perfectly happy. Even after everything, and even here in this house, she could not be more perfectly happy.

By ten thirty on Saturday night, they have all drunk too much but at least the atmosphere is less strained than it has been. It was wonderful to have David in her arms and bed and inside her last night and they had laughed and planned and giggled, but she could tell that David wasn't particularly impressed by Rob.

"He's shy," she told him as they curled up together, spooning amid the sweaty sheets.

"He doesn't say much. He's a bit odd," was David's verdict. "I can't see what you like about him so much."

But today has been different, and she's glad. When she'd got down to the kitchen this morning, Rob had already started cooking breakfast, and instead of sullenly staring at David as he had the day before, he'd been giving a comedy cooking demonstration, claiming to be a French chef called Francoise des Eoufs and making David laugh with his over-the-top performance, adding salt to eggs and frying sausages as if he were the top chef at the Ritz. David then joined in, pretending to be a very stilted BBC interviewer questioning him about his techniques, and the whole thing descended into a farce pretty quickly, both of the boys doing their best to make each other, and then Adele, laugh. As they'd eaten Rob had asked questions about university and was clearly trying to be more friendly, as much as that didn't come as easily to him when he wasn't putting on some silly performance. David had answered all the questions, and although he too still seemed slightly unsure, breakfast had definitely been a turning point.

Then they'd gone for a long walk through the woods and dicked around by the well, and it had been fine. She'd loved being out with the two of them, skinny little Rob and her big, strong, handsome David. She was lucky to have them. Rob was definitely trying and that was working. She can see the awkwardness going out of David slightly.

She feels quite content sitting in front of the fire with a gentle wine buzz humming in her head. It might not have been the perfect weekend she'd hoped for, but it's getting better. They're both protective of her, that's all it is, which makes them both wary of each other. She's lucky really.

David gets up to go to the loo and get another bottle of wine, ruffling her hair as he goes past. His fingers feel good and she smiles at him, watching him leave. Rob, lounging on the rug opposite her, sits up.

"How am I doing?" he asks. "Better than yesterday?"

She grins at him. Her other man. "You're perfect. Well done."

"Maybe you should go to bed," he says. "Give us some boy time."

"Male bonding?" She laughs.

"Something like that." He smiles back. One day he might be handsome, she thinks. When his spots have gone, and the braces are off and he's filled out. He looks so young compared to David.

"It might be good for us to talk without you here. No offense."

"None taken." A thought strikes her. "Don't talk about my money, though, will you?" she says. "David would hate that I've told you about that. Please don't mention it." Her words come out in a rush as David's footfalls come back toward them.

"Wouldn't dream of it," Rob says, looking into the mesmerizing flames. "Hadn't crossed my mind."

51

LOUISE

He looks like shit, but I probably don't look much better. His eyes are bloodshot and although he's wearing a suit, his shirt is crumpled. He hasn't shaved. He's given up, I think. He looks like a walking dead man. His eyes stray to the bar.

"I've ordered us a pot of coffee," I say. "I think we both need clear heads now."

"Louise, whatever this is, whatever you think you know about Marianne"—he's standing by the table, and he barely looks at me—"I don't have time for it."

"Sit down, David. Please." I take his hand, gently but firmly, keeping hold as he tries to pull away. It feels good to touch him. "Please. I have some things I need to say. Things you need to hear."

A barmaid brings over the tray of hot coffee, putting the cups out for us and pouring with a cheery smile, and David's natural politeness kicks in and I let him go so he can take a seat opposite me.

"I told you to stay away from us," he says when she leaves.

"I know. And I now know you were warning me, not threatening me. I know what happened with Marianne. I've been to see her."

He stares at me. "Jesus, Louise. Why? Why would you do that?"

I can see the fear in his snappiness. I can see him properly now and I'm filled with shame.

"Because I've been an idiot," I say. "Worse than an idiot. I've been . . ." I don't have the right words to cover it. "I've been fooled and foolish. I've done a really bad thing and I need to tell you about it." He's listening now, a wary alertness. A fox during the hunt. "But first I'm going to tell you what I know, okay?"

He nods slowly. This isn't whatever confrontation he was expecting and it's taking a minute to sink in. How much has he drunk today? How much does he need to numb out the awfulness of his life?

"Go on," he says.

"Okay." I take a deep breath. "I think your wife is crazy, a sociopath or a psychopath or something. I think you give her the pills because you *know* she's crazy. I think when you first realized, you were trying to help her and now you're trying to contain her. I think that's why you call home so often—to check up on her. I think Adele knows we slept together and she became my friend to turn me against you—I haven't figured out quite why yet—but she's definitely been playing with me—with *us*. She killed your pet cat just like she killed Marianne's and you can't do anything about it, because she's got something over you and threatens you with telling the police what happened to Rob. How he's still on her estate somewhere, dead. She told me that you killed Rob—"

He leans forward to say something but I hold my hands up, silencing him. "Let me finish." He slumps back in his chair, accepting the accusation. "She told me that you killed Rob," I repeat, "but *I don't believe that.*" He looks up, a first glimmer of hope. "I think whatever happened to Rob, *she* did it and maybe you protected her in the aftermath because you loved her and she'd just lost her parents. I think you made a stupid, terrible mistake and she's been holding that against you forever to keep you." Suddenly I feel weepy and I bite my tears back.

"I have been so awful for believing her over you because you didn't open up. I should have known. I should have *trusted* my feelings for you, but after Ian I've forgotten how to trust a man and I carried all that over into us."

"And it's not easy to trust a man who's cheating on his wife." He looks ashamed as he speaks and I don't want us to dwell on that. Not right now. That's not important.

"When you were so angry, threatening me to make me stay away, I should have seen you were trying to protect me from her," I say. "But I didn't. And she was *so* good at seeming fragile. She was *so* good at drawing me in. And I'm *so* sorry I let her." I lean across the table and take his hand. "I need you to tell me everything, David. I am on your side. I've been stupid but now I really need to hear from you what's going on because I'm so sick of Adele's lies and I'm going to end up crazy if I don't hear the truth."

He stares at me for a long time, and I hope he sees the trust in my eyes and the feelings I have for him.

"Whatever it is, David. I believe in you," I say. "But I need you to explain it all to me. The money, what happened with Rob. I need to know. Because then I'm going to tell you about the bad thing I've done and you're probably going to hate me for it."

"I could never hate you," he says, and then I really do feel like I'm going to cry. What a mess I've got myself into. *We've* got ourselves into. How could I ever have thought he was a killer? He sips his coffee and then clears his throat, his eyes drifting around the bar. Is he trying not to cry too?

"Just tell me," I say. One of us needs to be tough now, and that person is me.

"It all feels so sordid." He stares down at his coffee. I have a feeling he won't look up until this infected cyst of a story inside him is burst and all the poison out. "My whole life does. But it didn't start out that way. At first it was . . . well it was wonderful. God, I loved her. Adele was the most beautiful girl I'd ever seen. But not just that. She was sweet and funny. Her parents didn't approve. I was the poor farmer's boy whose father had pissed everything away drinking, and I was nearly five years older than her, and I'd known her, on and off, for pretty much forever. She used to follow me around while

I'd be working the fields around school, sometimes telling me about her nightmares."

"She was the little girl you gave the dream book to."

He nods. "Not that it helped much."

If only he knew. It must have been that book that taught Adele about the lucid dreaming and the second door. I want to mention it—I should mention it—but I want to hear the rest of his story first, before distracting him with something so hard to believe.

"But as she grew up," he continues, "well . . . it . . . it felt so right. She was this ethereal creature who didn't care about my rough hands and my shitty dad—she just saw *me*. She had faith in me. If it hadn't been for her, I'd probably never have scraped my way into medical school. We were so in love. I can't describe it. That way you can love so fully when you're young." He pauses. "And then there was the fire."

"You saved her," I say. "Your scars."

"Yeah. Yeah, I did. I didn't even feel the burns at the time. I remember the terrible heat. I remember thinking my lungs were burning as I breathed, but mainly I remember thinking she was dead. She was out cold. Fumes or smoke inhalation or something. I couldn't wake her up."

I remember thinking the same trying to wake Adele. Her cold hand. Shaking her. *How long has she had the second door?* I nod for him to continue.

"Did she start the fire?" I ask.

"I don't know. I didn't even consider it at the time, but since then . . ." He trails off. I imagine he's wondered about it a lot. "There was talk of arson. The police thought it could have been me. And even though I thought maybe someone could have started it, I never thought it could be her. Some disgruntled employee maybe—and there were many; Adele was too young to really grasp her parents' natures, but her dad hadn't exactly made his money without damaging a few people on the way. But I never thought it was her. She nearly died. If it *was* her she was taking a big risk."

"I think she likes taking those," I say.

"Perhaps. But she was so distraught. Wouldn't sleep. It was like she was fading away. Maybe that was some form of guilt. She said she should have woken up. She could have saved them."

Sleep. Dreams. Was Adele even there when her parents died? Had she set the fire and gone through the second door to make sure David was coming to save her? Or was she caught up in the smoke and passed out before she could escape herself?

"And then she met Rob?" I say. "At the therapy place?"

"Westlands, yes. She really liked him and being friends with him helped her. I hated it a bit at the time because I thought looking after her was my job, but I was still recovering from my burns and I had uni. Adele insisted I go back—she even got her lawyers to sort out all my finances as soon as she could, which made me feel uncomfortable, but we were planning to get married anyway, and so she said I was being silly. Anyway, meeting Rob was good for her. I understood that. He was there and I wasn't. I didn't like that he was an ex-junkie, and even though I never said it, I think she knew that. I sort of thought their friendship would be over when they left Westlands, but then she invited him to go and stay at the house. She was like that back then. Wanting to help people. Or at least that's how it seemed."

"So what happened?" *Rob*. The notebook boy. Finally, I'm going to find out his fate.

"I only met him once. Well, I went up for a weekend so I guess it's more accurate to say I knew him for a couple of days. He was a spotty, skinny kid with braces. Nothing special. I don't know what I was expecting. More charisma, I guess. He seemed young to me, for eighteen. He didn't speak a lot, at any rate not for most of the weekend. Just stared at me and muttered answers to my questions, and then would have these over-the-top moments of trying too hard. He did this terrible chef routine one morning that I went along with, but to be honest, it made me uncomfortable. Adele said he was shy. Not good with people. But I found him strange, not that I told her that. We ended up staying up chatting for a couple of hours on the Saturday night after Adele went to bed, but I couldn't click with him at all. He kept asking me stuff about our relationship. I was pretty sure he was jealous. When I left on the Sunday I was quietly wishing their friendship would come to a natural end soon." He pauses and swallows. "My wish came true, but there wasn't anything natural about it."

"Rob died," I say.

Eventually, he nods. "I wasn't there when it happened. That was ten days later."

For the first time he looks up, right into my eyes. "I know where Rob is, but I didn't put him there."

Rob is dead. There it is. Plain fact. It comes as no surprise and I realize I've believed that to be the case for a while.

"I know," I say, and it's true. I absolutely believe him. Too late, perhaps, but I do. "I know you didn't."

"She called me in a panic one morning," he continues, the story pouring out of him now. "She said that they'd been taking drugs, and she thought Rob had overdosed because when she straightened out, he was dead. I told her to call the police and an ambulance. She was crying. She said she couldn't. When I asked her why, she said she'd panicked and pushed his body into the old dry well in the woods on the estate grounds. She was almost hysterical. I couldn't believe it. It was just . . . just crazy, I guess. I drove up there straight away thinking I could talk her into telling the truth to the police. But she wouldn't. She said she was scared that after what happened to her parents and then this, they would lock her up. They'd think she had something to do with it all. She said she'd panicked but she couldn't undo it now. She said no one apart from us knew that Rob had even been there. No one else had seen him. His family didn't even know. She begged me not to tell. She said we could move away from the house and no one would ever know what happened."

"But *you* knew," I say.

He nods. "At first I thought I could do it—keep this secret for her. Protect her. And I tried. I tried so hard. We got married quickly, but the signs were already there that things were going wrong. I hated what we'd done, but I think I could have learned to live with it if I'd thought it haunted her, too, but she seemed absolutely fine, as if she'd forgotten about it already. This boy's whole life. Gone.

His death hidden. I thought maybe her reaction was a coping mechanism—trying to blank it out—but it wasn't. She really had breezed over it. She was *joyful* on our wedding day. As if we didn't have a care in the world. Then she found out she was pregnant and I thought she'd be even happier, but she totally freaked out about it and insisted on getting an abortion—to get this *alien thing* out of her." He pauses and his breathing is ragged. This is hard for him. Facing all this. *Sharing* it. "Love dies hard, you know?" He looks at me, and I grip his hand tight.

"It took a lot of time for my love to die," he says. "I made excuses for her, and I had to finish my training and specialism, so I didn't always see how much she'd changed. But she had. She was spending ridiculous amounts of money—even with her wealth—"

"And that's why you've got control of it?"

He nods. "I'd signed it back to her at the end of that weekend I'd been up at the house in Scotland—I had never wanted control of her money. But neither did I now want her to fritter it all away. What if we eventually had children? What if this was all some emotional response to everything that she needed to get past? What if she came to regret her spending? She agreed to put me in charge. She said she knew she had a problem and needed someone to manage it. Looking back, I think that decision was yet another knot in the noose she kept ready to hang round my neck. Anyway, we continued on for three or four years pretending everything was okay, but I couldn't forget about Rob. His body in the well. And I eventually realized that our love had died with him that night. I couldn't forget about Rob, and I couldn't accept how she could. I told her that it was over. That I was leaving and I didn't love her anymore."

"I presume she didn't take that well," I say, and for the first time, he gives a half-smile. There's no real humor in it, but it's there. *My David's* there.

"You could put it that way. She was hysterical. She said she loved me and couldn't live without me. She said she'd take all the money and I'd be penniless. I said I didn't care about her money and never had. I didn't want to hurt her but I couldn't live like this anymore. She went very quiet after that. A stillness that scared me. That *still*

scares me. I've come to recognize it as a sign of something dangerous inside her. She said if I left she'd tell the police what *really* happened with Rob. I was confused. I didn't know what she meant.
Then she said that truth was all relative. Truth often came down to
what is the most believable version of events. She said she'd tell the
police that Rob and I had fought and I'd killed him and thrown
him in the well. I was shocked. That wasn't true. She said it didn't
matter. She said the police would think it was jealousy and they'd
already been suspicious of me about the fire at her parents' house, so
they'd definitely listen to her."

I think about my letter. What I have to tell him when he's
finished. *Oh god, Louise, what have you done?*

"And then she played her trump card. The piece of evidence
that would place the police firmly on her side. Something she's held
over me for what seems like forever."

"What?" What could she possibly have done?

"My watch," he says simply. He sees my confusion and continues. "When I was burned I couldn't wear it. I gave it to Adele to
wear, as a kind of keepsake. Even on the tightest link it was too big
for her, but she liked having it and I liked her wearing it. I didn't
realize it would bind us together in this hell forever."

"What happened to your watch?"

"When she put Rob in the well, my watch slipped off her wrist.
It got tangled in his clothes." He pauses and looks at me. "My watch
is in the well with the body."

I stare at him. "Oh god." I feel slightly sick. Who's going to
believe David's version with evidence like that there?

"What I hate most is that I let her blackmail me like that. I was
too weak. The thought of going to prison—worse, of no one *believing* me—of everyone thinking I did this terrible thing—froze me.
What if Rob's death hadn't been an accident like she said? Had she
killed him for some reason? Would it look like murder if the body
was brought up? I couldn't face it. I was trapped. She promised me
she'd be good. She promised me we could be happy, that I could
love her again. She said she wanted a child. All the things she thought
would make me happy. It sounded crazy to me. I couldn't imagine

bringing a child into our marriage. Not anymore. In the end, I made my peace with the fact that my punishment for my mistake and my weakness was to be trapped in my loveless marriage."

God, they must have been long years he's spent with Adele, living on that knife's edge. I want a drink. I'm sure he does too, but our drinking days are done for now. He can't hide in the bottom of a glass any longer and I need a clear head.

"But she couldn't keep her mental illness under control for long. She played the perfect housewife but then she'd have these uncontrollable rages over nothing."

"Like with Marianne," I say.

"Yes, like that, but it started long ago. I was sure she was spying on me. She knew things she couldn't possibly know. She'd ring co-workers she thought I was too close to and leave them hateful messages. She had a job for a while but then when I made friends with the woman who ran the florist, there was a fire there. Nothing that could be pinned exactly on her, but enough for me to know it was her. Moving jobs every couple of years because of something she'd done. We'd make *pacts*. I'd promise to call her at least three times a day and she'd give up her credit cards. I'd come straight home from work and she'd give up her mobile phone. Anything to stop her wrecking our lives—or anyone else's—with her madness. She's an aggressive and disempathetic sociopath, I'm sure of it. She has a view of right and wrong but it's not like anyone else's, and she only loves, if that's what it is, me. She'll do anything to stop someone coming between us. And she's so convincing. Who would believe me?" He looks at me. "You didn't. You bought her stories hook, line, and sinker."

"I'm so sorry, David. I hate myself." I need to tell him about the dreams. About how Adele spied on him. How she knew things. I need to be honest with him. I open my mouth to speak but he's in his flow and he cuts me off.

"It's not your fault. She plays her part well, and I was a drunk cheat. I should have never spoken to you in that bar. I just wanted . . . I just wanted to be happy. And god, I should have *known*." He almost slams his hand down on the table with frustration, but instead grips the edge of the wood. "I should have realized when she was little. That insane stuff she would say."

"What do you mean?" I tense as I ask. It's going to be about the dreams. I know it. She loved David. Of course she'd have tried to share it with him.

"When we were first together we got drunk and she tried to tell me that she could do all this mad shit when she was sleeping. She was vague, but it sounded bonkers. Worse, it was probably my fault, because it sounded like she'd taken the ideas from the hippie book on dreaming I gave her and then made crazier stuff up. I just laughed and thought she was winding me up, but when she was upset that I didn't believe her, I should have known that these fantasist ideas were leading to something. She was too old for them to have been childish imaginings. She was clearly showing signs of some serious disorders brewing. I mean, who could possibly believe that you could leave your body when you sleep? It's the sort of thing people who've taken too much LSD say. So yeah, I should have seen the signs. At least remembered them when we got older." He looks at me. "It's why I was so glad to meet you. You're so *normal*." He grips my hands again as if I'm some lifeline. "You're so grounded. Your nightmares are just nightmares and you just get on with them. You would never believe in anything like that. You're *sane*."

Oh god, if only he knew. I can't tell him now, can I? *Actually, everything she told you is real. How else do you think she's spying on you?* I can't do that to him. I can't do that to *me*. Not now. Not when I still have to tell him about the letter I've sent to the police. He needs facts and reality. He can't cope with anything else.

"She's certainly got problems." It's all I can manage to say. "I'll give her that."

We hold each other's hand tightly and he stares at me. "You really do believe me, don't you?" he says, and I nod.

"Yes. I believe you." It's clear in my face anyway. I absolutely believe him. He didn't kill Rob.

"You have no idea how good that feels to hear. But I don't know what to do. I've told her I want a divorce. Who knows what she'll do now? She certainly won't let me leave. And I'm worried what she'll do to you. Jesus, this is all such a mess."

And now it's my turn to share my wrong thing. "It's a worse mess than you think," I say. My heart is racing. "*I've* made it worse."

"I don't see how it can be any worse," he says with a soft smile. "If you can still like me after everything I've just told you, if you can *believe* me, then everything, for me at least, is already so much better." He looks better too. There's more light in his eyes; a heavy load shrugged off, if only for a few moments.

And so I tell him. How I researched online and I sent the letter to Angus Wignall at Perth Police Station outlining all the reasons I thought Dr. David Martin was involved with the death of a young man called Robert Dominic Hoyle and how his body was probably still on Adele's estate somewhere. It's my turn to keep my eyes down in my coffee cup as my face burns. It's not even as if Adele told me to do it. This is all my own stupid work. When I'm finished, I finally look up.

"So you see, I *have* made it worse," I say. "Maybe they'll ignore it as a crank letter. Maybe that Wignall won't even *see* it." Oh, please, please, god, let that be the case.

David leans back in the chair and lets out a sigh. "No, I think he'll read it. He was like a terrier around me, trying to find some way to pin that fire on me."

"You must hate me," I say. I want the ground to open up and swallow me and never let me go. Why do I make everything worse? Why am I so impulsive?

"Hate you?" He sits up, his face somewhere between a frown and a laugh. "Have you listened to anything I've said? I don't hate you. I . . . well, it's more the opposite. I even like you for the way you believed in Adele. That urge to help her. It's one I understand. But no, I don't hate you for this. In many ways what you've done is a relief. It's made things clear."

"What do you mean?" He doesn't hate me. Thank fuck for that. We are still together in this.

"Adele doesn't know about this letter you've sent?" he asks.

I shake my head. "I don't think so." I can't really be more accurate. It's hard to ascertain what Adele does or doesn't know, but I
can't tell him that, not after what he's just said. "What are you going
to do?"

"I'm going to go up there," he says. "I'm going to go and tell
the police everything. The truth. I'm going to be done with it."

It's not what I was expecting and I'm momentarily dumb-
founded, but I know it's the right thing. "They'll believe you," I
say, even though I'm not entirely convinced. "I believe you. And
I can back you up. And so will Marianne, I'm sure."

He shakes his head, smiling softly. "I think it'll take more than
that to counter Adele's version. My watch is there, remember?"

"So why do it?" I'm afraid I'm going to lose him before I've
got him. "Surely there's another way. Why go up there if you think
they'll arrest you?"

"To *end* it," he says. "Once and for all. I should have done it a
long time ago. I'm so tired of carrying the guilt around with me.
It's time that boy got a proper burial."

"But we can't let her get away with everything," I say. "And
she's dangerous. Why shouldn't she be the one in trouble? She's the
one who's guilty here!"

"I might not be guilty," he says, "but I'm not innocent, either.
And this is a perfect punishment for her."

"What do you mean?"

I stare into his beautiful blue eyes. They're calm and clear. "All
Adele has ever wanted is me," he says. "In her own twisted, fucked-
up way, she loves me. She always has and she always will. She's
obsessive about me. If they put me in prison, then I finally get away
from her. She has no more hold on me. I'll be *free*."

I can feel tears coming again and this time I don't stop them.
"Can't you wait awhile? Can't we have a few days together first?"

He shakes his head. "If I don't do it now, I won't do it, and
spending time with you will make it so much harder. It's enough
for me that you *believe* in me."

"When are you going to go?" I don't care about Adele. I can

handle myself with her. I know her secrets now. I feel a twist of guilt. I don't mean to, but I have a secret I can never share with him, just like she couldn't.

"Today. Now. It's only two thirty. I can't go home first, she'll know something's up, but I can be halfway to Scotland by the time she realizes I've gone. I'll call you when I get there tonight."

"Are you sure you shouldn't think about this for a bit longer?" I'm being selfish, I want to keep him here with me, out of prison. "It's so quick. It's so . . ."

"Look at me, Louise."

I do.

"Honestly—isn't what I'm doing the right thing? Taking our feelings for each other out of it?"

From the calmness of his expression, I know he knows the answer already, and I nod. It *is* the right thing. Even if it gets the wrong outcome and no one believes him, the truth needs to be told.

"It's so unfair," I say. I'm burning on the inside, needing to do something. "Maybe I should go and see her and—"

"No. You can't do that. She's dangerous."

"But I have to—"

"She's a sociopath, Louise." He grips my hand tightly. "Do you understand that? You can't go near her. Promise me you won't go anywhere near her. In fact, I'd rather you took Adam and got out of London until I've done what I have to do. But at least promise me you'll stay away from Adele."

"I promise," I mumble. It's not fair that she'll get away with wrecking his life. It's not fair that she'll get away with wrecking mine, too.

"Good. I couldn't stand it if anything happened to you, and I don't want to be worrying about you while I'm facing up to this. I love you, Louise. I really do."

He gets up and comes to my side and then we're kissing. He tastes of stale alcohol, mints, and coffee but I don't care. He's warm and loving and strong and mine and fresh tears well up.

"It's going to be okay," he whispers when we break apart. "Really it is." He smiles at me. "How are you on prison visiting?"

I laugh a little through the tears that won't stop. "I'm all for trying new experiences."

He pays for the coffee, a mundanely routine act that makes everything else seem even more surreal, and then we head outside, where I cry into his chest some more, uncaring who sees.

"It'll be all right," he says.

It won't be. It won't be anywhere near all right, but I nod, and we kiss some more; tears and snot and tiredness and stale alcohol. What a pair we are. I press my face into his neck and suck in the warm smell of him, and then there's just cool air and traffic fumes and he's gone. I watch him walk to the tube station. He doesn't look back. I don't think he dares to in case he changes his mind.

This is all my fault, I think for the thousandth time as I lean against a wall and scrabble in my bag for my e-cig. Me and that stupid letter. I can't believe he's gone so quickly to face it all. How awful must his life be to feel a relief in going somewhere that will no doubt end in his arrest. The death of his career. His life and reputation in tatters and labeled a murderer. I wipe the tears from my face and let the breeze cool me. It's not my fault any more than it's David's. We're just pawns. Adele is to blame. Adele is to blame for everything.

I think of the one secret I've had to keep back from David—the dreams. The doors. The craziness of it all. Why did she even teach me about that if she hated me so much? I'm filled with anger for her and it drives out my sadness for David and my self-pity at losing him. I need to bait her. To taunt the truth out of her. Maybe when she realizes that she's lost David anyway, she'll say something, *anything,* that can help him. There must be some way to make her *see* what she's doing. How there are no winners here. And if nothing else, I need to tell her exactly what I think of her. It's time for an honest conversation with my so-called best friend. I haven't lied to David. I'm not going to go to the house. I'm not going to see her face-to-face. But I didn't promise not to *speak* to her, did I?

52

ADELE

I sit in the quiet of the kitchen with only the steady ticking of the clock for company. It's a strangely comforting sound. I wonder about that sometimes, the proliferation of noisy clocks in the world, each relentlessly marking out our lack of time. We should be terrified of them, and yet that repetitive tick somehow soothes the soul.

I don't know how long I've been sitting here. I'm listening to the beat of the seconds, not watching the minutes and hours. I feel sidelined in my own life now. Redundant. It's very nearly all over and I feel empty and sad.

They say if you love someone, set them free. Well, I'm finally setting him free. There are easier ways to have done it than the route I've chosen, but you can't fake trust and you can't fake belief and you can't fake the realization of a truth. It has to be *fresh*. He needed to see those clear in Louise's eyes. The shock of having misjudged the entire situation. His innocence. Those were things I couldn't give him.

He really does love her. I can't fight that admission any longer. Hey ho, c'est la vie. I've had a good run. I feel adrift as I sit and wait and listen to my life trickling away. Yes, I conclude, as the shrill tone of the cheap mobile makes me jump from my reverie, I could have done everything differently, but this way has been far more interesting. At least I get to have that as my swan song.

Louise is all energy and anger and upset down the line, the antithesis to my calm. It fizzes into my ear, radiating like heat.

"How long have you known?" she asks. I can hear it's taking all her control not to shriek the words at me. "I want to know what the fuck you've been playing at!"

She's seething with rage, and it infects me.

"I think I should be asking you that, don't you? After all, you're the one who's been fucking my husband."

"What I don't understand," she says, ignoring my barb, "is why you told me about the dreams. Why did you help me when there was a risk I'd find the second door? And if I did, that I'd figure all this out?"

The ungrateful bitch. "I didn't know then." I keep my own sudden anger trapped inside. "I thought you were my *friend*. I was trying to help you. I never meet anyone like me and you made me feel less alone." I can sense her distrust. A quiet hitch of breath at the other end.

"You can only use the second door to go to places you know." I speak slowly, making sure it sinks in. "If you haven't been there you can't *see* there. You have to visualize the details." I lean back against the cool wall. "It was only when I was alone and missing you one evening that I went through the door to your flat. I wanted to *see* you. But instead I saw him there with you." I pause and work up some attempt at tears. "That's when I found out. *Then* I knew."

She is an open book, Louise. I know she's working through the logic of what I've said. She's got too much in that head of hers right now to remember the conversation they had in the office that first morning about their drunken indiscretion. The office I'd had the tour of the day before. I remember it, though. Every word and action. Her nerves. His panic. Also, the heat from both of them at seeing each other again. I remember the absolute rage I had to manage until I forced our meeting and she told me about her night terrors. After that my anger melted into perfect joy. Potential enemy turned into a gift from God in those few moments. But for now, at least, what I've said makes sense to her. I've also given her some vital information. *You have to visualize the details.* Look at me, even now, helping her.

"Why didn't you *say* something? Why give me all this shit about David? Making me think all this stuff about him? These *lies*?"

Always looking for answers. Always needing to know. She should have been a detective. "Lies and truths are only perspectives. And why do you think?" I focus on the task at hand and raise my own voice slightly, upset and hurt. She wants a confession, I'm sure, but my game isn't over yet. "You were my best friend. My first proper friend in ages. I wanted you to hate him. I wanted you to choose *me*! Why should I lose both of you? How is that fair? I hadn't done anything wrong!"

That last might be pushing it a touch far given everything she knows, and I must sound like I'm crazy. Of course, as far as she's concerned, I *am* crazy.

"I wanted you to love me the most." My voice is softer now, as if my burst of energy has been too much. "But you loved him and you only ever felt sorry for me. Pity and guilt, that was all you ever felt for me while you merrily slept with the man I love." I may not have much moral high ground, but the wronged wife is one ledge I'm going to stand on.

"That's not true, and you know it." A defensive lilt in her voice. I imagine her face has flushed. She's so predictable. "I *was* your friend," she continues. "I thought you were mine, and I tried to stop it. It had started before I'd even met you. I didn't know he was married. I tried to end it. And it did end."

It's her turn to be economical with the truth. It did end, but only when I intervened and he found out about our friendship. Louise would have gone on guiltily spreading her legs for him behind my back if he hadn't panicked and finished it. Protecting her from me. That's David. Forever saving women. Of course that version of events doesn't suit her view of herself so she likes to think her guilt would have won out and she would have ended it anyway. I know people better than that. I know *her* better than that.

"Well, now you have lost both of us," she says, defiant.

"No, I haven't. He won't leave me. He'll never leave me."

"You don't get it." She's talking to me like I'm a child. "I believed you. I believed everything you said. I went to the police with it."

"You did what?" I emit an almost-gasp. Surprised. Or at least a good impression of it.

"I wrote them a letter. Addressed to the policeman who investigated the fire that killed your parents. The one who thought David was involved. I told them all about Rob and how I thought his body was still somewhere on your estate."

"You did what? Why would you do that? I never told you to do that."

"I did it because I'm stupid and I didn't know you were crazy then!"

"They won't believe you," I mutter, standing and pacing the hall, my head down as if I'm frantically thinking. She can't see me but she'll hear my footsteps. She'll sense my worry. "They won't believe you."

"No," she says, "maybe not." A breath. "But they will believe *him*."

I freeze and pause. "What?" I say.

"He's on his way to Scotland to speak to them. He's going to tell them everything. He's going to tell them the truth."

A long moment of quiet falls between us, only the relentless tick of the clock breaking the silence.

"But he can't!" I say eventually. "They won't . . . He can't . . . He wouldn't . . ."

"But he has. And no, they won't believe him. You're too good for that. They'll arrest him."

I can hear her momentary joy at how aghast I am. At how we're both hurting now. All that potential love for him that she's denied for so long, burning bright inside her.

"We both know he didn't kill Rob," she says. "Why can't you just say that?"

"They'll put him in prison," I say so quietly it's barely a whisper. "They'll take him away from me." Tears spring from the corners of my eyes. Just the thought of being separated from David can cause a physical reaction in me, even now.

"Why couldn't you have hated him?" It's my turn to shout. "Why? Why would you do this?"

She doesn't answer so I wail like an animal and sink to the ground. "You were just supposed to hate him," I cry into the handset. "You were supposed to choose me." I pull my knees up under my chin as I snivel snotty tears onto my silk sleeve, lost in my role. "What am I supposed to do now? He can't leave me. He can't. He won't."

"He has," she says, Louise now the calm one, now the one in control. "But you can stop this, Adele. You're the only one who *can* stop this. Tell the truth. At least tell me the truth, here and now."

Oh, no, little goody two-shoes, I want to hiss at her. *It's not going to be that easy.*

"You're sick, Adele."

Oh, bless you for that, Louise, you husband-stealing sorry excuse for a woman. We both know the word you're actually thinking is "crazy."

"The pills you haven't been taking will help you," she continues. "If you go to the police and tell them the truth—if what happened with Rob was an accident and you panicked—well, they'll be easier on you. All you did was hide the body. With David they'll think it was murder. They might think he murdered your parents, too."

I note that she's very carefully avoiding suggesting that perhaps I murdered all three—*psycho crazy Adele.*

"They'll be gentler on you. Mitigating circumstances. You'd lost your family and had been in therapy. They won't put you in prison, I'm sure of it."

Oh, what a honeyed tongue she has. No, they might not put me in prison, but I hear Broadmoor's no walk in the park either, thank you very much.

"Why would he do this?" I moan. "Why?"

"He doesn't love you, Adele. He hasn't for a long time. He's just been trying to look after you. To do the best for you."

I want to punch her in the face for her false sympathy and her presumption to know so much about our marriage. I dig my fingernails into my knees instead as she continues.

"Why make him suffer? If you really love him—and I think you do—you can save him from this. You can't keep him, Adele. You can't trap him with you. That's no life, not for either of you. But maybe if you tell the truth, if you protect him now when he needs you, then maybe you can put something right."

"You've taken everything from me," I whisper again. I will not admit to any guilt. Not at this late stage in the game. "What am I supposed to do without him?"

"You could do the right thing," she says. "*Prove* you love him. Let all this shit be over with. At least maybe that way he won't hate you. Maybe *you* won't hate you."

"Fuck off," I whisper, enjoying the crude language in my mouth. I sit there shaking for a moment until the rage bursts from me in a blaze of spit. "Fuck off!" I shriek at her again, and then burst into tears.

There's a click and a dead tone in my ear and I'm alone again with the endless ticking of the clock. God, she's a patronizing bitch at times, I think as I get to my feet, pocket the phone, and wipe my tears away. But she's right, though. It *is* time that I made everything better.

53

LOUISE

I'm shaking as I hang up.

Have any of my words sunk in? What will she do now? Call the clinic? Smash up the house when she realizes I wasn't lying? I think of how broken she sounded. No. She believed me. She knows he's gone. I try to ring David but his phone goes through to answerphone. He'll be on the train already and the service must be bad. I curse under my breath but then leave a message to tell him I'm safe.

Safe.

Adam. I'm supposed to pick him up in an hour. How can I play happy families with him tonight? With all this going on? Oh, my baby boy, I love him so much but I can't deal with him today. I'm too distracted. Also, there's Adele. She knows where I live. What if her awful upset turns to anger? *Sociopath.* That's how David described her. What if she comes after me when all this sinks in? I consider checking us into a hotel as David suggested, but that would require too much explanation to Ian when Adam sees him. Also, part of me wants to know how crazy Adele is going to get. If she comes after me I want to be prepared. I think she's going to lose control without David there. I almost hope she does. That would help support David's version of events.

I call Ian, silently promising that whatever else happens, tomorrow I'm taking Adam out for a special mother-and-son tea. "Hey," I say when he answers, mildly concerned. I never ring him at work. Those days are long gone. "Nothing to worry about. I just wondered if you and Lisa could do me a favor. It's a bit last-minute, though."

"What is it?"

"Could you have Adam tonight? Collect him from Day Play? Something's come up and I'm running late and I've also had an invitation out to dinner this evening that I'd like to go to."

"Sure!" he says. "I'll call Lisa, she'll go and get him."

I can hear the enthusiasm in his voice. He thinks I've got a date. Finally, his ex-wife is moving on.

"Thanks," I say. "You're a star."

"No problem. And have fun!"

We say our good-byes and hang up. How strange it is that love can turn to hate and then to this mild friendship.

I resist the urge to go and buy a bottle of wine on the way. As much as I tell myself I'd only have one glass, in the mood I'm in the bottle would be gone by the time David calls and I don't trust myself not to beg him to change his mind if I'm drunk.

And then, of course, there's Adele. If she turns up and I've been drinking I'll have no chance against her.

54

ADELE

Time marches on, that's what they say, isn't it? Tick, tick, tick. It marches through today. This last day. I hadn't expected it to be to-night. I hadn't expected to be alone when the final hour came. I'd planned to do it at the weekend when Adam was away and when David was here. Drugged and asleep, perhaps, but here. The stars have aligned for me, though, and Adam's at his father's and David, well, David is on his self-destruction mission to Scotland. Back to the homeland to clear his conscience. It's far better this way. Less complicated for one, and this is all about me and Louise after all. David is just the *prize* we've been in a tug-of-war over. We're both tired of pulling now. It's time for the game to end. A loser and a winner must be decided.

The stage is set and everything is ready. I prepare the bedroom and then write my letter and leave it in a sealed white envelope on David's desk. It's new stationery—expensive. Only my fingerprints on it. They won't be able to say David put me up to it. I've thought of everything and it all has to be perfect. To *look* right.

There are still hours to pass and once I've practiced everything over and over until I can't face doing it again, I simply walk around our empty house bidding my farewell to it. My heart races and my mouth is dry. I need the toilet almost constantly. For the first time, I realize I'm afraid.

The rain has stopped and I go out into the cool dusk of the evening and enjoy the prickle of goosebumps on my skin. It calms me. I must screw my courage to the sticking place and I will not fail. The tree branches hang low over the lawn and flowerbeds, but they're full and alive and the creeping autumn hasn't claimed the leaves yet. It's like a tamed version of the woods on the estate. Left alone, how long would it be until all this trimmed and clipped nature was wild? I feel like this garden. A clipped wild thing. I stay there for a while, savoring the smells and the breeze and the sight of it all, and then when the evening dips into night and my skin is shivering from the cold, I go back inside.

I take a long, hot shower, forty minutes, maybe more. Time seems to be moving more quickly now, as if aware of my mounting terror, and toying with it. I take deep breaths in the steam to counter my nerves. I am in control. I have always been in control. I will not become a weeping, wailing, fearful woman now, at the end.

I dry my hair, relishing its shiny thickness, and then study myself in the mirror before pulling on my best silk pajamas. I feel like crying even though that's absurd and makes me hate myself a little. I check everything is where it should be, even though I only prepared the room a couple of hours ago and *know* that it's all where I need it. Like David constantly checking his passport on the rare occasions we've gone away on holiday. I smile at that. The thought of David calms me. This is all for him. Everything has always been for him. I love him so very, very much.

I look at the clock. Ten P.M. In half an hour or so, it'll be time. I lie back on the bed and close my eyes.

55

LOUISE

He doesn't ring back until after ten and I'm almost crawling up the walls by then. The reality of what he's doing is slowly sinking in. The next time I see him it might be across a prison visiting table. I feel sick and jangly as if I've drunk too much strong coffee and hearing his voice is a flood of relief. He's in a hotel in Perth and waiting for Wignall, who's driving over to meet him. I'm glad I didn't drink. If he can be strong about this then so can I be. I tell him about my call to Adele, blurting it out in a tidal wave of words.

"I couldn't get her to admit it. She sounded guilty and she was upset but she didn't actually say you were innocent. I'm so sorry. I wanted to make her see what she'd done. I hoped she'd be honest. I wanted to try and persuade her to tell the truth about the watch, about what happened."

"It's okay, Lou," he says. He doesn't sound angry at all, just tired and resigned. I like the shortening of my name coming from his mouth, though. It sounds intimate. "She doesn't know *how* to tell the truth. But you have to be careful now. I don't think you really get what she's like. I couldn't stand it if anything happened to you."

"Nothing's going to happen to me. I promise. I'm going to be right here where you need me." I'm talking in clichés but I don't care.

"I think that's him," David mutters into the phone, someone

hundreds of miles away having caught his eye across the room. "I'll call you when I can," he says. "I promise. And please, get out of the flat tonight? Go to a neighbor at least?"

"David, I . . ." I don't know what to say. I love you? Something with the potential for that anyway. I've never been more sure that I can love someone than I am about David. But I don't get to finish my half-declaration of half-love. The phone clicks off in my ear, the policeman claiming him.

The tension drains from me in an instant. There's no going back now. No more time to change his mind. I feel hollow and empty and selfishly wish that Adam were here so I could go into his room and look at him sleeping and remind myself that I have had some good luck in the world. Instead, I go into the kitchen and reach for the gin bottle in the cupboard and the squash. It'll be better than nothing. I'm in the middle of pouring a stupidly large measure when I hear my phone pinging. A text.

I dart back into the sitting room, my heart in my mouth. Is it David? Has the policeman told him to go home and get his own head checked? Are they dismissing him without hearing him out? Thinking he's a time-waster?

It's not David. It's Adele. I'm so sure it's going to be him that I stare at the phone for a moment before really registering the name, and then my stomach tightens with nerves. What now? What's she going to do now? I press the button to read her message.

You were right. I have to make things better. Be honest about everything that happened. I can't live without David and they will take him away from me. But I can't be locked up, either. I can't do that. I don't want to be in some awful place with crazy people. It's my head. I don't want it messed with. I'm not strong enough for that, or to live without David beside me. So, I'm going to take the easy way out to save him. Maybe not easy but my only option. I suppose it's the right way too, after everything. I hope you're happy now. Maybe he'll be happy now, with me gone. I was your friend, Louise, for a little while. Please remember that.

I stare at the message, trying to make sense of it. What's she going to do? What's she saying here? Take the easy way out? What does that mean? The truth of it is screaming somewhere inside me while the rest of my brain tries to catch up. It's so far from what I'm expecting from her. But then I think of how she was on the phone, broken and crying. She might be insane but she does love David. She's never been without him.

The easy way out. She's going to kill herself. I think of all the pills in their cupboard. Is she going to take them all? Is that it?

I try to call her but there's no answer. Fuck, fuck, fuck. My ears hum with tension. What do I do? Call the police? And say what? What if it's not even true? This is Adele, after all. Is this some kind of test? A trick? But what if it isn't? Even after everything, I don't want this on my conscience if I could have saved her. How can I know?

There is one thing I can try, I realize. My own craziness that she's opened up in me. My new ability.

I neck half the gin and juice mix and sit on the sofa. If I can *see* her then I'll know. I slow my breathing. I let my neck relax. I think of nothing but the door. I focus as I never have before and there it is, the shimmering silver. I think of Adele's house. Her bedroom. The expensive metal-framed bed. The feature wall with three green stripes. The feel of the cotton bed set underneath me. The floorboards. For a moment I think I can get there but then the door pushes me back and vanishes. It's too far. I can't go that far. Not yet.

Cursing myself and her and everything, I finally sit up and grab my phone. I click on the Uber app. Cars within two minutes.

I was your friend, Louise, for a little while.

Fuck it. Fuck, shit, fuck, I have to go. I have to. I don't have any choice. I don't even grab my coat before rushing out into the cold night.

The cab is true to its word, arriving almost as soon as I'm on the street, and after barking an address at the driver, I leave a message on David's phone telling him where I'm going and why. If it's a trap and something goes wrong at least he'll know what happened to me. *Who* happened to me. I try her phone again. Still no answer. My foot taps and I lean forward in the seat, urging more speed from the engine.

How long has it been since that text came in? Ten minutes

maximum, I think. But maybe several minutes too long. Am I already too late?

I'm out of the car before it's fully stopped, calling back an absent good night. I fly up the thick stone steps and with a shaking hand press the buzzer hard. I hear the bell ringing out on the other side but I can't see any lights on downstairs. I push the buzzer again, holding it down for five seconds or more, but still nothing.

I crouch and peer through the letterbox. "Adele? It's me!" An acrid smell wafts out toward me. Smoke? At the far end of the corridor, from inside the kitchen, I see an orange flicker. Oh, shit. Oh, fuck. A fire.

What had Adele said? She was going to put things right? Was she talking about her parents more than Rob? A fire killed her family, and there was a fire at her job in the florist. Is this her thing? Is killing herself by fire Adele's way of somehow leveling things out? I ring the doorbell once more, my face flushing with panic, and then I remember the key and start to scrabble in the flowerpot, digging deep into the dirt before accepting that it's not there. She's taken it back. No way in for me.

I don't know what to do. What if she isn't inside? What if she's trying to get me arrested for arson or something? But then, conversely, what if she's upstairs in her room, drugged and waiting to burn or suffocate or however the hell else people can die in house fires? I bang on the door. She's so close and yet so far away.

So close.

I think of the second door. I'm close now. Maybe I can do it from here. I sit on the top step and lean back against the porch, propping myself up in the corner. I take deep breaths, shaky at first and then smoothing out. I clear my mind, focusing on the silvery doorway. I'm getting better at this now that I'm not afraid of it. I can *summon* it now instead of it coming to me unbidden.

When the edges are glittering bright in the darkness behind my eyes, I picture Adele's bedroom. The image is clear. The colors of the walls, the green of guilt-ridden woods. The en-suite in the corner. The coolness of air trapped in by old bricks. The mirror on the back of the wardrobe. I see it so clearly and then suddenly I'm through the door and—

—I'm there, hovering above the room. It's dark but I can see Adele, lying on the bed, still and perfect in cream silk pajamas. There's no sign of pills, or water to take them with, but I can feel a terrible emptiness coming from her as if she's already dead. A gray dullness hangs in the air around her body as the first trails of smoke come up from the hallway below.

She's gone, I realize. Not dead, but she's out of her body. She doesn't want to feel herself die. She doesn't want to be here when it happens. Is she scared she'd change her mind? Panic at the last minute? Is this what happened with her parents?

I move closer toward her as I hear crackling coming from down-stairs. Fires aren't silent as they spread, and by the noises I can hear, this one is growing fast. I should have called the fire brigade. I should have called the police. I should have done *something* practical. Some neigh-bor will notice the blaze soon, but it'll be too late. However Adele started the fire, it's taking hold. I need to get her out of the house. I automatically reach for her but I have no grip, I'm insubstantial, I'm nothing but energy. What can I do? How can I get her out of here?

A thought comes to me, cool and clear, as if the lack of a body's chemical reactions has subdued my panic. It's a crazy thought and I don't know if it's even possible, but it might be my only chance to save her.

Her body is empty. I'm right here. It would only take three or four minutes to run down the stairs and out of the house and then we'd both be safe. It's all I've got. Soon the stairs aren't going to be passable. There are wooden floors everywhere. Varnished. How fast will they burn?

I stare at her body, still mildly surprised at how beautiful she is, and then I think of her eyes. Hazel brown. I imagine seeing out from behind them. How it would feel to be inside that skin, toned and firm and so slim. I imagine *being* Adele, of slipping into that body, of controlling it, and then—just as I feel a terrible jolt of shock some-where in the core of me, a feeling that something is *very, very wrong*—I'm inside her.

56
AFTER

"She doesn't mention the fire in her parents' house in the letter she left," Inspector Pattison says, "but the reports state that it started in the fuse box." He's a thick-set barrel of a man whose suit has seen better days, but he has a world-weariness in his eyes that speaks of a career policeman. He's reliable. People trust him. He's calm.

"The fire she set in your home, Dr. Martin," he continues, "also started in the fuse box cupboard in the kitchen, so perhaps there is some indication of guilt in that."

"Do they know what she used?" David asks. He's pale and looks gaunt in that way people in shock do, but also so much *lighter* in spirit. Of course he is. *Ding dong, the witch is dead.*

"Turpentine and soaked tea towels."

David nods. "That makes sense. She'd been decorating."

"We found the letter she wrote—her confession of sorts—on your desk. In it she confirms everything you said in your statement to DCI Wignall in Perth. She put Robert Hoyle's body in the well on her estate and she'd been wearing your watch at the time. We've had confirmation from Scotland that the body has been recovered. Obviously it's in a state of extreme decomposition, but we expect dental records to confirm the identity. Also, given the manner of your wife's death—the heroin overdose—the same cause of death she gives for Mr. Hoyle—it would appear she was attempting to make some amends there. Perhaps she had a conscience to clear on both counts, her parents and Mr. Hoyle."

"But where did she get the heroin from?" David asks. "She was many things but she really wasn't that kind of person."

"Anthony," I say, as if the thought has just struck me. My throat is still quite raw from the smoke and I sound husky. "Anthony Hawkins. I saw him hanging around her a few times. Maybe she got him to get it?"

"Hawkins?" The inspector jots the name down.

"A patient of mine," David says. "An ex-patient of mine, I should say. Drug user and obsessive. Turned up at the house." I see the light go on then. "Adele answered the door. Maybe his obsession transferred to her. Adele is—*was*—very beautiful."

"We'll speak to him. As for your wife's letter, it was in her handwriting and only had her fingerprints on it so there is no doubt she wrote it." He looks up. "Which is very good news for you. Although you're lucky it didn't go up in the fire."

"Typical Adele," David says, a bitter half-smile on his face. "Even in her last moments she couldn't entirely set me free."

I'm barely listening. All I can think about is that David is holding my hand, squeezing it tight. I haven't felt that in such a long time. Last night, even though we were in day three of police purgatory, we made love and we laughed and smiled and held each other tight. I feel like I'm in a dream.

"Will David have to go to prison?" I ask, concerned.

"I can't comment on that until the investigation is over. Then if there are formal charges to be brought your solicitor will be informed. There are mitigating circumstances, however. She was fragile at the time of Mr. Hoyle's death and he was trying to protect her. Although even if the death was accidental, there is still the fact Adele hid the body and David was an accessory after the fact to that."

"I know," David says. "I won't be fighting any charges on that count."

"And I imagine you won't be practicing psychiatry any time soon either?" Pattison looks sympathetic. Of all the criminals he must have witnessed in his years on the force, David must be the least likely.

"No," David says. "I imagine not. That's another outcome I'm waiting on. I don't actually mind too much. Perhaps I need a change all round." He looks at me then and smiles, and I smile back so hard I think my face will burst. There's no need for us to hide our feelings from the policeman. The affair, the *love,* was all there in the letter.

I should know. I wrote it.

I push unfamiliar blond hair out of my face as we leave the police station. Louise's body—my body—still feels strange. To suddenly be carrying an extra stone of weight slows me down for a start, but I'm enjoying having more curves, and if David likes them then they'll stay. She needs glasses for distance, though. I don't think she'd realized that yet.

Oh, Louise, how perfect she was. How wonderfully she performed. And I have to give myself my due. My plan went perfectly. After my failed attempt to buy smack in that god-awful underpass that only resulted in a black eye and nearly losing my bag, Anthony Hawkins had fallen into my lap and was *so* pleased there was something he could do for me. Drugs, needles, everything I needed, he got.

I'd practiced with the heroin so I knew just how much I could inject myself with—between my toes and out of any track mark sight—and not fall into an immediate haze. I'd been practicing that day when Louise turned up and then blamed my state on the pills. An unexpected bonus.

I prepared the fire but didn't light it. When it got late enough, I texted her my wordy intent to kill myself. I *watched* her. I saw her trying to *see* me and giving up. Just before the taxi pulled up outside, I lit the fire and ran upstairs. On the first doorbell ring, I injected just enough heroin, and then hid the remainder of the drugs under the bed where I'd already placed a pair of David's surgical gloves. I went through the second door. I *saw* her outside. And here was the most tricky bit. Picking my time after she was empty to go into her. Waiting for the first tremble that something was wrong. A vibration in the air behind me to let me know she was going into my body. If she pulled back to her body, then I was sure I'd be kicked out.

But fortune favors the brave, and her skin became mine. I grabbed the key from on top of the door lintel where I'd hidden it and raced up the stairs through the thickening smoke.

She was moaning slightly on the bed, her eyes glazed. Unexpected heroin will do that to a girl. She focused slightly when she saw me. Louise there, behind my eyes, looking at me in her body. She was afraid then, even despite the high. I think she tried to say my name. She gurgled something, at any rate. I didn't pause for good-byes. We didn't have the time for that. I snapped on the gloves and retrieved the rest of the syringe. I injected it between her/my toes. Then it was good-night, sweetheart, and all over bar the shouting.

I dropped the syringe on the floor, stuffed the gloves in my pocket to get rid of later, and then hauled her up, thanking myself for having got so skinny, and thanking her for at least going to the gym a little bit. Then I half-carried her down the stairs and out into the night. Sirens were wailing in the darkness by then and the little old lady next door was standing in the street in her dressing gown clutching her yappy dog.

And that was that. When the fire engines turned up, I told them about the text and how I'd dug the spare key up from the plant pot and got in to try and save her. She was dead by then, though. She'd probably died halfway down the stairs.

Good-bye, Adele; hello, Louise.

If you love someone, set them free. What a load of bollocks.

57
THEN

"I was doing it when my parents died," Adele says. They're stretched out in front of the fire, the Shakespeare book she's been reading to him from abandoned. "Just flying everywhere. Like I was the wind or something. Soaring out over nature." She passes the spliff back to Rob, not that he needs it. He's been *chasing the dragon* as he calls it. Smoking some heroin. At least he's not injecting. That's something.

"It started when I was little," she continues. "I read about lucid dreaming in this old book that David gave me, and then once I'd managed that there was this whole other *thing* that started. At first I could only do it when I was sleeping. Maybe it was hormones or something. Maybe I didn't have that mental control as a child. But god, it was always so wonderful. This secret skill. At first it was only places I could picture. And at first I couldn't go very far at all. Then, as the years went by, I got better and better at it. Or it became more natural or something. Now I can do it at the drop of a hat, and soar. I tried to tell David about it once but he just laughed at me. He thought I was joking or something. I knew then that he'd never believe it, not really. So I've kept it to myself. Until I met you."

"That's why you wouldn't sleep," Rob says. He takes her hand and squeezes it and it feels good. It feels good to be able to *talk* about this with someone. To share it *all*.

"Yes," she says softly. "It was my fault my parents died. The fire was accidental, whatever anyone says, but if I'd been *there,* even if I'd been normally asleep, I would have woken up. I could have done something. But I wasn't. I was high up in the trees watching the owls and the woods and all the life that comes out at night."

"Sometimes shit happens," Rob says. "You have to put it behind you and get on with life."

"Agreed," she says. And then, more honestly, "And I don't think I could give it up if I tried. It's a part of me. Who I am."

"So that's what the weird second door is all about," he says. "I've had it a few times already but it weirded me out. I wrote about it in the notebook."

"Why didn't you say anything before today?"

"I didn't want you to think I was a freak."

She squeezes his hand back. She loves Rob, she really does. And David might not have liked him much—she could tell even if he didn't say anything—but she's sure he'll grow to.

"Well, if you're a freak, then you're a freak like me," she says, and then they laugh. She's happy. He's happy. And David's wonderful. Her future looks so bright. "I love that you can do it too. It's brilliant."

"Hey," Rob says, rolling onto his side and pushing himself up on one elbow. "We should try something. Something really mindfuck crazy."

58

ROB

We stand by the graveside, hand in hand. We're laying the past to rest by being here. Saying our farewells. There is little to see, just a name and two dates. What else could David have carved there on that black marble headstone? Loving wife? Hardly. And, anyway, it might be Adele's body but it's Louise who's really buried in this patch of earth.

Poor, sweet Adele. My tragic Sleeping Beauty. So caring and kind and yet so simple. I did love her in my own way, I really did. But it was like Romeo and Juliet. Romeo thought he loved Rosalind until he saw Juliet. Some love is so powerful it sweeps everything else away.

I remember everything about the moment I first saw David. Adele on the gravel, all girlish excitement, and me, lingering back in the shadows on the steps full of resentment at his impending invasion of our paradise.

And then he got out of that battered old car and he was . . . a *revelation*. For a moment I couldn't breathe. I felt blinded and enlightened all at once. It was love at first sight—a love that could never die. Adele and all her soft kindness paled in comparison. What I felt for her was simply dust on the wind. Gone in a second. David was strong. Clever. I loved the quiet way he had about him. All that calm. I finally understood why Adele loved him so much, but I could also in that instant see how she would hold him back. She was too damaged for someone as brilliant as David. He needed someone who was his equal. He needed *me*.

I could barely speak all weekend, just muttering answers to his questions, or making an absolute fool of myself trying to be funny, and wishing Adele would just fuck off with all her fussing and leave us alone together so I could revel in his presence. I knew then that I had to have him. I had to. It was fate.

I lay awake both nights listening to them laughing and fucking and it burned at me. I wanted to feel those strong farmer's hands on my skin. I thought of the blow job I'd given the nurse to get the weed at Westlands and I wondered how brilliant it would be to do that with someone like David. Someone I adored. I wanted to touch David's scars and remind him that if it wasn't for *her* he'd still be whole. I went through the second door and watched them for a while, torturing myself with the sight of his strong back over her as he thrust into her. I wanted to feel that passion. That love. That body pounding its lust into mine.

When he left to go back to university I felt as if my soul had been ripped out. I felt empty. I didn't want to live if I couldn't have him. Why should Adele have him? Simpering, weak Adele, who appreciated nothing? Who took his love for granted? Who had all this money and didn't even care about it? If I had that, and David, I would make sure his life *shone*.

And that's when it came to me. My simple and terrifying plan.

"Shall we go?" I say, and lean up to kiss him with Louise's full lips.

He nods. "Adam must be bored by now."

We stroll through the late sunshine back to the car, and I reflect on how wonderful life really is when you're in love.

It's easier to do a thing a second time. It was easier with Louise. My fear was all in the planning. The variables. With Adele my fear was that it wouldn't work even when she'd agreed to my crazy idea. *Let's see if we can swap bodies! Just for a minute! Haven't you ever wondered what it's like to have a dick?*

Louise would never have gone along with that, of course, but Adele was young and the young are notoriously stupid and she was stoned and glad to finally have someone to share her secret with. And, of course, she liked me. A perfect storm. I'd taken just enough smack but not enough for her to notice if I concentrated. We went out into the woods laughing—what was it she'd said? *If we're going to do voodoo magic it should be in a clearing at night.* That was it.

And then we swapped. Left our bodies, counted to three, and went into each other's. She didn't know what had hit her. The odd puff on a joint was no preparation for the power of a smack high. And within seconds, the needle was in. Overdose delivered. Just like I did killing Louise.

Good-bye, Rob; hello, Adele.

It was exhausting getting the body to the well. Women's bodies are so feeble and I hadn't been prepared for that. Dry leaves and mud were stuck to my jeans, and my weak body ached as my sweat cooled in the damp, chill air. I'd expected the world to be different afterward, but everything looked the same. The only thing that was different was me. The watch falling in with her was a fortuitous accident. I didn't care much. He'd given it to *her,* not me. I didn't care much about leaving my body to rot there, either. I'd never liked it. It never summed up what I was on the inside. I was far more glorious than that pasty, spotty shell. I kept the notebook, though. My one link to my old life. I tore out the pages with the second door— couldn't have David accidentally finding that—and then hid it in the box of remnants from Adele's parents' lives. I'm still keeping it. Who knew it would come in so handy? Maybe it will again.

I didn't handle the switch with Adele brilliantly in the aftermath. I should have shown more remorse over the body in the well. That was the first red flag for David, I think. And then, of course, the horrendous discovery of the pregnancy. I was having enough trouble adjusting to all the other quirks of the female body to even remember that I should have had a period, and there was no way I was ready for a whole other person to be growing inside me. Also, it was Adele's child, not mine. And I didn't want any part of her in my new and wonderful life with David. I didn't know enough about Adele either.

Their history. None of it was on my side when it came to David loving me. I had to fake too many breakdowns to hold him, and then, of course, resort to threatening him.

This time is different. David didn't know Louise that well, and I've watched and learned and memorized her life: her quirks, her tastes, her humor. He loves me now, though, I can see it in his eyes. He's free of the past. Maybe I'll give him a baby this time. Make us a proper family.

"Where do you want to go on our honeymoon?" he asks, when we're back in the car. "Pick anywhere you want."

We married a week ago, alone in a registry office. The day Adele in my original body was buried in a crappy little cemetery in Edinburgh. But only now that we're both officially free to do as we please have we started to think about what comes after. I pretend to consider his question for a moment. "The Orient Express," I say. "And then maybe a cruise."

"You hate boats." The small voice comes from the backseat, and I don't have to turn around to see the dark look in Adam's eyes. He knows something is wrong with me, he just can't figure out what. "You always say you hate boats," he says stubbornly.

"He's only being silly," I say, and squeeze David's thigh. "I think he's worried you'll take me away from him."

My teeth are gritted behind my smile. There is still one small obstacle to overcome for our happiness to be complete. David might not have known Louise well, but Ian does and Adam does. Those links need to be severed. It was easy to end the friendship with Sophie—a small mention to her husband of possible infidelities took care of that—but Adam's departure from my life will need to be somewhat more dramatic. It shouldn't be too difficult to arrange. Children are notoriously accident-prone. And anyway, grief can bring people closer together, can't it?

"I love you, Louise Martin," David says as he starts the engine and we drive away, leaving the past behind.

"I love you too, David Martin," I say. "More than you'll ever know."

ACKNOWLEDGMENTS

Oh my gosh, it's so hard to know where to start with this because the list of people I have to thank is long and humbling. In the UK, thanks to my fabulous agent and friend, Veronique Baxter at David Higham, and also to the entire foreign rights team there who have done such a great job selling *Behind Her Eyes* into different territories. And of course a huge thank-you to all those editors who bought it too! I am forever indebted to Natasha Bardon, my editor at HaperFiction, for giving me the chance to pitch to her and then for being such a great champion in getting this published. The same goes for the publicity and marketing teams, the art department, and everyone else who has been so enthusiastic. I'm very very happy to have a new home with you all. In the US, a big thanks to Grainne Fox from Fletcher & Co for doing such an amazing job and keeping such a cool head as I squealed and giggled through the process, and I am so delighted that Flatiron Books is my new home stateside. Big thanks to Christine Kopprasch, my editor, for wanting the book and having faith in it, and also to Amy Einhorn for her support of it. Again, as with HarperFiction, the whole team at Flatiron have been so lovely to work with and I couldn't ask for better people. Let's hope my book does you all justice. I'm lucky to have great editors who have given great notes. This book is so much better for your input.

I also have to thank Baria Ahmed, my buddy, for pointing out, when she read it after we'd been through several rounds of edits, that I'd referenced a hospital in Perth, Australia, instead of Perth, Scotland. Good catch!!

And also, of course, last but very much not least, huge thanks to all the readers who pick *Behind Her Eyes* up. I really hope you enjoyed it. You're all what makes the job worth doing.

Behind Her Eyes

by Sarah Pinborough

1. When Louise's life gets entwined with her lover, David, and her friend, Adele, she finds it difficult to give either of them up. Could you identify with her indecision and longing about either or both of them?

2. Adele, David, and Louise all keep secrets from one another. Whose secrets surprised you most?

3. What did you think of Adele and Rob's friendship? When you look back at Adele in the past chapters, how different does she seem from Adele in the present?

4. Louise loves David, but she becomes increasingly worried about Adele's welfare in her marriage. As Louise starts "to complete the jigsaw of their crazy marriage," what did you think was going on between Adele and David? Did you feel suspicious of David?

5. Under the guise of friendship, Adele begins to shape Louise into who she wants her to be, helping her to get fit, stop smoking, and quiet her night terrors. Through the book, did you feel like their friendship was real, even though both were clearly hiding things?

6. Now that you know the ending, what do you think of the book's title, *Behind Her Eyes*?

DISCUSSION QUESTIONS

7. From the start, Adele seems to know things that she shouldn't. How did you think that would be explained?

8. Adele talks about "this life I fought so hard for," and she believes that "I can never be happy until David's happy." In Adele's mind, everything she does is for David, and she keeps saying, "The course of true love never did run smooth." Do you think she really loves him?

9. Adele teaches Louise about lucid dreaming, a real phenomenon, but then takes her a step further, beyond the second door. Have you ever had a lucid dream?

10. The second door changes everything for Adele and Louise, and it introduces a supernatural element to this psychological thriller. How did you feel about the element of the second door?

11. Louise takes matters into her own hands and tells the authorities about Adele's suspicions that David had caused Rob's death, but after she meets Marianne, she figures out that Adele has been lying to her about many things. At that moment, what did you think would happen next?

12. The ending of *Behind Her Eyes* contains a huge twist. When you think back through the book, starting with the prologue, what clues did the author provide about what was really going on?

13. What did you think of the ending? Did you see it coming? What do you think will happen next?